What people are saying about *The Altar Boys*:

"Poswall has written a poignant and timely tale about deceit and corruption in the Catholic Church…. With finely-drawn characters and a well-developed ear for dialogue, Poswall takes us on a fast-paced, behind-the-scenes look at big-time, high-stakes litigation. J.J. Rai is a character worth rooting for. John Poswall is a new and compelling voice…."

—SHELDON SIEGEL, *New York Times* best-selling author

"*The Altar Boys* is a fascinating legal suspense novel by one of America's top trial lawyers, who has an authoritative grasp on his subject matter. On top of that, he can really write! This is a page-turner, a slam-dunk winner."

—JOHN MARTEL, *New York Times* and *San Francisco Chronicle* best-selling author

"*The Altar Boys* is right out of the headlines; indeed, a startling look behind the headlines by an author who has been there."

—STAN ATKINSON, Northern California news anchor

"I loved *The Lawyers*. This book, *The Altar Boys*, captured my attention to the point that I would take it into the bath tub with me. A real page turner….I am now anxiously awaiting its publication and to see *The Altar Boys* on the *New York Times* bestseller list."

—RUSS SOLOMON, Founder, Tower Records, Videos and Books

THE
ALTAR
BOYS

A NOVEL BY

John M. Poswall

JULLUNDUR PRESS
a Golden Temple Publishing company

This book is a work of fiction. Names, characters, places, and events are products of the author's imagination or are used fictitiously. Any resemblance to actual events, locations, or persons, living or deceased, is purely coincidental. We assume no responsibility for errors, in accuracies, omissions, or any inconsistency herein.

First printing 2008

ISBN 978-0-9729992-5-0
LCCN 2007935642

ATTENTION CORPORATIONS, UNIVERSITIES, COLLEGES, AND PROFESSIONAL ORGANIZATIONS: Quantity discounts are available on bulk purchases of this book for educational, gift purposes, or as premiums for increasing magazine subscriptions or renewals. Special books or book excerpts can also be created to fit specific needs. For information, please contact Jullundur Press, a Golden Temple Publishing Co., 1001 G Street, Suite 301, Sacramento, CA 95814. Fax: 916-449-1320; Email: goldentemplepub@aol.com

To

my three best friends

who died

during the writing of this novel

JUDGE JAMES T. FORD

who gave us his philosophy

of life:

"Find joy in every day"

WADE R. THOMPSON

who gave us "Andy"

and

my mother

LILLIAN VIOLET (BOWEN) POSWALL

who urged me

to retain my Catholic faith

"just in case."

Sorry, mom.

Prologue

He sat alone in the bell tower of the Cathedral of the Blessed Virgin. This was his favorite place, and night was his favorite time here, especially during Benediction, when the waft of incense permeated through the church's old plaster ceiling below, on its way to heaven. He was so high above the congregation that he couldn't really hear. But he didn't have to, for he knew the sounds from his earliest memories, the sounds of the chains carrying the censer, the incense burner, as the altar boy swung it toward the monstrance containing the Eucharist—the body of Our Lord Jesus Christ.

Smelling the incense, he instinctively made a small sign of the cross on his forehead, on his lips, and over his heart.

The sunset had been beautiful, as it so often is in Sacramento. He didn't mind the coming heat of summer. At this height, when the sun set, a light breeze invariably carried the coolness of the Delta up the Sacramento River, through the grated openings of the tower, and provided some relief.

He looked, from inside, through the face of the giant clock, with its Roman numerals, to the emerging stars and the sky beyond. Many a night he had sat in this place and watched the intricate and ancient machinery of the clock. He was fascinated by it. As its minute hand moved unalterably and reliably around the outside of the circle, it pointed to time—and to space. First, the time by minutes. Then, he had come to see, to the various stars and constellations beyond. And, because the clock was connected to the sound of bells, it would signal not just an exact time every night, but a different star or constellation in every season of the sky.

Now, the bells were electrical recordings. Soon, he hoped, with the coming restoration, the old cast bells of the tower would be back in use. He looked at the three large bells in front of him on the floor of the clock tower. Each, according to its marking, was made by the E.W. Vandozen Co. of Cincinnati and, from what he could see by rubbing a wet finger over the letters, was from the Buckeye Bell Foundry—one dated 1894, the other two 1895. He looked up through the darkness, to the giant bell, just twenty feet above, which he knew from inspection bore the name of the first bishop of Sacramento from when the cathedral was dedicated in 1889.

He could see, as he had studied it for hours, that a six-foot square opening—now covered—once existed from the ground, through each platform, to the top of the tower through which the giant bell had been hoisted. Probably, he thought, with a block and tackle, with oxen pulling the ropes to lift it into place, perhaps a half-dozen years after the cathedral was built. Or, he mused, Mexican farm workers instead of oxen. Some things hadn't changed much in over one hundred years in California. The floors, all the way down, still had the holes through which, he guessed, ropes once dangled in the cathedral entry to toll the bells. Soon, he imagined, these bells would once again be attached to the ropes, and he would toll the bells from the entry, calling God's children to celebrate the consecration of He who had given Himself for the sins of the world.

He saw the connection in all of this. God made time, and He made the universe. It was all here in this bell tower, in the hands of the clock—God's hands.

He breathed in the incense as the clock struck nine o'clock and smiled in satisfaction of his life. If he could chose a place to die, he thought, this would be it.

"*Dios mio*," he whispered, looking up at the sky above.

It was Saturday, May 7, 2004. Within days, his life would start to crumble, and in three months, to the day, he would get his wish—to die in this place—but under circumstances that would both shock and horrify the Sacramento community, impaled as he would be upon God's hands.

Dios mio, indeed. By the dictates of his faith—if there was a God—he was going to Hell.

Chapter 1

Judge Gerald Vincent of the Sacramento Superior Court was reviewing petitions and motions filed in his department to be heard
the following week. Unlike other judges, he did not use a law clerk. Rather,
he insisted on personally examining each document filed, judging even
their clerical compliance with the published Rules of Court. He was always polite to his staff but distant. No one ever laughed in his chambers.

He was meticulous in dress and similarly fastidious in his expectations of litigants. It started with the rules on the stapling of documents:
"One staple, three inches from the top of the left side, and one staple
three inches from the bottom of the left side, each ¾ of an inch from the
left edge of each document filed." Documents with one or three staples,
or two staples in different locations shall not be accepted for filing. Under no circumstances could a document be pre-punched to fit into the
court's file system, which relied upon the punching of two holes at the
top of each document. Only his clerk could do this, after the judge himself personally reviewed the staples, the margins, the overall appearance,
and, finally, the legal sufficiency of the contents of the document. In
chambers, his door was always shut, leaving his clerk and bailiff in the
anteroom. Inside, opera music played softly. A bone china cup, saucer,
and an occasional plate sat on his surprisingly crowded desk. But the
desk did not bear law books—well, not the law of California. Rather,
alphabetically arranged, were authors of ideas that inspired men and na-
tions. Eclectic, they had in common a search for meaning and order in
human experience. They scanned the early Greeks, from Epicurus and
Aeschylus to Plato, the Roman Cicero, and the Christian thought of St.
Augustine and Thomas Aquinas. The naturalist Charles Darwin was rep-

resented, as was the jurist Hugo Grotius. And great leaders from Hamurabi and Marcus Aurelius to Disraeli found favor with him, as did the historians Lord Acton and Gibbon and the philosopher Bertrand Russell. It was not unusual for a quotation from one or another of these great thinkers to find its way into his legal opinions. He wrestled with ideas.

Mixed among his books were magazines on art, antiquities, travel, and sailing. His desk was like an island, on a Persian rug, among the shelves of law books common to all judges that covered the walls. And even in chambers, he wore his judicial robe, over an expensive Thomas Pink shirt, dress slacks, suspenders, and a bow tie—all purchased in San Francisco.

Judge Vincent had come to the bench the usual way: He had known a governor. Sacramento was a notorious venue—locals called it a "dumping ground"—for a governor's political friends looking for a job, generally in the last two years of a governor's second term. Gerald Vincent had served Governor Pete Wilson well—one of the inner circle of advisors, even though he was not from San Diego like most, including Wilson's Chief of Staff and powerhouse Bob White. One of the least known publicly, Vincent had worked four days a week for the Governor, arriving Monday morning from his home in San Francisco and staying until Thursday night in a modest, two-bedroom townhouse he purchased in Campus Commons, just across the river from Sacramento State University. In his six years with the Governor, Vincent's picture never appeared in *The Sacramento Bee* newspaper, despite the fact that his legal work was behind every major initiative measure and legal defense or challenge advanced by the Governor. His name never appeared in a political or social column. To see him alone on the American River bike trail, in helmet with rearview mirror and expensive Italian racing attire, one would mistake him for a competitive cyclist. But one would be right in that he pushed himself to perfection in everything he did, even as he sought anonymity.

In his ten years on the bench, Judge Vincent had made no friends of his fellow judges. While he attended mandatory judges' meetings, he usually sat quietly, listening. The other judges had long ago stopped inviting him to dinner or even asking him to lunch with them. It was known that he had inherited wealth, including the family mansion in San Francisco near Land's End, to which he returned every weekend for a life unknown to his brethren. He had revealed his love of sailing on the Bay to fellow judge, Lloyd Johnson, an avid sailor and owner of a thirty-six-foot yacht, harbored at the San Francisco Yacht Club. Yet, with all of their talk of boats, neither had stepped foot on the other's boat or shared a drink at the Yacht Club.

Despite his isolation, no one doubted Judge Vincent's ability or his integrity. He had proven both, ruling against the Wilson Administration within months of taking the bench, on a writ brought by the Northern California Legal Aid Society on behalf of homeless and mentally impaired adults. In his ruling, he quoted Lord Acton: "Property is not the sacred right. When a rich man becomes poor it is a misfortune, it is not a moral evil. When a poor man becomes destitute, it is a moral evil, teeming with consequences and injurious to society and morality."

Polite, but unwilling to tolerate fools, he soon became known as a judge's judge, totally prepared, highly competent, precise but impatient—not someone who missed anything. He was also the Presiding Judge's dream, as he would take the many writs filed in the Sacramento Superior Court against the state of California since, Sacramento being the state capital, it was here that venue lay for all of the special interests and political squabbles that found their way into the Superior Court of California. But a writ, unlike a regular lawsuit, was an emergency action, heard by a judge without a jury, that took precedence over all other actions, and generally required a hearing, with a judge issuing—or denying—an injunction that could do anything from disqualifying a ballot measure to shutting down a prison system. Not a position for the ambivalent or the faint of heart. When he was not doing writs, Judge Vincent backed up other departments when there was overflow, so no one complained when, cases permitting, he left for his San Francisco home on Thursday night, after the commute traffic on Highway 80 had died down, giving him a clear shot to the City.

It was Thursday, and Judge Vincent was thinking that he would get out on time until the P.J.—Presiding Judge—called. "Gerald"—no one called him Jerry—"could you take Judge Kelly's probate calendar next week? He's out sick. I'd take it myself, but I have a Judicial Council meeting all week in Los Angeles."

Judge Vincent looked at the clock, a seventeenth-century French Renaissance piece at the front center of his desk. Two-thirty. He could read the filings for the court calendars of Monday, Tuesday, and Wednesday, and still get out by 7:00 P.M. He'd read the rest of the week's files on Monday afternoon.

"Sure, Roth. Have his clerk bring the files over right away," he told the Presiding Judge.

"Thanks, Gerald. I appreciate it. Have a nice weekend," the P.J. responded, acknowledging their understanding that Judge Vincent would have Friday off in return.

Most judges would rely on the Probate Examiner, a special court clerk, to review probate petitions. When the judge took the bench and was handed the files, each would have the examiner's notes accompanying the file. At that point, most judges would simply recite the notes to the petitioner without really having to have read the file ahead of time. Not Judge Vincent. He sat down to review each file personally.

His timing was right. At 6:00 P.M., he was on Wednesday's calendar, reviewing what was expected to come before the sick Judge Kelly next week. He had already found numerous problems with earlier files that had been missed by the Probate Examiner who had gone over them for Judge Kelly. This annoyed Judge Vincent. He knew Judge Kelly was not likely to have caught any of the errors since he spent more time joking with lawyers in the cafeteria than reading files. Judge Kelly, it was said, would sign a paper napkin if his law clerk put it in front of him.

Civil 123417—Doe 1, a minor v. R. Gutierrez, et al.

Civil 123418—Doe 2, a minor v. R. Gutierrez, et al.

The two files were attached with a rubber band. Each contained an order signed by Judge Kelly permitting the filing under a fictitious name. Each contained a sealed envelope, which, Judge Vincent knew, should contain the petition explaining why these actions were not fully public and why the minors were listed as "Doe" plaintiffs. The general rule provided that a lawsuit might be filed in the name of a "Doe" if it was necessary to protect the person's identity, generally because the nature of the proceeding was such that disclosure of identity would cause further damage to the "Doe" plaintiff. Of course, the "Doe" person would be disclosed to the defendant so that the defendant could properly prepare a defense against the allegations. The fact that each "Doe" was identified as a minor suggested a proper use of the Doe allegation to protect a child from further harm.

Judge Vincent looked at the petitions and saw immediately that they were virtually identical. Each specified that it was a "Petition for Minor's Compromise," citing Code of Civil Procedure, Section 372. Such a petition was necessary because only the Superior Court, through the Probate Division, had authority to allow settlement of a claim involving a minor. The purpose of the Code Section was to ensure that the minor's rights were protected, from his parents, legal guardian, or other persons— and his lawyer. Only after a court had satisfied itself that a settlement was appropriate and in the best interests of the minor could a defendant obtain a complete waiver and release of all future liability.

These petitions, however, were not filed by a representative for the children. Nor were the children represented by an attorney. Rather, the petitions were filed by an attorney representing a defendants identified only as "R. Gutierrez, et al." While legal, and specifically permitted by the Code section, such a petition could expect heightened scrutiny from a judge attentive to his responsibilities, since the only thing that stood between the proposed action requested by the defendant's attorney and a release was the judge assigned to hear the petition, which would have been Judge Kelly had he not been out sick.

Each petition sought the court's approval of a settlement of $15,000 to each minor in return for a complete release "of all liability of R. Gutierrez, his employer, and any and all other persons" for the alleged injuries. That was standard. A complete release. But what was the incident that had caused injury? What was the injury? Judge Vincent could find no explanation in either petition. Rather, each stated identically:

The minors allege the suffered injury caused by defendant R.

Gutierrez, for which no medical care was required, and the parents

of the minor agree that there is no continuing or future significant injury apparent or probable. While defendants do not admit liability, defendants have agreed to make the payments provided herein.

The $15,000 to each child was to be paid in three installments: $5,000 upon court approval, $5,000 in three years, and $5,000 at each child's eighteenth birthday—and, as they were twins and then twelve years old, this would not be for another six years. A confidentiality agreement was also specified as part of the settlement.

Judge Vincent was busy with his red pen.

"No facts to evaluate injury."

"No medical reports as required under Local Rules."

"Why a confidentiality agreement? Children are already protected with Doe filing."

"What is the $15,000 for if no injury?"

"Why is the $15,000 split into three payments over time? To maintain silence?"

In frustration, he pulled the Probate Examiner's sheet. It contained one word: "Approve." He was shocked. Not a single note about the obvious deficiencies in the petitions. What was going on?

He turned back and looked at the court files. Civil 123417 and Civil 123418. There were two regular probate departments and odd-number cases were assigned to Kenneth Hayashi and even to Judge Norm Kelly. By filing two separate petitions simultaneously a filer was guaranteed that, at the front desk, where they were numbered, one would be assigned to each department. Then the attorney would go upstairs to find a clerk to sign the temporary order allowing the Doe allegation. At this point, the attorney could choose to go to either of the departments—pick his own judge—then combine the two files together for hearing. Everyone knew Judge Kelly's reputation, and it appeared likely that the applicant had specifically sought him out to approve the petitions. Clever, but, like most things, the ploy did not escape Judge Vincent. He circled the numbers of the files with his red pen.

Then he circled the name of the law firm filing the petition on behalf of the cryptically named defendants, R. Gutierrez, et al.: "Dougherty, Andrews and Young."

Roland Dougherty, the senior partner, could be seen daily taking Communion at the Cathedral of the Blessed Virgin, just five blocks from the courthouse in downtown Sacramento. For a lawyer, he was soft-spoken but, in defense of Holy Mother the Church and his Catholic faith, he was passionate—a warrior for Christ. As long as anyone could remember, his firm had represented the Diocese of Sacramento. Young lawyers, like the one who had signed the petitions before the court, learned quickly that representation of the Catholic Church was a duty of all in the firm. Time was kept on all legal work for the church—but none was billed. Perhaps Dougherty judged the devotion of his attorneys by the hours; perhaps he wanted the lifetime calculation for his interview with St. Peter.

Legal issues involving land acquisition, zoning, contracts, homeless shelters, personnel matters—and the occasional embarrassment—were all handled by Dougherty himself. Anyone with a case—or potential case—involving the Catholic Church could expect to receive a pleasant, almost fatherly, call from Dougherty, seeking to dispose of the matter. Within the legal community he was known as "The Cardinal." Even bishops deferred to him, it seemed, as he had seen four or five come and go in the years he had served dutifully to protect his faith.

Judge Gerald Vincent could see through the documents before him. He knew what was going on. He knew what injury these two boys had suffered at the hands of R. Gutierrez. He guessed, correctly, that R. Gutierrez was a priest.

It was 6:30 P.M. He was alone in his chambers. He took off his judicial robe, went into his private bathroom, and threw up.

Chapter 2

J. J. Rai was sitting in his Sacramento law office, on the top floor of a
twenty-six-story building, with a spectacular view of the Sierras to
the east and the Sacramento River to the west, laughing at his law school
classmate, Andy Miller, who was on speaker phone from Las Vegas. Andy
was screaming: "Martha Stewart, for Christ's sake! Massive corporate fraud
threatening the very foundation of our democratic society and all the
United States government can do is go after Martha? This is insane, J.J.
We've got to do something."

"What do you suggest, Andy? Set up a defense fund for Martha
Stewart? Take up a collection?"

There was no stopping Andy.

"It's not about Martha. They're using her to distract America from
the conspiracy between the corporate elite and our political leaders. They're
all corrupt. They're in bed together."

"Well, at least they will have thousand-count sheets if they get in
bed with Martha," J.J. replied, taking a sip of his morning tea.

Andy ignored the comment.

"It's like the sixties. We've got to take back our country. Before it's
too late."

"Andy, I love your idealism, but I am just one tired lawyer in a
small town. Still, I'm behind you, Andy. You go get 'em."

"I will. I still believe one man can make a difference. Like Ma-
hatma Gandhi, Martin Luther King, Nelson Mandela...."

J.J. interrupted, reflectively, "Lee Harvey Oswald."

"Yeah, him too," replied Andy, without breaking stride.

"Andy, Andy," J.J. said, trying to stop his old friend, who was now on a roll, "I love talking to you, but I've got my daughter on the other line. I've got to run."

"Rebel? Well, say 'hi' from uncle Andy."

"Okay," J.J. said, as he switched to the next blinking light on his phone console and looked at the framed picture on his credenza of his daughter and her brother.

"Dad, I thought I'd wait till 10:30 to make sure you were in the office, especially on a Monday morning," came the voice of J.J.'s daughter.

He smiled. "I've been here since 9:00, smarty-pants. You know I'm the senior partner and have a staff of lawyers to supervise." He leaned back in his high-backed chair and put his feet on his ultra-modern style glass desk that rested on cement cylinders. He'd come a long way from the hundred-dollar rolltop desk of his civil liberties days as a young lawyer.

"Yeah, right, dad. Has your secretary brought your toasted raisin bread and tea yet?"

They were into a usual pattern of banter. He decided to break out.

"By the way, your uncle Andy says 'hi.' He's in Las Vegas for an aviation seminar."

"Right. He's in Vegas, drunk, probably with a hooker, chasing an air crash case for some law firm. Why do you put up with him, dad? He really is an alcoholic, a sexist, and a disgraced lawyer."

"Disbarred," J.J. corrected her.

"Huh?"

"You said 'disgraced.' He was disbarred. There's a difference."

"Well, he planted evidence. I'd say that's a disgrace."

"No, he was so committed to a burned child, and justice, that he risked his career. For that, he got disbarred, not disgraced."

"Whatever. I just called to remind you that graduation is June 12th."

"How could I forget, sweetheart. That's when I get to stop paying Harvard Law School for tuition, books, room and board—some of which, I might add, has been paid from fees earned on the occasional airplane crash case uncle Andy refers to this office. Which reminds me, you can pay me back by working here for a few years."

"Sacramento? Are you kidding? When I tell anyone back here in Cambridge I am from Sacramento, you know what they say?"

"What?"

"Sacramento? Is that near San Francisco?"

"It is the capital, sweetheart."

"Right, dad. Known for Kings basketball and Schwarzenegger—and even the Governor doesn't want his family to live there."

"What are you saying?"

"Dad, in the big world, Sacramento isn't even on the map. Have you looked at the daily *New York Times* weather map. It only shows San Francisco and Fresno in Northern California. No Sacramento." With that, she was off. "Gotta' go. Love you, dad. Bye."

J.J. smiled as he looked at his remaining piece of raisin toast. "Fresno?" he said to himself.

Sometimes it felt that, after a career at the pinnacle of the law, the only one left to whom he had anything to prove was his daughter. And, at 5223, 105 lbs., she was tougher than any opponent he had ever met in the courtroom. She was two years younger than her brother Charlie, but had called herself his lawyer even as a five-year-old. Whatever had to be negotiated between dad and son had to go through her. Even now, thirty years later, she still negotiated, intervened, stood up for her brother—and her mother. J.J. felt he was no match, even as one of the "best lawyers in America," for his daughter because she had the distinct advantage of being so loved by him.

And, there was the guilt—that he had broken up the family. Not that she had ever said it. Well, not that way. But they all blamed him for the divorce, didn't they? Back then, he didn't carry blame well. Their mother, he had to admit, was a wonderful person. She and J.J. had met as undergrads and married "in the Church." While he attended Berkeley's Boalt Hall law school, she embraced much of the counter-culture down campus. She studied meditation, Eastern philosophy, and veterinary medicine.

Returning to Sacramento after law school, J.J. and his wife, Rachel, started a family and something of a zoo. The children never wanted for pets: rabbits, snakes, a rhesus monkey named Jane Goodall, dogs, cats, and a llama named Dali Lama—the latter being the reason the family moved to ten acres in the foothills outside of town after the Sacramento city inspector served a zoning violation complaint upon them. But it had all been worth it, and now his son was a marine biologist, albeit a shy one who still relied upon his sister for help.

But as the home moved more distant from the office, so did J.J. and Rachel's lives. Then, the first big case, followed by another, followed by greater separation for longer periods as the cases—and his fame—grew bigger. What held the marriage together, it seemed, were animal shows, swimming tournaments, gymnastic meets—the children. So, when J.J. left, it was as if, perhaps to them, the children were not enough.

Then came the divorce. It got ugly. Not because of anything he or Rachel did, he believed, but because his wife's lawyer saw the case as an opportunity to go head-to-head with one of the top lawyers in town and make a name for himself. An attempt to resolve the divorce amicably by talking directly to Rachel resulted in J.J. being reported to the State Bar for unethical conduct in directly communicating with a client represented by an attorney. J.J. settled the divorce on the terms demanded—and waited.

Two years later, a headline in the *Sacramento Bee* announced J.J.'s latest case filing to make the paper: "Divorce Attorney Sued for Sex with Clients." Payback. It did not go unnoticed by most in the legal community that the attorney being sued had represented J.J.'s wife in their divorce. To those who kept count, J.J. had evened the score. To them, he had no choice if he was to maintain his reputation as a feared trial lawyer.

None of this had sat well with Rebel. As always, she was defensive of her mother and brother. Since the divorce, it seemed that J.J.'s life was an attempt to justify himself to her. It was made harder as the intervening years had brought girlfriends—and two brief marriages—to juggle as he fought to win her back.

J.J. was disappointed that during college Rebel no longer spoke of becoming a lawyer. Instead of the LSAT—the law school aptitude test—she opted for the Graduate Record Exam and took a masters in political theory at U.C. Berkeley. She did welcome his help in landing an internship in Senator Barbara Boxer's office upon graduation, which she left to join the Clinton reelection campaign, researching and writing policy papers on everything from environmental protection to trade policy—and her natural advocacy, women's rights.

On April 3, 2001—J.J. remembered the date and exactly where he was—Rebel called her dad and announced: "I've been accepted to law school. I start Harvard in August." Six months earlier, she had divorced her husband. It had been painful, and J.J. had begun getting more regular calls from Rebel.

Now, they were going to law school, together. J.J., while still feeling like he was on probation, held out hope that perhaps one day they could practice together: father and daughter, partners.

Chapter 3

*J*J. had become a legend in the legal community. His birth name was Jawaharlal Jallianwalla Singh Rai. His Indian father had in mind Jawaharlal Nehru, then the leader of the Indian independence movement, and Jallianwalla, the place in the Punjab known to every Indian school child, where in 1919, thousands of peaceful demonstrators were fired upon by British soldiers under the command of General Dyer. The massacre, Dyer proclaimed, was a "jolly good thing." Ironically, J.J.'s mother was English.

When he started first grade, the school admissions officer took one look at the name and wrote, "J.J. Singh Rai." The "J.J." stuck. When the mood struck him, J.J. would announce his complete name and use his best Punjabi accent, which sounded more like Peter Sellers in *The Party*, and add, "but, but…you may call me J.J." For a rural county jury, however, he'd skip the accent and just introduce himself as J.J. Rai.

He prided himself on looking fit in his preferred Armani suits. Just under six feet, he was the same 175 lbs. he'd been in law school, but now, through years of running and tennis, he seemed to wear them better. Perhaps it was the clothes that came with the success. Or, perhaps, he was just more comfortable with who he was. Yet, even in sports, he was competitive: in tennis, against an opponent; in 5k and 10k races, against himself. It was not that he didn't enjoy himself. He enjoyed competition.

J.J. didn't look Indian. That's why the name and the occasional accent were so surprising. He used them both. In some ways, they set him apart—or reminded him of who he was and whence he had come.

It seemed everyone had a "J.J. story." Often, when he was introduced to give a talk or to receive an award, a story of his exploits would be told. Sometimes, he recalled the events recounted; other times, he didn't. Some stories he knew to be true; other false. Lately, he realized, he wasn't sure anymore whether a given story was true or whether he had heard it repeated so often that he, too, had come to believe it.

Had he, as a young lawyer, really told a notoriously strict judge, when late for a trial, that, no, he didn't wear a watch because he found that it inhibited his creativity? Or had he really referred to a short attorney and a tall attorney for General Motors as Rocky & Bullwinkle during a jury trial involving a product liability case on behalf of a quadriplegic client? And had he put pictures of his children into evidence to frustrate his opponents when they found that the pictures had worked their way into the jury room?

But it wasn't the million-dollar jury verdicts he had won that were recalled on the walls of his office. Sure, there were mementos of past jury trials: guns, toy cars, scaffolding bolts, car parts, electrical power line conductors, and many other items marked with court exhibit numbers. What he prized most, however, were those matters for which he had never received a dime. Some were the subject of a plaque—from women with breast cancer for whom he had obtained treatment when they had been denied by their HMO. Others were small cards of thanks. Most of these people he had never heard from again, but he was satisfied that they turned to him when no one else could or would help. He was not their best friend; he was their lawyer.

If there was a theme to his fights, it was this: a struggle between the powerless and the powerful, David versus Goliath. He was the equalizer to the money and power of the adversary, usually government or corporate America.

Perhaps his identification with the powerless came, in part, from his family experience. His father had left India at age eighteen and worked to send money home to support siblings. His English mother was thrust into poverty when her father died, and she and her sisters became dependent upon Catholic school lunches and free clothes. His mother and father had met at an air raid shelter during the Blitz in England in World War II and struggled in the aftermath of the war to make a better life. Coming to America when J.J. was ten, they worked in the fields of California. Later, for most of her life, his mother was a housekeeper for wealthy Sacramentans, some of the same people with whom J.J. now associated in social settings. He was a millionaire uncomfortable with his wealth. He still identified with his roots and felt a stranger in his surroundings. For the affluent and powerful, having J.J. Rai around was like having a pet cobra: sooner or later, he would strike. It was in his nature.

As for Andy Miller, his Berkeley law school friend, J.J. recognized the distinction between "disgraced" and "disbarred," even if the law did not. Andy Miller had made law in California the hard way. His name was on the leading California case involving subordination of perjury by an attorney. Called upon to represent an eight-year-old child who had been burned and disfigured when he climbed into an electrical power substation, Andy had placed several bikes, Hot Wheels, and toys around the fencing of the substation. Witnesses had told his investigator that such evidence of children's presence was often seen at the site before the accident. But after the accident, this evidence had disappeared. Andy assumed, rightly, that the good folks of General Pacific Power had removed the evidence of its attractive nuisance. So, Andy had gone to Toys R Us, loaded up his trunk, and placed the bikes and toys around the fencing. Then he had taken pictures, which were later shown to a jury in support of the jury instruction on "attractive nuisance," wherein the jury was told that even if the little boy had climbed the fence, if General Pacific Power knew or should have known that children were attracted to the dangerous area, it should have anticipated that they would climb into its fenced transformer. The photos had proven that children sought out the fenced area in the woods to play: "Just look at the those toys," Andy had shouted to the jury, pointing to a large screen upon which the photos were projected. The jury verdict had been for a record $6 million. General Pacific Power had been furious. It had known that Andy had placed the toys at the site because it knew that its own investigators had previously removed the real evidence. But it couldn't admit the truth nor prove, during the trial, what Andy had done, so it had paid the judgment. But two years later, Andy was in a divorce action with his third wife, and his firm was breaking up. It was never clear who contacted whom, but an investigator for General Pacific Power obtained a signed statement from Andy's wife that he had told her of the false evidence. Immediately, General Pacific sued Andy for fraud—for the $6 million it had paid based upon the false evidence and for an equal amount in punitive damages. It seemed like a slam dunk. That's when Andy turned to his old classmate, J.J. Rai.

Together, J.J. and Andy established the law of California for liability of an attorney for fraudulently produced evidence. Some said it was a sad day for the reputation of lawyers. The California Supreme Court held that all actions of an attorney in trial—including manufacturing evidence—were absolutely privileged and could not be the basis of a lawsuit. Although there was clear precedent in a statute passed decades before by the California Legislature to protect citizens, even lawyers, in legislative and judicial proceedings, the decision outraged everyone. All the major newspapers in the state editorialized against the decision. The *Los Angeles Times* lamented: "What we all believed is now the law: Lawyers can manufacture evidence." The Supreme Court, in its opinion, had said that the only remedy was for the State Bar to discipline the attorney involved. The State Bar acted immediately: It disbarred Andy for life.

Andy was unrepentant. He had been caught but confessed he would do it again if faced with the same situation.

"I knew General Pacific had removed the evidence, and I wasn't going to let them get away with it," he told J.J. "Not with that little boy depending on me. You should have seen him, J.J. He had fifty thousand volts hit him and, fortunately, throw him ten feet off that fence. But first the electricity went into his hand, over his head, and through his body to ground out the back of his foot on the fence. The heat of the electrical current cooked a path through him, and the shock to his brain was irreversible. He spent five months at the Shriner's burn center in Galveston, Texas. Jesus, J.J., he looks like he's just smiling at you. His mom has to sit him up to wash him and keep his limbs moving."

Even now, ten years later, J.J. knew Andy still visited the burned boy monthly.

Chapter 4

J.J. had his eyes closed, in thought, when his secretary, Natalie, knocked and entered. The knocking was a formality she observed even though she had worked for him for nineteen years—half her life. At thirty-eight, married with three children, she was both a beautiful young woman and an extraordinary secretary. J.J. often told her if she quit, he would have no choice but to retire.

"J.J., there's a family here asking for you. I told them they needed to call and make an appointment, not just come in, but they said they were told to see only you."

It was not unusual that people would ask "only" for Mr. Rai. His was the reputation that floated the firm, but, at this point in his career, he hand-picked the cases he wanted and handed off the rest to younger members of the firm. Once clients got working with another attorney, with J.J. occasionally popping in to assure them that he was consulting on the case, they were happy. But nobody got into his office, past his secretary, without screening.

"Tell them to phone in. You know how it is. Once they're in the office, it's a guaranteed hour to get them out."

She nodded and turned to leave.

"What's it about anyway?" he asked as she reached the door. Since the prospective clients had apparently walked in, he figured they couldn't be too injured. Now, if they had wheeled in....

"A little hard to say. Mexican family. Parents with twin boys and an older sister. They have some papers for a hearing set for this Wednesday."

J.J. felt a bit of sympathy. "Probably getting evicted and waited till the last moment." But, along with sympathy, he also felt annoyance.

"Damn it! Why couldn't someone have helped them and directed them to Legal Aid instead of sending them to me?"

Again, the secretary started to leave.

"No. Natalie, tell them to have a seat. Just bring me the papers—maybe we can at least direct them properly."

She smiled as she left, knowing her boss was an easy mark for someone in need. She returned a few moments later with what he immediately recognized as petitions for compromise and settlement of minors' claims. He looked at them briefly and saw that the cases involved only $15,000 each. The two petitions appeared essentially identical. Small cases, he thought—not worth his time.

He read one of the petitions. Then he turned back to the caption page and the name of the law firm that had filed the petition, listed at the top left corner of the pleading papers: Dougherty, Andrews & Young.

Of the J.J. stories circulating in the courthouse, there was one often told by a devout, now-retired, Catholic judge that was completely true. As a young lawyer, J.J. had used any advantage for his client's causes, including an appeal to a judge's religious faith, if necessary, to obtain a favorable ruling. On one occasion, things had not been going well in a morning settlement conference before Joe Savage, a devoutly Catholic judge. Judge Savage couldn't be budged in his evaluation, in a car accident case, siding with the insurance company and against J.J.'s injured client.

Finally, after an impassioned plea, J.J. had thrown open his suit jacket. On the inside was a medal, with a hanging cross.

"Judge, you can't do this to me. I hold the Ad Altare Dei Award, the highest religious award in scouting. I was the chaplain of my Sea Scout group. And look…."

J.J. then had pulled a photo from his jacket pocket and placed it on the desk in front of the judge.

"I was an altar boy and an acolyte to the bishop at the Cathedral of the Blessed Virgin."

Sure enough, there in the picture was J.J. in his cassock, holding the tall candle of a bishop's acolyte, as he knelt on the steps of the altar.

The judge had taken the picture and told the insurance company to split the difference and settle the case. The matter had been promptly resolved.

Within days, everyone in the courthouse had heard the story of J.J. and his picture in altar boy attire. Judge Savage had had the photo framed and had kept it on his desk until he retired.

J.J. also had a framed copy of the photo, with his scout medals attached, sitting on a bookshelf in his office. He looked at it now.

Of course, the bishop had had more than one acolyte. The picture showed the bishop dressed in red vestments signifying the tongue of fire of the Holy Ghost at Pentecost. The bishop was administering the sacrament of Confirmation at the Cathedral of the Blessed Virgin. Four of the six boys attending to the bishop were clearly visible in the picture. Each had already received the light slap to the face from the bishop, as part of his confirmation and to make him strong in the fight between good and evil.

Of the boys, one was J.J. Rai. Next to him was Brian Thomas Riley, who had died in Vietnam. On the other side of the bishop was Donald O'Brien, who had entered the priesthood after high school and was now Bishop O'Brien of the Catholic Diocese of Sacramento. The fourth altar boy was Roland Dougherty. Even then, J.J. did not like Roland Dougherty.

"Natalie," J.J. said into the intercom, "I'll see the parents now. Please have the children stay with you in the reception area." He added, "And Natalie, what are the parents' names?"

The papers before him had listed only the children as Doe petitioners. They referenced the parents but did not specify their names.

"Octavio and Maria Sanchez," she replied.

Chapter 5

*O*ctavio and Maria Sanchez were born in Mexico and had come to the United States, illegally. They had had the good fortune to benefit from one of the amnesty programs of the late eighties and had settled in Delano, where it had also been their good fortune to meet Father Donald O'Brien, a tireless worker for the United Farm Workers. Fluent in Spanish, Father Don, as he was known, would say Mass at Our Lady of Guadalupe in Delano on Sunday but during harvest would take Communion to the fields so that his flock could receive the body and blood of Jesus Christ. In carrying out his mission, he recognized neither the boundaries of other parishes nor the lines of private property. He regularly joined protest marches, and, in the early days of the farm workers' struggle, he had fasted alongside César Chávez. He had also joined in litigation (sometimes against the directives of his conservative bishop) with California Rural Legal Assistance and its famous—or, if you were a grower, infamous—supervising attorney in Salinas, Ralph Santiago Aberscal.

J.J. had followed Father Donald O'Brien's career since they were in parochial school together. He admired him even though he himself had long ago set aside his own Catholic faith. The last time J.J. had been in a church had been at the Cathedral of the Blessed Virgin for the investiture of Donald O'Brien as bishop of the Diocese of Sacramento. The cathedral is the church of the bishop, where the cathedra, or bishop's chair, sits. The Pope, for example, is the bishop of Rome, and while he celebrates mass in the world-famous St. Peter's Basilica, in the Vatican, the cathedral for Rome is actually St. John Lateran Basilica, where his cathedra sat long before the papacy moved to the Vatican. Through the cathedra, bishops—including the Pope—acknowledge their succession to the Apostles of Christ and to the first bishop, Peter.

At the investiture, J.J. had watched as his old friend and fellow altar boy received the symbols of that succession—the mitre, the staff, the ring—and was made to sit upon the cathedra as only a bishop is permitted. They had each come a long way on divergent paths, seeking justice.

When Father Don was named bishop, he asked Maria and Octavio Sanchez to join him in Sacramento. He needed a housekeeper, and he found a position as a custodian at the cathedral for Mr. Sanchez. The move freed the Sanchezes from the fields and gave them both the security of year-round work, with benefits and a free Catholic education for their children. The twin boys were then only seven, and their sister, Carmen, was twelve. The school was on the same grounds as the cathedral, and the Sanchezes' living quarters were in a small house behind the rectory. They were surrounded by their faith, and their children were in a spiritual environment. They were honored by the offer and excited about the good fortune that God had bestowed upon them.

The arrangement turned out to be everything the Sanchezes had hoped for. Octavio revered the cathedral and loved Christ. He had systematically ordered his weekly mopping of the floors to follow the stations of the cross—starting with Jesus being condemned to death at the northeast corner, moving to Veronica wiping the face of Jesus at the end of the row, then crossing the three sets of doors at the entrance of the cathedral onto the south wall where Jesus falls for the third time and is thereafter stripped and crowned with thorns. Slowly, Octavio would push his mop, as Christ carries his cross to Calvary, until Jesus is nailed to the cross, dies, is lowered from the cross, and is laid in the tomb at the fourteenth station in the far northeast corner of the cathedral. Such suffering always made him cry, and he wished that he himself could suffer, in place of the Son of God, for the sins of man. Each time he resolved to do better in his own life. To resist sin. The sight of such suffering was made bearable by the inclusion of a fifteenth station, added in the sixties by a few churches, signifying the triumph of faith over death: the Resurrection.

"I am the resurrection," Octavio would repeat, in Spanish, through his tears, each time.

He spoke little English though he understood it well enough for his job. Still, he preferred Spanish. He always waited for Bishop O'Brien or a Spanish-speaking priest to take Confession.

On Saturday nights, after Benediction, Octavio would prepare the cathedral for Sunday morning Mass. Meanwhile, his wife would drive the short distance, across the parking lot, to the cafeteria, where, every Saturday night, Bingo—or, as some called it, the eighth sacrament of the Catholic Church—would be held. She could have walked, but she was just a little nervous walking home in the dark, in downtown Sacramento.

Maria's job was in the rectory, where she took care of the bishop and the priests of the diocese who lived there. Answering the door, she met those who came to see the bishop and served them tea or coffee and the cookies the bishop liked. All of the priests of the diocese sooner or later found their way to the bishop's home, as did many of the supervising sisters—nuns—some wearing the habits of old but more of them opting for civilian clothes. Maria preferred the nuns in uniform as she remembered them from her youth—"holy looking." Though it wasn't her job, she occasionally cooked Mexican food, of which the bishop was fond.

The Sanchez children wore school uniforms and thus were dressed as well as the Anglo kids. On occasional Sundays, the Sanchez parents would be embarrassed when the twins serving Mass, as altar boys, had holes in their shoes prominently facing the congregation as they knelt, piously, their hair slick with Brylcreem, their hands clasped, their eyes on the raised Eucharist. Still, as twins, they were special.

Juan and Felix had been altar boys for three years, starting in the fourth grade, when Father Ramon Gutierrez, had come to the boys' class— girls were in separate classrooms—and taken them to the cathedral. For the first time, the boys crossed the barrier that was the altar rail and had gone upon the altar. Father Gutierrez had explained that as altar boys they would deliver the water and wine that would be consecrated and transformed into the blood of Christ. The concept of transubstantiation—a priest changing ordinary bread and wine into the body and blood of the Savior, Jesus Christ—had struck awe and fear into the boys; awe that Father Gutierrez had such power and fear that they would be in the presence of Jesus reconstituted. But fear had been quickly replaced by excitement presented by the opportunity to "bang the gong"—as they called it—during Mass and wear the black cassock. Their parents had been pleased when the twins announced they were going to be altar boys. They did everything together.

The problem started a few months ago, Mrs. Sanchez told J.J. Every summer, Father Gutierrez would take the altar boys camping in the giant redwoods of the Santa Cruz mountains. For a week, the group would camp out, cook, sing songs around campfires, and hike redwood trails. They would go swimming in the river at Ben Lomond. At least one day, they would drive into Santa Cruz and play on the Boardwalk and at the ocean.

"This year, when the papers came to sign up, Felix said he didn't want to go," Mrs. Sanchez told J.J.

"Did he say why?" asked J.J.

"No. We asked him. He kept saying he didn't want to go. We asked his brother. Juan said he didn't know why Felix didn't want to go, but Felix got very upset, so his father and I said, 'Okay, you don't have to go.' But still he wouldn't tell us why he didn't want to go."

From the court papers, J.J. knew this wasn't the end of the matter. This was just the beginning. He had a feeling as to where the story was going, but he wanted the parents to tell it in their own way and in their own time since it was obviously very difficult for them.

He asked, "What happened next?"

Again, Mrs. Sanchez spoke up. Mr. Sanchez remained seated with his head down.

"Next Sunday, after that, Felix says he doesn't want to be an altar boy anymore. Again, we asked him why, and he has no answer. We are worried. We think maybe he doesn't believe in God anymore. Maybe he's losing his faith." Mrs. Sanchez paused.

J.J. recognized that it was not a language barrier that was causing the difficulty, but rather another barrier that had been breached.

Finally, she resumed. "Then, on Sunday, he won't leave the house—even to go to Mass. So Juan is the only altar boy because his brother won't come."

Mrs. Sanchez reached over and held her husband's hand. "After Mass, Father Gutierrez comes up to us and asks, 'Where is Felix?' So I tell him everything. That Felix doesn't want to go camping and doesn't want to be an altar boy anymore."

"What did Father Gutierrez say?" asked J.J.

"Nothing. He couldn't look at me. Mr. Rai, I knew then he had done something to Felix. I started crying. People were looking at me. Father Gutierrez just walked away without a word."

She was crying now and holding her husband's hand tight.

"Let's take a break. I'm going to get a cup of tea. Would you like some, Mrs. Sanchez? Mr. Sanchez?" asked J.J. He handed Mrs. Sanchez a box of Kleenex. She thanked him. "Water, please," she said. Mr. Sanchez said nothing.

"Let me get it," J.J. said, using the excuse to get out of the office. He needed a break for what he guessed was coming. He had children, and, as a lawyer, had never understood why, in times like this, people looked to the courts for justice. He was convinced, after seeing it all, that justice for the perpetrator, if it involved his children, would be with a baseball bat.

He walked into the reception area and saw the children. The boys, in parochial school white shirts and gray corduroy pants, sat quietly. Their sister had her feet on the coffee table and was on her cell phone. He walked over to them.

"Hi, guys. Would you like a cookie?" The boys answered in the affirmative, politely, sitting upright in their chairs. Their sister, with a naval body piercing, evident from the low riding pants, and a tattoo over her right, rather large breast, didn't answer. She looked at J.J. in a way that made him feel uncomfortable, got up, and announced she was going for a smoke.

J.J. got a cup of tea and Mrs. Sanchez's water and asked Natalie to get cookies for the boys. Then he returned to his office.

Time to get to the facts, he thought. "Did you ever find out what happened to Felix, Mrs. Sanchez?" he asked, after handing Mrs. Sanchez her water.

"Yes, the bishop told us."

"The bishop?" J.J. asked.

"Yes, when I knew Father Gutierrez had done something to Felix, I went to the bishop and told him everything that I told you. He asked to see Felix. So I took Felix, and they talked."

J.J. wanted to get some time parameters. "When was this?"

"About four weeks ago," she responded after looking to Mr. Sanchez for assurance. He nodded in agreement.

"And then did Bishop O'Brien tell you what Felix said?" J.J. asked.

"No, he just said that the boys did nothing wrong and that he was going to talk to Father Gutierrez."

"Did he do that, do you know?" J.J. was thinking that the bishop would clearly be a witness if in fact he had questioned Father Gutierrez about any improprieties. Of course, he anticipated that any lawyer for the diocese, especially Roland Dougherty, would claim one privilege after another to prevent J.J. from learning what had transpired during any conversation between Bishop O'Brien and Father Gutierrez. He was about to be surprised.

"Yes, I saw Father Gutierrez come to the rectory the same day," replied Mrs. Sanchez, "and he was still in there with the bishop when I left work a couple of hours later. And that evening, the bishop called me back to the rectory and told me that Father Gutierrez had admitted that he had touched both of our boys in their private parts, just like Felix had told him this had happened. He said he had to get some advice about what to do, but he wanted to make sure the boys weren't harmed and to help them with any problems."

"You said 'both boys?' He told you that *both* boys had been molested by Father Gutierrez?"

"Yes, he said that it was on the camping trips."

"But Juan had never said anything to you before Bishop O'Brien told you this?"

"No. Juan has never said anything."

J.J. made a note on his legal pad. He was amazed that a parent had complained of a problem with one child and the bishop had come forward to divulge to her that actually *two* children had been molested by a priest of the Church. But then, the bishop was Don O'Brien, not one to tolerate—let alone cover up—the sins of the Church.

"What about Father Gutierrez?" J.J. asked. "Did you talk to him any further?"

"He's gone. No one has seen him since that day," she replied.

Then she added, "Bishop O'Brien personally took the altar boys on their camping trip this year. My husband went for the first time, to help, and our boys did just fine."

J.J. picked up the court papers.

"I guess that brings us to these papers. How did the settlement come about?"

"Well, a few days after the bishop met with Father Gutierrez, he asked if I and Octavio would meet with him and the attorney for the Church, Mr. Dougherty."

Enter Roland Dougherty, Defender of the Faith, thought J.J.

"Where did you meet—at the attorney's office?"

"No, at the rectory. Mr. Dougherty was there with the bishop when me and Octavio came over. The bishop explained that he wanted to make sure the boys were not having any emotional problems that might cause them difficulty later in life. He said the Church would pay for a child psychologist to meet with them just to be on the safe side. And then Mr. Dougherty said the Church felt terrible that a priest had done this. They had fired him to make sure he never hurt others, Mr. Dougherty said. And they wanted to put some money aside for Felix and Juan to help with college. That's how they said it. We were still very upset, but we didn't blame the bishop or the Church. So we agreed."

"Have you seen the child psychologist's report?"

"No, but we were told that the doctor thought the boys were handling it all very well."

"And what do you think? Have you talked to the boys about what happened?"

"I don't know what to think. They seem all right, but they really don't want to talk about it, and we thought it better not to bring it up. So we haven't talked about it."

She turned to her husband, but he continued to look down at his hands. It was clear that this was not the kind of conversation that any parent would want to have with a child. Not knowing what to do, or what to say, they had said nothing.

After a moment, Mrs. Sanchez added, "I don't even think they talk about it between themselves."

"Why do you say that?" J.J. asked.

"Well, they seem a little quieter with each other. It used to be hard to get them to stop talking when they went to bed. Now they seem quieter, together."

J.J. put an asterisk next to the reply and then asked, "How did you and the bishop decide on $15,000 for each boy?"

"We didn't. It was never discussed. We got a call when the papers were ready, and we went to Mr. Dougherty's office and signed them. They were at the front desk, and the amount was typed in."

J.J. picked up the papers and looked through them again, briefly.

"Can I ask you, Mr. and Mr. Sanchez, why are you here?" The question seemed to surprise them.

"When Alfonso called on Saturday, he was very insistent that we should see you. He said the children would surely have a lot of problems in the future that the Church wasn't telling us about, and, after we sign these papers, we could lose our jobs. He said you could protect the children and us, Mr. Rai. We didn't know what to do, so we thought we should meet with you before we go to court. We don't know what is right, Mr. Rai. We don't want a lawsuit against the Church. The Catholic Church is the faith of our parents and grandparents. It's more important than money, but—" she paused and turned to her husband—"God gave us these children to raise and protect."

"Who is Alfonso?" J.J. asked.

Again, the surprised look.

"Isn't he with your office, Mr. Rai."

"No," answered J.J., and added, "Is Alfonso Mexican?"

"Oh. Yes. Definitely. From Mexico—not Mexican-American. Quite a difference in language. He spoke to us in our language."

"Well," J.J. said, puzzled, "we don't call people on the phone seeking business, but I do have some concerns regarding your boys and what happened to them. I hope they are just fine, and it certainly seems that Bishop O'Brien acted properly and promptly once this matter was brought to his attention. I am just not sure that the lawyer for the Diocese has been as considerate. I am not blaming you, but, as parents, you really need to know more about what happened to your children and what problems they might face. I don't think Mr. Dougherty has been as concerned about that as getting this matter quietly handled."

J.J. held up the papers and said, "I can tell you, just from what you have told me, that with what's been going on all over the country involving the Catholic Church, your boys should be getting more money and—"

Mrs. Sanchez interrupted him. "We don't care about the money. We don't want to sue the Church."

"And you haven't," responded J.J., "but these papers have been filed with the court to settle your sons' rights forever, and you really don't know how badly they are hurting or the problems they are going to have in the future. You need to know that; the court needs to know that, before any settlement is approved."

"But what can we do?" Mrs. Sanchez asked. "We've already signed the papers."

"That's not a problem. Only the court can approve a settlement. So nothing is binding yet. But you will need to show up on Wednesday and tell the court that you've changed your mind and that you need more information before you settle."

"Can we do that, Mr. Rai? I really feel like I'd be letting the bishop down if I did that. He's really been so helpful to our family all of these years. If we did that, it would be like saying we didn't believe him."

"Not at all. I know Bishop O'Brien very well. I'm sure he would agree. Like you said, he just wants what is best for the children. Mr. Dougherty, on the other hand, is a lawyer. He's trying to protect his client, the Diocese of Sacramento. He's not really looking out for your children."

"Well, could you do that for us, Mr. Rai? We couldn't do that to the bishop—go in there in court."

J.J. thought of walking into Roland Dougherty's little hearing, unannounced, and throwing in a wrench. If Dougherty hadn't been his notorious skinflint self but had put up $25,000 each, instead of $15,000, he might have saved himself a little embarrassment. Now, if J.J. intervened, Dougherty would find himself forced to put the contents of a few more collection plates into the kitty. Caught. Should be fun, J.J. thought.

He decided to help them. One visit to court should be enough to get the matter resolved in a fair settlement. Dougherty would see the handwriting on the wall. J.J. wouldn't even have to charge the family. It would be good public relations with the court.

"Okay," J.J. said finally. "Meet me at the courthouse on Wednesday. This is in Department 18, which is on the third floor. Judge Kelly is a very nice man, and I am sure we'll have no problem at all. You can just sit in the courtroom and wait for me. I'll be there by nine o'clock."

Mrs. Sanchez thanked J.J. profusely for his offer of help. Mr. Sanchez said nothing, and even when J.J. extended his hand to shake—and he took it—Mr. Sanchez never made eye contact.

As they were leaving, J.J. instructed them, "Don't mention to Bishop O'Brien or Mr. Dougherty, if he calls, or anyone else that I will be present at the hearing. I'd rather that they not know I'm coming."

Mrs. Sanchez agreed, although she did not understand this admonition.

J.J. wanted to see the shocked look on Roland Dougherty's face when he walked into the courtroom.

Chapter 6

One of J.J. Rai's oft-threatened, fantasy lawsuits, now that he had taken on most everyone else, was to sue God. Of course, to obtain jurisdiction over the person of God—just like General Motors—one has to serve legal papers upon the defendant. Only then could the court exercise "in persona" jurisdiction over the named defendant. Serving an individual is not complicated. A piece of paper, called a summons, is physically handed to the individual. Sometimes the individual will attempt to avoid the summons, i.e., run like hell when he sees the process server. Or refuse to take the piece of paper when it is handed to him. A defendant once left the paper thrown at him by a process server on his lawn and mowed around it for three months. But, it is said, the law is not stupid. It recognizes attempts at avoidance and provides, for example, that after throwing a summons at a person, a copy can be dropped into the mail to perfect service. A defendant can continue mowing around the papers on the lawn, but he has been successfully served. For people who had moved, however, the law is indeed really stupid. It provided that when a person had moved, and a document is required to be served by mail, the service could be effective by mailing it to the "last known address" of the person to be served. This is, of course, the one place in the world that everyone knows that the defendant is *not*. This, J.J. liked to refer to as "the beauty of the law."

Suing a corporation is a bit more complicated. A corporation is recognized as a legal person, much like an individual, but it has to be served by the serving of an officer or a person designated as its "agent for process." Then there is *where* it may be sued. A corporation can be sued only at its "principal place of business," where it is incorporated, or in any place in which it has "minimum contacts sufficient to satisfy due process."

J.J. thought of God as more like a corporation than an individual, certainly if one considered the Trinity similar to shareholders of a corporation or a board of directors, which together make up an entity, or in the view of the Catholic Church, the "person" of God.

People often say of an attorney that he "loved the law"—usually in an obituary. J.J. didn't love the law. He used it to certain ends. And, mostly out of boredom, he enjoyed messing with it. Starting with the Trinity.

"If we serve the Holy Ghost," he once asked a Jesuit priest, "but not the Father or Son, would a court have jurisdiction over God?" The Jesuit priest, Father Tom, confessed to being an agnostic.

Or, drawing upon the Gospels, he asked whether Jesus would be God's "agent for process," since the New Testament said that only through Him could anyone come to the Father. "Would that include a lawsuit?" he asked.

"And where is God's 'principal place of business'? The Vatican? Mecca? Salt Lake City? Waco?"

His ultimate fantasy was to file a lawsuit against God and have the process server take the suit to the Diocese of Sacramento and personally serve the bishop, on behalf of God, claiming that the bishop, as a successor to the Apostle Peter, was the agent of God.

The legal procedure after one has been served with the lawsuit, is statutory. Anyone served with process claiming that he is the agent of another must move the court to quash the service. Such a person must file a declaration under penalty of perjury denying that he is the agent for the person sued.

This, then, had been J.J.'s dream, much of his life, since he had left the Catholic Church. He would sue God, serve the Catholic Church, and, compel it to move to quash the Summons with a declaration, under penalty of perjury, stating:

Neither the Catholic Church, or the Diocese of Sacramento, its bishop, or its agents or employees, is the duly appointed agent of God.

Of course, the Catholic Church could accept service on behalf of God and acknowledge it was God's agent. Then, how would other religions react? J.J. wondered. Would they demand to be sued, each claiming it, and not the Catholic Church, was His true agent? A rush to be named *the* sole defendant? How wonderful; how pathetic, J.J. thought.

Perhaps, the Catholic Church would ignore the summons when served upon it. If so, J.J. imagined waiting the thirty days required and then asking the court to enter a judgment against God. J.J. could see the headline: "Catholic Church defaults; God ordered to pay."

What he had not yet determined was how he could sue a God in whom he did not believe. Or why there was something—perhaps anger—that made him want to sue God. And what were the damages that he could claim of this God in whom he did not believe? That he did not believe? But didn't such a suit against God, for not believing, imply the existence of God? Or was such a suit brought out of the despair of imagining human life without a God?

Chapter 7

$\mathcal{I}$t was already getting warm at 8:45 A.M. when J.J. walked the three blocks from his office, past City Hall with its clock that he still instinctively checked, to the Sacramento courthouse. Earlier, on the drive in from his home in the foothill town of Penryn, KFBK's Kitty O'Neal had predicted the first hundred-degree day of summer, and it was only the second of June. It was going to be a long, hot summer.

At sixty, with black hair—gray at the temples—and dressed in his Italian clothes, he looked the part of the successful trial lawyer. He no longer wore the off-the-rack suits that he had worn for years while addressing juries. He was rarely in court anymore; his reputation carried him forward. Now, opponents sought mediation and resolution and paid him handsomely out of court. And each multimillion-dollar settlement, especially if publicized, fed the myth of invincibility and contributed to the next out-of-court settlement. He saw to it that each was publicized.

If, however, an article didn't regularly appear in the newspaper, announcing another precedent-setting legal victory, people—especially lawyers—started talking. Was J.J. still taking cases? Had he died? Or worse: Had he retired? To still such rumors, J.J. occasionally liked to get to the courthouse even if only for a cup of coffee in the cafeteria, or, like this morning, to facilitate a matter where he could help the court and litigants expedite a settlement. If, in the process, he could earn the respect of the court—and embarrass a pompous senior partner of an opposing firm—so much the better. If all went well, it might even get him a blurb in R.E. Graswich's column in *The Sacramento Bee*—a column people hated but read to see if they were mentioned.

Climbing the first set of steps to the granite terrace of the Sacramento County Courthouse, J.J. noticed soap-like suds rising in the fountain, apparently from the churning action of the filter, to be knocked back down by the spray of a hundred cascading streams of water. He didn't know whether it was a maintenance problem or a prank, but it seemed to make a joke of justice.

Through the spray, J.J. could see the morning ritual of the sale of foreclosed real property "upon the courthouse steps," as the legal notice would say—a ritual that stretched back to the laws of England in the twelfth century under kings. A group of bidders stood circling the foreclosed property that was once someone's home, like vultures over a carcass, hoping to dine on the cheap.

J.J. joined the line going through the metal detector and took the black-and-gray speckled granite steps down to the central public elevators. The area was crowded as litigants, attorneys, and court staff made their way to the six floors of courtrooms for hearings on the nine o'clock calendar, which usually contained pretrial matters and began the court's day.

When J.J. got on a full elevator, he noticed Michael O'Reilly, a top trial attorney from San Francisco. They knew each other well from the American College of Trial Lawyers. O'Reilly gave just a nod of acknowledgement but said nothing. J.J. understood the lack of communication signaled that O'Reilly was in trial and one or more of the elevator occupants wearing the "juror" badge was on his jury. From years of trying cases, J.J. knew one misspoken word overheard by a juror could destroy an otherwise well-prepared case. And jurors were all ears and eyes—especially outside of the courtroom. J.J. gave O'Reilly a responsive nod and a slight smile that said "good luck."

J.J. straightened his collar, which was wet from the walk, as he got off the elevator on the third floor of the courthouse. He was a few minutes late, but everyone knew that Judge Kelly never started on time. He walked the long hallway, jurors standing against the walls waiting to be called, reached Department 18, and pulled on one of the large double doors. It was locked. A sign said, "Department 18's calendar will be heard in Department 22." Judge Gerald Vincent, he thought. He turned, picked up the pace, and headed for the stairwell, pulling open its fire doors and taking the plain cement steps two at a time. Department 22 was on the fourth floor and at the other end of the long hallway. Everyone knew Judge Vincent did not tolerate anyone being late in his courtroom.

As he entered Department 22, J.J. saw the Sanchez family sitting at the counsel table and a young man addressing the court from the other end, next to the jury box. J.J. was disappointed that Roland Dougherty was not present to see his entrance. He decided to sit just outside of the wooden railing, in the public area, to take stock of the proceedings, instead of entering the area reserved for attorneys. Perhaps he wouldn't have to say anything. Certainly, Judge Vincent would have a lot more questions than Judge Kelly would have had, particularly since the petitions were patently insufficient under the statutes and local rules.

Judge Vincent looked at J.J. as if he had been expecting him. Perhaps the Sanchezes had told the judge they were to meet Mr. Rai here. The judge looked at the clock situated on the wall above his bailiff's desk.

"Mr. Rai, you are late," said the judge, as J.J. sat down on the wooden benches used by members of the public.

"Yes, Your Honor, I went to Department 18."

"So did everyone else, Mr. Rai, but they all managed to get here on time."

"I apologize, Your Honor."

"And you will pay $100 to the clerk before you leave."

"Excuse me, Your Honor, but I am not on your calendar. I am not counsel of record and have made no appearance in this matter." J.J. stood to make his point.

"Then why are you here, Mr. Rai?"

"I thought I might help, Your Honor, since it appeared that the petition filed by Mr. Dougherty's office was clearly inadequate. I told the Sanchez family that I would bring this to your attention, or rather Judge Kelly's—in whose court I anticipated this was to be heard."

"Well, since you knew the petition was obviously inadequate, did you call Mr. Dougherty and explain that to him, Mr. Rai?"

"No, Your Honor. I really didn't think I needed to explain the law and the local rules to Mr. Dougherty. He must have known himself that these petitions were insufficient."

"Mr. Rai, I suggest it was your duty to meet and confer with opposing counsel before allowing a matter to come up on my calendar that is, as you say, so clearly insufficient. You've wasted the court's time this morning by not taking this up with Mr. Dougherty before the hearing. I should sanction you for that, also."

J.J. was now both frustrated and a little annoyed. "Your Honor, I am not counsel of record. I came here today merely to help these people and to see that their children's rights are protected."

"Thank you, Mr. Rai," responded the judge, his tone indicating that the "thank you" was sarcastic. "On a Minors Compromise Petition, it is the court's job to make sure that the minor is protected, including from attorneys."

The judge seemed to become even more impatient: "Mr. Rai, are you going to represent these two children or not? If not, you are wasting the court's time by being here. Yes or no, Mr. Rai?"

J.J. felt challenged. He did not feel that he could walk out of the courtroom, in the face of the judge's comments to him, and leave the Sanchezes to the mercy of Roland Dougherty, the Diocese of Sacramento, or the impatience of this judge.

"Yes, Your Honor, I will represent the children." He entered the counsel area and stood next to the seated Sanchez parents.

For the first time, and somewhat strangely, the judge smiled.

Turning to the young lawyer, who had remained standing during the confrontation without saying so much as a word, the judge asked: "Do you have any medical reports to offer?"

Hesitating, the young lawyer answered, "Well, we have a consultants report, but that's privileged."

"Give it to Mr. Rai," the judge instructed him without hesitation.

"But, Your Honor, I'll have to check with Mr. Dougherty," said the young attorney, clearly more afraid of his firm's senior partner than of this judge, but knowing that he had reason to fear both.

The judge immediately decided not to waste any more time with the young attorney. "Mr. Rai, I am ordering you to meet and confer with Mr. Dougherty and agree upon a proper petition, the medical documentation required, and a proposed resolution consistent with the injury."

The judge then turned to his clerk, seated at a desk below the judge's bench. "Madam Clerk, do we have an hour next week to hear this matter?"

"Yes, Your Honor," she replied, checking the computer screen in front of her. "Next Wednesday at 10:00 A.M."

The judge directed his next question to the Sanchezes, "Where are the children?"

J.J. interrupted. "Your Honor, I told them not to bring the children today, given the problems with the petition."

The judge tapped his finger and looked over the top of his glasses at J.J. "Mr. Rai, I know your reputation. Perhaps you think the rules don't apply to you. The rules require the children to be present. To do my job, I must meet the children. Next week, bring the children. And young man," he said, addressing the attorney from the Dougherty office, "I want Mr. Roland Dougherty—not you—personally present to explain this petition. Is that clear?"

"Yes, Your Honor," came the crisp reply, perhaps signifying relief that he could pass the case back to the firm's senior partner.

The judge closed the files and moved them to the left side of his bench. As he did, he reached for another file from the pile to his right. Looking directly at J.J., but addressing his clerk, he announced, "Call the next case. Perhaps its counsel will be better prepared."

The young lawyer—J.J. never heard his name—interrupted. "Excuse me, Your Honor, but will next week's hearing be back in Department 18 in front of Judge Kelly?"

Nice try, thought J.J. Roland would have done the same.

"No," said the judge, "you gentlemen have wasted my time. I'll see it through to the end."

The young lawyer seemed to flee the courtroom, although, J.J. surmised, he could expect much worse when he returned to his office and reported what had occurred. J.J. held the gate to allow the Sanchezes to exit. He whispered to them to go outside and that he would talk to them in the hall.

J.J. went to the end of the bar and handed the bailiff his business card. The bailiff, a uniformed and armed deputy sheriff, not a civilian court attendant used by some of the less formal judges, handed the card to the clerk, and she entered J.J.'s name on the docket. He was now, whether he wanted to or not, under the prodding of Judge Vincent, attorney of record for the Sanchez family. The clerk gave him a wink after making sure that the judge was not looking. J.J. smiled. Always nice to have a friendly face among the court staff. When he was trying cases, it was often the bailiff and the clerk to whom he would look for advice as to how he was doing with a jury. They watched while he worked and reported the reactions.

As J.J. turned to leave the court, he noticed an attractive woman, typing on a laptop. She was sitting in the shadows of the back left corner, where, if there had been a jury empanelled, she could see their faces. He guessed she was in her mid-forties. When she looked up, she stared directly ahead toward the judge as if following the proceedings, but she was no longer typing. He walked down the aisle to the door and took a last look at her. He was disappointed that she did not look back at him.

When J.J. exited the courtroom, he found that the Sanchez parents had been joined by their daughter. Together, they were standing in the hall. Mrs. Sanchez introduced Carmen, and it was clear that both she and her husband were embarrassed by their daughter's appearance. Her spiked bleach blond hair had shades of pink, her lipstick was black, and she wore a rabbit-skin wrap, complete with connecting furry rabbits. Her miniskirt, over fish-net stockings and four-inch heels, screamed hooker.

Carmen was clearly aware of the stares she was getting. Her only comment was, "I got tired of waiting in the car."

J.J. quickly explained the contemplated proceedings of the following week as court personnel and others looked on. He cut it short and told the Sanchezes that he would call them later in the day. An old friend walked by and rolled his eyes at J.J.

J.J. waited for his new clients to leave and walked slowly down the hall to the bank of elevators on the fourth floor. He didn't want to encounter the Sanchezes again on the ground floor or walk out of the courthouse with them and their daughter, past attorneys, litigants, and court personnel flooding in for the ten o'clock trial court docket. He knew the teasing he would get from fellow attorneys. He made a mental note to ask the Sanchez family to leave Carmen at home in the future, but, as the judge has instructed, to bring the boys.

J.J. pushed the button on the far wall and turned as he waited for an elevator. There she was again. Now, in an opposing elevator, looking directly at him. The door shut slowly, and she was gone. He felt better. So, she had noticed him. He smiled.

He saw her again as she pulled out of the courthouse parking lot in a brand new Lexus convertible. He recognized the signature plates. The car was a rental from the airport.

What would cause someone to fly into the Sacramento International Airport, rent a car, sit through, and take notes at a nine o'clock hearing before Judge Gerald Vincent? For a brief moment, he allowed it might be him; but then, he hadn't been listed as attorney of record so neither Dougherty—or she—could have known he would appear. Nor was there really anything of consequence in the record, at least that anyone could tell from the virtually anonymous filings by the Diocese regarding the boys.

Well, whoever she was, she was good looking—and gone.

He would have been flattered to know that, as she took her seat on the United flight to New York, she pulled out an article about him: "Are We Who We Were—and Were We Ever?" It was his speech at the 30th reunion of the class of 1969—his law class—of Boalt Hall, reprinted in the *California Lawyer* magazine at the insistence of Dean Herma Hill Kay, the first woman dean of a major American law school.

Her stepfather had given her the article, and now that she could associate J.J.'s face with the master of ceremonies of the reunion, she settled in to read it.

Are We Who We Were—and Were We Ever?

[What follows is the speech of J.J. Rai to his fellow classmates on the occasion of the 30th reunion of the law school class of 1969]

Thirty years! Thirty years! We come together and all the dean can talk about is whether we're going to include Boalt in our wills. It's nice to know that Boalt is following our careers, if only in the obituaries.

How can we forget those days when we first came together? In 1966. The last graduating class of the sixties. At Boalt. In Berkeley. During those tumultuous times. "The war" to us will always be Vietnam. The protests: "Hey, hey, LBJ, how many kids you kill today? Black Power. With Huey and Stokely. We are on a first-name basis, right? And then there were Martin, John, and Bobby: "Some people see things as they are, and ask why? I dream things that never were, and ask why not?"

My kids ask me of those days and I wonder, as we reach fifty-six, thirty years later: "Are we who we were—and were we ever?"

I have to confess to some nagging doubt, which I wish to confront tonight. Actually, I am confronted with it by my children, especially my daughter, Rebel, to whom cross-examination is instinctive.

"Dad," my daughter Rebel asks me, "were you at Woodstock?"

"Well, no, but I was at Berkeley in the sixties," I answer with pride, my eyes moistening as I look into the distance, or at least the blur left when I remove my glasses.

"So you were in the Free Speech Movement?"

I bask. "Ah, the FSM."

"Well?" she asks, bringing me back.

"Well, no. That was Mario Savio in 1964. I didn't get to Berkeley until 1966, so they went ahead without me. By 1966, I think Mario was a mailman."

"Mario? You knew him?"

"Well, no. But everyone called him Mario. He came back during the People's Park Protest in 1969. Or, as we call it, the PPP."

"So, Dad, you were in those protests when Reagan called out the National Guard. Wow!"

"Well, no. But Brian Jacobs went down and got beat up and arrested, so we all wore 'Free Brian' buttons as Reagan gassed the university."

"You were gassed by Reagan, Dad?"

"Well, no. But Boalt Hall is upwind from the campus, and it kind of blew up. We could smell it so we protested finals."

"Really, you refused to take finals?"

"Well, no. We delayed them. It actually gave us a little more time to study. We couldn't refuse to take them. After all, we needed the grades to get jobs in those big law firms. You can't go messing up your whole career for some cause."

"But you did oppose the war, right?"

"Of course. We all did."

"And refuse to go to Vietnam? You stood up to Nixon and Kissinger?"

"Well, actually, I took this draft class and got a 1-Y classification. See, the wife of a classmate got TB, and I exposed myself to her."

"Dad, does Mom know you exposed yourself to a classmate's wife?"

"That's not what I mean, and you know it."

"Well, at least you went to a law school that recognized the equality of women."

"It was hardly equality. Rose Contreras was number one in the class, all three years. I'd call that female dominance."

"It's natural for us to lead, Dad. But I thought Mom said you worked for the poor when you got out of Boalt."

"No, she said we *were* poor when I got out of Boalt. My first job paid $750 a month. Later, I did work for the ACLU—hey, did you ever see Peter Fonda in the movie *Easy Rider*?"

"Who?"

"He would pronounce it really slow, with a Southern accent: Aaa-Cee-L-You—and I had an Afro for a while. I represented a gay lib group and even shut down a nuclear power plant while making a little money, of course, in accident cases. How do you think we afforded all those big houses and travel and the money I paid your Mom? The PSAs."

"What Public Service Announcements?"

"No, Property Settlement Agreements, the divorces."

This is usually where it gets ugly.

"Face it, Dad. You're an ambulance-chasing yuppie. Look at those $4,000 Armani suits, those $600 shoes."

I become defensive.

"Damn it, I named you Rebel, didn't I? I worked hard to send you to an all-girls school. I even wrote the essay on your application: 'Why I want to go to Mills College.' So leave me alone."

"Dad," she begins with the patience of a person saying the same thing for the hundredth time, "it's a women's college, not a girls' school. And you wrote the essay because you are so controlling. Chill out."

"Listen, kid," I say, my voice rising, "I was politically correct before you were born. I rode with the Black Panthers in the streets of Oakland. I faced the po-lease. I can say any damn thing I want. I went to Berkeley in the sixties."

Last month, I was invited to a thirty-five-year Woodstock reunion party. I don't know if any of the insurance defense and corporate attorneys present were at Woodstock. I know I wasn't. But that evening, they were all wearing polo shirts, shorts, and expensive sandals. Being a graduate of Boalt, at Berkeley, I decided it was time to dress appropriately.

I wore an American flag as a cape, over a bare upper torso on which I hand-painted "Fuck Nixon" in bright colors. I even personally made a peace symbol, as best I remembered, out of cardboard, painted it black, and put it on a leather string around my neck. I wore a black wig with hair hanging past my shoulders and a red, white, and blue bandana around my forehead. I went barefoot.

To impress my children, I had my picture taken and sent it to them.

At the party, I enjoyed being someone I had never really been.

As I was leaving, I overheard an older woman say, "Why is he still so angry with Nixon?"

My daughter called me the next week, at my office. She had the photo I had sent in front of her.

"Dad," she asked, genuinely perplexed, "if you're so politically correct, how come you didn't know you were wearing a Mercedes hood emblem around your neck?"

"Well, I still cling to an image of the law student at Boalt Hall, at Berkeley in the sixties, that perhaps never was. The one my children think I might have been. But there must be a reason the image is so important to me that I refuse to give it up. Maybe it's the lawyer that I wish I had been. I know that as a law student in the sixties I was never really comfortable with the concepts of personal wealth and country clubs. And here, thirty years later, we are at a country club, many of us wealthy, and it still doesn't feel right.

"The only explanation I can give you is summed up in a few words that I have uttered with pride over these years: 'I went to law school at Boalt Hall. Yeah, Berkeley.'"

Power. Peace.

She looked up and smiled. The flight attendant appeared over her shoulder.

"A glass of champagne, please."

She was still smiling, her hand on the article, when her champagne arrived.

Chapter 8

*I*t didn't take Roland Dougherty long to call. J.J. had expected the call and was pleased with himself when it was announced. As he picked up the phone, he put a finger to his lips to signal the young associate in his office to sit and watch him work Dougherty.

"Good morning, Roland. Sorry to have missed you in court this morning."

"J.J., how have you been? I thought you would have retired by now with all of your money. Writing your memoirs maybe," responded Dougherty in a jocular, if forced, fashion.

J.J. laughed. "No, still looking for something memorable enough to put in them. You know, that last, great challenge." He rolled his eyes at the young associate.

"Well, J.J., I'm sure you figured out that this case is no challenge. It's a terrible thing that a priest would improperly touch a little boy…"

J.J. interrupted. "Two little boys. Altar boys."

"Right," said Dougherty. "Two little boys, but Bishop O'Brien immediately undertook an investigation and took instantaneous disciplinary action against the priest. I'm sure you understand, under these circumstances, that the Church is not liable for these terrible acts. But I'm not calling to argue the law. We just want to do the right thing for these children."

Right, thought J.J. You just want to do the right thing. You're not concerned about the law. Then why did you just tell me that the Church has no liability if we're not talking about the law?

"I don't know, Roland. These kind of cases are being brought all over the country against the Catholic Church. There seems to be an epidemic caused by fondling priests. And you, of all people, must know that it's been covered up for years."

Dougherty understood the charge directed at him. He didn't take the bait.

"Well, there is certainly an epidemic of lawsuits. I don't think, in context, there is a disproportionate number of what you call fondling priests. And I wouldn't call what has occurred a cover-up. I know you personal injury trial lawyers like to use that term. But it's much more complicated. The Church has a responsibility, beyond the temporal, for the salvation of all sinners, even priests."

Save it, J.J. thought. Somehow, with the admonition that "God hated the sin but loved the sinner," the Catholic Church had acted as if its priests were the victims in sexual assault cases or, at the very least, were the lost sheep that needed to be brought back to the flock. The biblical parable of the shepherd leaving ninety-nine to the wolves to go after the one that was lost always seemed odd to J.J.—not to mention a bad way to manage sheep.

J.J. was in no mood for a sermon. Especially from a lawyer.

"Roland, as a Catholic, doesn't it just make you sick that the same person who, on the one hand, professes that he can turn a wafer into the body of Christ is jerking off altar boys, with the other hand? Sorry for mixing metaphors, but doesn't that shake your faith just a little bit, Roland?"

This time J.J. did not look at the young associate. He was not asking for effect; he was asking because he genuinely wondered how anyone could reconcile the two such that he could have any faith in the teachings of these "fathers" of the Church.

Dougherty did not respond directly. He was unshakable in his faith, as he always had been. He was not calling to argue about either the teachings or the leadership of the Church. He was calling as an attorney arguing a client's case.

"J.J., we are all human. We are all capable of sin. In the last fifty years, between 1950 and 2002, about 4,400 priests were accused of abuse in the United States. That's about eighty-eight priests a year out of thousands of parishes with millions of Catholics. You need to put it in perspective, J.J. I bet Wal-Mart has more sexual harassment claims per year than the Catholic Church."

"Roland, Wal-Mart is not the voice of God on Earth. If I were to follow a religion, I would want it to be not just 'no worse than,' 'comparable to,' or 'a bit better than Wal-Mart.'"

Finally, J.J. had gotten to Roland Dougherty. He raised his voice. "J.J. what do you want? To embarrass the Church? To take down Bishop O'Brien, who you know very well is a decent guy who has done everything you would want from a person faced with this kind of situation? You want to go after headlines at the expense of the Sanchez parents and their children? Is that what this is all about, J.J.?"

"Roland, I don't have a plan, except to do the job the court insisted I do. If you had filed a proper petition and presented the court with appropriate medical records, I doubt that I would ever have heard about this case."

"Right. The way I heard it, you had one of your runners call the family and chase the case," said Dougherty.

"That's bullshit. Who told you that?"

"Well, actually your client, Mrs. Sanchez, told that to the bishop. I would assume she knows how she came to find herself in your office."

"Wrong, if she said that. My office doesn't chase cases. And while we're at it, my office doesn't settle lawsuits without proper medical documentation, especially when it comes to a minor. So, Roland, why don't we start by you sending me the medical reports that Judge Vincent told your young lawyer to give me?"

"We don't have any reports," said Dougherty.

"What do you mean, you don't have any reports? The young lawyer from the firm said that you had one, but he couldn't turn it over without talking to you."

"Well, he was wrong. I have a psychologist's consultation comments. But if our attempts to settle this case amicably are going to be resisted and the matter becomes adversarial, then we are claiming the work product privilege for our consultant's work. You can go and get your own expert to examine the boys."

Well, thought J.J., that didn't take long. No more Mr. Nice Guy.

"How did you ever expect this to get approved, Roland, without a report for the court regarding these boys?"

"I had spoken briefly to Judge Kelly about the matter. We were prepared to meet *in camera*, out of the public courtroom, and discuss our psychologist's findings. That would have protected the boys from any embarrassment. Of course, that was before you got involved."

"And I'm sure good old Judge Kelly had told you that he would approve the settlement. Unfortunately for you, Judge Kelly was sick and Judge Vincent took over the matter."

"Look, J.J., these kids are fine. The priest shouldn't have touched them on camping trips, but come on. When we were kids, we all did this kind of harmless grabbing and groping, show and tell. It's part of boys growing up. It never hurt anyone. Don't try to make a bigger deal out of it than it is."

"I don't know about you, Roland, but I never got grabbed by any adult, let alone a priest."

"J.J., there's $15,000 on the table for each boy. Your people don't want a lawsuit challenging their Catholic faith, and we don't want the publicity of a lawsuit, even though, as you know full well, under California law the Church is not liable for the priest's acts if we didn't know or have any reason to know in advance that he was doing this kind of thing and if we took immediate corrective action as soon as we found out. Are you going to sue Bishop O'Brien and say that he knew or should have known that this priest was engaging in this kind of conduct? It's not true, and you know it. Your clients know it, too. And, J.J., we both know that the Sanchez family would never allow you to bring such a lawsuit. So let's be reasonable and get this matter settled, okay?"

J.J. knew he was caught between his obligation—that Judge Vincent would strictly enforce—to assess the injury to the boys and the Sanchez's unwillingness to sue the Church or the bishop under any circumstances. There might be a little wiggle room; but he knew there wasn't much.

"You get the medical report to me and then maybe we can talk," J.J. answered.

"Get your own damn medical report!" said Dougherty, and hung up.

As J.J. sat, holding the phone, he was sorry he had let his young associate listen in on a conversation that had not gone as planned.

"What do you do now?" asked the young lawyer.

"When they give you lemons," J.J. answered, pausing to draw the young man in, "use them in a gin and tonic."

Chapter 9

$\mathcal{I}$n the afternoon, after the court hearing, J.J. Rai called Sally Conrad and left a message on her machine. She would usually call back at the top of the hour, between patients.

Sally was his go-to expert on matters psychological. He used her as a resource to test his instincts and to find the right expert to testify. There were experts who would tell you what you wanted to hear, and there were experts who told you what you needed to know. Sally was the latter. She was an L.C.S.W.—Licensed Clinical Social Worker—by title, and although that hid the breadth of her knowledge and experience, J.J. knew he would need an expert with a pedigree of publications—preferably a psychiatrist with an M.D. and board certification—should the matter go to trial. However, he was not anticipating a trial. He was anticipating an evaluation and settlement. Right now, J.J. wanted to know what he needed to know about child molesters, child abuse, and what damage to look for in the lives of these two boys. And, if he could ever get his hands on the psychological report that Dougherty had, he needed someone to evaluate the report and its objectivity.

Sally was generally comfortable in her role as a consultant with the caveat that she would not be disclosed as an expert witness and would not testify in any legal proceeding. She wanted to be free to be completely candid, not an advocate for one side or another, and to possibly become a treating therapist but only, she insisted, after a case was over. She wanted nothing to do with litigation. She had very little faith in the adversarial system as a manner of diagnosing or treating patients.

Part of J.J.'s trust in Sally came from a few years of therapy with her, which therapy began with his involvement with a future wife and ended promptly after the divorce. When J.J. suggested that perhaps the marriage was the source of his problems, given the timing of the treatment, Sally snapped her fingers over her head and exclaimed "Bingo!" at the insight. She then threw a couch pillow at him, they hugged, and thus ended his treatment.

He had been back once, but only to drop off his law school buddy, Andy Miller, whose life—with divorce, disbarment, and dissolution of his law partnership—had imploded. J.J. had counted each day that Andy didn't kill himself a success. And he had credited Sally with that success. Andy—Macho Man Andy—was such a mess that he had been two years into therapy before his condition had allowed him to see beyond himself. At that point, he had realized that his therapist was a lesbian. The shoes had been a giveaway. By then, however, he had become as dependent upon her as J.J. had once been.

It was five o'clock when the call came in. "J.J., Ms. Conrad on the line," announced his secretary.

"Sally," he said, sitting back and loosening his tie. He suspected she was sitting, as he remembered her, on the large stuffed chair, her feet curled under her, the lamp on next to her, a coffee cup, her constant companion. In fact, at sixty-two, her hair had grayed a little, but she still wore her dishwater blonde hair short, her shoes sensible, and her smile mischievous.

"You're getting married!" she exclaimed.

"No, Sally. I wouldn't do that without talking to you."

"You've got that right, J.J. You are capable of learning, after all."

"I need your help."

"I told you that you would come crawling back to me."

J.J. laughed. "Not right now. This is about a couple of children who have been abused." He added, "By a priest."

"Jesus, J.J., no disrespect intended, but I don't treat children," she quickly reminded him.

"I know, Sally. I don't want you to treat them. I have a week to satisfy myself that they are doing all right so that I can recommend a settlement to the court. I don't have time to find an expert in these matters and do a formal work-up. I may have a report for you to review from the other side. In any event, I just want you to size up the situation and give me an assessment after meeting the boys."

"J.J., I don't even like children." She had no trouble admitting what might seem an unacceptable characteristic for a woman.

"Well, Sally, they are really nice kids. Really well-behaved. They're twins. Altar boys. I don't even want a written report—just your sense of whether there is anything there to worry about. Okay? Same rules. You are not a witness. Just give me your impression. You know I rely on you."

"Don't you have anyone else more qualified? What about that psychiatrist you used to go fishing with."

"Sally, he's dead. You're it. I looked through my old list of local psychiatric consultants. They're all dead."

"So what are you saying, J.J.? That you're calling me because I'm old but not dead? Come on, J.J. There are a lot of witnesses on this clergy abuse stuff. This is happening all over the country. You can get on the phone and, within an hour, find one to fly out here and give you whatever you want."

"That's exactly why I'm not going to call any of them. I don't want them to give me what I want. I trust *you*."

He was fully aware that many psychiatrists, as well as other experts in law, were available to testify to whatever an attorney wanted. It was also a fact, in psychiatry, that the diagnosis of a patient often had more to do with the therapist's own biases than any objective fact about the patient. Even an "honest" psychiatric opinion was often a personal bias hidden behind psychiatric nomenclature.

"Look, Sally," pleaded J.J, "if you tell me there is a problem, I'll bring in the best expert I can find. I just don't want one of these guys coming in, messing around in these kids' brains, and creating something that isn't there. I want to know if there is a problem—not compound it."

She knew exactly what he meant. She had seen it in child custody and other court battles. Psychotherapists who were the problem. Dueling "experts" caught up in the litigation, saying anything to help their side in an adversarial system. After a minute of silent reflection, she relented.

"Okay, J.J., but you owe me big time. I really don't like kids."

J.J. breathed an audible sigh of relief. "Thanks, Sally. I know it's an imposition. This is a really scary area for me. Molested children. This isn't like my other cases where I can see the injury, the broken bones, the burns, the scars. These kids just look like sweet, normal"—he paused—"altar boys."

Sally had seen all forms of abuse in her practice. Because she dealt with adults, she usually saw the consequences of childhood abuse rather than contemporaneous symptoms of abuse. She was convinced that childhood sexual abuse did have long-term and devastating effects. She was also aware that the controversy in the psychiatric literature was less a debate between peers and more of a war between advocates of different positions.

Fortunately, she knew that she would be looking at the children from the point of view of a therapist and not from the point of view of an advocate. Nor would she have to defend her views in court. She had agreed simply to deliver her opinions to J.J., as she had done in previous cases.

J.J. gave Sally the family's phone number and asked that she get back to him by the following Monday. He didn't need to tell her how to handle her inquiry or interviews. He left it up to her, trusting that she would do whatever she felt necessary and then give her honest opinion.

He hung up and immediately called the Sanchez family to let them know that Sally Conrad would be calling and meeting with them. He told them she was a Licensed Clinical Social Worker and would be evaluating the children for him to determine an appropriate settlement. Because of their apprehension, he assured the Sanchezes that this had nothing to do with the filing of a lawsuit against the Church. Rather, Sally was ultimately helping him and the judge in protecting the children.

As he got off the phone, J.J. realized that his control of the matter was limited. Clearly, Mrs. Sanchez was in contact with the bishop and, through the bishop, with Roland Dougherty, who had a clear idea of what the Sanchez family would and would not do. J.J. felt like a gambler whose cards could be seen by his opponent.

As soon as he was off the phone, his secretary's voice came through the intercom. "J.J., Bishop O'Brien has been holding for you. Shall I put him through?"

Chapter 10

"Bishop O'Brien, I hope you are not calling about the Sanchez matter," J.J. said as he answered the phone.

"J.J., it's still Don, not Bishop O'Brien. And yes, I am calling about what happened today in court."

"Bishop…Don…I've talked to Roland Dougherty. He's representing you, and I am prohibited from talking to an adverse party who is represented in litigation by counsel," J.J. said, reciting the State Bar rule.

"Well, J.J., we're not adverse. We're both concerned for those boys, aren't we?" The bishop had a point. There was no lawsuit pending.

"Look," interjected the bishop, "let me come over to your office. I have some reports and documents for you. I am sorry if you and Roland got off on the wrong foot. As I recall, the two of you never got along when we all were altar boys together."

"You didn't like him much either. As I remember it, he always sold more *Catholic Herald* subscriptions than both of us."

"I don't think he sold any, J.J. His parents would just give him the money to turn in so he could win each time," laughed the bishop.

"I never knew that. Now there's another reason to hate him. You and I could have used a new bike or some of the other prizes they gave out."

Finally, J.J., laughing, relented. "Okay, come on over, and you can say whatever you want. I am not communicating with you without your lawyer—even if he is an asshole."

Bishop O'Brien laughed, too. "Shall I bring the sacramental wine or do you have some Scotch there at the office?" The memories flooded back. He and Don O'Brien would serve early morning Mass and take a little swig, on cold days, out of the wine bottle that sat in the sacristy before they ran down the back stairs of the cathedral, into the parking lot, and across to the school. The wine seemed very bitter back then, but it warmed the throat and chest. And then, unlike now, J.J. actually believed that the wine would become the blood of Christ through consecration by the priest. He had never tasted consecrated wine but assumed that it became sweeter.

"My stash is better than what you have behind the altar, and you don't have to drink out of a screw-top cap," J.J. said, remembering those days together.

Then he added, "I'll have the secretary leave the front door open. It's the twenty-first floor—the top—directly across from César Chávez Park."

As he waited for his old friend, J.J. poured a drink for himself. Alcohol was a staple of trial work. Since it was after May 1st, his tradition of white alcohol for summer and brown for winter dictated a gin and tonic. He walked into the conference room with his drink and looked across to the magnificent landmark that was the Cathedral of the Blessed Virgin with its distinctive three towers, the taller being the center clock tower upon which stood a large gold-leafed cross. Behind these towers he could see the huge copper cupola, reminiscent of St. Peter's Basilica in Vatican City. It was just three blocks away and just one block from the equally impressive State Capitol building that had been completed close in time to the cathedral. In their day, J.J. thought, in the new state of California, these two buildings must have dominated the Sacramento skyline from a great distance in the open, flat Sacramento valley.

Even now, they were impressive among the modern buildings, in part because the city fathers had placed height and sight limitations upon buildings around the State Capitol. Looking down at César Chávez Park below, J.J. saw a priest, the white of his Roman collar caught by the sun, through the palm and magnolia trees, as he walked briskly from the southeast corner into the park. Tall, thin, gray hair in a close-cropped military cut, the priest stood out now as he had in the marches with César Chávez. The last time J.J. and Bishop O'Brien had been together was to march around this very park in a funeral procession for their mutual friend, Mayor Joe Serna, who had died much too soon. J.J. felt a sense of sorrow that Bishop O'Brien was now marching though the park named for César Chávez to a personal injury lawyer's office in order to make amends for the sins of a priest. It seemed beneath him.

J.J. heard the elevator "ding" and knew that Bishop O'Brien had arrived at his floor. Then he heard, "J.J.? Hello?"

J.J. went out to greet his old friend. They shook hands warmly and then fell into a hug in which they slapped each other's back. As they parted, the bishop, smiling, surveyed the high windows looking west to the evening sun and, through the glass of the conference room, east to the Sierras.

"What a beautiful place, J.J. You have certainly done well. And from what I hear, you deserve it," said the bishop.

"Well," J.J. said as he led the bishop to his office on the southwest corner, "we've all done pretty well for parochial school kids and altar boys, haven't we? I mean, you're the bishop, Roland Dougherty is the senior partner of one of the most respected business firms in town, and I…well, I've made some money."

"Don't diminish what you've done, J.J.," said the bishop. "I'm sure you're not listed in *Best Lawyers in America* just because you've made money."

"Actually, for that publication, it is exactly because I've made money. In civil litigation, Don, it's all about the size of the verdict." J.J. added, "See, size does matter." He immediately felt a little uneasy with his own joke, even with his childhood friend, who was sitting across from him with a collar of a Roman Catholic priest.

The bishop smiled. "It's the same with bishops. How big a congregation he has; how much money can he raise; how many schools can he build."

J.J. jumped up. "I'm sorry, Don. I forgot your Scotch. Let me get it."

He walked to the wet bar, dropped some ice into a heavy Wexford glass, and poured a splash of Johnnie Walker Blue Label Scotch. "Water back, as I remember from your civil rights days, right?" J.J. asked.

"Yes, I remember the article that described me that way. My superiors at the time were not only unhappy with my Scotch drinking, but also my civil rights activities." He watched as J.J. poured the drink. "A little more on the Scotch if you don't mind, J.J. I'm off duty, and, on my salary, I don't get a lot of opportunities to drink a good Johnnie Walker Scotch."

J.J. returned to the seating area in his office and handed the bishop the Scotch and the glass of water as the bishop laid an expanded folder on the coffee table at the foot of the couch. Then he leaned back and took a sip of the Scotch. "Ahh," he said.

They sat quietly for a few moments until the bishop finally asked, "Remember Sister Eileen?"

J.J. nearly choked on his gin and tonic and leaned forward, coughing. When he stopped, he said, "My God. Sixth grade. Wasn't she something? You never knew what hand she was going to slap you with. Sometimes, both hands would come flying from behind her habit and hit you on each side of the head at the same time and knock you into next week. I don't remember that we really did anything wrong. I think she just liked hitting boys. I wonder whatever happened to her."

They laughed together until the bishop said, "She's probably in hell." Again they sat silently. J.J. was looking into his gin and tonic.

"Do you believe in hell, Don?" he asked.

"No," the bishop said after long reflection. "The belief that a loving God who created the beauty and intricacies of the universe would feel the need to eternally punish His creations for some failure to follow His rules or recognize His majesty demeans the very concept of a loving God. 'Love me or else.' What kind of a love is that? What kind of a God is so insecure that He has to demand that we, mere mortals, have to love Him? Love is something that is given freely, or it's not love."

"Well, good, Don," said J.J. "I've been worried since I left the Church. I would hate to die and find out I've been wrong all these years and hell really does exist after all. It would be a little late for me at that point."

"I understand, especially for a lawyer," mused the bishop. Again, the two old friends laughed. Again, they sat in silence. Again, it was the bishop who broke the silence. "Give me another drink, J.J., and I'll tell you about heaven."

The bishop was talking; J.J. was listening. It was a habit that he had acquired from years of negotiating. Let the other side talk. You don't learn anything when you're talking. He had also developed a pair of corollaries to this rule, which he taught young attorneys: The first person to speak in a negotiation loses; and, the party that cannot walk away from the negotiation loses. He handed the bishop his refill of Scotch.

Again, the bishop took a swig and expressed his appreciation with an audible "ahh." He lifted the glass up in front of his eyes, and, looking at its contents, said, "J.J., this is heaven."

"The Scotch?" J.J. asked.

"No. Well, yes, that too. Now, this is not official dogma, you understand, and you are not to quote me, but I have concluded that we are living in heaven."

"What do you mean? *This* is it?"

"This is it, J.J. This is as good as it gets. This is heaven."

"Then what happens when we die?"

Again, the bishop took a sip of his drink and held the question as he savored the Scotch.

"We die," replied the bishop.

"That's it? Thousands of years of philosophy and religious thought, summed up as a statement, 'We die'?"

"What do you want from me, J.J.? Immortality? Immortality is for gods, not for men. Isn't that the distinction?"

"Yes, I suppose so, but if that's all you're offering, what's the point?"

"The point is living. It is also living with the unknown and the unknowable."

"Don," asked J.J., "have you considered that perhaps you're in the wrong business? You're a bishop of the Catholic Church, for Christ's sake, and you're sounding like me!"

"Well, J.J., we were both raised in the same Church, with the same priests and nuns. Maybe I'm just not as smart as you. You believe there is no God. I believe that God is a concept beyond human understanding. That doesn't make me give up on the Church as a teacher of the precepts of Jesus Christ. I believe in His message of love. It's not the message that I have a problem with; it's the messenger in the form of the Church."

"How can you be a bishop if you believe the Church is the problem?"

"Some people, a lot of people, need the heaven thing to make sense of or give meaning to life. They can't deal with the idea of death as the final act. Fine. No harm. If that's what it takes to have them stop obsessing about death and concentrate on living fully, I'm for it. Christianity is about living like Christ. Living. Not avoiding death."

J.J. pondered the surprising expressions from a bishop of the Catholic Church.

"What about you, J.J.? Do you believe in the law?" asked the bishop.

"Of course, I believe in it. It exists. My job is to get around it."

"Mine, too," said the bishop. "Sometimes I have to get around the Church to find Christ."

The bishop leaned forward and reached for the folder on the coffee table. "I have some things for you. First, the memo from the psychologist, Dr. Frank Mandel, who interviewed the two boys, together. Second, the complete personnel file of Father Ramon Gutierrez, including my letter to the superior of his Order, terminating him from his assignment here at the Sacramento Diocese and recommending that he be separated from the priesthood. Finally, I have included a memo of my own investigation and the confession of Father Gutierrez."

Bishop O'Brien pushed the folder toward J.J.

"Does Roland Dougherty know that you're giving me these documents?" J.J. asked without touching them.

"I told him if he didn't give them to you, I would. I am the client. It is my choice—over his objection I might add."

J.J. picked up the file.

"I am sorry for the way this matter has been handled," continued the bishop. "However, once I reported it to our liability insurance company, and the Conference of Bishops, I had to cooperate with legal counsel and, as you know, that's Roland. I wanted the children to get more, $25,000 each, but Roland was handling the legal aspects."

This time the bishop stood and got his own Scotch and water. "Just a splash," he explained.

After returning to his seat, he added, "I feel responsible for these boys. I have known this family for years. I brought them to Sacramento with me. I have watched these children grow. I blame myself for not knowing that one of our priests could do this kind of thing, for not being more vigilant."

"I don't think Dougherty would want you talking like this."

"I don't care about the law, J.J. I just want these children not to suffer. I want to take care of them. I am glad you're involved, J.J. You tell us what to do, and I'll see that it's done."

J.J. saw a tear in the bishop's eye. Feeling uncomfortable in the presence of his friend, under these circumstances, J.J. stood to signal the end of the meeting. "Listen, thanks for these files. Let me read them through. Maybe we can wrap this thing up by next Wednesday's hearing," he said in an attempt to ease his own discomfort.

As they walked out, J.J. asked, "So what happens to the priest in a situation like this?"

"Usually, he'll be sent for an evaluation at a place that the Church maintains for these kinds of situations. Then it's up to his Order. With what has happened nationwide, you can understand the Church's hierarchy is very sensitive about reassigning someone like this anywhere else. I would assume that he would be assigned to a monastery for a lifetime of prayer or be discharged from the priesthood."

"Do you have any information that he did anything like this to other children?" J.J. asked.

"He said he didn't. But I don't believe him. Once these guys start, they don't stop. I know Dougherty quotes those statistics about *only* four thousand-something priests in fifty years. What he doesn't tell you is that those priests molested over ten thousand separate victims. And these are just the reported cases. I am sure that many more, if not most, were never reported. So, to answer your question, no, we don't know whether Father Gutierrez has ever been involved in anything like this before. But I would not necessarily believe his denials. My only hope is that we caught him in time," said the bishop.

"Mine, too," said J.J. Rai.

Chapter 11

J. J. knew that Sally Conrad would do her part. He was reassured on Friday when his secretary told him that Sally had picked up the bishop's notes and the psychologist's report. "She is seeing the family again over the weekend," the secretary told him. So it was no surprise when Sally called on Monday morning. What was unusual, however, was that she asked to meet with him, in person, at his office. Normally she would simply share her observations, thoughts, and opinions on the phone.

"What's going on?" he asked.

"That's what I'd like to know," Sally said. "I think we need to talk."

"Okay, come on in at 1:00."

As he hung up the phone, he was both confused and concerned. During the rest of the morning, he tried to concentrate on the article he was reading as part of the continuing education requirements of the California Bar. The deadline was coming up, and he had put off taking classes or even listening to tapes. Why did he need to study the law, he asked himself with some irritation. He was *making* the law. But his thoughts kept coming back to the two altar boys. Was he really protecting their interests or just trying to squeeze Dougherty for the fun of it? Was it just another game to him that he had to win? Were the clients just pieces on the board? He was espousing justice for the children, but where was his sense of outrage? Had he become so good, so professional, that he had grown detached and no longer identified with the individuals he represented?

Sally was prompt and direct. Before he could sit down, she dropped the bishop's file on his desk and asked, "Have you read these?"

"Yes, of course," said J.J.

"Okay, then tell me your understanding of what happened to these two little boys."

"Well, it's all there. Admitted by the priest. As the boys said, the priest groped and fondled the two of them, together—and I think exposed himself, too—on the altar boys' summer trips. I believe there were two trips, and this all came to light when Felix refused to go on the camping trip this year."

"Anything else?" Sally asked.

"Like what?"

"Anything," Sally repeated.

"I don't think so."

"And since both boys were involved, did they each acknowledge the priest's conduct?"

J.J. looked at her a bit impatiently. He was not used to being cross-examined. "Yes, I believe so. What difference does it make? The priest admitted it."

He leaned forward, his arms on the desk in front of him. "What's going on, Sally? What's wrong?" He'd had enough of this question-and-answer routine.

"I don't know, but something is seriously wrong," she said. "Let me tell you about the sequence of my interviews, and you'll see what is bothering me."

"Okay," J.J. said. "Do you mind if I take notes?"

"No, but I'm only a consultant. Not a witness. We agreed," Sally reminded him.

"Right," J.J. agreed.

Sally immediately began to describe her interview process. "I started with the parents, together, to get an overview and a bit of history. Date of birth, marriage, when they came to the United States, children's birthdays, any childhood medical or psychological disorders or learning problems. They told me how they worked in the fields, how they met Bishop O'Brien when he was just a priest with the farm workers, and how they came to Sacramento with his help."

She looked down at her notes and continued. "Dad is a custodian at the cathedral, and mom maintains the rectory for the priests as a house-keeper and all-around helper. The oldest child, Carmen, age seventeen, has been a problem to them since they moved to Sacramento when she was between eleven and twelve. Alcohol, drugs, boys, shoplifting, tru-ancy, you name it. The twins, on the other hand, have been model children. Well-behaved. Done well in school, not great, but no behavioral prob-lems. And, for about three years, they've been altar boys." Sally stopped and looked up at J.J. to signal the end of the history portion of her notes.

"Then I got to the question of what happened to the boys," Sally said.

"And?" J.J. pressed her.

"They don't know. The parents never asked."

"But they went to the bishop," J.J. said.

"The mother did," Sally corrected him, "but only because she sus-pected something had happened on the camping trip when Felix refused to sign up this year and Father Gutierrez acted guilty when she told him outside the cathedral."

"But she was right. Father Gutierrez confessed," said J.J.

Sally held up her hand. "Let's go to my next interview."

"Okay," J.J. said, moving down his legal pad to put the next name.

"Felix. When I first spoke to him, I asked him ..."—Sally paused to read from her notes:

Felix. Did something happen on the camping trip that made you not want to go back again?

Yes.

What happened, Felix?

Father made us take our pants off and touched us.

Where did this happen?

In our tent.

Who was there?

Me and Juan and Father.

J.J. looked at her as if to say, "See."

"Let me tell you about my next interview, with Juan," Sally said. "I should preface this with the comment that I interviewed the boys separately. I asked Juan the exact same questions I had asked Felix. 'Juan, did something happen on the camping trip that made you not want to go back again?'"

She looked up at J.J. "You know what he told me?"

"What?"

"He told me he wanted to go on the camping trip this year."

"But why would he want to go on the camping trip if he had been molested by the priest," J.J. asked.

"Well, that's the other part. I asked him if the priest did any of the things his brother said. He told me he doesn't remember any of those things happening."

"But the priest confessed!" J.J. exclaimed. "And the Church's psychologist, hired by Daugherty, met with the boys and confirmed this happened to both of them."

"The psychologist had the bishop's statement of what had reportedly occurred. He met with the boys together—not separately, as he should have. The psychologist didn't ask questions because he thought he knew what occurred and Felix readily agreed to everything he said."

"What about Juan?" J.J. asked. "Didn't he concur with his brother in the presence of the psychologist?"

"I asked him. He said neither the bishop nor the psychologist asked him what had happened. The bishop didn't even talk to him because he had already heard the story from Felix. The psychologist assumed that these events occurred, and Juan simply sat silent. I think Juan's probably telling the truth when he says this because both the bishop and the psychologist assumed the fact of molestation."

"What are you telling me, Sally? Did these boys get molested or not?"

"Oh, there is no doubt in my mind they did. But no one is asking the right questions."

"Like what?"

"Like, why is Juan denying the conduct of the priest? Does he truly not remember? And if he doesn't remember, is this a repressed memory situation? If so, what happens when he does remember? Those are some of the questions that I would be asking."

"Repressed memory? Are you serious? How can a twelve-year-old not remember something as shocking as a priest molesting him and his brother, together?"

"This is why I told you to get an expert in child abuse in the first place. This is a highly controversial area in child abuse matters. But the concept generally isn't new. Freud talked of hysteria. It's the same thing. Imagining something that is not there or suppressing an event that is too shocking to remember. There's lots of literature on this," Sally answered.

"Do you think he has really repressed the memory, Sally?"

"I doubt it. I went back and re-interviewed the parents—I even spoke to Carmen. I have another theory."

"What is that?"

"Well, since Felix raised this, and it has all come out—and Father Gutierrez has been fired—the relationship between the boys has changed markedly. They are quiet with each other. They don't talk for hours at night as they used to after going to bed. And Juan wanted to go on the trip. I think these are highly significant facts," said Sally.

"What is your theory?"

"I think Juan is angry with Felix."

"Why?"

"For bringing the molestation to an end."

J.J. looked at her in shock. "Jesus, Sally, that's sick. This is a twelve-year-old who has a priest groping him and his brother while camping, and you're telling me the kid wants it?"

"J.J., I don't think it was limited to the annual camping trip—or just groping."

J.J. covered his mouth. He suddenly had the feeling of standing in a mine field without a map. Sally didn't leave him there long.

"Did you know that, in addition to serving as altar boys together on Sunday, from time-to-time each of them served alone at daily Mass before school? Because there are less people, and only a few take communion on weekday mornings, just one altar boy is assigned. Also, the side altar is used, which is in a deep alcove and out of sight of most people in the church. A small group of altar boys from the school—including Felix and Juan—rotate on these early morning assignments. Felix didn't want to go on the camping trip; he didn't want to be an altar boy anymore, either."

Sally looked at her notes. "Some mornings, Felix said he would drink wine."

J.J. felt relieved. Clearly, Sally had never been an altar boy. "We all did that when we were altar boys. It means nothing."

"Did the priest make you drink the wine to get the bad taste out of your mouth?" Sally asked.

"Oh, Jesus, Sally. Did Felix tell you that?"

"Yes."

"Did he explain or describe anything else?"

"At that point, I asked only whether there were other things the priest did at the church that he thought were wrong. He said yes, and I elected to end the conversation."

"And do you think he was also doing things to Juan, also at the church?"

"I don't see why not. In fact, I think that is what's behind Juan's anger. Twins are special; identical twins—like Felix and Juan—are even more so. There is a bond, but there is also a competition between them. It starts in the womb as a competition for nourishment, and it continues through life. This priest brought them together in a forbidden act and then played out a singular relationship with each—probably unbeknownst to the other—to make one feel special as the other is left out. When all of this comes out, as I think it will, it's going to have a profound effect upon the boys' lives and on their relationship as twins. I think we're seeing the beginning of that."

"Where do we go from here?"

Sally closed the file on his desk. "I go nowhere. My job is over. You asked for my opinion; I've given it to you. You better get these little boys some real professional help. They're going to need it."

J.J. thought of the steps he would now have to take. Foremost, he would need to get the boys into immediate treatment. He would also need to know what had actually happened to each of them. If the boys were reluctant to talk or were repressing any of the events, there was only one other source of information: the priest. J.J. realized he had to locate the priest.

"Sally, you mentioned a meeting with the parents. Have you told them any of your thoughts about what the priest did to their boys?"

"No, J.J. I figured that was your job. Sorry."

He knew he had to tell the parents. Also, with what had occurred at the last hearing, he knew he had better give notice to the other side and to the court that he could not recommend settlement at this time, in any amount. There was too much more he needed to know. The judge is not going to be happy, J.J. thought.

"Was the sister any help? You talked to her too, right?" J.J. asked.

Sally stood up to leave. "She's a piece of work, J.J. She had driven the boys to my office and was waiting for them. After talking to the boys, I invited her in. She walked in, wearing jeans and a halter top with spaghetti straps. Backless. The top was so loose that you can see her breasts through the side when she leaned forward. And she made a point of leaning forward frequently. She sprawled out on my couch, put her feet up, and proceeded to light a cigarette with a lighter. I told her my office was a no smoking place. She just looked at me and blew smoke over her shoulder while she used a soda can as an ashtray."

J.J. shook his head. He had seen Carmen in court and understood the spectacle that she made of herself.

Sally continued, "I asked her in a general way whether she had noticed anything unusual about her brothers' behavior in the last few months. She smiled at me and said, 'I know this is all about the court case and the priest whacking them off. I'm not stupid.'"

J.J. made a mental note that Carmen should under no circumstances be called as a witness for the boys. She seemed totally unpredictable and uncontrollable. Some witnesses he could send to Macy's and dress up. This one, even dressed appropriately, would generate little sympathy for her brothers, talking of them being "whacked off."

"I asked her if the boys had talked to her about any of the events, and she said, 'No.' Finally, I asked if she had ever seen Father Gutierrez do anything she thought was unusual or inappropriate."

"What did she say?"

"She said, 'How would I know. I don't go to church.'"

"Not very responsive," said J.J.

"The whole time she is sprawled out on my couch, she was clicking this tongue piercing against her front teeth and making a point of showing it to me. She was obviously trying to aggravate or shock me. Finally, when I didn't respond, she said to me 'You know what this is?' I replied, 'It's a tongue piercing.' She said, 'Do you know what it's for?' I answered 'To improve your verbal skills?' She laughed, took a drag on her cigarette, and said 'You're close. It's for fellatio.'"

Chapter 12

The last thing J.J. wanted to do after talking to Sally Conrad was to deal with Roland Dougherty. He prepared a brief letter to the court and had the runner take it to Judge Vincent's department immediately; but he waited until 5:00 P.M. to fax it to Dougherty's office. Then he left for an early dinner at the Firehouse restaurant in Old Sacramento. The weather was warm enough for a meal under the vined arbor of the brick-floored patio garden. One thing that Sacramento had was long, warm, beautiful evenings in the summer with outdoor dining to take advantage of the weather.

Old Sacramento bordered the Sacramento River and represented a valiant attempt by the City to turn what was once a wino area, complete with prostitutes and flop houses, into a tourist Mecca of "historic buildings." The effort was not helped by its isolation caused by a major, elevated interstate highway slicing it off from the rest of the downtown. The Firehouse restaurant managed to survive even the tourists as one of Sacramento's finest restaurants. With horse carriage rides clacking on the rubbled stone roads, the Old West raised wooden sidewalks, and the railroad museum, J.J. patronized the Firehouse in the hope that it would not fall prey to the tourists and begin serving "authentic" Union Pacific beans or General John Sutter hot dogs on a stick.

As J.J. pulled into the parking lot in the alley behind the restaurant, his car phone rang. It was the firm's answering service paging him. Ever since missing out on a big accident case when a family had called at 6:00 P.M. on a Friday, J.J. had insisted that a person, not a machine, answer the phone twenty-four hours a day, seven days a week. Lawyers rotated "on call," just like doctors, and often, like doctors, responded to emergency rooms or trauma centers. This call was marked "urgent" and "personal."

He should have known better. As soon as he pushed the button, a voice started yelling: "What are you pulling, Rai? This is bullshit!" J.J. recognized the voice of Roland Dougherty.

"Roland, the letter is self-explanatory. It appears, from discussions with my psychological consultant, that these children have been subjected to more than we've been told, and we need time to investigate and report to the court. What's your problem with that?"

"You know my problem. You're just trying to jump on the bandwagon and cash in on the abuse hysteria," he shouted. "There's nothing wrong with these kids. We are not going to pay ransom, Rai."

"Nobody is asking you to pay ransom, Roland. We just need to know what happened and assess the damage to these children," responded J.J. as calmly as he could.

"It's not going to work, Rai. The offer of $50,000 is withdrawn. Tell your clients that. See how they feel about your games."

"Fifty thousand? Gee, Roland, you only offered me $30,000 for both boys. Have you been holding out on me?" J.J. asked, feeling he had scored a point.

Dougherty slammed the phone down. J.J. was left with a dial tone and a smile. He could always get to Roland Dougherty, even when they were altar boys and he would tilt his candle until it dripped hot wax on Roland's head and sent him running off the altar during Mass. Even Don O'Brien would laugh so hard that he would ring the bells early from shaking so much.

* * *

On Wednesday morning, J.J. met the Sanchez family early in front of Judge Vincent's department, as planned. He wanted to tell them about the delay before court began so that they clearly understood it was in their sons' interest. Carmen was there—apparently as the family driver again—and he asked her if she could take the boys to the sixth-floor cafeteria. He handed her a $5 bill and said, "They have donuts up there." The boys looked pleased. Carmen looked bored.

He explained to the Sanchezes the possibility that there was more abuse than reported, that it may have affected the boys much more than anyone suspected, and that they could develop emotional problems later in life. "We don't know for sure exactly what happened yet, but the boys need help. Treatment. And we need to investigate more."

The Sanchezes asked no questions. But then Mr. Sanchez spoke up.

"No mas. No court," he said in broken English.

His wife explained: "We don't want to sue the Church. We want to settle today for the $50,000."

J.J. was taken aback. They had come to him asking what to do. He was used to taking over and doing what needed to be done. He had been right to investigate and to make sure that the children—and this immigrant family—were not being taken advantage of by Roland Dougherty and the Church. The investigation was uncovering more abuse, but now they were demanding he discontinue his efforts and settle immediately.

Then it struck him. "They only offered you $30,000. Who told you they would settle for $50,000?" he asked.

Mrs. Sanchez answered without hesitation, "The bishop."

Before J.J. could respond, the bailiff opened the courtroom door and announced, "All persons having business in Department 22, please step in and be seated. Remain quiet."

J.J. directed the Sanchez family to the front seats of the gallery. As they sat, the bailiff bellowed: "All rise. The Superior Court for the County of Sacramento is now in session, the Honorable Gerald Vincent, presiding. Be seated."

J.J. entered the counsel area and sat in one of the chairs reserved for attorneys. The Sanchez matters were seventh and eighth on the docket, so he sat and listened to the various cases before him. The first was a motion for summary judgment by the City of Sacramento against a citizen who had fallen on a sidewalk. The argument seemed to be that Sacramento was a city known worldwide for its trees; tree roots raise cement; therefore, anybody in Sacramento should know that sidewalks are dangerous places to walk. The City lost. Next, the City attorney sought an injunction to require that a dilapidated sailboat, upon which a family with goats lived, be moved from its location under the "I" Street Bridge. The patriarch of the family, representing himself without an attorney, rambled on about the Declaration of Independence and the Magna Carta—why does every nut who represents himself mention the Magna Carta? J.J. wondered—and finally told the judge that the family would be happy to move if somebody would just tow them upriver. The judge suggested that the City attorney and the gentleman go out in the hall, work it out, and come back with an agreement.

By the time that "Doe 1 v. R. Gutierrez" and "Doe 2 v. R. Gutierrez" were called by the clerk, J.J. was still considering his dilemma. His consultant had told him that these children needed help and that they could face serious psychological problems in their future. The parents, on the other hand, had instructed him to take the $50,000 offer and settle without further investigation.

"Mr. Rai," said the judge, addressing him as J.J. approached the counsel table, "it appears from your letter to the court that you are, again, not prepared to proceed. Am I correct?" The emphasis came down upon "again."

"Your Honor, I immediately notified the court, and counsel, when information came to me that indicated that these children have been subjected to more abuse than the defendants suggest in the pending petitions."

Roland Dougherty rose immediately.

"Your Honor, we reported to the court exactly what these children told the bishop and a trained psychologist. We 'suggested' nothing. It appears that if these children have now been subjected to 'suggestion,' it is by counsel, Mr. Rai."

"Oh, come on, Roland. Your papers to the court reveal nothing other than you want to sweep the whole thing under the rug, quietly, and on the cheap. They don't even mention that R. Gutierrez is a molesting priest and that the settlement is on behalf of the Catholic Church."

"We were protecting your—"

The judge shouted them down.

"The next word addressed to anyone but the court is going to cost $500 in a contempt fine. Each of you will address only the court, not each other," admonished Judge Vincent.

They both fell silent. They knew Judge Vincent's reputation. The judge turned to J.J.

"Mr. Rai, what information do you have that is not already before this court?"

"From her investigation, our consultant believes that both children were sexually molested over a long period of time at the cathedral itself, not just on isolated camping trips from year to year. It appears that the conduct of Father Gutierrez has been repetitive and may have involved more than touching—that is, actual sexual acts."

"Mr. Dougherty, do you agree this information is not before the court in your petition?" asked the judge.

"Yes, Your Honor, because it never happened. There is no such evidence. Mr. Rai has provided us with no report from any qualified person proving these new allegations. At best, this is speculation; at worst, it is subordination of perjury because someone is now coaching the boys to build a better case."

"Your Honor," replied J.J., "we are concerned enough about the credibility of this information that we are seeking to find the priest for HIV/AIDS testing."

That brought a gasp from Dougherty, but he held himself in check until the judge nodded at him.

"Mr. Rai's statements are outrageous, Your Honor. Now he's trying to inflame these proceedings, sensationalize for the media, and scare the Sanchezes into not settling. They don't want this lawsuit, Your Honor. It's now all Mr. Rai's crusade."

"Crusade? A strange choice of words, Roland," shot J.J.

"That's $500, Mr. Rai," thundered the judge. "I warned you. You can write a check to the clerk before you leave or be escorted out of the back door by the bailiff; your choice. You will address the court and not counsel. Is that clear, Mr. Rai?"

"I apologize, Your Honor."

"It's still $500, Mr. Rai," said the judge, his voice suddenly quiet under the circumstances. He knew he was in control of his own courtroom.

This time J.J. raised his hand. He wasn't about to risk another fine.

"Yes, Mr. Rai?"

"Your Honor, Mr. Dougherty said that the Sanchez family doesn't want a lawsuit. I believe that he or his client is in direct communication with my clients and has informed them directly of an offer to settle for $50,000, which has never been submitted to me or to the court. This kind of communication is illegal and intolerable. I ask that you admonish Mr. Dougherty to stop such contact immediately."

Roland Dougherty was up, again, but this time he waited for a nod and then addressed the judge.

"Your Honor, Mr. Rai has been communicating directly with the bishop, behind my back. I ask you to admonish *him*."

The judge held up his hand. "Gentlemen, if you wish, I will report both of you to the State Bar or you can do so yourselves. They are the ones who enforce the Rules of Professional Conduct. While you are before me, however, you will obey my rules. Don't bring your personal squabbles into my courtroom."

The judge then motioned for the Sanchez parents to come forward. J.J. moved his chair to make room for them at the counsel table. As he did, he saw her again, sitting in the back, where the room was partially shadowed. On her lap you could see a laptop computer. Who was she? Damn, she was good looking. This time, she didn't avoid his gaze.

"Mr. and Mrs. Sanchez, I am sure this is very difficult for you," began the judge, "but the Church has submitted a settlement proposal—what we call a Minor's Compromise—to this court. It is my job to evaluate it. Only I can decide, under the law, whether a settlement is reasonable and thus release the defendants from all liability—forever." He seemed to linger on this last word, "forever."

"I appreciate the fact that you want this matter settled. This may be hard to understand, as parents, but you no longer get to make that decision. I do."

Seemingly as an afterthought, he asked, "Are the children here?"

J.J. answered, "Yes, Your Honor. You ordered their presence. They are in the cafeteria with their sister. They are available to you at any time."

Judge Vincent seemed genuinely burdened with the weight of the matter before him. He called his clerk for a sidebar and leaned over to speak to her. They spoke quietly as everyone strained for a word or a phrase. As Judge Vincent straightened back up and rolled his chair to the center of the bench, he announced, "We are going to hold an evidentiary hearing. I see no way to resolve this matter other than through an evidentiary hearing. I cannot evaluate the church's offer anymore than I can assume the truth of your unproved accusations, Mr. Rai. As I stated to the parents, I must satisfy myself that the children are fully and properly compensated for their injuries."

Addressing Roland Dougherty, the judge asked, "Mr. Dougherty, do you agree on behalf of the Diocese of Sacramento that I may establish the proper amount of compensation by way of an evidentiary hearing?"

Dougherty was happy to hear the judge refer to J.J.'s comments as "unproved accusations." He knew the Sanchez family was not happy with J.J. and would likely be even less cooperative with the delay. He also knew that Judge Vincent was a tough judge. He'd never let J.J. Rai pull any of the stunts that were so persuasive to juries. J.J. had already been sanctioned twice by the judge.

"Yes, Your Honor," he answered.

"Very well," said the judge. "That is how we will proceed. Wednesday, August 4. A full evidentiary hearing." The judge started to gather and close the files.

"Excuse me, Your Honor, don't we get a say?" asked J.J., now on his feet.

"No, Mr. Rai. You have made certain serious accusations. I am taking your word, as you are an officer of the court, that you have evidence to support those charges. I am giving you the opportunity to prove your case. I suppose, if you don't want to avail yourself of that opportunity, you can, in the seven weeks between now and August 4, file lawsuits on behalf of the children and proceed in the normal manner. Otherwise, Mr. Rai, I suggest you be ready to present evidence on the date, before this court."

The judge paused—for effect, it seemed.

"Is that clear to you, Mr. Rai?"

Automatically, J.J. responded, "Yes, Your Honor," although he did not understand how he could be required to submit the children's cases to a binding decision by a judge and give up their right to a jury trial.

Certainly, the judge must know better, he thought. Then, why was he ramrodding these cases through? J.J. wondered. It concerned him.

Dougherty spoke up. "Your Honor, in light of the new claims, we want an opportunity to have our psychological expert examine the children again."

The judge looked at J.J. for concurrence.

"The Code is clear: The defendants are entitled to 'an' exam. One. They've had it," J.J. objected.

"He's right, Mr. Dougherty," the judge agreed.

"Your Honor, we are being blindsided. We don't even know what supposedly happened," protested Dougherty.

"Mr. Rai, I assume you will have psychological testimony?" asked the judge.

"Yes, Your Honor."

"I am ordering you to file a written psychological report with this court and with opposing counsel ten days before the hearing so that we will all know the proposed testimony and the defendants can properly prepare for cross-examination and offer their own expert opinion."

He didn't wait for comment from either side. He nodded to his bailiff who announced, "This court is now adjourned."

J.J. picked up his file as Dougherty brushed by.

"Stay away from my bishop," said Dougherty in a hissed whisper.

J.J. turned to confront him. The bailiff, sensing a problem, moved quickly toward them. But J.J. let Dougherty go by and looked to the back of the courtroom. She was gone.

When J.J. exited the courtroom, the Sanchez parents were waiting. Mr. Sanchez grabbed J.J.'s arm: "No mas. No more court."

His wife added: "We came to you. You're supposed to be our lawyer. We want this settled, now. No hearing."

With that, Mr. and Mrs. Sanchez walked away, leaving J.J. alone in the hallway.

Chapter 13

*O*n Friday, J.J. flew back to Boston for his daughter's graduation from Harvard Law School. Rebel had gone to Mills College—"a women's college, not a girls' school," as she reminded him from time to time— and made a name for herself in political circles both on the West Coast and in Washington. Her internship with Senator Barbara Boxer of California brought her into contact with many of the Clinton administration's top officials and political operatives. One, a lawyer ten years her senior, she married—and divorced two years later. A brief conversation during President Clinton's reelection campaign resulted in an offer of employment on Hillary Clinton's staff. The conversation concerned Rebel's masters thesis chronicling the rise of women to positions of power through their fathers or husbands throughout history, including, in recent times, Indira Gandhi, Benazir Bhutto, Margaret Chase Smith, Elizabeth Dole, Mary Bono—"Well, maybe Mary Bono isn't a good example, but you see my point. Women take advantage of the opportunities available to them."

But Rebel was not looking to be handed success by any man, including a husband or a father. Nor had she picked just any law school; she picked Harvard. For at least ten years after being rejected by Harvard Law School, J.J. had carried the rejection letter on his person at all times. His daughter knew this. Perhaps that's why she applied: competition with dad. And she managed to win a round.

Competition aside, J.J. was proud of his daughter. Not only had she been accepted, done well, and was now graduating from Harvard, she had lined up a judicial clerkship with the federal Ninth Circuit Court of Appeals in San Francisco. Again, something that had eluded him when he had graduated: a prestigious clerkship. Another round for his daughter.

Her success had come on top of his own. As the first family member to go to college, he had graduated *cum laude* from Boalt Hall Law School in 1969—the last class of the sixties at U.C. Berkeley. He often reminisced to those who commented on her name, "Why do you think we named her Rebel? Her mother and I were in Berkeley in the sixties."

On the plane to Boston, J.J. carried with him copies of a dozen or more articles forwarded by Dr. Peggy Leibowitz of the Department of Psychiatry at U.C.S.F. School of Medicine, along with her book titled *Understanding the Abused Child.* Dr. Leibowitz had been recommended to him as an expert witness by Sally Conrad, and J.J. had asked the doctor to forward some reading material for him to better understand the psychological issues involved in his case. The doctor had also run a computer search on MED-LINE to give him a feel for the literature and issues in the area of childhood sexual abuse. He quickly found the lines drawn between advocates who believed "the victim" and those who railed against "False Memory Syndrome." Dr. Leibowitz, along with Elizabeth Loftus of the University of Washington, seemed to be among the most competent and professional in their approach. They recognized that the issues were complex, not compatible with a one-dimensional formula, and presented a minefield for the treating clinician. This was the kind of help J.J. was looking for with the emphasis on "expert" and not "witness."

"Does it tell you something about our society," he asked his daughter on the ride in from Boston's Logan Airport, "that we have a *Journal of Child Sexual Abuse* and a separate *Journal of Child Abuse?*" He scanned the pages of the MED-LINE computer search. There were hundreds of articles listed. He was reading off titles as Rebel drove: "'Is there touch in the game of Twister?: The effects of innocuous touch and suggestive questions on children's eyewitness memory.'"

"Dad, didn't we play Twister?" his daughter asked.

"'Remembering and Reporting by Children: The Influence of Cues and Props.'"

"And, dad, didn't we have a pool table with cues?"

"'False Memories; Lasting Scars.'"

"So, dad, even if I'm lying, you owe me money?"

"'Recovered Memories: Sexual Abuse Amnesia.'"

"Dad, I can remember all of my sexual activity—except when I was drunk."

He looked up from his list of titles. "Rebel, I'm your father. There are some things I don't want to know."

"Dad, I'm your daughter. It's your fault."

"Why is everything my fault?"

"Because I am just like you, and mom is too nice," she said. J.J. had to acknowledge, despite their divorce years ago, mom was still the nice one.

They were quiet for a while. She usually got the last word. After a few miles of silence, she spoke but in a more serious tone. "Dad, why are you researching false memories and recovered memories? I thought this priest admitted molesting the boys."

"It's a bit weird. The priest admitted to certain conduct on a couple of camping trips. One boy says more happened. The other boy says nothing happened, not even on the camping trips, or at least nothing he remembers."

"So?" she asked.

"So, should the one who remembers get money and the other get nothing? Or is the one who is denying that anything occurred more in need because he is repressing memories—or at least is unwilling or unable to talk about conduct that will potentially have a devastating effect upon him later in life? And how do I prove the consequences of acts that he says never happened or that he doesn't remember?"

"How old is he?"

"Twelve."

"And all this happened when?"

"Maybe last summer. Maybe since."

Rebel was, as always, blunt in her evaluation. "I'm not buying that he doesn't remember. Forget all that psychobabble. He just doesn't want to talk about it. It's too embarrassing for a preteen boy."

"You may be right."

"I mean, did *you* want to talk to adults when you were twelve about playing with your wanker?"

"La la la la la," J.J. sang, holding his hands to his ears. "I am not having this conversation with my daughter."

"Well, dad, I want to thank you, after all."

"For what?" he asked.

"For not bringing me up in the Catholic Church."

"You couldn't have been an altar boy anyway."

"Thank God," she muttered and, again, had the last word.

When they arrived at Cambridge, Rebel drove him directly to his hotel. He had visited her enough; he didn't need a tour of the campus, although tomorrow, he promised himself, he would take a final walk around the law school that had eluded him as a young man. How would his life have been different, he wondered.

"Mom's already here with C.R.," Rebel said, as she pulled up to the hotel, referring to her brother by his nickname from early age. "I hope you don't mind; I put both of them on your credit card."

"Mind? Why should I? If I can't claim credit for your success, the least I can do is claim all of you on my credit card."

"I knew you would understand, dad. Oh, and we are having dinner together tomorrow night, after graduation."

"Also on the card?"

"Of course."

"Why not?" J.J. smiled.

Graduation was held in the quad, just north of Harvard Yard, with chairs arranged on the grass in front of Langdell Hall, the enormous columned edifice that housed the largest academic law library collection in the world. J.J., Rachel, and C.R. opted to sit on a blanket Rebel had provided under one of the large old trees that lined the quad instead of on the chairs. In this location, they avoided the bright sun and were closer to the stage.

Dean Elena Kagan presented the diplomas to the 550 graduates in caps and gowns—a long afternoon procession across the elevated stage on the steps of Langdell Hall. J.J. and C.R. couldn't help standing and yelling as the dean announced: "Rebel Rai, graduating *magna cum laude*."

Rebel held her diploma up, in response, in what appeared to J.J. and Rachel as the Black Power salute of the sixties. They saluted her back.

J.J. looked at his former wife, Rebel's mother, and shook his head. He had tears in his eyes.

"Our little girl. I knew she was doing well, but *magna cum laude* from Harvard Law."

"It was probably inevitable, J.J. She is your daughter," Rachel answered, smiling back.

"She's our daughter, Rachel."

"Don't blame me for bringing another lawyer into the world," she said, as she hugged him.

They met back at the hotel, as agreed, knowing it was virtually impossible they could find each other in the bustle of bodies in the quad once the ceremony was over. When Rebel entered the hotel's restaurant, J.J. and C.R. stood and applauded.

"She just graduated from Harvard Law School," J.J. announced to those at the tables around them looking on. Dutifully, most of them stood and joined in the applause. On cue, the waiter appeared carrying a tray with a bottle of Dom Perignon, two champagne glasses—neither Rachel or C.R., both vegetarians and health conscious, drank alcohol— and two glasses of sparkling water with pomegranate juice.

"To family," Rebel toasted, as she sat at the head of the table seat reserved for her.

"Why didn't you tell us you were graduating *magna cum laude*?" J.J. asked, barely able to wait to let his daughter sit.

"You were *magna cum laude*, too, weren't you, dad" his son asked.

Rebel interrupted. "Yes, but dad's class at Boalt Hall had only 265 students. I did it in a class of 550 students. Twice as many competitors."

"But you didn't tell us," J.J. responded.

"Well, I suspected I would be in the group, but we don't get class rank until graduation, so I didn't know for sure."

"So what was your ranking in the graduating class?" J.J. asked.

"What was yours?" she asked back.

"Fifteenth, upon graduation," J.J. responded. Law students never forget, not even thirty-five years later. "I was higher the first two years, but being on Law Review took a lot of my time, and I dropped third year. But you know all this, don't you, Rebel?"

She was smiling at him.

"So what was your ranking?" her brother asked her.

"Twelfth," she said triumphantly. "Out of 550. And I was an editor of the *Harvard Journal of Law and Gender*."

"Well, I had the highest grade in Contracts and Real Property," J.J. responded.

"I was selected by Dean Kagan to help her on her address to the New York City bar on the status of women in the law," Rebel replied.

"That was nice, by the way, seeing Harvard law with a woman dean," said J.J.

"The first woman dean at Harvard in 186 years. I'd say that wasn't nice, dad; it was overdue."

"So would I, but my point is that we, at Boalt Hall at U.C. Berkeley had Herma Hill Kay, our first women dean about ten years before Harvard."

Rachel interrupted. "All right, you guys. Knock it off."

"He started it," Rebel said, sounding much like the little child she once was.

"You did,' J.J. replied.

"Concede," Rebel demanded.

"Never," J.J. replied.

They all laughed.

"Dad," Rebel said, downing a good portion of her champagne, "it's like they say about Fred Astair and Ginger Rogers dancing together. She did everything he did, but she did it backward and in high heels."

She finished the rest of her champagne.

"I beat you, dad, wearing high heels."

J.J. conceded with a gesture of his champagne glass. He had never felt so good being beaten.

Chapter 14

*D*r. Peggy Leibowitz had agreed to examine the children and testify at the hearing. She made it clear, however, that in the time available, the most she could do was a preliminary evaluation, if that.

"You have to understand that while you and the law are concerned about the external conduct, we therapists are more concerned with the internal: how the child perceives and processes what has occurred to him. Each child is different. Unique. This is true of identical twins. You can see already, they are reacting very differently to what you believe are the same external events," she told him. "Since the response is profoundly personal, one may interpret a very negative experience in a favorable manner in order to explain it to his conscious mind or unconsciously repress it because it is too terrible to imagine, while another may verbalize the abuse and recognize it as such. Unfortunately, just because one talks about it doesn't mean the consequences of abuse will be alleviated sooner. Either way, you have to understand, the effects of sexual abuse are complex, enter into every relationship thereafter, and can be potentially devastating to a child."

The arrangement with Dr. Leibowitz was that she would come to Sacramento once a week for the next six weeks and meet with the children and the family, as she deemed appropriate, depending upon her progress.

"Would it be possible for you to treat the boys in any way or assist them or reassure them during this period?" J.J. entreated her. "I realize it would be difficult for you to treat them full time from San Francisco; however, is there something you can do for them now?"

"It's not the distance; it's the problem you lawyers have created," said Dr. Leibowitz.

"Which is?"

"Patients in litigation turning around and suing their therapists for allegedly inducing false memories of abuse. The *Textbook of Clinical Psychiatry* recommends that a psychotherapist avoid occupying both roles of treating therapist and expert witness. One of the editors of the textbook is the Chair of the Department of Psychiatry at your school of medicine in Sacramento. I can just see him testifying against me if your case goes south and reminding me of the admonition in his textbook."

J.J. pondered his predicament. He had a private consultant in Sally to advise him on psychological matters. He had an expert witness in Dr. Leibowitz to evaluate the boys and to testify. Yet, the children still had no one treating them and likely would not until the case was over. Ah, the beauty of the law once again, he thought and sighed.

At least, J.J. felt a sense of relief that he now had on board a distinguished psychiatrist with an impressive *curriculum vitae* boasting numerous publications on child abuse. Her evaluation would meet Judge Vincent's demand that he produce competent evidence of abuse and its likely consequences. Now, however, in order to back up a claim that he had impulsively made to the court, he needed to make an effort to find the priest—or at least appear to. J.J. knew it wasn't likely that the priest would ever appear in the jurisdiction voluntarily and risk facing criminal charges. For the same reason, he expected the priest would have nothing to add to his so-called confession to the bishop. Dougherty would see to that. He would make sure that the priest had a lawyer, with no obvious ties to the church, who would invoke the priest's Fifth Amendment right against self-incrimination. But J.J. wanted at least to show Judge Vincent that he had tried to locate the priest. Also, he wanted to make clear to the court that Roland Dougherty was playing games with his Petitions for Minor's Compromise. Dougherty did not really represent Father Ramon Gutierrez, whose name appeared on the petitions. He represented the Catholic Church, and it was the Catholic Church that was offering money to settle the sexual abuse claims of these altar boys. So J.J. sent a Notice of Deposition to Dougherty's law office demanding that Father Ramon

Gutierrez be produced twenty days hence for a deposition, which, the notice stated, would be videotaped at the office of J.J. Rai. He also sent a letter to Roland Dougherty asking about the priest's whereabouts so that he could contact him to discuss the facts of the abuse. In doing this, he was baiting Dougherty to either claim that he represented the priest—in which case it would be improper for J.J. to communicate with a party represented by counsel, but Dougherty would have to produce him for a deposition—or to end the charade and acknowledge he represented only the Catholic Diocese of Sacramento.

To annoy Dougherty further, and to indirectly communicate with Bishop O'Brien, J.J. had a process server go to the Chancellery of the Diocese and serve a subpoena for Father Ramon Gutierrez's attendance at the deposition. It was both unnecessary and of no legal effect, but he could claim that he did everything he could, to no avail, to find the missing priest. The bishop would be the person who received the subpoena at the Chancellery.

Dougherty didn't take the bait. He waited a week and wrote J.J. that he did not represent the priest personally, that the Diocese had terminated him immediately upon learning of his immoral and illegal behavior, and that he had no idea of the priest's present whereabouts. He even threw in a last known address:

R. Gutierrez, c/o Holy Trinity House
374 Morgan Hill
Baltimore, MD

The same day he received Dougherty's letter, J.J. received a disturbing phone call from a prominent trial lawyer in the community.

"J.J., this conversation isn't taking place," began the lawyer.

"Okay. What is it?"

"Your clients, the Sanchezes, they're looking for an attorney. They were referred to me. I turned them down."

"Why would they be looking for an attorney?"

"To take over the case you are handling for their boys, or to sue you, or both," came the reply. J.J. was silent. He knew the Sanchezes were unhappy. He had convinced them, despite their reluctance, to cooperate with Dr. Leibowitz by telling them that the judge would approve a settlement only after reviewing her report. He had promised them that upon receipt of the report he would attempt to negotiate a settlement before the hearing, but he had emphasized that he had no power—and nor did they—to settle the children's cases without going to the judge and obtaining his approval.

Obviously, the explanation that J.J. had given the Sanchezes had not satisfied them.

"And J.J., do you know who referred them to me?"

"Who?"

"Roland Dougherty."

Chapter 15

*A*ndy Miller was back in Vegas. Not for an aviation convention this time. He was there to alternate between the pool in the morning, the spa in the afternoon, and the craps table in the evening. The Bellagio was his second home. When in Vegas, he never left the property. In the mornings, the showgirls would be by the pool getting a little tan before the heat of the day. At the spa, which offered a fully equipped exercise gym, a steam room, a Jacuzzi, massage, a big-screen television, and even a juice bar—Andy never stepped foot in the exercise gym—he could read *The Wall Street Journal*, catch up on his investments in the market, walk around in his monogrammed robe and rubber shower shoes, and watch sports events from everywhere in the world on satellite T.V. And, of course, in preparation for the evening, he would take a nap while being massaged by the trained hands of a young woman—he never allowed a male masseur to touch him. For dinner, he had a choice of some of the best restaurants in the nation. As he had a rule never to gamble before 10:00 P.M., he dined, and drank, leisurely.

For all of his divorces and his disbarment, Andy Miller had bounced back, financially, quite well. As an attorney, he had developed a knack for landing the biggest of cases, especially mass torts. The massive explosion of a chemical plant in Bhopal, India, had changed the practice of tort law. Since then, American lawyers had raced to Third World countries, rounding up clients among those injured or killed by exploding gas tanks and petrol-chemical plants, plane crashes, or environmental disasters like off-shore oil or toxic spills, and bringing the injured of the world, figuratively, into the courts of the United States. They usually did this by suing multinational corporations whose subsidiaries, though many times removed, may have contributed to the devastation. For the people of Bhopal, India, Andy Miller filed suit in the United States District Court in New York. What did New York have to do with India? Nothing. But since the companies operating the plant were, many intermediaries removed, owned by multi-national corporations residing in the United States, compassionate attorneys saw to it that Third World suffering had First World justice. Andy Miller had been a leader in this humanitarian effort. It took years, but it netted him millions, and the race was on. Whenever a tragedy occurred anywhere in the world, especially air crashes (as they were the most common), American lawyers were there.

When Andy was disbarred, he just changed hats. He became an "aviation litigation consultant" or "investigator," instead of an "attorney." Most people meeting him and signing a retainer agreement didn't really know the difference. He was as charming as ever, confident, and persuasive. He was the face of whatever firm would handle the case; the firm to which Andy handed the case for a percentage of the fee. It was actually easier than sitting in an office and suffering the drudgery of reviewing tens of thousands of documents and endless pages of testimony that made up air crash litigation. Everyone knew that after a suitable period of litigation, when the attorneys hired by the airlines had made enough with their hourly fees, the case would settle. The real investigation was done by the N.T.S.B.—the National Transportation Safety Board. The lawyers just tagged along, repeated the process laid out before them by the government, followed the same witnesses and testimony, and collected millions. Meanwhile, Andy sat by the pool in Vegas, when he was not traveling the world in search of a catastrophe, and enjoyed the showgirls and the alcohol.

Tonight, he was at a small bar off the floor of the casino. The news was on. He was talking to the bartender.

"You've been married *four* times?" the bartender asked.

"Yeah, four wonderful women. At least when I married them," Andy mused, tapping his drink.

"So what happened?" the bartender asked.

Andy noticed a couple of customers had stopped talking to listen to his conversation. He didn't care.

"Same thing every time," he began. "I'm a better lover than a husband, I guess. I met my second wife on a flight to New York. A flight attendant. Wined and dined her for three days in New York. Then I'd fly in and meet her all over the country on her stopovers. Torrid affair in beautiful hotel suites, which, by the way, has the added benefit of room service." He shook his head. "I left my wife for her."

The bartender asked again, "So what happened?"

"It wasn't the same—having sex in just one city. And she wouldn't go back to work so we could, you know, just take it up again like we used to, in different cities." Andy tapped his glass to signal a refill. Bourbon. He never varied his drinks. Too hard to keep track. The bartender brought his drink, and Andy resumed the conversation.

"When I met Vivian, a masseuse, it was love at first touch. Three years of marriage, with the massages getting further and further apart and…well…then Mychelle came into my life. Literally. I showed up one day at the office, and there she was. The new secretary. Gorgeous. Very young. Maybe a bit severe, but I thought I wanted that, at that time in my life. I just flipped."

"Number four?" asked the woman sitting two stools down.

Andy looked over at her. "Yeah, number four."

"The last one," said the bartender. "Where is she now?"

"On her third husband since me. Can you believe it? She left me." Andy looked at the woman two stools down as though the thought somehow strained credulity. "And for a young partner at my own firm, who promptly stole my best cases—along with my wife." He shook his head. "So here I am. Single."

A hint of sarcasm was intended, but missed, when the woman asked Andy, "So why not put your love skills back into play?"

His voice rising, Andy said, "After what Mychelle did to me? No. My therapist says I have a fear of commitment."

She asked, "How can you have a fear of commitment? You've been married four times!"

"Yeah, that was what I told her. But those were on my terms. I was getting them to commit *to me*, not me committing *to them*. Mychelle broke the rule. She dumped me."

"So you're in therapy with a woman?" asked the bartender.

"Yeah, kinda. My therapist is a lesbian, but I think I can cure her."

On the television, Andy saw the image of Martha Stewart, followed by some men in suits at a podium in front of what appeared to be a courthouse. "Turn it up," he loudly asked the bartender. Martha Stewart had been indicted.

"You limp-dick motherfuckers!" Andy shouted at the television, as prosecutors announced proudly their collar of Martha Stewart—as if it had been hard to find her between her daily appearances on her own television shows, her numerous houses, her magazine publishing house, and the headquarters of her worldwide empire. Martha had been indicted for some "chicken-shit charge" warranting a parking fine while Ken Lay was walking the streets—actually being chauffeured in his limo—after the massive Enron fraud that had decimated thousands of retirement funds and destroyed employees' lives.

The bartender asked Andy to keep it down.

"That's what's wrong with America's legal system. There is no real justice. It's a charade. It sucks," continued Andy. The other customers moved away from him. He hadn't drunk so much that he didn't notice. In fact, he kept a reasonable watch on his drinking, at least before playing craps. He decided it was time for dinner. He walked over to La Cirque in the Bellagio and, being alone, sat at the bar as he often did and ordered dinner. Sitting at the bar, the service was faster, the servers were always available, and he could watch the beautiful women enter and leave since the bar was at the front of the restaurant. The bartenders were always good for stories. What happens in Vegas might stay in Vegas, but that didn't stop everybody in Vegas from talking about it.

After dinner, precisely at 10:00, he left for a leisurely walk to the craps tables. As always, he moved from table to table, observing the play and the players. He liked to be around happy people. Fun people. Loud people. That's why he didn't play blackjack; it was too quiet.

He found his table, nodded to the pit boss, and signed a marker for $10,000. The stick man smiled and said, "Good evening, Mr. Miller." He corrected the young man: "It's Andy." Then he laid down $300 on the pass line to test the table.

By midnight, he was having fun, and the table was with him. He was up about $30,000, so he allowed himself a few extra drinks and was making dumb "hop" bets, hard ways, and other sucker bets—but still winning—when he spotted a beautiful young woman at the edge of the crowd, which had gravitated to all the noise the table had been generating. Even at sixty, Andy's testosterone (or at least his habits of a lifetime) kicked in. Like a peacock, he stood a little more erect, even if his feathers were graying, damaged at the ends, and limping to attention. And, as with all men, he looked at her through the same eyes with which he had viewed women in his younger days, which did not reflect back the much older man that she was looking at. He smiled at her.

"Gorgeous, get in here. I need someone to blow on my dice," he said.

A player moved to allow her to come forward, which she did, hesitantly, holding a bucket of quarters from slot winnings. "Come here," he motioned. Play on the table had stopped as he was the new "come-out roller"—the next player to throw the dice. As she edged forward, Andy noticed a freckled-faced, sandy-haired, young man—"boy" would be the term Andy would use—who didn't look old enough to be in a casino. He was, Andy realized from a glance at their matching rings, her husband. A good trial lawyer, Andy was trained to look for visual clues about people: a ring, a limp, a fiction versus a nonfiction book, the conditions of shoes, an open or closed body position. But a beautiful young woman, especially when Andy had good bourbon on board, could always send mixed signals to Andy.

He realized his mistake instantly and adjusted to the new circumstances.

"Young man, quickly, bring your beautiful bride in here," he said.

Andy laid a $100 black chip on the pass line next to his own bet and announced, "A wedding present." A group at the other end of the table started singing, "Here comes the bride." Everybody got into the mood.

"What's your name, sweetheart?" Andy asked.

"Priscilla."

"Priscilla. Like Elvis' wife. Wonderful. Okay, Priscilla, you blow on the dice and yell 'Oh, Andy,' and we're gonna win some money together. You and I—and your husband," he added.

She blew on the dice and said in a quiet voice, "Oh, Andy."

He threw the dice. The stick man announced, "Eleven, Yo, 'leven. Front line winner."

She shouted with joy. The table resounded with the words, "Oh, Andy."

By the third come-out roll, the crowd—and Priscilla's husband—was yelling, "Blow—Oh, Andy," and people were leaving other tables to watch the run of good luck.

It all ended abruptly after a long run of numbers, not because they lost, but because an Asian man at the other end of the table placed a "don't pass" bet with five black chips: $500. Andy didn't mind Asians, at least at a craps table—although he would never leave one on a jury—but he took it as a sign when one bet against him. He picked up his winnings, urged Pricilla to do the same, and left the table.

Andy invited Pricilla and her husband to join him at the bar at La Cirque—he was still mad at the bartender at the other bar from earlier in the evening. Under Andy's instruction, and with his stake, the couple had left the craps table with about $2,800. And, for blowing on the dice, Andy saw to it they were comped into a suite at the Bellagio when he had left the table, a big winner. He knew that hotels liked to keep winners on the premises, so that they could have a chance to win back the money. Odds had a way of playing out. If the hotel could keep a player on the premises, gambling, long enough, it would win. The suite was a small price with the odds favoring the house, and it was also done as a courtesy to Andy, a regular at the Bellagio, and a big gambler.

They turned out to be a sweet young couple, and, yes, his instincts were right. They were honeymooners, on a bus tour that included two nights in Vegas at a cheap hotel, a view of the Grand Canyon and the Hoover Dam, and three days on a "working dude ranch"—the whole package running $700 each, round trip, London.

Priscilla and her husband, Blake, were from a little suburb outside Southampton, in England, called Totton—she pronounced it "Tot-un"—

where he worked in an insurance firm by day and a health club in the evening. Andy took a second look at him. Perhaps "wiry" could be substituted for "scrawny." He must have something, thought Andy, to command Priscilla's allegiance. There were a few times, when she blew on the dice and smiled at him, that Andy thought he saw more in that smile. But then, he reminded himself each time, this young girl was younger than his own daughters and was somebody's daughter, too.

He had introduced them to dice, given them winnings and a suite at one of the most beautiful hotels in the world, but he wanted to give them something more meaningful in their final moments together. Advice. Advice to newlyweds from an old, four-time loser.

Now on straight bourbon, without ice, he stated, apropos of nothing but loud enough for the bartender to stop and pay attention, "That reminds me of this one time I was in Elko."

Blake put his drink down in front of himself, and Priscilla held hers below her miniskirt on her exposed knee of her crossed legs as she sat on the bar stool between Andy and her husband. Andy couldn't help but glance at the legs one more time before turning as if to address the bartender.

"My fourth wife, Mychelle—Mychelle from hell—had left me for my partner, with half of my assets and an order for $15,000 a month in alimony, and I find myself in a whorehouse in Elko, Nevada. I don't know to this day how I got there, but I'm sitting on a stool, in the middle of this room, with this hooker on her knees in front of me giving me a blow job, and nothing is happening."

Andy started to get animated. "I mean nothing. And I can see she is getting a little irritated, like she's on overtime and not getting paid time-and-a-half or something. And then she just stops and says to me, 'Do you want me to put a finger up your ass? Would that help?'"

Andy stopped, shook his head, and took a sip of his bourbon, letting the image sink in. The bartender smiled. Blake and Priscilla looked straight ahead, afraid to look at each other. To their horror, Andy continued.

"So, I say, 'Wouldn't that be kinda messy?'"

"And she says, 'I'd wear a condom. I ain't gonna ruin this manicure just to get you off.' Now, I've never seen a hooker with a manicure. Maybe a call girl, but not a hooker in a whorehouse."

The bartender nodded, agreeing that this was indeed unusual in his experience also.

"I look down, and sure enough, she's got those really fancy colored nails, and they are really long, too, and I'm thinking they might be sharp, but I figure what the hell, so I say, 'Do whatever you think will work. You're the professional here.'"

Andy shook his head. "Of course, she says, 'That's $50 extra,' and I say, 'Fine.' You know, she had me where I didn't figure it would help the mood to negotiate."

Again, the bartender nodded, acknowledging the reasonableness of the observation.

Andy took another sip of his drink, as if getting ready for the climax—at least of the story. "That seemed to be the right thing to say, because then she takes charge and the next thing I know, she's back at it with a vengeance, but with a sharp finger up my ass," he continued. "After a minute or two of that, she stops and yells, 'Damn it, concentrate!' And I say, 'On what?' She says, 'Doing it to some women you hate.' Well, that does it. I think of Mychelle-from-hell and wham!" said Andy, slamming his fist on the bar.

The bartender seemed to understand. "It sounds like you have unresolved issues with Mychelle," he said. "Hate is not the opposite of love; indifference is. See, it wouldn't work if you were over Mychelle because—"

Andy looked at him, puzzled by the interruption.

"What the fuck are you? A bartender or a therapist?" he asked.

"Both," said the bartender, and then shut up.

The young couple sat, frozen, wondering whether they had stumbled into an American horror film that featured them.

Andy eased off his stool and threw a black chip on the bar in front of the bartender. He turned to the honeymooners.

"Happy life, you two wonderful kids. Blake, love your wife. Don't end up an old man with some hooker's finger up your ass getting you off to hating an ex-wife."

He hoped he had helped them by sharing the story of his life. It was more likely that they would never have sex without apprehension and fear at their respective sphincter muscles.

When Andy got to his suite, he put on his monogrammed Bellagio robe, took a small bottle of a bourbon out of the minibar, and poured some over ice. And, as was his routine, he put all of his money in the room safe and turned the dial, knowing that he would immediately forget the combination and not be able to get the money out tonight to return to the casino should he wake up in the middle of the night.

He threw cold water on his face, rubbed some over the back of his neck, and ran the cold tap on his wrist. He found this tended to wake him up, if only momentarily. Then he went to his briefcase and found the map of Houston and laid it on the bed. He had circled the Enron headquarters, along with Ken Lay's condominium, golf course, and favorite restaurants. He had learned all of this, and more, through a lengthy web search. Now he was ready to put his plan into action. On the ground.

Andy's conclusion that Ken Lay needed to die arose out of an academic—well, inebriated—discussion among strangers at a bar. Deterrence works only with those bright enough to be deterred, opined one. The death penalty for some schmuck stealing from a lumber yard in Boise, Idaho, who panics and shoots the fat security guard riding around in his Cushman golfcart, isn't going to deter a liquor store robber in Memphis, Tennessee, reasoned another. But—and it made perfect sense to everyone at the bar at the time—if you whack a Wall Street robber baron, in broad daylight, as he steps out of his limo, preferably at the steps of the New York Stock Exchange, CEOs throughout the country are going to pay attention. They would perceive it as the rising of the proletariat, or a new Shining Path, all over America, whose slogans might include: "Don't fuck with our 401Ks," "No more phony IPOS," or "Don't game me." Not, perhaps, as noble as "Give me liberty or give me death," but, with a bullet in the forehead, a similar message would be conveyed.

Andy Miller had a passion for justice. Drunk or sober, justice was justice. It seemed obvious to Andy. Ken Lay needed to die. Justice demanded it. And Andy was going to Houston to stalk Ken Lay, plan the moment, and see that justice was done.

He noticed the message light was on. In his state, it took him a while to figure out what it was, but he successfully lifted the receiver and pushed the button.

"Andy, call me. I need a favor. I need you to find someone." He recognized the voice of J.J. Rai. And, from habit, he didn't erase the message. Again, he knew he wouldn't remember it in the morning if he did.

Andy laid down on the bed as carefully as possible and began chanting, very softly, until he fell asleep: "Kill Kenny. Kill Kenny. Kill Kenny…."

Chapter 16

*A*ndy, it's J.J."

"What?" Andy responded. He looked around his suite, saw his clothes on the chair, and thought he might be in Las Vegas. He turned and looked over at the pillow on the other side of the bed. He was alone. He was both relieved and disappointed. The sun was shining through a sliver of open drape.

"Who?" he asked, running his hand over the remaining hair around the sides of his head and scratching the bald top. He looked down and saw that he had slept with his black socks on.

"God, I hate that," Andy said.

"What?" asked J.J.

"Sleeping with my socks on. I never get a good night's sleep with my socks on."

"Andy, it's the middle of the afternoon. Did you get my message? I need you to do something."

Andy got up and peeked around the drape. He could see the pool area. The showgirls were gone. Must be after lunch, he thought.

"Let me call you back, J.J. I need some coffee and breakfast."

"Okay, Andy. Don't forget."

"I won't."

It was late afternoon when Natalie put the call through to J.J. "It's Andy, from Las Vegas. He says he's at the spa and ready for you."

J.J. got on the phone. "What are you doing, Andy?"

"Pedicure. Have you ever had a pedicure, J.J.? And a foot massage. It's great."

"I need you to find someone for me," J.J. said.

"Who?"

"A priest."

"You're getting married again, J.J.?"

"If I was, it wouldn't be by this guy. No, Andy, this guy has been molesting little boys. I need you to find him."

"Why is it always the priests and never the nuns?"

"You know, Andy, I've never given any serious thought to sex with a nun. Don't make me think about it."

"I was just wondering."

Remembering his parochial school nuns, it was a visual that J.J. was eager to avoid.

"Anyway, I want you to do what you can. I don't expect to find this guy. The Diocese says it doesn't know where he is. Even if that is a lie, he's probably hidden. If we were to find him, he'd likely not tell us anything anyway."

"So why am I looking for him?"

"So we can say we did."

Andy understood: positioning, trial tactics. One could hardly claim the other side was hiding someone if one didn't at least make an attempt to look for him or pretend to look. Sometimes it was better not to find someone. The speculation as to what he might have said, if found, would be unlimited.

"J.J., I think you have forgotten something. I'm not a real investigator. We both know what I do," Andy reminded him.

"Andy, I need someone I can trust. I only have a few weeks. There are limits on what a licensed investigator can do. You aren't licensed."

"Well, that sounds both ominous and exciting. Who do I have to kill?"

"No one. Just check out this underground railroad that the Catholic Church has for priests who molest kids. It seems they send them to a halfway house back East, and then the priest disappears. See if he's really gone. At least make it look like a good faith effort."

"Okay, but I need to go to Houston for a few days. Can this wait?"

"Not really. Let me fax over all the information I have on this priest, and you can start working on the phone from Vegas and see what you can come up with." After a moment, J.J. added, "What have you got going in Houston?"

"Oh, it's a planning matter. I have to check out some facilities, some sites."

"Can it wait?"

Andy thought about it. "I suppose, but you know what they say: Justice delayed is justice denied."

Chapter 17

*D*r. Leibowitz gave J.J. an oral preliminary report on her psychological findings after four weeks of consultation with the children. Speaking on the phone with her, J.J. had previously made it clear he did not want a report in writing until she was ready to file her final report. Even then, he wanted to go over her conclusions and opinions before she put them in writing. She had enough experience in litigation to understand that a preliminary report could be devastating on cross-examination if an expert opinion were to be modified or changed at a later time. She cautioned J.J., however, that, putting aside the legal and tactical considerations, jumping to early conclusions regarding child abuse had its own pitfalls. It took time for the child to internalize the abuse and form a response and for the therapist to break through the response to the truth.

"There is no single psychoanalytical theory of abuse or treatment applicable to all children," she told J.J.

"Will we ever know what really happened?" asked J.J.

"It isn't important what really happened. It's how each child perceives what happened and internalizes the perceived experience. A child might have a memory that was created in fantasy, added to, repressed, and later recalled, fully or partially, on a conscious level but only as a memory. Abuse brings into question the whole concept of memory."

"What do you mean?" J.J. asked. "What happened happened, didn't it?"

"Well, take, for example, the famous tests on eyewitness identification. Students in a police science class will see someone run in and 'shoot' the professor and run out. They are then asked to recount what happened and describe the assailant. In their shock, their mind confabulates—tries to make sense of and put together what it thinks happened. The experience is then described very differently by each of the students although each witnessed the same events. What was real? What did they see or what did they *think* they saw?"

"But real things happen in life. There is such a thing as reality, isn't there?"

"Is there?" Dr. Leibowitz asked. "Have you ever had a memory, strong and reoccurring, without knowing if it happened or if you dreamt it and merely remembered the dream? Or, the *déjà vu* experience, where you remember a place, event, or conversation, and you know what is going on has happened before, and you know what will happen next. The experience might be triggered by a phrase, a smell, or just a feeling deep inside you. Such 'memories' may be internally generated, fantasized upon, or distorted, rather than being externally generated by what you call 'reality.'"

"But, how can we know?"

"We can't. Children don't come equipped with TiVo. We can't run the reel back and freeze frames. We can only look for outside corroboration of what the child tells us happened. I'm sorry, but for psychological purposes, we are frankly not concerned with what actually happened but with how it is perceived by the child, since the child's perception is his reality—and that is the reality we have to deal with."

"But that could lead to false accusations, couldn't it?"

"Yes."

He was waiting for her to qualify her answer. She didn't. Instead, she used his silence to change the subject.

"I'm concerned the parents are not being very cooperative. That is never a good sign in therapy."

He knew it wasn't a good sign, legally, either. He was losing control of the case. He was fighting not only the Church, but also the parents. Was it because of the pressure that they were feeling from the bishop? Was it because of their anxiety over confronting the church of their faith? Or was there something else? He didn't know. And this bothered him. He was used to knowing everything about his case and being in control at all times.

"By the way," said Dr. Leibowitz, "it is also standard in abuse cases to have a physical exam. I set that up with a pediatrician. Felix underwent the full exam. Juan refused to undress. I thought you should know."

"What does that mean?"

"I don't know," admitted Dr. Leibowitz. "I'll have to reflect upon it."

J.J. was agitated as he got off the phone. This was a clear case. It should have been going better. Something did not feel right. He decided to call his daughter, who had moved to San Francisco after graduation.

"What are you doing?" he asked. He leaned back in his chair and put his feet on the desk.

"It's the summer after graduation from law school. What do you think I'm doing? Studying for the California Bar exam."

"Really? I thought you went to Harvard. You still have to take the Bar exam even if you went to Harvard?" he teased.

"So, dad, how is your case going?"

"I don't know. I have the Church admitting abuse; a client denying abuse; parents who don't seem to care if their kids were abused; and, now, an expert witness who, at $300 an hour, wants to 'reflect upon' the situation," he said, his voice rising with frustration.

"Is that all?"

"No, I also have one mean and angry judge who thinks I'm wasting his time and fines me every time I appear before him."

"Dad, chill out. The law is about discovering the truth. It will all come out in time," she said calmly.

"Sweetheart, truth usually has little to do with the law, and, if an attorney does his job, it rarely sees the light of day."

"And to think I want to grow up and be just like you, dad."

He smiled. "Okay. Okay. Let me see if I can make you proud and find some truth here. I just hope it doesn't sink my case. I don't get paid for losing."

"Maybe I can come up and watch some of the hearing."

"Great. Maybe you can help me," he said, pleased that she might spend a little time in court with him.

"Sure. But right now, I've got to get back to contracts. Boring. Bye, dad."

J.J. next dialed Andy's cell phone number. He got a voice mail and left a message: "Andy, call me. I think I really need to find this priest—for real."

Chapter 18

The final report of Dr. Leibowitz, with its attached pediatric exam, six-page *curriculum vitae*, and a comprehensive list of psychiatric authorities cited, vindicated Sally Conrad's referral, if not the accompanying $7,000 bill.

Summary and Conclusions: Both Juan S. and Felix S. have been subjected to multiple acts of molestation over a three-year period. These acts included sexual touching and fondling together, and separately, by Father Ramon Gutierrez, on annual camping trips. Also included were acts of oral copulation between Father Gutierrez and Felix alone on a number of occasions during the school year before and after morning mass. This conduct was kept secret at the direction of Father Gutierrez from others, including the sibling Juan. It is also the opinion of the therapist that it is probable that similar conduct occurred between Father Gutierrez and Juan, alone, and was kept secret from his brother Felix. Physical examination of Felix was inconclusive for other forms of penetration. Juan refused a physical exam. Both children tested negative for HIV/AIDS.

The report then noted the need for treatment:

Both children are in need of long-term psychotherapy to deal with their abuse. Both children will, in the therapist's opinion, have long-term consequences in their lives, including in their relationship with each other and with other significant persons. The full extent of problems cannot be known, but based upon the literature, all forms of intimate contact, with friends, lovers, and spouses will be difficult. Their relationship with children, should they have them, will also be significantly, adversely, affected. The fact that the abuser is a male, and a priest, and that the children are at a developmental age of pre-adolescence, carries very special problems of sexual identity, dealing with authority figures, and trust.

Long-term problems, in this therapist's opinion, for each of the children, are, with reasonable medical certainty, rated from very disruptive to devastating. Such children are at high risk of anti-social and destructive behavior, including everything from alcoholism, drug use, and crime commission, to suicide.

The attachments to the report included three lists. The first was entitled "Effects of Sexual Abuse," the second "Sexual Difficulties Resulting from Sexual Abuse," and the third "Psychic Responses and Disorders Associated with Sexual Abuse." Each list gave a full page of potential problems. Each consequence was followed by extensive citation to the psychiatric literature.

J.J. looked through the citations: S. Freud, "3 Essays on the Theory of Sexuality," *Complete Psychological Works of Sigmund Freud*; Chu, Frey, et al., "Memories of Childhood Abuse: Dissociation, Amnesia and Corroboration," *American Journal of Psychiatry*; Green, "Comparing Child Victims and Adult Survivors; Clues to the Pathogenesis of Child Sexual Abuse," *Journal of American Academy of Psychoanalysis*; Schaaf, et al. "Childhood Abuse, Body Image Disturbance, and Eating Disorders," *Child Abuse and Neglect*. A final one caught his eye: "Soul Murder: The Effects of Childhood Abuse and Deprivation."

J.J. pitied Roland Dougherty having to cross-examine Dr. Leibowitz. Dougherty was a charger. Right up the middle. You could see him coming. Two yards and a cloud of dust, as they say in football. With Dr. Leibowitz, every question would likely dig a deeper hole for the Church.

Just like the admonition, "Never argue religion with a preacher;" never argue psychiatry with a psychiatrist. Both can always find support in the literature for their position, whatever it might be. And in child abuse, a tie goes to the victim—not the abuser.

Dr. Leibowitz's summary was followed by twenty-four pages of very detailed notes of each meeting with the family, the children individually, and one meeting with the boys together. J.J. wondered why Dr. Leibowitz had brought the boys together on that one visit, so he looked at the notes of the joint meeting.

As with Sally Conrad, Juan had not admitted any of the conduct in the joint meeting with Dr. Peggy Leibowitz. In fact, he was now being adamant that Father Gutierrez had done nothing wrong and that Felix was making it all up. He had argued with his brother in front of Dr. Leibowitz. At the same time, he had refused to discuss specifics.

In an individual session, Juan had related to Dr. Leibowitz that he enjoyed being an altar boy and that he had thoughts of becoming a priest because he felt "close to God." Dr. Leibowitz had written in her notes that the level of "religiosity" was unusual for a twelve-year-old boy and evidenced a very close relationship with the abuser, who himself was a priest. She suspected that the priest had used religion in a way to justify his relationship with Juan. She added that Juan had a gift from Father Gutierrez, a rosary, that he constantly handled, like prayer beads, during the course of the session.

Felix, on the other hand, had gone further in his sessions with Dr. Leibowitz and had explained the "bad taste" in his mouth by describing oral sex with Father Gutierrez that took place before or after morning Mass when both were in ecclesiastical robes, he in his altar boy cassock and the priest in vestments of Mass even as they had their pants and underwear around their ankles. On one occasion, Felix described kneeling before Father Gutierrez on a prayer bench, as the priest recited the Confiteor in Latin, with his robes over the boy's head.

Apparently, Father Gutierrez had been careful enough to limit all contact with the boys to the morning Mass when only one of the altar boys and no other priest was present. Felix had said that Father would give him a special blessing and a pat on the face when he poured the water and wine upon Father's fingers and gave Father the towel to dry his hands after the consecration. Otherwise, there would be no touching during the Mass itself. That usually would occur before or after and most often in the altar boys' changing room, just off of the altar, where the cassocks were hung, across the altar from where the priest prepared himself for Mass and hung his vestments. Afterward, Father would return to his side of the altar and hang up his vestments, and Felix would go down the back corridor to the door that led down the stairs to the parking lot and on to school.

Outside of the cathedral, Father Gutierrez would be quite discreet, even on Bingo night, when the boys would come with their mother. Father Gutierrez would never seek them out as he turned the wheel and called out the letters and numbers, which was one of his regular assignments.

The report noted that Felix was now afraid of his brother because Juan had physically attacked Felix one evening, hitting him and calling him an apostate. Felix hadn't known what the word meant. Juan had denied the incident. When Dr. Leibowitz had asked Juan whether he knew what the word "apostate" meant, he had looked at her in anger and answered: "Someone like Felix."

Chapter 19

J. J. received the call in his car.

"J.J., it's Andy."

"Where are you, Andy?"

"Houston."

"I thought you were going to do that work for me first. What are you doing in Houston?"

"I told you. I have some research to do here."

Andy wasn't about to tell him that at the moment he was also in his car—actually a rental—sitting outside of Ken Lay's condominium building, watching the tailpipe exhaust of a limousine as it sat waiting for its owner.

"What have you got for me?" asked J.J.

"Bad news. There isn't any conspiracy. I found your priest by calling the place on his resume. You know, sometimes the best source of information is the phone book. You should try it, J.J."

"So where is he?"

"Laredo, Texas. He was at that naughty priest place up in Baltimore for a few weeks until his Order decided to defrock him. They gave him a plane ticket back to his first parish in Laredo, where his mother still lives. I called the parish—it's on the resume—and the priest there gave me his mother's name and even looked up her phone number for me in the Laredo phone book. I called her, but she doesn't speak English. I got someone who speaks Spanish, and the mama told me, through the interpreter, that her son had been staying with her but now has an apartment across the border in Nuevo Laredo. Apparently, he goes back and forth. She said she'd give him a message when he comes by. So, J.J., if he's hiding, it appears that it's out in plain view. Sorry."

J.J. had to rethink his tactics. If the priest was this easy to find, the other side had to know that he would be found. If so, they probably had nothing to fear from what he might say. Most likely, he wasn't about to talk to anybody about "touching" little boys. What would be in it for him? So, thought J.J., what would be the point of actually finding him if he was so easy to find?

But he had gone this far, he thought; he might as well spend the price of a phone call.

"Andy, this case goes to hearing in a little over a week. Check in periodically with the mother and see if you can at least set up a recorded phone interview with the priest. Just see what he has to say, if anything."

"Okay. You want the recording surreptitious or with a beeper?"

"Use your own judgment, Andy. Maybe if there is anything that we can use in court, you could add the, you know, 'and I've had your permission to record this conversation' at the end. If you say it up front, he might not talk to you at all. Play it by ear. It might be illegal, but I don't think anyone is going to come after you on behalf of the privacy of a child molester living in Mexico."

"I could just say I was drunk and didn't know the machine was on," Andy said. "Did I ever tell you about the time I left my cell phone on at Mustang Ranch? Boy, was my wife pissed!"

"Which wife?"

Andy thought for a moment. "You know, I honestly can't remember."

Chapter 20

*I*t was starting out as a very hot summer in Sacramento, which is as redundant as saying that Death Valley is a desert. For Sacramento, hot is measured by the number of days when the temperature hits one hundred degrees. As August approached, it appeared that the record would be broken. Another measure is the number of people, mostly teens, who drown at the confluence of the Sacramento and American rivers at the Discovery Park beach. This year, that record was also in danger. The saving grace of the heat, if there was one, was that mosquitoes tended to disappear when temperatures went over one hundred degrees. But J.J. was taking no chances with the threat of the West Nile virus. He sat inside his screened porch, overlooking his pool and tropical gardens, sipping a gin and tonic, and rereading Dr. Leibowitz's report.

Occasionally, he looked up to make sure he didn't miss the sunset. Sitting on the west side of a hill in Penryn, five hundred feet above and thirty minutes away from Sacramento, J.J.'s home gave an unobstructed view of the western sky, the horizon, and the setting sun over Sacramento. The hearing was scheduled for the following morning. No matter how long he had been a trial lawyer—now over thirty years—he could never get ready or feel ready until the last moment. Invariably, he would be up until 2:00 A.M. the night before the first day of trial, jotting notes on the edges of lined paper in his three-ring binder, highlighting reports and depositions, and tabbing exhibits. He had concluded long ago that this last-minute ritual was not from a lack of preparation or planning, but rather was the accumulation of adrenaline necessary for a contest. He had to reach his peak of readiness for the contest at the starting line—not sooner, not later.

Someone, a litigator early in J.J.'s career, had described to him the "bathtub" theory of trial work. For trial, you fill up the tub. When the trial is over, you pull the plug and go on to the next trial, refilling with new information. But it is also true, the water needs to be hot when you get into the bath, not tepid or cold.

Earlier in the day, Dougherty's office had hand-delivered a copy of a report by one Dr. Jonathan Mandel, M.D. The report summarized the doctor's involvement in the case, including an account of his meeting with the boys and a summary of his opinions. While J.J. had been ordered to provide Dr. Leibowitz's findings to the defendants, they had not been ordered to provide him with anything. This, he realized, was an oversight at the first hearing. He wondered why Dougherty was sending him the report on the eve of the new hearing. He quickly dismissed "good faith" as a motive.

He read the report, then reread it. It was only two pages.

On May 10, 2004, I met with Bishop O'Brien. He told me that information had come to him from the mother of twin boys, age twelve, that one of the boys was refusing to go on a camping trip supervised by Father Gutierrez. The mother brought this to the attention of the priest, who apparently acted in such a manner as to make the mother believe that some improper conduct had occurred on previous camping trips. The bishop immediately undertook an investigation and spoke to the boy, Felix Sanchez, and was informed that the priest had, indeed, engaged in inappropriate sexual touching of Felix and his brother, Juan, on previous camping trips. The bishop then confronted the priest, who admitted the abuse. The bishop also met with both boys, assured them that they had done nothing wrong, and was otherwise supportive of them. At that time or shortly thereafter, Bishop O'Brien voluntarily offered to personally lead the camping trip for the altar boys, which is an annual event, and both boys did attend the camping event in the presence of Bishop O'Brien and their father, who was also invited by Bishop O'Brien to participate. Both boys did well on the trip.

Bishop O'Brien immediately took disciplinary action and dismissed the priest from his assignment at the Cathedral of the Blessed Virgin. He also directed a letter to the head of the priest's Order strongly suggesting that the priest be dismissed from all priestly duties and be discharged from the Order.

At no time prior to Bishop O'Brien's meeting, or at any time prior to the initiation of the present motions with the court, did either boy offer any new or different information to his parents or anyone else to suggest that there was any other abuse that occurred at any other time.

On May 12, 2004, I met with the boys. I recited the information provided as to the nature and timing of abuse involving them and the priest. I also made it very clear to them that they were totally innocent of any blame and that they should feel no guilt for what had been done to them by an adult abusing his position of trust. I did this to comfort them, to provide emotional and psychiatric support, and to establish a relationship with them wherein they felt safe and secure.

I continued the meeting with the children for approximately one hour, during which we discussed school, family, sports, and other interests. (Felix enjoys soccer and team sports; Juan is more of a loner and spends much time on his computer.)

Both boys appear well adjusted and have a very good relationship with and respect for their parents and family (although their older sister is not really part of their lives because of an age difference and a pattern of anti-social behavior on her part). Their parents are very religious, and this abuse claim has left them very conflicted.

I understand now that new and more serious claims of abuse have been made by one of the boys. I saw nothing in my initial exam to suggest anything other than inappropriate touching, which, while disturbing, did not appear to warrant immediate psychiatric intervention. In fact, it is my opinion, that adult intervention and overemphasis on the conduct can create false memories or fantasies, whether consciously or unconsciously, through the power of suggestion, which can overwhelm any real occurrence and be more harmful than the original occurrence. Unfortunately, children who participate in therapy where inquiry is made of them about sexual misconduct often create memories either to satisfy the therapist or, because they are "primed" by the questions themselves, to believe that events occurred which are not, in fact, a part of reality. Unfortunately, this "false reality" can take on a life of its own and cause problems for the child who, in time, comes to believe that the false reality is the real one, in the same manner that persons often can have a dream that seems so "real" that later in life they are not sure whether events actually occurred or are recollections of a dream.

In conclusion, I believe it is reasonably medically certain that these two boys will continue to need the supportive environment provided by their parents as they deal with the abuse that they first reported. It may also be appropriate that they receive some supportive counseling in the future, at a time of their choosing, when they are better able to articulate and understand what in fact occurred and what feelings they harbor about those events. Earlier, forced therapy could well be counter-productive and create fantasies and embellishments beyond the actual original abuse.

I would estimate the cost of future counseling would not exceed $3,000 for each child. I do not anticipate serious consequences, in the long run, from the acts of touching, which are not particularly uncommon for adolescent boys during their development.

The report was signed by Jonathan Mandel, M.D., and set forth his title: "Diplomate, American Board of Psychiatry and Neurology."

The other document Dougherty's office had delivered was a formal offer of settlement, called a "998" after the Code of Civil Procedure section for which it was named. Such an offer specifically requires an acceptance or rejection. Failure to accept the offer at the time it is made can result in significant sanctions at the end of the case should the person to whom it is made not be more successful than the offer made. Again, J.J. wondered, why was Dougherty doing this? He could have phoned J.J. and made the offer. No, it would have killed Dougherty to offer him more money personally. Why not a letter? A letter is informal; a "998" offer is very formal and requires that any acceptance be filed with the court.

The only good news, in a way, was that the formal offer was now for $50,000 per child or a total of $100,000. The sums were inadequate, J.J. thought, but the higher the offer, the more pressure he felt to be right. He stuck the offer in the file and kept preparing, taking a break only to watch the sunset, as he did every night, and to get a refill on his gin and tonic. At this time of day, his two rules merged: Never miss a sunset because no two are alike, and, once missed, will never be there again; and, in alcohol, drink clear in summer, dark in winter.

He almost missed the phone ringing for the clinking of ice from the ice-maker into his glass. He looked at the clock. It was 11:30 P.M. He picked up the phone.

"I just got served with a subpoena at my front door. I told you, I don't testify; I'm only a consultant!" exclaimed a voice without introduction.

He recognized Sally Conrad's voice. "You got a subpoena? For what? Records?" he asked.

"No, to appear and testify tomorrow morning! I've got clients tomorrow morning. What am I supposed to do?"

"I can't tell you to disobey a subpoena, Sally, but I can tell you I am planning on calling witnesses to the stand all morning, so if you happen to be late, like not there all morning, no one should notice. By lunch time, I'll have this thing figured out for you."

"But I'm not an expert on this stuff. I told you. I was just advising you. I am not an expert witness in this case. Get me out of this!"

"Okay. Okay. I'll bring it up with the judge right away," J.J. assured her. "They are just playing games," he added.

"This is why I don't do litigation. I don't play these kinds of games. They scared the shit out of me, J.J. This guy was waiting at my doorstep when I got home from the k.d. lang concert at Arco Arena. Isn't there some rule that they have to serve you at your business office, not come stalking around your house?"

"No, there is no rule. Like I said, they're just playing games. They wanted to scare you off because they know you've been helping me."

After he hung up, he wondered not just how Dougherty knew where Sally lived, but how he knew she was working as a consultant on the case. He had never mentioned her name to the court or opposing counsel.

He realized he'd better be ready for the unexpected. It didn't help him sleep.

Nor did the phone that rang at 6:00 A.M.

"Who is it?" he mumbled, unsure whether he was having a dream.

"It's me, dad. Your daughter."

He sat up. "What's happened? Is your brother all right?"

At this hour, he feared, it had to be an accident.

"It's 9:00 in the East, dad. *The Wall Street Journal* has been on the newsstand for some hours. My law school roommate in Boston called to tell me."

"So?"

"You're in it, dad! Front page. You just put Sacramento on the map. I'll fax you a copy in a few minutes. I'm not going to miss this. I'm driving up for the hearing."

Chapter 21

J.J. didn't mind publicity. Usually. He was of the Melvin Belli—the famed San Francisco trial lawyer—school of thought that said there is no such thing as bad publicity for a lawyer, as long as your name is spelled right. It was still publicity. People remembered your name long after they forgot what the story was about. He was always available to reporters and to the media, for a good quote or story or expert advice. He was called frequently and always made a point of calling back. Reporters had a job to do, like everyone else, and he knew they appreciated it if someone made it easy for them. J.J. made it easy by being a source, by giving good quotes, and by alerting them ahead of time to breaking stories—usually arising out of his own cases.

But he had always felt that he had some control over the publicity related to his cases. So, it was with apprehension that he viewed the pages coming through the fax, as he had no knowledge of the story or what it might be about or why he had not been contacted. Even in an attack piece, a professional journalist was bound to give an opportunity to rebut charges before they were published. In fact, even a journalist who was unprofessional would make the contact, if only to claim that the target was uncooperative or take a quote out of context to fit his point of view. In this instance, J.J. had received no contact whatsoever. Nor, frankly, was it customary for *The Wall Street Journal* to publish articles about his cases. Certainly not about a local matter in Sacramento, California.

This had to be part of Dougherty's hardball tactics that had started the day before, with the service of a subpoena on Sally and delivery of the formal offers, he thought. Now it started to fit into place for him. The formal offers were being made so that they could be disclosed, looking as they did like court documents. But when he saw the headline, it was clear that this was not a story planted by Dougherty or one that the Church would want in the newspaper, let alone a national newspaper with the reputation of *The Wall Street Journal*. His eyes went to the byline. He always checked for the reporter on a story. "Maureen McReynolds, Journal Staff Writer." He didn't recognize the name and was sure he had never spoken to any such person.

His eyes moved back above the byline to the headline:

Priest Abuse Case to Explore Depth of Damage to Children

He began reading the story.

Beginning this morning, in a courtroom in Sacramento, California, a judge will hear testimony on the extent to which two young boys have been or will be affected by sexual abuse inflicted upon them by a Catholic priest. Some say the damage can last a lifetime.

"We are only beginning to understand the ways in which children are harmed by sexual abuse and its long-term effects," said Dr. Freda Thurmond, a child psychologist at Harvard School of Medicine. "It cannot be swept under the rug. It has profound effects."

In the Sacramento case, the Diocese of Sacramento admits that the priest, Father Ramon Gutierrez, abused the boys, both of whom were altar boys. The boys, 10 years old when the abuse was alleged to have begun, and now 12 years old, are not identified in court papers in order to preserve their anonymity and reduce further damage to them by publicity. However, recently, they were at the courthouse cafeteria and appear, to all external observation, to be polite, well-behaved, pre-adolescent boys from a reportedly very religious family. They reveal none of the pain and psychological damage that experts say they can expect to endure in coming years, and possibly throughout life.

There is a dispute as to what exactly happened, but a psychiatric report filed by well-known child abuse expert Dr. Peggy Leibowitz notes the exact acts of abuse are not as important as the fact of abuse and how the boys internalize it. According to information available on www.survivorsofsexualabuse.com, some children will act out, while others may withdraw. Dr. Frank Parkinson of Duke University, an expert on child abuse, has written that the response is unique to each individual: "There is not a set of signs for all abused children. Some children may fear being left alone; others withdraw altogether. Some develop physical problems like stomach aches or overeating. Others may become bulimic or anorexic. Depression, phobias, anxiety, nightmares, flashbacks, suicide attempts, alcohol and drug abuse, and self-mutilation are some of the many listed observations in children who have been victims of sexual abuse."

Most experts agree that sexual abuse often leads to difficulty in intimate sexual relationships for the victim. Again, the response may vary from a total inability to have a sexual or close personal relationship to a preoccupation with and a penchant for a promiscuous sex life. But, Dr. Michael Johnson of UCLA warns, "When young boys of age 10, 11, 12, are subjected to sex with a male figure, especially someone of the status and reverence of a priest, they can become very confused about their sexuality, especially if they derive pleasure from the act. This confusion can result in self-loathing for having enjoyed the physical pleasure and can lead them to questions their own sexuality. This period is a sensitive sexual developmental stage for a young boy."

Attorney Michael Blanfield, who is handling a nationwide class action sexual abuse case against the Catholic Church, advises Catholic parents not to let their boys, under 16, be altar boys. "They are too impressionable, too vulnerable, and just too attractive to priests," he says. He also suggests perhaps it is time to allow Catholic priests to marry and young girls to be "altar girls." Some, however, have suggested that if girls are allowed to be "altar girls," this might double the incidents of sexual abuse in the Catholic Church.

Recent cases of child sexual abuse against the Catholic Church throughout the United States have resulted in multimillion-dollar settlements and awards. The Sacramento case is unique in some respects in that it was actually brought to the court by the Church itself, in an attempt to settle with the immigrant parents of the boys. The Church suggested the amount of $15,000 to each abused boy. The parents, at the time, were unrepresented. The court put the matter over for an evidentiary hearing upon the agreement of the Church to be bound by the court's award. The court also appointed counsel to represent the two boys (see box, titled "The Altar Boys").

Well, J.J. thought, not bad. Of course, he noticed that he wasn't even identified in the story, thereby violating his first rule of publicity. Plus, he could have provided a quote or two if the reporter had had the good sense to call him. He was always good for a newspaper quote or ten-second newsworthy—some would say incendiary—blurb for radio or television. On newsstands on the East Coast, before he even got up in the morning, and not even mentioned by name.

"Damn."

Then he looked at the box. There was his picture. Actually, it was the picture of the three of them at the Cathedral of the Blessed Virgin, from the 1950s: the one that he had shown to Judge Savage at a settlement conference years ago; the one that had circulated around the courthouse for years; the one that was on the wall in his office.

He read the contents of the box:

The Altar Boys

When the cases of two little boys abused by a priest are called this morning before a court in Sacramento, California, it will pit two other altar boys from the Cathedral of the Blessed Virgin against each other—with a third occupying the cathedra of the cathedral as its bishop.

Roland Dougherty, the senior partner of a prominent Sacramento law firm, will once again represent the Diocese of Sacramento, as he has for years. Known as the "Cardinal" among Sacramento's Bar because of his representation of and identification with the Catholic Church, he is a devout Catholic from his days as an altar boy at the cathedral.

The altar boys will be represented by J.J. Singh Rai, who was himself an altar boy with Dougherty and their mutual friend Donald O'Brien. J.J. Rai is listed in *Best Lawyers in America* and "Super Lawyers of Northern California."

Bishop Donald O'Brien, who immediately fired the abusive priest, appears to have sought, without success, a compromise between his two fellow altar boys. According to people who have known them since childhood, nothing much has changed in their relationship with each other.

Despite his Indian name, Jawaharlal Jallianwalla Rai—known to his friends as J.J.—was raised Catholic and attended parochial school. Immigrating with his family from England, he lived in wooden World War II tenements in Sacramento, which were subsequently pulled down to make room for the Interstate 80 freeway where it crosses the Sacramento River on its way to San Francisco. He worked his way through school, starting in 7th grade delivering *The Sacramento Bee* that now often heralds his legal exploits, graduating with honors from both Sacramento State College and U.C. Berkeley's Boalt Hall School of Law.

Roland Dougherty is the son of former District Attorney Timothy Dougherty and grandson of former State Senator Denton Dougherty. He attended Notre Dame University and Stanford Law School. The Doughertys have been a leading family in the Sacramento community since the 1860s and trace their wealth to early land acquisitions in an area now called Citrus Heights.

Donald O'Brien returned to Sacramento five years ago as bishop, after serving as a priest and a monsignor in the Central Valley. He is known for his dedication to issues of social justice, his identification with the poor and immigrants, and his long association with César Chávez and the United Farm Workers of America. He speaks Spanish fluently.

The three will meet in court this morning. Rai, now an ex-Catholic—one might say a fallen altar boy—is cast as the avenging angel. Dougherty relishes his role as defender of the faith for Holy Mother, the Church. It is apparent that Rai and Dougherty do not like each other. Bishop O'Brien will have his work cut out for him to keep the two combating altar boys apart. Our prayers are with him.

Who was this writer? He looked back at the byline. Didn't ring a bell. And how did *The Wall Street Journal* get wind of the case? He knew enough, after thirty years of practice, to know that "investigative journalism" was, for the most part, a joke. People with an angle, like him, took stories to reporters. Reporters didn't find them on their own. Often, reporters and editors would never leave the newspaper building in writing a story. A well-drafted news release, with quotations, could frame the story. In effect, a lawyer could pick the media, direct the story, frame the issue, and provide the quotes. If he was really good, a lawyer could almost write the headline.

So, who leaked the story? he wondered. Why on the East Coast? The stodgy *Wall Street Journal*? And, where did the reporter get the information about Dr. Leibowitz's report? It was not public. The story wasn't half bad, he thought. Accurate. Researched. He knew Dougherty would be outraged and blame him. J.J. smiled. Not only couldn't Dougherty prove anything but, for once, J.J. wasn't guilty.

Chapter 22

*I*t was ten to ten when J.J. walked up the steps, past the fountain, and through the front doors of the Sacramento courthouse. Few people realized the building had been dedicated, many years after its construction, to the memory of Dean Gordon Schaber, a dynamo in Sacramento legal and political circles from the late fifties until his death in 1997. The Dean, as he was affectionately known, had transformed an unnoticed, unaccredited night school called McGeorge into a prominent, university-affiliated law school from which most Sacramento practitioners of the last ten or fifteen years were graduates. McGeorge's early claim to fame was a collection of Perry Mason books and films because the Dean was a close personal friend of Raymond Burr, the actor who had portrayed the famous television attorney. By the time Dean Schaber—who had also been Presiding Judge of the Sacramento Superior Court and a confidant of U.S. presidents, California governors, and rich and prominent leaders worldwide—died, McGeorge could boast a United States Supreme Court Justice, Anthony Kennedy, as one of its former professors.

Often, as J.J. entered the courthouse, and especially when he stopped to look at the pictures of Gordon Schaber and read of his accomplishments, he thought how the practice of the law had changed in Sacramento. Back when the Dean had been the Presiding Judge, lawyers had numbered only in the hundreds; now there were thousands. Then, agreements would be made with a phone call or a handshake; now, everything had to be in writing through "confirming letters." Often, the letters did not "confirm" anything; rather, they took a one-sided view of a conversation in anticipation of filing a contentious motion with the court. Perhaps, he thought, the situation was just like fish in an enclosed area. When there are too many fish, the growth of all is stunted, and they turn on each other. The practice of law was no longer fun; it was not the profession that he had entered.

He put his briefcase on the conveyor belt of the machine that would examine and sniff it and walked through the metal detector, picking up his car keys on the other side from the plastic container held by the deputy sheriff.

"Good morning, Mr. Rai."

"Good morning, Tony. Thanks."

No cameras. No reporters.

While waiting for the elevator, in the marble walled entry, he was greeted by a few of the regulars, court clerks carrying files for their judges, and the blind operator of the coffee shop on the sixth floor.

"Are you coming by for a donut and coffee today, J.J.?" the blind man asked, picking J.J.'s voice out of the crowd.

"Maybe, Mark. Have to see if Judge Vincent gives us a mid-morning break."

"With Judge Vincent, you'll be lucky if you still have a case by the mid-morning break," replied one of the regulars. That brought laughter.

No one signaled any knowledge of J.J.'s special hearing.

On the fourth floor, he moved to the front of the elevator. As he passed Marty Jorgensen, an old-time criminal defense attorney and fixture at the courthouse, he smelled vodka.

"In trial, Marty?"

"Yeah, double murder."

"How are you doing?"

"D.A.'s killing me," he sighed and shrugged.

J.J. hoped that none of the jurors were on the elevator.

He patted Jorgensen on the shoulder and exited the elevator. The smell of vodka lingered as the doors shut behind J.J. Some lawyers swear they are at their best with a bit of a buzz: "calms the nerves...increases confidence." At least for the lawyer. Maybe not for the client.

The Sanchez family was not outside the courtroom. Nor were any media representatives.

The story was on the newsstands all over the East Coast and, here in Sacramento, no one knew what was going on at the courthouse in the middle of town, thought J.J. Rebel was right: Sacramento is nowhere.

J.J. opened the heavy wooden door and stepped inside the courtroom. Roland Dougherty was standing a few feet away, talking to someone J.J. didn't recognize. Dougherty looked up from the papers in his hand and, staring at J.J., loudly announced, "Bailiff, Mr. Rai is here. Please tell the judge I wish to have a meeting in chambers."

Dougherty then turned, walked to the bailiff, and handed him a fax copy of *The Wall Street Journal* article. "And please give the judge this article," he said.

J.J. wasn't particularly surprised. He acted amused. If he was going to be blamed, at least he would act a little guilty. Draw Dougherty in. Really get him aggravated.

"Good morning, Roland," he said and proceeded to counsel's table, placing his briefcase on the first chair. "Read any good papers lately?"

He walked over to the Sanchez family—the parents and all three children were in the courtroom—and said, "Good morning." Then he asked the Sanchez parents if they would step into the hall for a moment so that he might talk to them before the hearing started. The person whom J.J. had not recognized earlier speaking to Dougherty stepped forward.

"Excuse me, Mr. Rai. We have a matter to take up with the court. I would ask you not to talk to the Sanchez family until the judge rules."

"Who are you?"

"I have been hired by Mr. and Mrs. Sanchez to represent them."

He handed J.J. a card. Larry Feldman of O'Reilly, Feldman & Cane of San Francisco. So they had to go out of town to find someone to replace me, thought J.J. Could it be that he was feared locally but his reputation extended only ninety miles to San Francisco, he mused to himself.

"Are you Catholic, Larry?"

"Presbyterian, why?"

J.J. smiled. "No reason."

"All rise," announced the bailiff. "The Superior Court for the County of Sacramento, Judge Gerald Vincent, presiding, is now in session."

The judge entered the room, ascended to the bench, and placed two files before him. Roland Dougherty had remained standing. He was looking at the bailiff and, alternately, the judge.

"Excuse me, Your Honor," he said.

The judge held up his hand. "One moment please, Mr. Dougherty. Madam Clerk, could you call the matter?"

The clerk stood and, in a loud voice, stated: "Civil Number 123417, Doe 1 versus R. Gutierrez, et al. Civil Number 123418, Doe 2 versus R. Gutierrez, et al."

The judge leaned back. "Now, Mr. Dougherty, we are on the record. What were you about to say?"

"Well, Your Honor, that was my point. I requested of the bailiff that he inform you that we would like to meet in chambers to take up an important matter."

"What matter?"

"This morning, *The Wall Street Journal* published an article about the petitions pending before this court. The article was clearly inflammatory, designed to influence these proceedings, and to embarrass the Catholic Church. The content shows that the reporter was given information that only the lawyers and parties would have. Clearly, the Church did not do this. That leaves Mr. Rai, who, frankly, is known for his insatiable appetite for publicity. We have made every effort to protect these children from the harm of publicity—naming them only as Doe 1 and Doe 2—yet their own lawyer exposes this matter through the media. We can only assume he is putting his own interests ahead of the children's or trying to extort money from the Church with the threat of more publicity," said Dougherty. He remained standing.

"Well, Mr. Dougherty, you have expressed yourself on the record. I see no reason to go into chambers for a private chat, do you?" asked the judge.

"Your Honor, I don't see how we can continue in this matter if Mr. Rai is going to go to the newspapers every day and disclose every detail of what is obviously very sensitive and sexually explicit testimony involving children."

"What do you suggest I do, Mr. Dougherty?"

"First, close the hearing to the public; second, issue a gag order on all parties, attorneys, and witnesses; and third, remove Mr. Rai from representing the children," Dougherty answered, clearly prepared for the question.

J.J. spun his chair around and looked at Larry Feldman. If this had been well orchestrated, this would be the time for Mr. Feldman to approach. He winked at Feldman. Feldman looked away and stood.

"Your Honor, may I be heard?"

"Who are you?" asked the judge.

The attorney walked forward to the counsel table. "Larry Feldman, Your Honor. I have been retained by the Sanchez family." With this pronouncement, he walked to the clerk, handed her a business card, and returned to the counsel table. There, he continued addressing the court.

"The Sanchez family is very unhappy with the tactics being used by Mr. Rai. This article today was the final straw. Despite his duty to do so, Mr. Rai has not informed them of an offer in the amount of $100,000 that was made yesterday and, I believe, lodged with the court. The Sanchez family wishes to settle this matter at this time. They ask that I be substituted for Mr. Rai as their attorney and that Mr. Rai be discharged."

"Your Honor," came a man's voice from the back of the courtroom. The interruption from the public seating section of the courtroom prompted the bailiff to stand.

"Step forward, please," said the judge.

As a gentleman left the back row, J.J. saw the attractive redhead who had been sitting next to the now-approaching man—obviously a lawyer with his monogrammed briefcase—the same young woman he had seen at the prior hearings.

"Your Honor, I am Martin Epstein of O'Melvany & Catchott of Los Angeles. I represent *The Wall Street Journal* and Ms. McReynolds, who is present here in court. She is the author of today's story in the *Journal*. We oppose closing this hearing or issuing any gag order as an unconstitutional abridgement of the freedom of the press. If an order is issued, we would request a delay in these proceedings to seek a Writ from the Third District Court of Appeal. If this court needs authorities, I am prepared today to provide a brief, as there is no authority to exclude the public from these hearings."

"These are minors, Your Honor," protested Dougherty. "Juvenile proceedings are regularly closed."

"Juvenile *criminal* proceedings are closed, Your Honor," Epstein responded. "This is not a juvenile court proceeding. This is a civil action against the Catholic Church on a matter of enormous public interest and concern. It cannot be hidden from the public, no matter how embarrassing the attorney for the Church feels these disclosures may be."

The courtroom door opened. All eyes went to the door. The bailiff moved forward, and the court reporter prepared for another intrusion into the proceedings. The entrant was about 5' 2" 23, not much over a hundred pounds—a nicely dressed young woman. J.J. immediately recognized the summer blouse he had bought his daughter, Rebel. It was as close as he could get her to wearing color: rust.

To the lingering question, J.J. stood and introduced the intruder: "My daughter, Your Honor. Rebel Rai." He added, "Harvard Law, 2004." He looked at the woman in the back row to see if she had taken note of this achievement. She wasn't typing.

"Mr. Rai, is your daughter appearing in this matter as counsel of record?" the judge asked.

"No, Your Honor. She will be assisting as my paralegal. She is about to take the California Bar later this month."

"Well," replied the judge, "she can assist from outside the railing as she has not yet been admitted."

J.J. turned to Rebel, rolled his eyes, and directed her to a seat in the public area behind him but outside the area reserved for attorneys. She excused herself as she edged past the Sanchez family to her seat, one down from the daughter, Carmen. As she sat, Carmen leaned over and said, "Your dad's the man."

Rebel thanked her. Mrs. Sanchez tugged on Carmen. Carmen pulled her arm away, saying, "Leave me alone." The bailiff stood to indicate that he had heard the commotion and that there was to be no talking in the courtroom.

"Mr. Feldman," the judge said, addressing the attorney newly retained by the Sanchez family. "You say the Sanchez parents want to accept the $100,000 offer to settle? Is that right?"

"Yes, Your Honor," he replied, standing next to Roland Dougherty.

"As the retained attorney for the Sanchezes, do you recommend that sum?" asked the judge.

"Yes, Your Honor," Feldman replied.

"Why?" asked the judge.

Feldman was momentarily stunned. "Because that's what they want to do, Your Honor."

"Mr. Dougherty," the judge asked, "do I understand that the petition you filed for compromise and settlement is now amended to reflect an offer of $100,000—$50,000 per child?"

"Yes, Your Honor," Dougherty said immediately, anticipating that matters were now proceeding as he had hoped and had in fact arranged.

"And aren't you the same Mr. Dougherty," asked the judge, "who earlier asked this court to approve $30,000—$15,000 per child, and aren't these the same Sanchez parents who were in agreement and asked the court to release the defendant priest and the Catholic Church, forever, for that amount?"

Dougherty didn't say anything.

"Mr. Feldman," the judge said, turning to him once more, "I have already explained to the Sanchez family that it is my duty to evaluate any settlement. I have conflicting reports of injury. Which should I believe?"

Feldman wasn't about to give up. "Your Honor, I think you should believe that the parents know their children best and know what is in their children's best interest. Money is not the only issue here. There is the question of their faith. The parents feel they can deal with this matter best within the family and within the continuing comfort of their faith. The amount being offered is more than sufficient to provide professional assistance, should that prove necessary."

J.J. gave him a look. Not bad, he thought—for a Presbyterian.

Dougherty was nodding in agreement with Feldman.

The judge was clearly annoyed. "I am going to take a recess, gentlemen. Neither side has presented me with any authorities for its position.

Mr. Epstein, you have a brief on keeping the hearing open. Give it to the bailiff. I am going to read the relevant code sections and Mr. Epstein's brief and rule. We will reconvene at 11:00."

With that, the judge left the bench for his chambers.

J.J. looked at the court clock. "Let's go to the cafeteria," he said, turning to Rebel. By way of explanation, he added: "Trial work: Nothing goes as planned."

"Maybe you should have planned better, dad," she replied. "I can't believe you didn't even know you were going to be on the front page of *The Wall Street Journal.* That's not like you. You always call me the day before you are in the paper so I won't miss it."

J.J. didn't like the feel of a case out of his control.

Promptly at 11:00 A.M., Judge Vincent resumed the bench. He was carrying a law book and the court files. The murmuring in the courtroom stopped, and all eyes were upon him. In the silence, J.J. heard a low, rhythmic tapping. He looked over to see the angry face of Roland Dougherty and, looking down, saw the heel of what he guessed was at least a size 13 shoe violently tapping at a frantic pace.

That guy is tightly wound, J.J. thought.

"All right," said the judge. "I'm ready to rule."

J.J. had been around long enough to know that if a judge was about to rule and had not called upon him, it was likely that the ruling was going to be in his favor. For a judge to rule against a party, due process requires that the party at least have an opportunity to be heard. The judge had asked J.J. nothing.

"Section 372 of the Code of Civil Procedure," the judge began, "requires the court to approve any settlement with or on behalf of a minor in order that it may be effective and release any and all persons responsible for the damage to the minor. In order to perform this mandatory function, the court must have the facts of injury, the consequences of the injury, and the terms of the settlement. To determine if a settlement is fair, the court must also be presented with evidence and must evaluate the evidence. In this case, the evidence is conflicting. I can only perform my duty if I hear and evaluate the evidence of the psychiatric experts and of the parents. Therefore, we will proceed with the evidentiary hearing on the petitions before me."

What had started out as a hearing to approve a compromise settlement, where only the Church would be represented, had suddenly turned into a full-fledged evidentiary hearing in which evidence, from both sides, was about to be heard. This was not how it was planned. Dougherty was up immediately.

"Your Honor, I respectfully request that you remove Mr. Rai from further representation."

"On what grounds, Mr. Dougherty?" the judge asked.

J.J. knew Judge Vincent had a reputation for being meticulous in all his proceedings. However, J.J. got the distinct impression that the judge was now carefully protecting the record and requiring that objections be concisely stated so that his rulings would be specific to the objection. A judge protecting the record this carefully was either one concerned about his reputation or one with an agenda. J.J. didn't know which it was in this case. He knew nobody got anything past Judge Vincent. He also wondered when it would be his turn and whether the judge would be coming down on him. So far, nothing had been asked of him, despite the charges flying from every direction. He knew he had nothing to hide, so he continued his silence, as difficult as it was for him not to take a poke at Dougherty.

"First," replied Dougherty with reference to the grounds for disqualification, "is the leaking of confidential documents about these children; second is Mr. Rai's attempt to influence these proceedings through media coverage; and, third, as Mr. Feldman has stated, the Sanchez family does not want him. They should not be forced to be represented by an attorney that they do not want, especially one who appears to be on a personal crusade...." He stopped, remembering the prior use of the word "vendetta," and corrected himself, "against the Catholic Church."

Finally, J.J. thought, I get to deny the charges and defend myself. He stood.

"Your Honor, Mr. Dougherty—"

The judge interrupted. "Mr. Rai, do you mind being sworn?"

J.J. thought about it. Normally that would be the last thing he would want. He could not remember a time in over thirty years when a judge had asked him to be sworn while he was representing a litigant in court.

"No, Your Honor, I have no problem whatsoever being sworn," said J.J. almost reflexively.

"Good. Madam Clerk, swear Mr. Rai."

She did. J.J. started to walk to the witness box.

"Mr. Rai, you may remain at the counsel table. I have just a few questions for you."

J.J. returned to his place and remained standing.

"Have you leaked documents to the news media?" asked the judge.

J.J. hesitated. "You mean in this case, judge?"

Rebel smiled.

"Yes, I mean in this case—and specifically, did you leak information or documents to *The Wall Street Journal* or any other persons for the intent that they would be delivered to *The Wall Street Journal*?"

"Absolutely not, Your Honor."

"Did you have anything whatsoever to do with this story in *The Wall Street Journal*?"

"No, Your Honor."

"Do you know or have you ever met Ms. Maureen McReynolds, the *Journal* reporter who is sitting in the back of the courtroom?"

J.J. turned and looked at her—as if he needed to—again. This time, he thought, he had the permission of the court and would likely get a responsive look from Ms. McReynolds. He was not disappointed. They shared eye contact for a moment, and then he turned and addressed the court.

"Your Honor, I saw her in the back of the courtroom on the first day; thereafter, we rode separate elevators together, from this floor to the main floor. I then also observed her in her car as she left the court parking lot. However, we have never shared a word on this or any other subject."

"Mr. Dougherty, do you have any questions of Mr. Rai regarding your claim of leaking this material to the news media?" asked the judge.

"Yes," said Dougherty. "Mr. Rai, have you spoken to any other media people about this case?"

Now J.J. was enjoying himself and decided at least to deliver a slight jab at Dougherty. Of course, he had to be mindful that the judge would not tolerate anything more. "Let's see, I told news anchor Stan

Atkinson I wouldn't be playing golf with him in his charity event today because I had a hearing. I didn't tell him what it was about. That's it. I think that's the only media person I can remember mentioning this hearing to."

"What about *The Sacramento Bee*?" Dougherty asked, his rising voice betraying both disbelief and frustration.

"If I had spoken to *The Sacramento Bee*, there would have been a story in the *Bee*, and I guarantee you that my name would have been in it with great quotes that I would have provided. So, no, I have not spoken to *The Sacramento Bee* about this case."

"Do you plan on talking to the media about these matters?" asked Dougherty.

"Well, you never know. I would like to meet Ms. McReynolds," J.J. said, pointing to her. "I mean professionally," he added. "I think that was a fine piece of writing she authored in the *Journal*. I always admire fine writing."

Both Rebel and Carmen turned and looked at Maureen McReynolds.

"Your Honor," said Dougherty, "that's the problem. Mr. Rai is uncontrollable. He'll talk to any microphone, camera, or reporter he encounters."

"Anything else?" asked the judge. He was getting agitated, everybody could tell. No one said anything further.

"Mr. Dougherty, you said there were three grounds for removing Mr. Rai. The first two related to leaking information that contributed to a news story. We have disposed of those. He didn't do it and—"

Dougherty interrupted the judge. "Perhaps the court should ask Ms. McReynolds who *did* leak these documents to her. She didn't just happen upon them in New York while sitting at her desk at *The Wall Street Journal*."

"Ms. McReynolds, step forward," said the judge. As she rose, her attorney, Mr. Epstein, also rose and accompanied her forward, holding the low gate to allow her to enter the area reserved for litigants and the attorneys. Epstein stood close, prepared to defend her from any citation for contempt because he knew that she would not answer any questions from the judge relating to her sources.

"Ms. McReynolds, I don't suppose you would like to volunteer the source of your information for the story in today's *Wall Street Journal*," said the judge.

"No, Your Honor. I would go to jail first," said Ms. McReynolds.

"No point in that, is there, Mr. Dougherty?"

The judge waved his hand to Ms. McReynolds and said, "You may return to your seat."

J.J. moved in his chair enough to watch her return to the back of the courtroom.

"Mr. Dougherty, I should also add for the record that your claim that these articles are inflammatory and designed to influence these proceedings is of no consequence to the court for a number of reasons," resumed the judge. "First, there is no jury present and no one to influence but me. Second, while you have handed a copy of this article to the bailiff, I have not read it and have no intention of reading it while these proceedings are pending. Nor will I read any other articles or publication or listen to or view any broadcast related to this case. That disposes of this objection also, I believe."

The judge looked at his notes. "As to the suggestion that both you and Mr. Feldman have made that these articles could embarrass the Catholic Church and perhaps harm the parents' faith in some way, I don't believe those are matters over which I have any power. Nor can I say that I am authorized by statute to take such concerns into consideration when ruling upon the adequacy of monetary compensation for specific injuries to minors. The embarrassment to the Catholic Church, if any, is occasioned by the conduct of its priest, which you admit. It is not occasioned by anything that this court, or I might add, Mr. Rai, has done.

"As to Mr. Rai's conduct, there is nothing in the record that in any way appears inappropriate; nor, for the reasons stated by Mr. Epstein on behalf of *The Wall Street Journal*, do I feel that I can issue gag orders or any order of the kind to prevent future discussion by either of you with the media of a matter that is obviously of importance in public debate." The judge paused, and added, "Nationwide."

Good, thought J.J. Finally, someone is protecting my constitutional right to make a living in as flamboyant a way as possible—if only to bug Dougherty.

The judge continued, "So, Mr. Dougherty, we are left with your third point. The Sanchez parents do not want Mr. Rai; they want Mr. Feldman. Apparently, you too want Mr. Feldman. That bothers me." The judge looked to Larry Feldman.

"Mr. Feldman, you may represent Mr. and Mrs. Sanchez in these proceedings if you wish, but you will not represent the children's interests. I find that the interests of the parents in minimizing damage to the Church or their faith is inconsistent with the interests of the children in being fully protected and compensated with regard to sexual abuse suffered at the hands of a priest. Therefore, I am disqualifying the parents to act as Guardian *ad Litem* in the petitions. That means they will not be making the decisions regarding the handling or settlement of this litigation on behalf of their children."

The judge turned to J.J. "Mr. Rai, you are appointed Guardian *ad Litem* for Doe 1 and Doe 2. This means that you will have complete authority as it relates to the handling of this litigation, subject only to this court's approval, of course. While you may recommend settlement or other disposition in this matter, the final authority is with this court. Is that clear, Mr. Rai?"

"Yes, Your Honor," replied J.J. He remained seated.

Feldman jumped to his feet. J.J. had to admire them: Feldman and Dougherty. They had this tag-team routine down pat. Perhaps they had used it before in other cases where things had gotten a little out of hand for the Church. But this time they were losing badly, and J.J. could not even take credit for what was happening. Their act had been botched by Dougherty and caught by the judge with virtually no involvement by J.J.

"Your Honor, an attorney must have the trust and cooperation of his clients. I realize that the parents are not the primary clients; the children are. But a lawyer needs to prepare his witnesses. That will be very difficult with the breakdown in the relationship between the Sanchez family and Mr. Rai," said Feldman.

J.J. stood. He, too, was getting impatient. "I assume Mr. Feldman will act professionally and make the parents available to testify, as necessary. As to the boys, Your Honor, my clients"—he looked at Dougherty and Feldman now to make the point clear—"I don't plan on calling them as witnesses."

"He has to call them!" said Dougherty, jumping up next to Feldman.

J.J. answered Dougherty directly. "No, I don't. I am going to be calling Dr. Leibowitz, the expert, to discuss her findings. I don't have to subject the children to you."

Again, the judge cut them off. "Gentlemen, I've ruled. We have lost the morning. We will convene at 1:30 P.M." He closed his file and announced his one final ruling.

"On the matter of closing the hearing, as with issuing gag orders, or contempt orders to the media, the motion is denied. This is a public courthouse, and these proceedings cannot constitutionally be closed. While I cannot issue a prior restraint on the press to respect the confidentiality of the victims' identities, it appears that they have acted responsibly to date, and I would urge and expect that they will continue to do so in the future."

The judge nodded to all, got up, and appeared to linger a moment watching J.J., who had risen and hugged his daughter, Rebel.

There was a sadness in the judge's face.

"We're adjourned," said the bailiff.

Chapter 23

"Good thing I arrived when I did," said Rebel, as she and her father walked out of the courtroom. "You seem to have been in a lot of trouble."

"Like you helped?" J.J. asked his daughter.

"You always told me to control the courtroom. The judge sure seems to be in charge of this one."

"That's an illusion. As long as things are going my way, why mess with success?"

"Well, maybe it's an illusion, but I don't get the feeling you have much control over the proceedings or the media."

J.J. had to admit that *The Wall Street Journal* article had taken him by surprise and remained a puzzle. Nor had he ever lost control of a case, to the extent that a parent was removed as Guardian *ad Litem* and he was appointed in their stead. In reality, whether he was called guardian or attorney, he had always exerted his judgment in deciding how to handle litigation in his clients' best interest. Now, however, he had sole judgment, subject only to the court's supervision. He couldn't hide behind the parents to get out of a case that he had doubts about.

Outside the courtroom, Larry Feldman was huddled with the Sanchez family. J.J. walked over to them. "Mr. and Mrs. Sanchez, I think it would be better if you took the children home during lunch. It's possible that some local media people might show up, and we don't want them catching the children on camera. They won't be needed today. I will let you know if they are needed at any time to come to court." He didn't wait for Feldman to speak. He put his arm around his daughter and walked toward the elevators.

As J.J. and Rebel walked out of the courthouse, she said, "You know, dad, I think Mr. and Mrs. Sanchez are really trying to do what they think is best for their children. Their religion is really important in their lives."

"They're blinded by faith," J.J. replied.

"Spoken like a true ex-Catholic. What does it benefit a man to inherit the whole world but lose his soul?"

"I thought I kept you away from religion," he said, "and now you are quoting scripture to me? Well, paraphrasing: You're not *that* good."

"But Feldman is right," she insisted. "It's not just about money. We're talking about the potential of a loss of faith, of belief in God, and for these children this could mean a loss of eternity. Isn't that as important as money?"

"Assume it is. No court, no jury, and certainly not I, can restore or cause faith to flourish in these children. If they lose their faith, or their souls, because of what the Catholic Church did to them, denying them compensation isn't going to change that. It might make the parents feel less guilty for challenging the Church—and maybe for not supervising their children well enough—but compensation and faith have nothing to do with each other."

He still had his arm around his daughter as they walked down the courthouse steps. "Rebel, we're at the courthouse. Here, we deal with worldly matters like justice and the law. If you want eternal justice or salvation, you'll have to go elsewhere. And, as this case suggests, not to a church."

"God, dad. What happened to you in the Catholic Church to make you so cynical?"

"Roland Dougherty would be a good place to start. If he is a paragon of Christian values, then I don't want to be one."

"Well," she observed, "so far, he's losing badly in this case. Every ruling has been against him."

"Don't count him out," J.J. warned as they entered the lobby of his building. "Dougherty is a zealot. He truly believes he's doing the Lord's work. And, if you're working for the Lord, anything is permitted. God can't lose, or else he wouldn't be God, would he?"

"So, dad, you're telling me that Dougherty sees this as a battle be-tween those who want to further the mission of the Church and those who want to harm it?"

"Well, that is how he might see it, yes."

"How about you, dad, how do you see it?"

"As a battle between good and evil—and they are evil."

"Amen," she replied.

Chapter 24

"We've had a busy morning, Mr. Rai, while you've been in court. Seems you are a media celebrity," said Natalie, his secretary, as J.J. and Rebel entered the office.

"Who is calling?"

"Everyone. NBC, CBS, local stations, *L.A. Times*, *USA Today*, and a bunch of others. They all want interviews."

"What about *The Sacramento Bee*?"

"No, I guess they haven't heard that you've gone national. Of course, it's only noon, and they probably haven't had their afternoon editorial meetings to review national media and competition to assign stories for tomorrow."

J.J.'s staff knew the routine of *The Sacramento Bee* and all media outlets throughout the state. He often had to make deadlines to guarantee the type of coverage he wanted, even timing the filing of lawsuits to fit the media's schedules. With newspapers, this usually meant the day before. With radio and television, however, an interview might be scheduled to catch the noon news, knowing that it would be repeated on the evening news and augmented with additional film or comment on the eleven o'clock news. To get a story to run two days, J.J.'s staff would stage a television event of a late afternoon filing for the evening television coverage. This would guarantee that the story would appear in *The Sacramento Bee* the following morning and would result in radio coverage throughout the second day, as most radio news personalities simply read from the newspaper on air.

"Anything from *The Wall Street Journal*? Ms. McReynolds?" he asked.

Natalie looked through the phone messages. "No, doesn't ring a bell."

J.J. walked into his office. Ms. McReynolds was still in town. That meant she intended to file more stories on the case. *The Wall Street Journal* would not have gone to all the trouble of flying up one of its high-paid lawyers from Los Angeles if it did not intend to print further stories. Yet, the reporter had not contacted him at all for information or an interview. Strange behavior on the part of a reporter, he thought.

Natalie followed him into the office. "What do you want to tell all of these news sources?" she asked.

"No comment."

"J.J. Rai," she said in amazement. "No comment!"

He laughed. "Timing. It's all about timing. Let's see how things shake out. Right now, I don't want to get the judge mad at me. But keep all the messages. We'll be calling everybody back at some point. This is just too good to let go of, especially with Dougherty on the other side."

"You need to talk to Dr. Leibowitz," she said. "She's on court standby. Do you want her to testify this afternoon?"

"No, I want to give her a whole day. The more Dougherty goes after her, the better for us. He can't help himself. He'll charge right into the psych world and won't be able to shut her up. Probably Thursday morning would be a good time. We'll know by the end of today. Give her a call and update her on the schedule, will you?"

She made a note to call the witness. Natalie's job was to hold hands of all the witnesses, and she did it well. Trials were evolving events that changed hourly, and she had to be on top of the witnesses, making sure they were at the courthouse when needed.

"Andy called," she said.

"What did he say?"

"He said he's found your priest."

"Great. I need to talk to him before I go back to court today."

"And Sally Conrad called," Natalie added. "A couple of times. Same message." She looked at the message slip and read from it: "Get me out of this thing. NOW, DAMMIT!" She handed J.J. the slip. He handed it back. "Call Sally and tell her to meet me at Judge Vincent's courtroom at

1:30. I'll take up the subpoena matter with the judge at the time. Then get Andy on the phone."

"Okay. You want some lunch?"

"No, I'm too hyper," J.J. replied, as he grabbed a handful of Jelly Bellies from the jar on the credenza behind his desk.

"Stop eating the candy. You're gonna kill someone, someday, on a sugar high," said Natalie.

"Well, if it's Dougherty, that may be."

As J.J. reached for the phone, Rebel signaled that she was going out to eat in César Chávez Park across from the building and would see him back in court.

"How is the trial going, J.J.?" Andy asked as soon as he got on the line.

"It's a hearing. Not a trial."

"Don't kid yourself, J.J. With the Catholic Church, it's a trial. I just read the story in *The Wall Street Journal*. This thing is national. Nice placement, by the way, J.J."

"Andy, you may not believe this, but this is one story I didn't place. It might even be the closest thing to news gathering I've ever seen."

"Well, somebody placed this thing with the *Journal*. It didn't get there by itself. If it wasn't you, then it was somebody else doing you a favor."

"What have you got for me?" J.J. asked.

"Damnest thing. I talked on the phone with the priest. Father Gutierrez. He's upset that they threw him out of the priesthood. He seems willing to talk, but there is no way he'll come back to testify. He knows he can be arrested."

"Did you record his statement?"

"No. I didn't want to push him too far. He seems cooperative, but he could skip at any time. He told me I can reach him through the address we have for his mother. He was a little skittish at first. Asked if I was a cop. Can you believe these guys? Criminals think cops can't lie. No wonder they get caught."

J.J. knew he was playing a precarious game with an admitted child molester. It was odd that the priest would actually talk to an investigator for the abused children's attorney. But the fact that he spoke to Andy didn't mean he would ever testify or even give a signed statement. And, if he did, what was there to assure that he would actually tell the truth? What would be his motivation? What incentive would he have to help the children? Other than, perhaps, to get even with the church that had defrocked him. Would that be enough for Andy to play on and get a statement? After all, this was a hearing, not a trial, and the rules of evidence could be bent when dealing with the approval of a minor's settlement.

Of course, there was always the media. J.J. smiled. Dougherty was right, in some respects. Sure, attorneys used the media and the threat of publicity to exert pressure for settlement. So what? Ultimately, all a lawyer could do was reveal what had occurred. It was just that the Church, and most defendants, didn't like to see it in writing, in a newspaper, for everyone to see. They preferred settling quietly and burying their dirty laundry.

"Let me see where Dougherty is going on this case," said J.J. "If he is going to concede the conduct ultimately, we won't need him. But if they really fight us on it, we may need to find a way to get something from the priest that will back us. Let's just keep his whereabouts—and the fact that we are in communication with him—in our back pocket. Maintain contact but don't push him for now."

While J.J. was thinking of tactics, including use of the media, he also knew he needed a genuine basis for the admissibility of the priest's statement in case the court insisted on formal rules of evidence. He had learned long ago that the best attorneys—who allegedly "flaunted" the law—were those who knew the rules of evidence and knew when they were stepping over the line. Those who didn't even know where the line was, ultimately, were just lousy, if loud, lawyers. A written statement, or even a taped conversation, would normally not be admissible into evidence without an opportunity for the other side to cross-examine the person who had given the statement. However, J.J. reasoned, a statement by the priest could be admissible into evidence as an exception to the hearsay rule, either as a "declaration against interest" or an "admission." Still, technically, the defendant in these hearings was the Diocese of Sacramento, not the priest personally. But then, in their effort to hide this fact, Dougherty and the Church had listed the priest as the defendant in the Petitions: Doe 1 and Doe 2 v. R. Gutierrez, et al. Of course, when J.J. had called their bluff and scheduled the deposition of the priest, Dougherty had declined to produce him on the basis that he represented only the Church and not the priest. But he couldn't have it both ways, reasoned J.J. He'd have Andy try to get a statement from the priest, which, if favorable, J.J. would present to the judge. If nothing else, it would enhance his negotiating position by undermining Dougherty's efforts to deny the conduct and require the Church to change its petitions to specifically name the defendant as the Catholic Diocese of Sacramento and not some unrecognizable "R. Gutierrez."

To obtain a ruling of admissibility of the priest's confession, J.J. would have to present the confession to the judge, and the judge would have to read it. Even if he ruled it was inadmissible, he would know its content.

You can't unring a bell, J.J. knew. This old objection of trial lawyers, when someone says or does something improper and then argues it was harmless, came to mind. A confession from the priest. Better yet, a confession with an admission that the priest had told Dougherty or his investigators of the additional conduct. If Judge Vincent knew such a document existed, well—ring, ring, dong, dong, boom.

No better way to beat the Catholic Church than with a bell, J.J. thought. He liked the symbolism.

"Andy, stay in touch. I may need you to record a statement after all."

"You got it, J.J. Best to catch me during the day. Most of my other work here is in the evenings."

"Where are you today?"

"Houston."

"What are you doing in Houston? I forgot."

"I told you. It's a research project."

"Andy," said J.J. and, in a measured and deliberate tone, repeated, "what are you doing in Houston?"

There was a long silence. Finally, Andy said, "Did I mention to you about the injustice of Martha Stewart being indicted while the executives of Enron, WorldCom, Halliburton, and all the others go free or get a slap on the wrist? The United States is being sold, J.J., piece by piece, to the highest bidder. Soldiers are dying. People are unemployed. Others have lost their retirement accounts. These guys cheat and steal millions and billions. And what does our government do? Decide to make an example of—get this—Martha Stewart! J.J., these charges against Martha Stewart are just a distraction from the real corporate fraud that is ruining this country. Martha Stewart, for Christ's sake!" he repeated. "For some chicken-shit, chump-change stock sale. Can you believe this? It is just wrong, J.J."

"What has this got to do with you, Andy? Or Houston?"

"Ken Lay lives here," Andy said without further explanation.

"So?"

"He's the poster boy for corporate corruption. He's the one someone should make an example of."

"Jesus, Andy. You've really gone over the edge this time. Tell me it's just a game. You're following him just to see if it can be done, right?"

Again, there was silence. Long enough to make J.J. feel very uncomfortable. Then Andy answered, "Sure, J.J."

J.J. did not feel any more assured. But he really couldn't deal with Ken Lay's problem right now, except indirectly. "Andy, will you promise me you won't do anything, like get arrested for stalking, until you get my statement and this case is over?"

Andy thought about it. "I owe you that much, J.J. I know you're depending on me."

J.J. contemplated his options and obligations. Did this fall close enough to the *Tarisoff* doctrine, where a therapist had a duty to notify a potential victim of their impending demise if the therapist were presented with such information by a patient? If he reported Andy, J.J. would undermine his own case. He concluded that his first duty was to his clients, two young altar boys who had been molested by a priest of the Catholic Church, not to Ken Lay, who had molested investors and pension plan participants and deprived many of their life savings.

Posited that way, the decision was easy. But he had one final question to satisfy his conscience. "Andy, are you armed?"

"Absolutely not," Andy answered immediately.

J.J. felt assured that at least he had done his duty. Andy, for his part, smiled as he hung up the phone. He was in Texas, home of the Alamo. He could walk into any sporting goods store and, with no questions asked, walk out within minutes, with a high-powered hunting rifle, mounted with a scope, and full of ammunition capable of dropping a bear at two hundred yards. As far as Andy knew, there weren't even bears in Texas.

Chapter 25

*R*eturning to court after lunch, J.J. saw the elevated satellite dishes on vans parked in front of the courthouse and knew the case had probably made the noon news with direct feed from the vans. He decided to enter on the opposite side, on 8th Street, to avoid the media. Again, he mused on how unusual it was for him to avoid the media. Dougherty made the mistake of being dropped off by a driver at the front steps, on the 9th Street side, and cameras set up at the fountain immediately turned upon him. Looking irritated, he walked through a gauntlet of media, repeating, "No comment, no comment, no comment."

At Department 22, J.J. was met by Sally Conrad. "How long till you get me out of here?" she asked immediately.

"I'll take it up first thing with the judge. Just go ahead and sit in the courtroom. No point in hanging around outside where a reporter might spot you."

"I don't need that, either," Sally agreed as she quickly entered the courtroom. As confident as she was in her personal life and as successful in her professional one, she still harbored a phobia when it came to dealing with the media.

J.J. started to follow Sally into the courtroom but saw Maureen McReynolds, *The Wall Street Journal* reporter, coming down the corridor. He let the door shut but kept one hand on the handle as if prepared to open the door for her. She smiled at him.

"Mr. Rai, isn't it?" she asked.

"As if you didn't know," he smiled back. "And I'm sure you know people refer to me as J.J."

"I have heard that, yes. But we have very established rules at the *Journal*. We always refer to subjects by last name. Mr. Rai, Mr. Hussein, Mr. Bush," she said, continuing to smile at him.

"Since you broke the story, I am saving an exclusive interview for you, Ms. McReynolds. I have given no quote to anyone else," J.J. said, offering exclusivity to encourage a working relationship—at least.

"Oh, you don't have to do that, Mr. Rai. I don't really need to interview you. I can observe the proceedings. Feel free to do interviews with others."

He opened the door for her and added, "Well, if you have any questions—"

She interrupted, still smiling, obviously enjoying herself. "I'll know where to find you," she said, finishing his sentence.

A slight fragrance as she brushed by.

The Sanchez parents were already in the courtroom sitting with their new attorney, Larry Feldman. While the boys were absent, J.J. was surprised to see that Carmen was sitting with her parents. Since he didn't anticipate calling her as a witness, he saw no reason to raise the question of her presence.

As the participants waited for the judge, a dozen or more people came in and sat in the public section of the courtroom. J.J. recognized the anchor of Fox 40 News and a number of other media faces. Sitting at counsel table, J.J. turned in his chair, leaned over, and pretended to look into his briefcase, but looked instead toward the back of the room where Ms. McReynolds sat in what had become her regular seat. He ran his eyes over the other reporters and back to her as if to say, "I might give them an exclusive interview; here is your competition." She shrugged to signal, "I don't care. Interview away." They were communicating—even if only with their eyes and shrugs. He was enjoying her.

The judge entered. Everyone started to rise. "Remain seated," said the bailiff to people already bent at the waist. He seemed to relish the power of his pronouncements. He alternated between "please stand" and "remain seated" just to keep everybody guessing.

Both J.J. and Dougherty rose to address the court. The judge held up his hand.

"I have an announcement of which the bailiff will be providing copies to all media." He then read aloud from a sheet of paper.

There will be no televising or oral recording of these proceedings in order to protect the identity of the children involved. I can only control what goes on in my courtroom and with the attorneys and participants, and then in a very limited way.

I request that all media reporting on these public proceedings involving minors subject to abuse do so in a manner to not add to their injury. Specifically, I ask that they, their parents, and siblings, not be identified by name, initials, birth date, ethnicity, or in any other manner that would make them known to members of the public, their schoolmates, or fellow church-goers.

I believe there is a code of conduct to which most media adhere. To date, only one article, that of *The Wall Street Journal*, has appeared and has been consistent with both the right of the public to know and the protection of the privacy of the children. I hope that all other reports will similarly be sensitive to this balance.

The judge nodded to the bailiff, who then handed copies of the statement to counsel and to all media representatives who had filled the courtroom.

"I think we can proceed," said the judge. "Is there anything else before we call our first witness?"

"Yes, Your Honor," said J.J., standing. "Mr. Dougherty went out in the middle of the night and served a subpoena upon a psychological consultant that I retained to assist me in this matter. She is not to be a witness in this case. She has not been declared as an expert witness, and I have no intention of calling her to testify as such. Her role was solely to assist me in understanding the psychological issues of the case. Clearly, this is privileged work product of an attorney, and her efforts are not available to opposing counsel, and she cannot be called as a witness by them."

Unlike the normal reaction that J.J. had come to expect, Dougherty did not rise to the challenge. In fact, he didn't rise at all. He waited for the judge.

"Mr. Dougherty, what is the legal basis for subpoenaing an advisor of Mr. Rai?" the judge asked.

Now, Dougherty stood. "Your Honor, after receiving the psychological evaluation and conclusions of Dr. Leibowitz, which recounted stories of sexual abuse substantially beyond anything ever told to any representative of the Church or the therapist that we had examine the children, I discussed this matter with our psychiatric expert, Dr. Jonathan Mandel. You may recall that Dr. Mandel examined the children at the request of the Diocese on May 12. He found no evidence of the type of abuse subsequently reported by Dr. Leibowitz. The only person, to our knowledge, who discussed the nature of the abuse with the children between the examinations by Dr. Mandel and Dr. Leibowitz, was Sally Conrad, a therapist—but one who admittedly is not competent enough to qualify as an expert on child sexual abuse for these hearings. Yet, after she talked to the boys, we are confronted with accusations of sexual acts, never before asserted."

Dougherty looked at J.J. J.J. knew immediately where he was going with this explanation.

"It was Mr. Rai himself who came to this court and said that information had come to him, apparently from Ms. Conrad, of these new accusations. Our expert, Dr. Mandel, will testify that abused children are very susceptible to manipulation—even by inadvertence and innocent questioning—by inexperienced therapists, despite their best intentions."

J.J. knew he was in trouble. Or at least that Sally Conrad was in trouble as a result of his request that she examine the children. Dougherty was not accusing J.J. directly of manipulating the children to bring false claims in order to build a case, as he had originally charged. Of course, if there had been a jury present, he would have implied, at the very least, that J.J. had directed this scheme against the Church. After all, everyone hates trial lawyers. But, no, he was now before a judge, so better to blame a therapist than a reputable attorney. Dougherty even tempered his charge

with the suggestion that the therapist might have done it innocently—
"with the best of intentions"—because of her "inexperience."

When he stood, J.J. knew he was dead on the law. He might have
slid by with another judge. Not with Judge Vincent. But he had to make
an argument, mostly so Sally could see that he did all that he could. And,
also, to limit the scope of her testimony. He realized he had let Sally step
across the line from advisor to witness.

"Your Honor," he began, "Ms. Conrad began her assistance in this
matter to advise me. Nothing else. She did so on the basis that she would
not be designated as an expert witness and would not be asked to testify.
We are not basing any of our case upon her testimony. We will prove our
case completely without any opinions she holds or observations that she
may have made. Our testimony will consist of independent observations
by a trained psychiatrist knowledgeable in sexual abuse. Of course, any
opinion that Sally Conrad may have provided me would clearly fall within
the attorney/client and work product privileges, not subject to disclosure."

He sat down. Dougherty started to stand to respond. Judge Vincent
didn't need it.

"Mr. Rai, I agree that opinions expressed to you by your consultant
are privileged. Mr. Dougherty cannot inquire into what Ms. Conrad said
to you. However, her observations of the children, the conversations she
had with them, what they said to her, and what she said to them are not
privileged. She may have been in these meetings as a consultant, but she
was also a participant and, therefore, a witness to what the children said
occurred. As I understand Mr. Dougherty's offer of proof, which is set
forth in the report he filed with the court and counsel the day prior to the
commencement of these hearings, he contends that she was not only a
witness to what the boys said occurred, but also an active participant in
getting them to say things that no prior therapist or person had previously heard. Is that your position, Mr. Dougherty?"

"Yes, Your Honor," Dougherty replied immediately.

"Is Ms. Conrad in the courtroom?" asked the judge.

"Yes, Your Honor." J.J. turned as Sally Conrad stood. Immediately,
the reporters in the courtroom also turned to look at her. Some scribbled

notes, which obviously would have included her name and the accusations being made concerning her role in the children's claims of sexual abuse.

"Ms. Conrad, you will be required to testify in this matter. Please have a seat," said the judge. All in the courtroom had turned to see Sally Conrad—except the Sanchez parents. Carmen Sanchez was still looking at her as Sally sat back down. In fact, Carmen gave her a slight wave. Sally couldn't help but notice that Carmen looked much more presentable than she had in Sally's office and showed no sign of the tongue piercing hardware.

"Can we finally proceed?" asked the judge.

"Yes, Your Honor," said both J.J. and Dougherty, rising. J.J. looked at Dougherty and wondered why he was standing.

"What's going on?" said the judge.

"Your Honor, I was going to call Mrs. Sanchez as our first witness," said J.J., still looking at Dougherty.

"Your Honor," responded Dougherty, "I was going to call Mrs. Sanchez as *our* first witness."

"We are the plaintiffs," said J.J.

"This is not a trial, Your Honor; it's a hearing upon a request by the petitioner to approve a minor's compromises. The petitions were filed by the Church; therefore, I believe that it is appropriate that we proceed to ask the court to approve our petition," said Dougherty.

"One way or another, gentlemen, we are going to hear from witnesses," said the judge. He thought for a moment. "Mr. Dougherty is correct. You are the petitioner. Call your first witness, Mr. Dougherty."

J.J. sat down as Mrs. Sanchez came forward and took the oath. She was directed to the witness chair. Dougherty gave her a smile and led her through some preliminary questions dealing with the time she and her family had come to the United States, the number of children she and her husband had, and how they had lived as migrant workers before coming to Sacramento. It was at this point, as he began to sit, that Dougherty noticed the daughter, Carmen, in the courtroom.

"Your Honor," said Dougherty. "I notice that while the boys have been excused, their sister, Carmen Sanchez, also a minor, is in the courtroom. Perhaps, given the nature of the accusations, she should be excused."

"I think that would be appropriate. Thank you for noticing, Mr. Dougherty," said Judge Vincent.

As Carmen left the courtroom, she stole another look at Sally Conrad.

Dougherty returned to questioning Mrs. Sanchez, bringing out how the family had moved to Sacramento and become totally involved with the Diocese. The children went to parochial school. Both Mr. and Mrs. Sanchez worked at the cathedral. In fact, they lived in a house on the premises of the rectory and participated in all of the religious and social functions of the church. The Catholic Church was their life and had been good to them, as had the bishop.

Dougherty finally got to the boys. "Juan and Felix, the twins. When did they become altar boys?"

"When they were ten," she replied.

"And was Father Gutierrez in charge of the altar boys at that time?"

"Well, he taught a class after school, where they would practice being altar boys. But they would serve at Mass for other priests, too," said Mrs. Sanchez.

"Did they usually serve together, the boys?"

"Most of the time, I think. Not all the time."

"And were you often at Mass when they served?"

"Yes, most of the time. Especially on Sundays."

"Did you ever smell alcohol on their breath at any time after they served Mass?" Dougherty asked, looking over at J.J. He had obviously practiced the question with Mrs. Sanchez and had no doubt about the answer.

"Never."

"Never?" he asked loudly.

"Never," she repeated.

"Did you know Father Gutierrez well?"

"Yes. I knew him since we came to Sacramento."

"And, working at the Diocese rectory, you would see him daily, wouldn't you?"

"Yes, I would."

"Did you ever see him act inappropriately with your children?"

"Never."

"Did your children ever say anything to you to make you feel uncomfortable about them being around Father Gutierrez?"

"No. Well, not until Felix said he didn't want to go to camp," answered Mrs. Sanchez.

J.J. sat looking at the witness. He didn't bother taking notes. It was clear that Dougherty was attempting to establish that no information came to the parents or, by the same token, to the Church, to suggest that these boys were being molested prior to the time Mrs. Sanchez contacted the bishop and expressed her concerns. All of this testimony was not to deny the abuse, but rather to limit it and, more particularly, to make clear that the Church had no prior knowledge or legal "notice" whatsoever and, arguably, no legal responsibility for the unlawful conduct of this fallen priest.

"And when Felix said that he didn't want to go on the camping trip, you confronted Father Gutierrez with this fact?" Dougherty asked.

"Yes, immediately."

"And there was something in the way that Father Gutierrez acted that told you, led you to believe, that perhaps something bad had happened on the camping trip? Is that correct?"

Clearly, Dougherty was leading Mrs. Sanchez in her testimony. J.J. could have objected, but what would be the point? This information was going to come out one way or another, and it really was not contested. If Dougherty felt comfortable, perhaps even too comfortable, leading the witness in this manner, J.J. could throw him off base later, when it really counted.

"You immediately went to the bishop with this information, didn't you?" Dougherty asked, continuing his leading form of questioning.

"Yes, immediately."

Finally, an open question with which Dougherty was comfortable: "Would you tell the court why you trusted Bishop O'Brien with this information?"

Dougherty moved to allow the media to see the witness better and to hear the anticipated endorsement of Bishop O'Brien and his conduct.

"Whenever we've had a problem, Bishop O'Brien has helped us. He brought us to Sacramento from our life as migrant workers in the Valley. He gave us jobs here. He saw to it that our children got a good education. When we've had any trouble, he's always been the one to help us."

J.J. thought about the answer. Very nice. Don O'Brien was a great guy. No question that he had been helpful to the family. J.J. was not about to say otherwise.

"What kind of trouble?" Dougherty asked, as if he really didn't know.

"Well, our daughter Carmen—the one that you asked to leave the court a little while ago—has been our problem child. Not like the twins. She has been the one that has always been in trouble. Alcohol. Drugs. Running away. Boys. The bishop has had to help, many times, to avoid her getting arrested for shoplifting, loitering, cutting school. Lots of things. We always say that the twins have been our gift from God; Carmen has been our burden."

Strange, J.J. thought. A mother, yet speaking of the loss of a daughter without emotion. Flat affect was the psychological term that occurred to him.

"So the moment you suspected any problem with your boys, you immediately contacted the bishop for help?" Dougherty continued.

"Yes, and he called in the priest immediately and fired him. Then he insisted that the boys get some professional help so they could be taken care of in case there was any problem from all of this."

"And, as their mother, can you tell us how they are doing?"

He looked to the judge, as if to argue again, with his gesture, that the best witness about the effects of sexual abuse on young boys was their mother.

"Felix was the one that was having stomach aches and making excuses not to go on the camping trip. He's better since Father Gutierrez was fired. Juan has had no problems. They both know that this thing is in court, and they are both worried that maybe their friends will find out about it and tease them. I think that's the biggest problem right now."

"No problems in school?"

"No."

"Have they returned to church?"

Mrs. Sanchez hesitated. Apparently, Dougherty had thrown this question in without having spoken to her about it. Perhaps in his devotion, the children's faith was his overriding concern.

"No, they haven't returned to church, and they haven't gone back to being altar boys." She saw the frown on Dougherty's face. "But," she added, "I think that might just be because they're afraid that other people might know about this, and they are embarrassed."

Dougherty consulted his notes. He was not going to deviate from the script again. He checked the last question and asked it.

"Mrs. Sanchez, do you ask His Honor to approve these petitions in which each of your boys would receive $50,000 and the case would end right now?"

She addressed the judge directly. "Yes, I do, Your Honor."

After a long moment of silence, Dougherty said, "No further questions, Your Honor."

J.J. stood and went to the front edge of the jury box. He leaned on it with one forearm. He had no notes. He wanted to appear both non-threatening and understanding.

"Mrs. Sanchez, you feel a great deal of gratitude toward Bishop O'Brien for all that he has done for you and your family over the years, don't you?" he began.

"Yes, he has always been there for us."

"And you certainly wouldn't want him to be unfairly criticized for the conduct of one of his priests, would you?"

"No. He didn't know what Father Gutierrez did at camp. He would never allow anything like this to occur."

"Right. I know Bishop O'Brien, and I agree that he would never permit anything like this. But you also don't want the Church and your Catholic faith to be held up in an unfavorable light in the media, do you?"

"No," she agreed.

"But what happened to your boys was a sin, wasn't it?"

"Yes, definitely," she answered immediately.

"But you really don't know what happened to your boys personally, do you, because you've never spoken to them about it. Isn't that true? The only thing you know is that Felix got sick and said that he didn't want to go on the camping trip anymore."

"Yes, but I could see it in Father Gutierrez's eyes when I told him. He did something to the boys on the trip. That's why they didn't want to go," she said, as if to show the truth of the notion that a mother always knows without being told.

"What did he do to your boys?"

"I don't know," she admitted, "but I knew right away it was bad."

"Actually, only Felix got sick and said he didn't want to go on the trip, isn't that true?" asked J.J. in a soft voice, "Juan wanted to go."

"Yes. But Felix said it happened to Juan, too."

"Who told you that?" J.J. asked, knowing the answer.

"Bishop O'Brien. He talked to Felix, and Felix told him that it was both of them."

"So if something happened on the trips over the two summers before this one, you never suspected anything. Is that right, Mrs. Sanchez?"

"Not until Felix said he didn't want to go this year," she agreed.

"But Felix also said he didn't want to be an altar boy anymore, right?"

"Yes, because of what Father Gutierrez did on the camping trips."

"But if something happened to the boys at the cathedral, during the last two or three years, you never suspected anything there either, isn't that right?"

"Because nothing happened. It was on the camping trips."

"But you didn't know about the camping trips. And you don't know for sure whether anything happened when they were serving as altar boys, do you, Mrs. Sanchez?" he asked as gently as he could.

"No," she finally relented in a quiet voice.

"And your boys wouldn't lie about something this serious, would they?"

"No," she said. "They are honest boys."

J.J. had gotten everything he wanted or needed. At the same time, he had to leave her on a positive note, rebuild her, even if she now harbored doubts that would likely follow for life any parent whose children had been abused, right under her nose, for years.

"Mrs. Sanchez, you only want what is best for your children, isn't that right?"

She grabbed the life preserver. "Yes, Mr. Rai. That's all we want." She looked at the judge.

"We'll take our afternoon break," said the judge. "Ten minutes."

Dougherty went out to make a phone call.

Sally Conrad caught J.J. halfway to the door. "How long do I have to sit here?"

"I'll insist Dougherty tell us whether he's calling you today. If not, you can go."

"I wish you'd done that at 1:30."

Rebel was next. "Is it me, or are things not going well?"

"Don't shoot until you see the whites of their eyes," J.J. responded.

"What?"

"Old Hickory. The Battle of New Orleans. I guess it was a bit before your time."

"Yeah, 1800-something or so, wasn't it?" she said.

"No, the song. He recited part of the jingle as best he remembered it: "Old Hickory said we could take 'em by surprise if we held our fire till we saw the whites of their eyes."

"Dad, I think you make this stuff up as you go along."

"I do, sweetheart. Or, as my Moot Court Professor, Ed Heafey, Jr., at Boalt Hall used to say, 'When they put a spear through your chest, and the jury turns to look at you, just act as if it belongs there.'"

"So, dad, you're saying we just took a spear in the chest this afternoon?"

"Pretty much, grasshopper. Now, smile for the media, and pretend it belongs there as we walk out of the courtroom." J.J. put his arm on her shoulder and guided her through the door, with a confident smile on his face.

166

Carmen Sanchez was sitting outside the courtroom on one of the benches in the corridor, alone. She looked at Rebel with a plaintive look that made Rebel uncomfortable.

"What's her story?" Rebel asked.

J.J. looked over at Carmen and whispered to his daughter, "She's a weirdo."

When J.J. and Rebel got to the cafeteria, they saw Larry Feldman sitting with Mr. and Mrs. Sanchez. Roland Dougherty was nowhere to be seen.

Returning on the elevator to the fourth floor, J.J. saw the reason for Dougherty's absence. He was in the company of Bishop Donald O'Brien, his client and star witness. J.J. and the bishop met as each got off his elevator.

"J.J., good to see you," said the bishop, offering his hand.

"Bishop. Nice of you to join us, finally," J.J. said, shaking his hand.

"Well," said the bishop loudly enough for the media now gathering around them, "this is a terrible ordeal for everyone. The Church wants to help these young children in whatever way it can. Our prayers are with them and with their family." He added with a smile, "And we pray for your soul too, Mr. Rai."

"Why, do you think that my soul is in danger, bishop?"

"We are all sinners. We can all use prayer, J.J."

J.J. turned to Dougherty. "Do you have a second, Roland?"

Dougherty separated from the bishop. "What?"

J.J. didn't really expect more of him. He tended to be abrupt whenever he wasn't seeking something himself.

"Who do you plan on calling this afternoon?" J.J. asked. It was a simple request—ascertaining the order of witnesses. Normally, attorneys share this information, so that they do not have to stay up all night reviewing prospective testimony and cross-examination of every witness in the case. Instead, an attorney can prepare for just those scheduled to appear the next day. Occasionally, a court will order disclosure, if there is a problem. Dougherty gave J.J. a bored look. "Wait and see," he answered.

"Look, all I want to know is whether you plan on calling Sally Conrad. She's been sitting here since 1:30, and if you're not planning on calling her today, let's let her go. She has clients to meet with."

Dougherty shrugged his shoulders to suggest that Sally Conrad's clients were not his problem.

"Okay," said J.J. "We can take it up with the judge. That way, he'll know you're just jerking her around and being an asshole, as usual."

Dougherty stepped past him, without another word, and walked down the hall and into the courtroom. J.J. followed, aggravated. As he reached the courtroom door, Carmen Sanchez, who was still alone on her bench, stood and approached him.

"Mr. Rai, can I talk to you?" she asked politely.

"I'm sorry," he responded, impatiently. "I have got to get into the hearing." He walked in and saw Sally gesturing. He knew she wanted to know what was happening. He raised his hand to signal "wait."

Rebel had been right behind her dad and had seen Carmen approach him. When they both were in the courtroom, J.J. asked "What do you think she wanted?"

Rebel shook her head. "She's a freak. Stay away from her."

As the judge entered, Dougherty stood as if to call his next witness. Instead, he announced, "Your Honor, we plan on calling Mr. Sanchez, Bishop O'Brien, and possibly Dr. Mandel this afternoon. I understand Ms. Conrad is here pursuant to subpoena. We will not be able to get to her today. I request that the court direct her to appear tomorrow morning."

"Ms. Conrad," said the judge. Sally stood as he addressed her. "You are excused today. Please return Friday morning at 9:00 A.M."

Roland Dougherty smiled at Sally. It was all she could do not to flip him the finger. She pushed open the door and walked out. In the corridor, she was approached by Carmen Sanchez.

"Ms. Conrad, can I talk to you? There are some things I never told you."

Inside the courtroom, J.J. assumed Dougherty would next call Mr. Sanchez to follow Mrs. Sanchez. Mr. Sanchez didn't have anything to add. He really knew nothing. But Dougherty was methodical to a fault. Sometimes the hardest thing for an attorney is to say, "No questions."

"Your Honor, the Diocese of Sacramento calls Bishop Donald O'Brien," Dougherty announced. It was said as if Moses was about to enter with the stone tablets. J.J. smiled, not only because his old friend was about to take the stand, but also because Dougherty had acknowledged that the "Diocese of Sacramento" was calling the bishop. After all the attempts to hide the Diocese behind the name of "R. Gutierrez" in the petitions, Dougherty just could not help himself but had to exclaim grandly and announce before the media that the bishop of the Diocese of Sacramento, the Reverend Donald O'Brien himself, was about to take the stand, under the direction and guidance of Roland Dougherty, Defender of the Faith and of the Holy Catholic Church.

They were lawyer and bishop now, but once they had been altar boys, and there was still something about being boys that made them engage in pranks. As Bishop O'Brien walked behind his chair, J.J. pushed back slightly, and the bishop ran into the chair. Immediately, J.J. jumped up.

"Oh, I'm sorry, Don," he said putting one arm on the bishop's shoulder and the other on the bishop's leg as if to massage it and relieve any pain that he may have caused.

"That's okay, J.J.," the bishop muttered as J.J. continued rubbing his leg.

"Let me help you," J.J. said, making a pronounced effort to assist the bishop, making it appear the bishop needed assistance walking around the counsel table.

"I'm fine," the bishop said. The bishop put his hand on J.J.'s hip and inconspicuously pinched him hard. In an earlier time, they would have been on the floor in a wrestling match. But now, in the courtroom, they released each other and assumed their present stations in life.

J.J. looked at his daughter. She had a hand covering most of her face, suppressing a laugh. He glanced at Ms. McReynolds; she rolled her eyes.

Well, he thought to himself, so much for Moses. He's just a clumsy priest named Don.

The clerk asked the bishop to raise his right hand to be sworn.

"There's no Bible?" he quibbled.

"No bishop, we affirm under penalty of perjury," said the judge. "'So help me God' went out a long time ago."

"That's a shame," said the bishop, as he prepared to take the oath.

J.J. admired the little joke. Bishop O'Brien was taking control of the courtroom, just as he had taken control of a picket line, with a bullhorn, in the face of angry growers in the Central Valley. He would be a formidable witness.

Standing in the witness box, Bishop O'Brien raised his right hand almost as if he were about to make the sign of the cross over the congregation. His left hand, perhaps by habit of delivering the blessing, was across his heart. In this posture, he was sworn.

"Bishop, how long have you known the Sanchez family?" Dougherty began. He wasn't going to waste any time on preliminary questions. Everyone knew that this was the bishop of the Diocese of Sacramento. He was used to appearing before groups. He did not need to be settled as a witness before being asked important questions.

"My goodness," began Bishop O'Brien, "I've known them since they came to the United States and joined my parish in Delano. That must be, I'd say, twelve, thirteen years ago."

"And how long have you known the boys, Juan and Felix?" asked Dougherty.

"Since birth. Shortly after I met the Sanchez family, the twins were born. In fact, I baptized them."

"We've heard testimony from Mrs. Sanchez that you have been a supporter of the family, assisting them with employment, finances, and family problems," said Dougherty.

It wasn't really a question, but, again, J.J. saw no point in objecting.

"Well, they are very kind. These are decent, devoted, and hardworking people. I value their service to me and to the Church. That's why I asked them to come to Sacramento with me when I was named bishop five years ago. Mrs. Sanchez has been invaluable in the rectory, and Mr. Sanchez is an excellent custodian of our beautiful cathedral."

"Was it unusual for the Sanchez family to come to you with family problems—specifically, problems involving the children?"

"Not at all. The family lives on the premises, behind the rectory. So, in some ways, we are like a large Catholic family, living, serving, and working together. From time to time, they would ask my assistance with the children. This might involve school—initially, getting them into parochial school and the financial problems related to that—as well as any problems that arose from time to time."

"So, if Mrs. Sanchez had concerns about Father Gutierrez and her boys, would you expect that she would seek you out?"

"Definitely. As I mentioned, I've known the boys since birth. I feel I have a very good relationship with them. If any harm came to them, I would want to know. I believe the Sanchezes know that. Of course, I am also the bishop, and Mrs. Sanchez, from her work with me at the rectory, knows that I am the one to discipline a priest within the Diocese, should that become necessary. So, yes, I would expect her to come to me if she had any problem involving her children or a priest and certainly if it involved both."

"When Mrs. Sanchez came to you, exactly what did she tell you about the boys?"

"She said she was concerned because Felix did not want to go on the annual altar boy camping trip. He also told her he did not want to be an altar boy. She had told Father Gutierrez that Felix did not want to go on the camping trip. Apparently, there was something in Father Gutierrez's reaction that led her to believe that something bad had happened on a prior trip. She was very upset, and I told her I would immediately find out what happened, if anything, and I think I also told her that Felix didn't have to go on the camping trip, so that he would stop worrying. Obviously, I was concerned for the child."

The bishop bit his bottom lip, as if thinking hard. Then he added, "I think that's about it for that conversation."

"What did you do then, bishop?"

"I did what I'm required to do—what I would have done anyway, as a supervisor of employees. I picked up the phone, called Monsignor Jenkins, who schedules all Diocese activities, and informed him that I was suspending Father Gutierrez immediately from all duties. I asked that he have Father Gutierrez confine himself to his quarters, pending my investigation."

Nice, thought J.J. The Catholic Church has finally gotten the message. A bishop is no different than the C.E.O. of a corporate franchise. Separation of church and state does not mean a church shepherd can fondle his sheep with impunity, answerable with a few rosaries for penance. If you, as a church official, chooses to grieve for the errant shepherd—to comfort the sinner—then he's your sinner, baby. You have just ratified or covered up. Take your pick. O'Brien was obviously well versed in the law. He knew that while a priest would be personally liable for molesting boys, the Church, like any employer, would not be liable for the illegal acts of its employee unless it either knew or should have known in advance of the priest's propensities or failed to exercise proper supervision or failed to investigate complaints promptly or ratified the acts after they occurred. These were the acts of a lowly priest and not the acts committed by an officer or managing agent of the Diocese. And, of course, the priest, with his vow of poverty, was long gone, and liability insurance did not cover him for his illegal act.

"And did you promptly investigate Mrs. Sanchez's suspicion?"

Dougherty was adding all the right words to the questions: "promptly investigate," the "suspicion." The reality was that J.J. had no doubt that his long-time friend, Bishop Donald O'Brien—Don—would do the right thing when confronted with a child-molesting priest. This presented J.J. with a problem: How was the diocese legally responsible? Not a problem for a newspaper story or public consumption but a problem for a lawyer charged with establishing legal responsibility of a church for the acts of a priest.

"Yes, I met with Felix. At that time, he was my main concern," answered the bishop.

"Solely based upon a mother's intuition? Her suspicions arising out of her knowledge of her children?" Dougherty asked.

"Your Honor," J.J. said, standing, "I've been patient with Mr. Dougherty, but now he's laying it on a little thick. Could he just ask what the boy said?"

"Mr. Dougherty, there is no jury; just me," said the judge. "I get the point. Just ask your question."

"Yes, Your Honor. What did Felix tell you, Bishop O'Brien?"

"Well, it wasn't that easy," answered Bishop O'Brien. "As I said, I've known these boys since birth. They are comfortable with me, but this is a delicate subject with young boys. So I started by asking Felix if it was true that he didn't want to go on the trip. When he said yes, I assured him that was fine. I said his mother and I were concerned that perhaps the reason was that Father Gutierrez had done something wrong on the last trip. He nodded. I told him he could tell me anything. Then I asked, 'What did Father do?' He said, 'He touched us.' I asked if there was anything else, and he said, 'He made us touch him.' I again asked if there was anything else, and Felix said 'No.'"

"You used the plural, 'us,' bishop. Did you mean to?"

"Yes," replied the bishop. "I, too, was shocked and asked Felix whom he was referring to."

"What did he say?" asked Dougherty, playing out the drama for all it was worth.

"He said he and his brother, Juan, were compelled by Father Gutierrez to do these things."

"Was this the first time you received any information to suggest that something had happened to Juan on one of these camping trips?"

"Yes."

"Bishop, prior to the conversation with Mrs. Sanchez, had you received information from any source whatsoever that gave you any suspicion of improper sexual conduct on the part of Father Gutierrez toward these boys or anyone else at any time during your bishopric?"

J.J. thought, upon hearing the word 'bishopric' of asking the court reporter to read back the testimony, but he thought that might be pushing it. But by the quick raising of his head and glance to Bishop O'Brien, he knew he had telegraphed his amusement with the use of the archaic term to denote the witness's tenure in office. Clearly, Bishop O'Brien was avoiding his eyes to maintain his own decorum with his old friend.

"Absolutely not," replied the bishop. "Had I received any such information, I would have immediately investigated and, if warranted, discharged Father Gutierrez, as I did upon receiving Mrs. Sanchez's information."

"What did you do with the information you received from Felix, Bishop O'Brien?" Dougherty asked, his brow furrowed as if he were genuinely concerned.

"Well, first I brought the boys together and assured them that God would not blame them; that this was a grievous sin by Father Gutierrez. I told them they would never have to see Father Gutierrez again and that if they wanted to go on the camping trip this year, I would personally go with them and invite their father."

"And did you, in fact, lead the altar boy trip including Felix, Juan, and Mr. Sanchez this year?"

"Yes, we went in late May to the Santa Cruz mountains. We had a very nice time. It was the first time, I believe, that the boys had been camping with their father."

Mr. Sanchez smiled at the bishop as if to thank him. The bishop nodded back.

J.J. couldn't help smiling also. The annual trip to the Santa Cruz mountains had been a tradition of Cathedral of the Blessed Virgin altar boys for half a century. He, Dougherty, and O'Brien had taken the trip together in the mid-fifties. I wonder how it ever started—the abuse—J.J. thought. And how many other altar boys were abused over the fifty years of trips? He looked at Dougherty at the defense table and O'Brien in the witness box and wondered whether either of them had been abused. Then another thought entered his mind: I wonder whether I ever was?

J.J. had never been camping before becoming an altar boy. His parents were too busy working to ever take vacations. He had gone twice, remembering priests driving as cars full of boys sang "one hundred bottles of beer on the wall" and other traveling songs. Together they had pitched camp in the giant redwoods, hiked, stayed in tents, sat around campfires, showered in public facilities in the woods, engaged in songfests with other young campers, swam in the river and swung on ropes at Ben Lomond, and were taken for a day on the Boardwalk of Santa Cruz. It was a wonderful trip that every altar boy looked forward to, and a tradition that had endured for all of these years.

J.J.'s attention returned to the courtroom as he heard the bishop state: "Then I confronted Father Gutierrez at my office in the rectory."

"Did Father Gutierrez admit any improper conduct on camping trips?" asked Dougherty.

"Yes, he did. He acknowledged mutual masturbation between the two boys and himself. He actually defended it as not really harmful."

J.J. could hear the murmur from the media and the rush of pens and pencils on paper. This was a revelation that the bishop did not have to make and, J.J. thought, judging from the media representative's reaction, would raise the question: How could the Catholic Church have harbored such a sick fucker.

"What was your response, bishop?"

"I was astounded by the idea that a grown man, let alone a priest, could attempt to justify this behavior or suggest that it was not harmful. I told him to pack and leave immediately, that he was relieved of…that he was fired…and, as far as I was concerned, his life as a priest was over. The next day, I called his Order and notified its director of my actions and recommended that Father Gutierrez be defrocked as a priest. At that point, he was under the direction of his Order, the Silicians, and I fully expected that they would deal with him, as I no longer exercised control or supervision over him once I terminated him at the diocese level."

The bishop looked to the Sanchez family. "I then went to comfort the Sanchez family."

Dougherty was satisfied.

"Thank you, bishop. Mr. Rai may have some questions," he said, in the coy way in which attorneys sometimes challenge their opponents to take on a star witness.

J.J. looked at Bishop O'Brien. Despite J.J.'s slight smile, the bishop maintained his composure, almost elegance, as a bishop of the Catholic Church in his priestly garb, with the small dash of crimson at the neck that marked him as a bishop and successor to Peter and the Apostles. There was clearly more the bishop could have said and probably would, if questioned. Dougherty was inviting—almost daring—J.J. to ask questions so that the bishop could unload prepared responses. But what the bishop had said so far only pertained to what he had been asked about: camping trips. Nothing else. Leave it alone for now, J.J. thought.

"No questions at this time," J.J. announced. "I ask that the bishop remain available in case we need to recall him."

J.J. wasn't taking the bait any more than Dougherty had when J.J. had dangled it previously. Dougherty was up immediately.

"Your Honor, if Mr. Rai has any questions, he should ask them now. The bishop is a very busy man. He can't just be at Mr. Rai's beck and call."

"I just don't have any questions right now, Your Honor. I don't doubt Bishop O'Brien did everything he said. Why should I then be forced to question him?" J.J. protested, mustering his most earnest expression.

"If you decide you wish to recall Bishop O'Brien, Mr. Rai," said the judge, "you are to give Mr. Dougherty twenty-four hours' notice. You may call your next witness, Mr. Dougherty."

"We call Dr. Jonathan Mandel."

A thin, balding gentleman, with a goatee and wire-rimmed glasses, wearing a jacket but no tie, walked into the well of the court and raised his hand to be sworn. He had a file under his left arm. He was clearly at home in a courtroom. When he was seated in the witness box, Dougherty started his questioning of this most friendly paid professional witness.

"Dr. Mandel, can you recite for the court your medical and psychiatric training, education, and experience?"

"Yes," said the witness. He faced the judge. Another sign of a professional witness. "I received my medical training and M.D. degree at the University of Utah. Thereafter, I served a rotating internship at Queen's Hospital in Honolulu, Hawaii, and then entered the U.S. Air Force, as a captain, serving as a general medicine officer at Hickam Air Force Base in Hawaii. I returned to the mainland and pursued a psychiatric residency at the Langley Porter Neuropsychiatric Institute at U.C. San Francisco. Upon completion of my residency, I entered the practice of psychiatry, first with the County of Sacramento, at the old County Hospital, then at DeWitt State Hospital in Auburn, and thereafter in private practice. Since returning to Sacramento in 1972, I have been an advisor to the courts on psychiatric issues, both in adult and juvenile proceedings. I am also an assistant clinical professor of psychiatry at U.C. Davis School of Medicine, located here in Sacramento."

Dougherty interrupted, to appear to be asking questions instead of just letting the doctor talk.

"Doctor, are you a member of any professional organizations in psychiatry?"

"Yes, actually both medical and psychiatric associations," the doctor replied. "The American Medical Association, the American Psychiatric Association, the California Medical Association, the Sacramento County Medical Association, the Central California Psychiatric Association—I'm a past president—and, of course, I am board certified by the National Board of Psychiatry and Neurology."

"Are you familiar with the psychiatric literature relating to reports of childhood sexual abuse, the manner of handling such reports, and the proper role of therapists relating to such reports?" asked Dougherty.

"Yes, I am. I have taken a special interest in this area. As you know, judging from what you read in the newspapers, it would seem that there is an epidemic of childhood sexual abuse in America, driving people to seek out childhood memories to explain all sorts of adult dysfunctions."

"Doctor, let me ask you directly: Do you believe that these two boys were sexually abused?"

J.J. mused to himself at the question. An old trial lawyer had once told him about an expert. He had said that the expert was "basically honest." J.J. had asked, "What does that mean, 'basically' honest?" "Well," the lawyer had said, "he won't lie about the obvious." This witness was about to admit the obvious.

"Yes, I do, Your Honor," he said, seriously, looking at the judge, as if he had provided a profound psychiatric revelation.

"What do you believe, based upon your training and experience, happened to these children?" Dougherty asked.

"Exactly what they first told a trusted adult, Bishop O'Brien. Apparently, Father Gutierrez joined them in what is, frankly, not all that uncommon in the development of pre-teen boys—mutual touching."

That's why you hire an expert, thought J.J. "Mutual touching." An educated non-expert would probably call it "mutual masturbation." A truck driver—and most kids—would probably call it "jerking off." But an expert witness, for a fee, could almost make it sound like sensitivity training.

"Why do you believe that this was the extent of the sexual conduct?"

"Well, a number of reasons." Again, the witness turned toward the judge. "First, the precipitating event for the discovery here was the impending camping trip. This was the catalyst that provided the response in Felix. Second, when the boys were in a trusting environment with an adult whom they had known their entire lives and were free to tell all, this is what they said happened. Third, Father Gutierrez admitted to conduct exactly as the boys described it. Finally, the boys did not disclose anything else to me in my psychiatric interview, nor did I detect anything in their responses to suggest a more serious form of abuse. It was not until they were subjected to multiple legal consultations with a person not well trained in handling childhood sexual abuse that they quote 'remembered' unquote a long history of abuse. Actually—and I think it is significant and supports my opinion—only one of the boys 'remembered' what they both supposedly did with the priest."

Dougherty looked down at his notes. Obviously, he had been provided the questions and the sequence by the witness.

"Do you believe that these later reported acts were truly repressed memories that had somehow come to light though not immediately disclosed by the boys?"

"No, I don't. Twelve-year-olds don't 'forget' current, ongoing sexual abuse," said the psychiatrist firmly and without hesitation.

"Where do you believe these new allegations of abuse came from?"

"I believe they came from suggestions during the interviews conducted by Ms. Conrad, the legal consultant to Mr. Rai," he said, glancing at J.J. as if to assess the impact of his testimony.

An experienced expert witness, thought J.J. He had not referred to Sally as a licensed clinical social worker or even as a lesser-trained therapist, but rather as a "legal consultant."

The witness continued. "Children, especially those subjected to sexual abuse, are very susceptible to suggestion. Unfortunately, untrained therapists will often jump in with conclusions about the occurrence or the nature of the abuse. You know the old saying, 'If you're a hammer, everything looks like a nail.' Unfortunately, there is a serious problem in psychiatry today, especially with children. Too many therapists attribute adult thought patterns, adult conduct, and adult fantasies to children. A child might say, for example, that a person gave him wine because of a bad taste in his mouth. The adult therapist, looking for child abuse, immediately thinks of oral sex instead of halitosis. The therapist's fantasy gets transferred to the child. Pretty soon, the child has confused memory, exaggeration, fantasy, and suggestion with what actually happened and, in what we call 'pseudo-memory,' may repeat the new accusation to the next examiner as his own memory. He may even believe it himself by then. He may also feel he has to defend this 'pseudo-memory' as his own for a whole host of reasons, not the least of which is secondary gain and the emotional support and other consequences that being a victim may bring."

The witness would have gone on forever had Dougherty not interjected a question: "And is that what you believe accounts for the new allegations of abuse that appeared in the psychiatric report of Dr. Leibowitz, the expert hired by Mr. Rai?"

"Yes, I do. It is my medical opinion, with reasonable medical certainty, that we are dealing with pseudo-memories that are the consequence of adult intervention and might, frankly, continue to grow with further intervention."

Smart, J.J. thought. He had to concede Dougherty wasn't stupid. Dougherty had realized that he couldn't take on Dr. Leibowitz directly, so he was undermining her testimony before she took the stand by blaming Sally Conrad for planting false accusations in the minds—or mouths—of the boys. The judge was right: Sally had become a critical primary witness—and the weakest link in his case. He should never have put her in this position. He should have known better. But at the time, he had thought he was dealing with a clear and admitted case of clergy abuse. He had just wanted a sense from someone he trusted as to how seriously these boys had been affected. He never anticipated that there would be new and different accusations arising from Sally's interview.

J.J. could see that it was crucial that he get a statement from the priest and find a way to get it into evidence. If he could no longer count on the boys' testimony, through psychiatric reports, to establish what had occurred, there was only one other person who knew—the priest.

"Doctor, in your professional opinion, what did Ms. Conrad do wrong to lead to these new, false accusations?" Dougherty asked.

"Objection, Your Honor," J.J. said, rising. "There is no proof that the accusations are false. There is just this witness's testimony."

"Sustained," said the judge.

"Well, doctor, you don't believe these accusations, do you?" responded Dougherty, becoming more aggressive in the face of the objection.

"No, I don't."

"And the boys never told you any such thing, did they?"

"No, they did not."

"Back to my question. In your professional opinion as a medical doctor and a board certified psychiatrist, what was wrong with what Ms. Conrad did that led to these new accusations?"

"The first thing," the witness said, "is that a therapist must maintain what we call 'therapeutic neutrality.' She was not neutral. She didn't just listen. She suggested abuse. Second, a therapist must document the memory process. I have seen no notes at all of Ms. Conrad's meetings. Third, she clearly was in a situation beyond her professional competence. Having Ms. Conrad meet with these boys and with the other members of the family was, in my professional opinion, a recipe for psychiatric disaster."

There was a long silence. Finally, the judge said, "We'll be adjourned until tomorrow morning at 10:00 A.M." He gave a hard look at J.J. before leaving the bench.

Dougherty met J.J. at the gate on the way out of the attorneys' area of the court. "You should have taken the $100,000, Rai. I'm recommending to the Diocese that it be withdrawn tonight," Dougherty said with a smile. He then pushed himself ahead of J.J. and out the swinging gate.

Ms. McReynolds was waiting alongside the last row of seats. "Sounds like Ms. Conrad is in for a rough time on the witness stand tomorrow," she said to J.J. "Is it true she is just a licensed clinical social worker?"

J.J. put down his briefcase. He looked around the courtroom. They were alone. "Listen, could you do me a favor? Hold off on mentioning her name until after she has testified. These types of accusations can unnecessarily ruin a person's career. At least give her the chance to answer the charges before you crucify her."

"The *Journal* doesn't crucify people," she replied.

"You know what I mean," J.J. pleaded. "Blame me instead, if you want. After all, I asked her to help me. It was never intended that she be a witness, and I can assure you that she absolutely did not suggest anything to these boys, and neither did I."

"Let me ask you something," she said.

"Sure."

"Have you found the priest?"

"Off the record?"

"Depends."

"How about off the record for now, but if I were to have a statement from him about what happened with the boys, I'd give it to you before I presented it in open court?" he offered.

"I can do that," she agreed.

"And Sally Conrad's name doesn't go into your national publication tomorrow morning on these accusations alone. You'll at least give her a chance to respond in open court before you run a story with her name in it?"

She nodded. "I'll just refer to her as a psychotherapist hired by the boys' attorney. But she will be named after she testifies in court. I am not agreeing to keep her name out permanently."

"We have a deal then," he said. "We've located the priest in Laredo, Texas. It was his original parish. His mother still lives there. He's staying with her. I have an investigator who is in Texas at this moment trying to nail down a statement. He's talked to the priest already, but we delayed getting a statement until we could see whether the Church was going to deny the abuse. Obviously, after today, we're going to actively seek a statement from the priest. As soon as I get it, you get it."

"Can I trust you, Mr. Rai?"

"With your life."

She sensed the topic had changed.

"What brought you out to Sacramento, anyway?" J.J. asked.

"If I wouldn't tell the judge, who has the persuasive power of prison to make me talk, what makes you think I would give up my sources to you?"

"Well, I was thinking perhaps dinner."

"I don't think it would be journalistically appropriate during the trial, Mr. Rai."

"Perhaps after the case is over?"

"I guess we'll have to see, won't we?"

"See what?"

"Whether you win or lose the case."

"Why would that make a difference?"

"I don't date losers." She smiled. She moved closer to him and waited for him to open the courtroom door. That fragrance again. He opened the door, and they walked side by side, down the hall, into the waiting elevator; they rode down in silence together, occasionally flashing a look at one another. At the ground floor, as they exited into the lobby, she offered her hand in a formal handshake. "Well, Mr. Rai, I'm on deadline. See you in court tomorrow."

To anyone watching, the handshake appeared as a business meeting ending except perhaps for the delay in letting go of her hand. Not that she resisted.

Chapter 26

"We are in serious trouble in this case," J.J. told his daughter, when he arrived at the office.

"What do you mean 'we,' dad? I've got to get back and study for the Bar exam. It's only two weeks away. But I'd say you're getting your head handed to you on a plate."

"Is this another one of your biblical allusions? 'Head on a plate.' John the Baptist? Didn't I tell you to stay away from religion? Read Nancy Drew, Erica Jong, Anaïs Nin, like other young girls."

"Find Andy," he shouted to his secretary, as she walked by his office. "I've got to talk to him, now!"

"Sally Conrad has called four times. Says it's urgent," Natalie shouted back.

"Why aren't we using the intercom?" he shouted.

"I don't know. You started this."

"Get Andy. Sally can wait," he yelled one final time.

"What are you going to do?" Rebel asked.

"Have a drink," he said as he took off his coat, loosened his tie, and poured himself a gin and tonic from his bar. "Want one?" he asked.

"I don't drink."

"Where did I go wrong with you? You spout religion; you don't drink—and you expect to be a lawyer?"

He sat at his desk, swiveled his chair to look at the western sky, with the sun still high above the horizon. People would be on the river after work, in ski boats, drinking. In the summer in Sacramento, it seemed that weekends started on Wednesdays because of the heat. Everyone was outside in the evenings: on the river, in pools, at barbeques, or, as he preferred, sitting dockside at the Virgin Sturgeon, watching a beautiful sunset. The owner, Lori, wasn't bad to look at, either.

"You know the problem with this damn trial?" J.J. asked. "It isn't a proper trial. We haven't had the normal months of preparation. Somehow, which to this day I still don't understand, I got drawn into a hearing that suddenly turned into a knock-down, drag-out, heavyweight prize fight. I don't like being this unprepared, and I don't like surprises," he said. "Unless, of course, I'm delivering them."

"Dad, you just don't like not being in control. And, of course, we Rais hate to lose. That's why I've done some computer research." She dropped a stack of papers on his desk. "I Googled this guy: their shrink. Amazing what you can find on the web with a few computer strokes, dad. You really have to learn to use a computer."

J.J. stared at the stack and read the first few pages. Then he remembered, and shouted, "Where is Andy, Natalie? Get me Andy!"

Natalie came on the intercom, breaking the shouting match. "Okay," she said, "I'm trying. But Sally Conrad called again. She's really upset. You haven't called her back. She says she's coming down to see you. She'll be here at 6:30, and she says you better wait. It's important."

"Where's Andy?" he asked.

"His cell phone has been off. I have left messages at his hotel. He's at the Four Seasons in Houston. You know Andy; he likes to go first class."

J.J. picked up the phone. He thought he'd better cool Sally down before she came in with flames for breath. As he did, Natalie announced, "Andy—line four." J.J. switched lines.

"Andy, where in hell have you been? We've been calling and calling. The shit is hitting the fan here."

"I have been on silent surveillance. Had to switch the phone off," Andy explained. "What do you need?"

"All hell has broken loose here, Andy. I need you to get down to Laredo tonight and get a statement from the priest. He needs to tell you about everything, and I mean everything sexual he did with these two boys—places, times, the works. Get him to admit to everything you can:

oral, anal, sideways, on top of each other—anything, but specifics as to what he did and where he did it. We're not buying this story that he did it only on camping trips. He did it at the cathedral. I want this sick motherfucker admitting that he wasn't just playing doctor on a camping trip. Got it?"

"I'm your man."

"What do you think the chances are of getting a statement?"

"No problem. He's a weird dude. I think he'll tell us anything we want to know. He just doesn't seem to give a shit."

"If I thought for sure you could get it by phone, I'd say do it. But this has gotten to be too important. Without him, we're sunk."

"I'm on it," Andy promised. "I'll call as soon I get something. And sorry about the phone thing. I'll call Natalie with my hotel number as soon as I make a reservation in Laredo."

"Great. Thanks, Andy." J.J. was very relieved. He got up and re-filled his drink.

"You drink too much, dad."

"It's only my second drink."

"I'm just repeating what mom says."

"Give me a break. Of course, I drink. I have you to deal with," J.J. said, smiling.

She smiled back. "I realize I'm just a law school graduate, but how do you plan to get whatever the priest says into evidence without the priest in court?"

"Well, let me explain the rules of evidence in the real world. This isn't Harvard. If evidence is totally inadmissible, then you put it in your opening statement so everyone will hear it no matter what the witness later can or cannot say. If it would be admissible, if a witness was available, then give it to an expert witness who can rely upon it in forming his opinion. That way it gets into evidence through the expert even though the witness is unavailable."

"Who are you going to give the priest's statement to?"

"Sally. She can defend herself with it and make Dougherty eat shit. He won't even know it's coming," J.J. said as he sipped his drink, finally feeling an element of control.

"Doesn't Sally go on tomorrow morning?" Rebel asked. "And you don't have a statement. You just have a wino heading for Laredo."

"Andy is not a wino; he is a drunk. But he is a reliable drunk."

Somehow, this sounded like a distinction without meaning and less than persuasive. They both laughed.

"Okay, I'm cutting it close," J.J. admitted, "but this is how real trial work is done. It's a dynamic thing. The issues you go in with often are not the ones you litigate. You keep adjusting. You go out on a limb occasionally and hope no one cuts it off before you climb higher up the tree. What I will need to do tomorrow is to stall until we get the statement. This stuff that you pulled up on the computer is great. There are enough articles here to cross-examine their good Dr. Mandel all morning. That means Sally won't get called until the afternoon session. By then, I hope, we'll have a statement."

His daughter rose from her chair and lifted a heavy backpack. "I've got to get studying, dad. I expect to be up most of the night. Maybe I'll come back tomorrow afternoon to see Sally testify."

"Thanks for the help, Reb," he said as he kissed her on the forehead.

"Good night, dad."

"Good night, Reb," he responded, pantomiming the nightly ritual of putting her to bed as a young child. Except as a child, "Good night" was only a prelude to "Rub my back; rub my head; get me a cold wash rag." He put his arm on her shoulder to walk her out.

"Hello?" he heard someone calling at the reception area. He recognized the voice of Sally Conrad. The staff had gone home. There was no one to meet her at the front desk.

"Oh, shit. I should have called her," whispered J.J.

J.J. walked out. Sally glanced briefly at Rebel passing by and told J.J., "We need to talk."

Chapter 27

$\mathcal{J}$J. fully expected Sally to be upset. He had put her in an untenable position. Her name would soon appear prominently in national media as that of a person accused of planting false claims of sexual abuse in the mouths of altar boys. She hadn't bargained for any of this. She didn't deserve it. She had reluctantly agreed to help him and, being Sally, she had taken the assignment seriously. She had been thorough. Too thorough, it seemed.

"Look, Sally, I never anticipated that the Diocese would accuse you of planting false claims with these kids. It's really an undeserved, low blow, and I am going to prove it's not true and demand a public apology for you," J.J. said, defensively, immediately upon greeting Sally.

Sally looked at him quizzically. "You think that's why I've been calling you all afternoon, J.J.? That what they say about me is urgent?" She shook her head. "I can take care of myself," she added. "I am in this thing now more than you know."

"Well, just so you know, I have spoken to *The Wall Street Journal* reporter, and she will not mention you by name in tomorrow morning's paper. She is going to give you the opportunity to testify fully before reporting any of these accusations."

"I don't practice in New York, J.J. I practice in Sacramento, and I have already heard my name mentioned three times on the radio and once on television since court was out today. I even heard it on a call-in show as I was driving over here. Thanks, but you can't manage the media."

She was right, he knew. Starting with the first *Wall Street Journal* story, he had never had control of the media in this case.

"I'm sorry. I did what I could, Sally."

"J.J., you needn't worry about tomorrow's story; you need to worry about the next day's headline, after I testify."

"What might that headline be," he asked, as they entered his office and he sat at his desk.

Sally remained standing. She held up her hands to indicate a banner headline: "Sister of abused altar boys claims priest raped her," she said.

Chapter 28

"Are you serious?" J.J. asked Sally, who had now taken a seat in front of his desk. He had covered his face with his hands upon the revelation of Carmen's claim to have been raped by Father Gutierrez. Sally's arms hung around the sides of her chair as if she, too, was flabbergasted by her own statement.

"She said it started shortly after she arrived in Sacramento from Delano and continued until she was a freshman in high school. That would mean it ended about a year before the first camping trip with the boys."

"When did she tell you this?"

"She was waiting in the hall outside the courtroom when I was excused, just after the afternoon session started. When I came out, she asked if she could talk to me, saying that there was something that she hadn't told me previously. I assumed it was about her brothers because that is all that we had ever spoken about, and she certainly hadn't been very forthcoming in our initial meeting."

J.J. chimed in. "She asked me, too, if we could talk as I was going into court. I brushed her off."

"Maybe that's why she tried me," Sally said. "Anyway, I told her to follow me outside, where we sat on the cement benches in the shade alongside the building. We sat. I waited. Finally, she said, 'Father Gutierrez raped me.'"

"Just like that?"

"Yeah, just like that. You think I'm making this up?"

"No, I mean, she actually said raped?"

"Yeah. Raped. Repeatedly. At her parent's cottage behind the bishop's residence."

"Come on, Sally. How in the hell could she be raped repeatedly in her own house? Where were her parents? Why didn't anyone see or hear anything? And why didn't she tell anyone?"

"Well, it didn't start out with rape. He worked up from friendly touching, with a kiss of the cheek, after Mass in the presence of her parents, to ambiguous touching on the side of her breast or when his hand would drop below her waist and touch her butt. She thought, at the time, it had to be inadvertent. After all, he was a priest. But things happened, and it progressed."

J.J. was frustrated. Everything about the case was out of control. "Being raped by a priest isn't a natural progression from inadvertent touching. It's rape, damn it!"

"Look," said Sally, growing angry with J.J., "I'm just reporting what she told me, okay? Don't shoot the messenger. And I don't like being cross-examined by you. You have a question, ask her yourself."

"I'm not getting anywhere near her." He sat thinking. When he finally spoke, it was quieter and as if to himself. "Why? Why now? Why is she, all of a sudden, telling us this? Why didn't she go to her parents? Or the bishop? Why us?" he repeated. He stood and walked behind his high-back leather chair. He hit the chair, knocking it sideways, exclaiming, "Damn!"

J.J. stood with his back to Sally, looking out of his window. His instincts told him that Carmen's disclosure was a trap.

His immediate thoughts turned to Dougherty: Had Dougherty put Carmen up to this? Dougherty's theory was that all of these new and false accusations were coming through Sally Conrad. Now, a further unsupported charge was about to be made, and its source was to be—once again—Sally Conrad. If this was a set-up, it would totally destroy Sally Conrad as a witness and make it appear like J.J. was suborning perjury—knowingly putting on a witness to testify to false facts.

J.J. also realized that the last thing he could do, as an attorney, was to meet with Carmen and question her himself. He had to maintain a distance from her, if only for his own protection, so he could truthfully claim that he had never discussed her accusations with her or encouraged her in any manner to testify to the new, unsupported, charges.

At the same time, however, there was no way he could ignore her allegations. If they were true, they would add credence to the accusations of the boys, would support Sally Conrad's testimony about wide-spread molestation, and would establish that the course of conduct by this priest had been going on for many years—long enough that the Diocese should have known or discovered it.

J.J. explained his concerns to Sally.

"What can I do?" she asked. "I can only tell the truth."

"Sally, I am not telling you to lie. I would never tell a witness that—and certainly not you. But I can tell you not to volunteer a thing. I will not ask you anything whatsoever about Carmen, except as it relates to the boys. As for Dougherty, listen very carefully to each of his questions. Unless he specifically asks you about Carmen, stick to the boys. Volunteer nothing. On the other hand, if he specifically asks about Carmen, you have to tell the truth. Then again, if he asks about Carmen, it is likely that he knows anyway and probably put her up to it."

"What do I do in that situation?"

"You tell the truth. She approached you. You never encouraged her. Don't express any opinion about her truthfulness. Report only what she told you. Before you get that far, however, I will be objecting that the hearing is only about the boys and not about Carmen. I don't represent her. No one does. Also, I'll object to Dougherty's asking your expert opinion about Carmen. He already has told the court he is not calling you for expert opinions, only your recall of conversations. If nothing else, my objection will demonstrate to the judge that we are not pushing this testimony as we would be expected to, if we had invented it."

J.J. could see that she was not comfortable. He knew she was not experienced in trial testimony. "If you have any doubt, look at me. I'll give you a little nod if you are to answer. I'll look away if you're not. Don't volunteer anything! Got it?"

"You're the legal beagle," she said.

"Right. The one who got you into this mess. Oh, by the way, did you make any notes of your conversation with Carmen?"

"Are you kidding. After that jerk, Dr. Mandel, criticized me in his report for not having notes—yeah, I've got pages of notes."

"Well, put them in a separate file marked 'Carmen Sanchez' and keep out any reference to it in the boys' files."

J.J. hesitated. As much as he didn't want to hear it, he knew he needed to know what was in the file marked "Carmen Sanchez."

"Can I see your notes?"

Sally handed him two sheets of lined paper that appeared out of a spiral notebook. "It's all I had with me," she said, as if needing to explain. The notes were written in pencil.

In the top left-hand corner, Sally had written "Carmen Sanchez." The first sentence began with the abbreviation "Pt."

"Why did you refer to her as your patient?"

"I consider anyone who approaches me in my official capacity to discuss their emotional or psychological problems a patient in the sense that what they say is privileged. Isn't that true with attorneys?"

"Yeah, but then why are you here discussing her privileged communications with me?"

"Because Carmen asked me to tell you."

"You mean you asked her permission to tell me?" J.J. asked, to clarify.

"No, I mean she specifically asked me to communicate this information to you."

Again, J.J. didn't like the feeling he was getting. He looked back at the pages and began reading:

Pt. 17 year Mex-Amer female, sister of abused altar boys. 8/4/04 met outside courthouse. Stated "Fr. Gutierrez raped me."

History: Started about age 12. Touching side of breast (developed). Kiss cheek. In public. After Mass. Parents present. Sometimes arm around, would drop to buttocks. Assumed "accident" or "imagining." But showed more attention. Holding hand. Rubbing back. Putting her hand on his thigh on bus, school outing but still talking to other kids. Later, giving her rides in his car and putting her hand on the front of his pants. Erection. Progressed to sitting on his lap, and he would put his hands in her panties or bra and "massage" her. He also put her hand inside his pants "so she would know what a boy felt like."

About age 13, he started coming to her home on Cathedral grounds in the evening—Bingo night—when mom and boys gone. Dad working. Weekly. Told her to wait in bed for him. Undressed. Mutual touching first then "taught how to do things." Would position her to look for lights of mother's car returning from Bingo.

Included intercourse—"Everything. I learned it all from him." (Condom)

Last time. Pt saw lights on ceiling. Said nothing. Almost caught by mother. Fr. Never returned. Ended. Recent flashbacks.

Admits to drug, alcohol, promiscuity. Blames priest.

Impression: Sexual abuse victim; personality disorder; drug, alcohol abuse; anti-social behavior.

Having told her not to venture any opinions or to volunteer any information, he nevertheless asked, to satisfy himself: "Do you think Carmen's telling the truth that she was sexually abused?" He finished what was left of his gin and tonic.

"Do I get a drink, too?"

"Oh, I'm sorry. What would you like?"

"White wine."

He walked over to the under-counter refrigerator. "Mt. Eden Chardonnay all right?"

"Anything."

He poured her a glass and brought it to her. She took a large gulp. J.J. felt she probably needed it. Instead of returning to his desk, he sat on an accompanying chair, hung a leg over the side, and chewed on his ice cubes.

"You know, it fits," Sally began. "I've wondered about her since day one. She's a misfit in the family. She has a history of drug and alcohol abuse at an early age. Visits to Juvenile Hall, some runaway activity, and promiscuity. She seems very hostile and angry, especially toward her parents. She's dropped out of school. That's why, in part, she's the family driver. It's the only way they can keep an eye on her. From what her parents told me previously, the problems seemed to have begun when they came to Sacramento. Apparently, in Delano, she was a good student, well liked, and not the wild, erratic, body-pierced, over-sexed teenager we see now."

She took another sip of her wine. "So, yeah, my sense is, I believe her. I think she has probably been sexually abused. But," Sally hastened to add, "you can't diagnose abuse from a list of symptoms. If you have sexual abuse, these are the kinds of things you often see. But the fact that you see them doesn't necessarily mean that you can diagnose sexual abuse. Lots of teenagers act out without any history of abuse—just because they are obnoxious teenagers. It's hard to work backwards from symptoms to abuse. But you can predict forward the probable consequences of childhood sexual abuse."

She finished her wine and put her glass on his desk. "But that's just one woman's opinion. And, as Dougherty would say, only a licensed clinical social worker at that."

"With the best instincts of anyone I know," J.J. offered. "But why do you think she would be angry at her parents if she was abused?"

"It's not unusual for abused children to feel anger toward those who they counted on to protect them. She even mentioned that she had not wanted to leave Delano. So coming to Sacramento, the place where she was subjected to abuse, perhaps relates back in her mind to leaving Delano despite her objections. Her parents brought her to the place where she was abused."

J.J. nodded. In law school, one of the early lessons was about proximate or legal cause—that is, the cause of an event for which someone would be held legally accountable. It was true, in fact, that if someone didn't get up in the morning then he could not have gotten into an accident later in the day. But getting up was not the cause of the accident. Similarly, parents moving a child to Sacramento, where a crime occurred, was not the cause of the criminal act of molestation for which responsibility would attach. But a child could easily make that leap: "I didn't want to leave Delano; if I hadn't left Delano and come to Sacramento, I wouldn't have been abused." Thus, in the child's mind, the crime would be the parents' fault.

"What about the fact that the priest likes little boys? How does that fit in with molesting a girl?" J.J. asked.

"The homophobia in our society contributes to the myth that pedophiles are homosexuals. Sexual orientation should not be confused with child abuse. Many young boys are molested by so-called straight males, including married heterosexuals. We are talking about abuse, possibly pedophilia, not necessarily hetero—or homosexuality."

"What a mess," J.J. said, as he stood to lead Sally out.

"I feel sorry for these children," Sally replied.

"Well, perhaps if you put them in your prayers, Sally."

"Yeah, right. I think they are better off with a good lawyer."

Chapter 29

*M*s. McReynolds had been waiting for him outside the court-room. She handed him a copy of the *Journal* story, with her byline, of that morning. "Battle of Psychotherapists in Priest Abuse Case" was the title. He looked quickly at the lead.

> SACRAMENTO, California—A case of two altar boys pur-portedly molested by a priest took a twist Wednesday when a psychiatrist charged that the most serious allegations of sexual abuse were the product of suggestion by a social worker who had inter-viewed the boys as a consultant to their attorney, Mr. J.J. Rai. The court has ruled that the consultant must testify as to her conversa-tions with the boys.

There was no mention of Sally by name in the *Journal* story. *The Sacramento Bee*, the only daily newspaper in town, playing catch-up to *The Wall Street Journal*, carried an initial story, which recited only the facts of the case and its allegations. No summary of testimony was in-cluded because, J.J. suspected, the news editors hadn't read the *Journal* article until late morning and hadn't assigned a reporter until the after-noon. Now, the *Bee* was scrambling to cover a story in its own backyard. The *Bee*'s court reporter was in court this morning. Television, on the other hand, needed visuals and, without interviews from the participants, most stations were content to run pictures of the cathedral and the court-house building with a caption: "Priest Accused of Sexual Abuse with Altar Boys." Somewhere, for the morning news show, Channel 10 had found footage of altar boys kneeling at Mass and a choir singing "Ave Maria" to organ music.

Most morning radio hosts read from *The Sacramento Bee* story, but one station announced that "famed talk show host Christine Craft" would be taking calls on her afternoon show, so "call and tell Christine how you feel about priests molesting altar boys." J.J. wondered how many callers would call in favor of abuse by priests.

But Sally did not go unscathed. Those local stations that had picked up the Maureen McReynolds initial report early enough the day before to assign a reporter blasted Sally's name over the radio, and Fox 40 television introduced its report with the caption "Therapist Plants False Sex Charges Against Priest?"

"Do you have a statement for me, counselor?" asked Ms. McReynolds of J.J.

"As promised, you get it the minute I get it. My guy is in Texas this very moment. He does not have it yet. I haven't heard from him this morning," J.J. replied. He gave her a roll of his eyes, and she understood that he was playing for time, in the courtroom—not with her.

"Okay, I get it when you do?"

"That's a promise. You've lived up to your end. I always live up to mine."

The bailiff got them once again. Both he and Dougherty had been caught half-risen by the judge's appearance only to be told to "remain seated." As J.J. looked back at his seat, he noticed Ms. McReynolds pulling on her right ear. She stopped and rubbed her face and smiled when their eyes met. J.J. looked at Dougherty. He was now seated. Had she been signaling Dougherty, he thought, or am I being paranoid?

"Gentlemen," said the judge. "Are we continuing with Dr. Mandel?" Dougherty stood. "Yes, Your Honor. He is in the courtroom. I have completed my exam. I assume Mr. Rai wishes to cross-examine."

"That's correct, Your Honor," said J.J., as he pulled a large stack of psychological articles from his briefcase.

"Dr. Mandel," said the judge. "Please resume the stand. I remind you, you are still under oath."

As the witness was walking to the box, Judge Vincent made an announcement.

"Counsel, we will complete this witness, if we can, this morning. However, a matter has come up that will require my attention this afternoon. So we will be dark after lunch. I hope this doesn't inconvenience you or your witnesses, and I apologize for not being able to notify you sooner. We will start tomorrow, Friday, at 8:30 A.M. to get in a full day. Please plan accordingly."

J.J. breathed a sigh of relief as he felt the tension dissipate. He would only have to stall the morning and would not have to worry about Sally testifying in the afternoon or Andy getting the statement to him in time to give Sally before she took the stand. Having been granted this reprieve, he could enjoy the morning with the good doctor on cross-examination.

"Good morning, doctor," said J.J. "Or would you prefer 'professor' since you mentioned being a clinical professor at U.C. Davis Medical School?"

"No, Mr. Rai, 'doctor' is fine."

J.J. had a lot of experience with psychiatrists in trial. Once they were committed to a position, there was no budging them. If medicine was an art, psychiatry was voodoo. A practitioner, as a witness, could pretty well fashion a psychological explanation for anything. What J.J. needed to do was attack the doctor, not the testimony directly. Chip away, indirectly, like chopping at a tree until it falls.

"I guess as a professor, it's still 'publish or perish,' isn't it?" J.J. asked, smiling at the witness.

"Well, like I said, I'm really a practitioner. A clinical professor just means I supervise young doctors and share my professional experience in a clinical setting."

"So, publish or perish, that doesn't apply to you?"

"No. I don't receive a salary from the university," the doctor said, laughing and noticeably relaxing.

"So, you're not really here as a professor of medicine and psychiatry, then, are you, because you don't really teach on the faculty, is that what I understand?" Chip, chip.

"I am here as a practicing psychiatrist, Mr. Rai, who has been asked to provide an opinion about these children."

"Yes, let's start there. Who paid for your opinion?"

"I was contacted by Mr. Dougherty's office," he replied, pointing at Dougherty sitting at the counsel table. Dougherty kept his head down, writing. "He pays for my time, Mr. Rai. Not my opinion."

"Have you done a lot of legal work for which you have been paid by Mr. Dougherty and his office before this case?"

"I've worked for them before. I wouldn't call it legal work. My role is as a psychiatrist, rendering an opinion."

"In a legal setting, though," corrected J.J. "I mean you weren't treating any of these people about whom you rendered opinions for money, were you?"

"Well, there was no lawsuit in this case when I was asked to see these boys."

"Right, it was all hush-hush, wasn't it?"

"Objection, Your Honor," Dougherty's voice boomed. "Argumentative. The Church brought this matter openly to the court."

"Sure, Doe vs. R. Gutierrez. Real open," quipped Rai.

"Sustained; rephrase your question, Mr. Rai," ruled the judge.

J.J. moved into the well of the court, where he could move like a caged lion, stepping toward the witness when making a point, or leaning back against the front of the counsel table, with his arms folded, when pleasantly chatting, setting up the witness.

"Doctor, are you critical of Ms. Conrad because she was acting as a legal consultant?"

"That may have influenced her judgment," the witness responded.

"But you were hired by a lawyer as a consultant. Did the fact that you were hired by an attorney who represented the Catholic Church influence your judgment?"

"No, I call them as I see them. On the facts. It doesn't make any difference who hires me."

"Right, doctor. And from whom did you get the facts?"

"Mr. Dougherty, initially. But I independently confirmed them in my interview with the boys."

"You didn't talk to the bishop?"

"No. Mr. Dougherty told me what the bishop said."

"You didn't pick up the phone and call the priest at the halfway house, under the protection of the Catholic Church, and ask him what happened?"

"No, the bishop already had spoken to the priest. I had no reason to believe the priest didn't tell the truth since he readily admitted to abusing the boys on these camping trips."

J.J. nodded his head, as if assuring the witness that everything he had done was appropriate.

"On direct examination with Mr. Dougherty, you said that"—J.J. hesitated, looking at his notes as if quoting—"'twelve-year-olds don't forget abuse.' Remember saying that?"

"Well, not when the abuse is chronic. Ongoing, like Ms. Conrad claimed."

"But they can forget they were *not* abused? Is that your testimony?"

"I assume you mean Juan. He may not have been aware that he was being manipulated."

"Oh, so a child may have the presence of mind to not forget, but it's their memory of abuse that you have problems with? Is that what you're saying?" J.J. asked, appearing confused.

"Mr. Rai, the literature is full of examples, including lawsuits and false criminal charges of abuse that never happened. Children have come forward claiming that they were taken into basements of schools and subjected to devil worship and sexual abuse or were lifted into spaceships by alien life forms and sexually abused."

"Doctor, do you feel Felix is lying when he says that he was abused repeatedly at the Cathedral of the Blessed Virgin while acting as an altar boy?"

"No, he may not be lying. He is a young person involved in a traumatic event, a very disturbing event, with a priest, and in this emotional state he can be vulnerable to suggestion, fantasy, confabulation, confusion, and guilt, all of which can contribute to false memories to blame, excuse, or express anger and the like. I have no reason to believe that he is intentionally lying."

"All of these psychological phenomena you suggest work in favor of more memories, not less, is that what you're telling us?" J.J. asked.

"I didn't say that. Sometimes it takes trained psychotherapists time to discover the full extent of abuse because of the victim's pain in discussing the matter. That doesn't mean that the patient doesn't know what happened."

"So, it's Juan who is lying when he denies all of the abuse at the cathedral itself, is that now your testimony?"

"No, I have no reason to believe he is lying, Mr. Rai. Maybe the fact is, as I believe, most of it never happened."

"And maybe the fact is, doctor, that he wasn't ready to talk about it to a trained psychotherapist who only spent an hour with the two boys, together. Is that possible?" J.J. asked.

"I don't believe that is the case."

"Possible, though, isn't it? Isn't that one explanation? You just told us—'Sometimes it takes a trained psychotherapist time to discover the full extent of the abuse because of the pain of discussing the matter. That doesn't mean the patient doesn't know what happened.' Wasn't that your testimony?"

"Yes, but—"

"But, you are critical of Ms. Conrad for putting in the time to learn the truth, aren't you?" J.J. pounced.

"Objection! There is no evidence Ms. Conrad learned the truth," Dougherty bellowed.

"Sustained. Let's take a break," said the judge as he read a note handed him by the bailiff. "I have to take a phone call."

J.J. made a quick exit, through the doors and down to the stairwell at the end of the corridor—where, occasionally a lawyer would, illegally, take a few puffs to stop the shakes, despite the "No Smoking in Stair Well" sign—and got on his cell phone to the office.

"Natalie, any word from Andy?"

"Nothing. I left messages at the hotel in Laredo. He knows we're desperate," she answered. "I assume he will call and fax the moment he gets a statement."

"Call Sally, will you, and reschedule. The judge has another matter this afternoon, so she won't go on until tomorrow morning at the earliest."

"So that gives us a little more time," said Natalie. "I'm sure we'll hear from Andy, one way or the other, shortly."

One way or the other wouldn't be good enough, J.J. thought. He was holding his own, but, without the priest's admission, the judge could easily find that the evidence supported only the fondling abuse on the annual camping trips, not the more serious, pervasive sexual abuse.

J.J. returned to the courtroom. He was pleased to see his daughter there. "Caught the first act, dad. When do you go for the jugular?"

"Now," J.J. replied. "But with a little more rope."

"Dad, I think we just mixed metaphors."

J.J. didn't hear her. His mind was on what was to come. He walked into the counsel area, looked at his notes, and moved next to the jury box, where he stood looking at the witness who was sitting in the first row of the public area. Dr. Mandel declined to look back at him as J.J. placed himself in the witness' peripheral vision. The witness could not help but know that J.J. was staring at him.

"Remain seated," said the bailiff as the judge resumed the bench. The witness walked forward, glanced at J.J., and returned to the witness box. J.J. began immediately.

"Doctor, I believe you told Mr. Dougherty that you were familiar with the psychiatric literature on sexual abuse?"

"Yes."

"And that you have taken a special interest in child sexual abuse matters. That was your testimony?"

"Yes."

"Well, doctor, aren't you being a bit modest?"

"I'm sorry, Mr. Rai?"

"Doctor, I know you told us you weren't a real professor—publish or perish—but you've made your own contribution to this area of your 'special interest,' haven't you?"

J.J. walked to the counsel table and made a point of picking up a large folder.

"I've done some writing in the area," said the witness.

"My goodness, doctor, that's what I mean by modest. 'Some writing in the area.' In fact, you've been very prolific in your opinions about the diagnosis of childhood sexual abuse, haven't you?" said J.J., waving the thick file at the witness.

"I've written a number of papers," the witness allowed.

"You didn't mention that in your recital of credentials. Is there some reason you left out all of these writings in your 'special interest?'"

The witness was watching J.J. but didn't answer.

"Now, let's see," began J.J., putting the file down and picking up one article at a time: "'False Memory Syndrome: Exaggerated Claims of Child Abuse.' Did you write that?" J.J. asked, holding up the first article.

"Yes."

J.J. put it on the table.

"'The Coming Epidemic of False Memory Claims Against Catholic Priests.' Did you write that?"

"Yes.

J.J. put this article on the table.

"'Innocent Priests: The Real Victims of Sexual Abuse Claims.' Did you write that doctor?"

"Yes."

J.J. put it on the pile.

"Oh," J.J. said, picking the article back up, "this is my favorite." Quoting from the paper, he read, "'The child abuse industry is fed by hysteria, poorly trained do-good therapists with wacky psychological theories, and an out-of-control court system.'" J.J. looked at the witness while holding the article. "Did you write that, doctor?"

"Yes, but let me explain," began the witness.

"Your Honor, could the doctor be instructed to answer the questions? Mr. Dougherty had his chance to advise the court of these various publications by this witness and will have another opportunity to examine the witness when I am finished."

"Just answer the question, doctor," said the judge.

"But, Your Honor, he is quoting these articles out of context," protested the doctor.

"You're right, doctor. I apologize," said J.J. "Let's put them in context. None of these articles have ever appeared in a scientific or psychiatric publication, have they? They have appeared only in newsletters for groups such as the False Memory Syndrome Foundation and the Foundation for Truth and Religious Tolerance, and on websites like www.truthinrealityandreligion.org, right?"

"Well, I have no control over where they appear. But they are consistent with my readings of the psychiatric literature in over thirty years of practice," declared the witness.

"Do you think this court is out of control, Dr. Mandel?" J.J. asked.

"Objection, Your Honor. This is argumentative. Mr. Rai is just pandering and groveling," proclaimed Dougherty loudly.

"Overruled. I'd like to hear the answer," said the judge.

"Your Honor, I have no criticism of this court. But I think courts generally have allowed so-called therapists to get away with accusations of sexual abuse that are not true and are produced by inappropriate methods. I am not alone in this. The Royal College of Psychiatrists in England published a report in the *British Journal of Psychiatry* in 1998 indicating that, under certain circumstances, there is a high probability that memories produced through therapy are false."

J.J. continued, "Doctor, do you remember that you were critical of Ms. Conrad for not maintaining 'neutrality' in this matter? You've been an outspoken critic of childhood sexual abuse claims for years, haven't you? In fact, you are one of the leading critics of such claims in the nation, aren't you?" J.J. thought it would be hard for a witness not to acknowledge that he was a "leading" something.

"I don't know if I am the leading critic, but—"

"Doctor, we put the words 'childhood sexual abuse' and 'false memories' into a Google search last night, and your name came up with 1,013 hits. I believe that's what you call them—hits." J.J. looked at his daughter for confirmation. Rebel nodded her head. "Did you know you were that famous, doctor—worldwide?"

"I haven't counted, Mr. Rai."

"Let me ask you about one specific group with which you seem to have affiliation, if not a collaborative relationship: The False Memory Syndrome Foundation. As I understand it, this is a group whose stated purpose is to defend those accused of child abuse and to expose what it claims are myths about recovered memories. That appears to be what you also advocate, isn't that true, doctor?"

"No one should be wrongly accused," said the doctor.

"We all agree with that," J.J. said, smiling at the witness, "but I'm wondering about your 'neutrality,' doctor. When you approach a case of alleged abuse, based upon your writings and your involvement with the False Memory Syndrome Foundation, you do so from the point of view of not finding abuse, minimizing it, or disproving it, don't you?" J.J. asked, his voice rising and his finger pointing at the witness.

"No, I just want to know the truth—not what some therapist suggests."

"Doctor, if you wanted to know the truth, why didn't you take a little time to get to know these boys, like Ms. Conrad did? Rather than just relying upon the facts given to you by Mr. Dougherty and, secondhand, from the bishop?"

"I had no reason to believe that the boys hadn't told the truth already, and they certainly were free to volunteer any contrary information to me."

"Really, doctor? So I guess that you would disagree with Dr. Nathan Szajnberg, preeminent psychiatrist and professor at U.C. San Francisco that it is 'not unusual for teenagers to be evasive with adults about anything that has guilt or shame connected with it.'"

"No, I would agree with that as a general statement. However, these boys had no reason to be evasive with the bishop. Even if they might be reluctant to speak to me, he has known them their whole lives."

"But, doctor, we're talking about your so-called psychiatric exam, not the bishop's reassuring chat."

"I was asked to evaluate the boys' adjustment to the situation. No one told me to ask them what happened. We already knew."

"Because the bishop told you?"

"Well, through Mr. Dougherty, yes."

"Ah. So, doctor, that explains it. You just never asked. You just took what Mr. Dougherty told you as gospel."

J.J. turned and looked at his daughter. She gave him a smile and a slight nod. He walked away from the witness, "Thank you, doctor. No further questions."

Dougherty was up immediately. He wasn't happy with the undoing of his witness. But what got him was J.J.'s final dig. "I object to Mr. Rai's suggestion and to his anti-religious characterization," said Dougherty.

"I'll withdraw 'gospel,' Your Honor."

"The words 'as gospel' will be stricken," said the judge. J.J. was disappointed. He thought it was a good phrase. He didn't blame the judge for striking the reference—just for not seeing the humor in it. This guy is a tough nut, J.J. thought.

"And we are in recess until Friday morning at 9:00. Please note the earlier time. I want a full day of testimony, uninterrupted, for a change, gentlemen. Who is our next witness, Mr. Dougherty?" the judge asked.

"Sally Conrad, Your Honor," Dougherty snapped.

Dougherty said "Sally Conrad" in a way that implied that the witness was the reason the court and counsel had to waste their time and the taxpayers' money. It was going to be a rough Friday morning. J.J. only hoped that he could give Sally the information she needed to hit Dougherty squarely between the eyes.

Chapter 30

"Andy called," J.J.'s secretary told him as soon as he returned from court. "He's in Laredo but says he'll be driving across the border to Nuevo Laredo in Mexico this evening."

"Why is he going to Mexico?"

"The priest has agreed to meet Andy, but thinks it would be safer in Mexico. He's still not sure Andy isn't working for the cops. But Andy says he's real talkative."

"Can you get a hold of Andy now?"

"No, but he'll fax a statement by tonight if all goes well. There is a two-hour time difference, so the statement shouldn't be too late."

J.J. wanted to tell Andy about the complication with Carmen and her accusations against Father Gutierrez. But he wondered how to handle it. Maybe one statement about the boys and a separate statement about Carmen. That way, Dougherty wouldn't be tipped off about Carmen's accusations, and J.J. could use either, or both, depending on how the testimony went and what the priest said in each. If he couldn't get a hold of Andy, he would just have to settle for a statement about the boys, since Andy didn't know about Carmen, unless the priest volunteered the information. J.J. wanted to save Andy a second trip. Friendship only went so far. Andy was having fun, playing crime—or church—buster. J.J. thought they were one and the same at this point, but Andy would probably be too bored for a second trip to see the priest. He had a short attention span.

J.J. called Sally and let her know about the cross-examination of Dr. Mandel. It had gone well, he felt. While Dougherty challenged Sally's "neutrality," it was clear that the witness the Church had obtained was a zealot "for False Memory Syndrome" and a witness paid not to find abuse and to attack those who did.

"He basically acknowledged, as you suspected, that he didn't ask the boys what had happened. He assumed that whatever the Church admitted was what had occurred and, given his bias, didn't want to go looking for any more," J.J. told her. Again, he felt he needed to apologize to her. "Sally, I'm sorry for getting you into this."

"J.J., I'm in now. Let me explain something. It's not that I'm afraid to be involved or doubt my judgment. I avoid forensic work because it requires professionals to be advocates for a position. Psychological issues are not well served by the type of advocacy that litigation engenders. It makes prostitutes out of professional witnesses or professional witnesses out of professionals, who are then paid to take a particular position. I would like, in this or in any other situation, to be able to take in what others say, consider it, and be able to change an opinion, if appropriate. From what I can see of the legal system, that would make me a lousy, and unemployed, witness."

That's what J.J. liked about Sally Conrad and why he called upon her often for advice: She was a no-bullshit straight shooter with good psychiatric instincts and judgment. She was probably right, he agreed. She generally wouldn't make a good witness, which is why he had sought her out for her judgment but hired someone else to express an opinion in court.

They discussed, again, Sally's testimony for the morning and particularly that she make no reference to Carmen's accusations and volunteer nothing about Carmen.

"Since you were asked to consult about the boys, I think you can keep the separate file on Carmen and what she told you about her alleged abuse. Leave that file at your office. Don't bring it to court because, at some point, Dougherty is going to ask to see your file on this case, and we don't want him looking into your notes about Carmen.

Sally agreed, although he knew that her hesitation questioned the propriety of his suggestion. "Don't worry. It's perfectly legal. These are separate files, separate people. You have only been asked by me to testify about the boys at this point."

J.J. added, "I am hoping to have a statement from the priest to-night. If all goes well, I'll give that to you in the morning before court. Come by the office, and we'll walk over together. We'll put the statement in your file if it is supportive. That way, Dougherty will stumble upon it and go ballistic." J.J. imagined his fellow altar boy screaming as he had when J.J. spilled hot candle wax on him during Mass.

"See?" Sally said. "This is what I was saying about the legal process. It's like a game with you guys."

"My job is to do everything I can to support your credibility so that your testimony will be believed. The statement from the priest say-ing that much more occurred than admitted by the Church—as you believe—will show that you are right and that their expert is wrong."

"That's fine, but why not just give it to the other side and the judge? Why plant it in my file just to see Dougherty go ballistic?"

"Oh, that part. That's called drama. It's for the fun of it. Trial work would be incredibly boring without the drama and gags. Good lawyers even appreciate it when the other side gets them with a good one. Dougherty, on the other hand, he'll just go ballistic. He'll be like a roman candle on the 4th of July. He doesn't have the ability to appreciate good lawyering."

"Men," Sally said.

"I think that was my cue to say goodbye," J.J. said. "I'll see you in the morning."

During the afternoon, J.J. tried to do some work on other cases and return some of the phone calls that inevitably built up during trial. But his mind returned to the Sanchez family. What must it be like to have all of your children abused? And, as claimed here, by a priest of your church? What does that do to faith? What does it do to the relationship between a child and the parents who brought the child to this faith? Can the child reject one—the parents or the faith—without rejecting the other? Will the child blame the parents? Do the parents blame themselves? If so, how can they—like Mr. and Mrs. Sanchez—stay committed to the church?

J.J. wondered about the priest, too. Schooled in religion, a teacher of morals, a preacher of the word of God, who raises the Eucharist during Mass and says, "This is my body"—to transform bread into the body of

Christ, but then lifts his cassock over the head of an altar boy kneeling before him. How does the priest reconcile these two acts? But being a representative of God, thought J.J., must make it pretty easy for a priest to have his way with a child.

By 6:30 P.M., J.J. still hadn't received anything from Andy. He was getting concerned. He owed it to Sally to get her proof. Damn it, he thought, I should have insisted that Andy tape the priest when Andy first spoke to him by phone. Perhaps the priest has been contacted by officials of the Church—Dougherty was too smart to do it himself—and told not to talk. Maybe he had been given a plane ticket to a nice rainforest resort in Costa Rica for the duration of the litigation. He might have even been promised a position in an orphanage for boys. J.J. was getting mad at himself.

He decided there were better places to wait than at the office, alone. He walked over to Frank Fat's restaurant for a drink and Chinese food in the bar. Rebel had headed back to the Bay Area to study when court had let out around noon. When alone, J.J. liked to eat at the bar at Fats, in the splendor of a million-dollar makeover to the Sacramento landmark twenty years ago when a million dollars was actually a lot of money. The small tables in the bar area lined up against the dragon-embossed banquette that ran the length of the bar had darkened mirrored walls above and were softly lit with fixtures that resembled rice paddy peasant hats. The bar area provided a wonderful place to see everyone who entered or left. Fat's was a place to see and be seen.

J.J. was nursing a gin and tonic when the executive editor of *The Sacramento Bee* entered and smiled broadly at him. They had known each other for years.

"J.J.," Arlen McCluskey announced, "look who I've got with me."

Behind Arlen, taking off her sunglasses and adjusting to the dark lighting of Frank Fat's, was Maureen McReynolds, the reporter from *The Wall Street Journal*. She was not in her business clothes, which were stylish enough, but in a brightly colored Mexican skirt and an off-the-shoulder beaded top that hugged her body, with her red hair pulled up and off her neck. She wore bright lime sandals.

"Well, Mr. Rai, having dinner alone, are we?" she asked, as she slid her arm into the fold of Arlen's elbow and smiled.

Her tone was playful, but J.J. couldn't help feeling that "alone" meant "without her."

"We aren't. I am," he said, smiling back, although he had a feeling deep inside himself that he immediately recognized as jealousy.

"Ah, yes, but then you are in trial, and I am sure your mind would be fully occupied even if you had a guest for dinner," she said, her lips closing as if to purr.

"Depends on the guest," J.J. answered, his eyes dropping to her lips.

"And I suppose the trial as well," she said, throwing back her head with a laugh. "But don't let Arlen and me disturb your trial preparation. I am sure you want to win. I'll see you in court tomorrow, Mr. Rai. Meanwhile, Arlen has promised me a great mushi pork and a fabulous tour of Sacramento's night spots; right, Arlen?" she asked, without taking her eyes off J.J.

"Right, Maureenie," he answered, as he wrapped an arm around her waist and moved her toward the rear of the restaurant.

J.J. remained standing, with his napkin in his hand, as they moved away from him. Ten feet away, she looked over her shoulder, smiled, and winked at him. She was captured in the light of the Buddha in an illuminated circle of glass that peered down at them, her hair glowing, as if on fire, from the reflection of the blood red painted upper walls and ceiling. Hundreds of dragons' red eyes, everywhere, were looking at her. J.J. laughed and said, loudly, "Waiter, I need another drink."

Then he sat down to order, and, after the experience of Maureen McReynolds, focused on items with the asterisk: "Hot and Spicy."

"Chili Beef Chow Fun," he said, when his second drink arrived. He wasn't sure what it was, but it promised to be "hot and spicy" and had the word 'fun' in its name.

After dinner, he debated waiting at his table to see her one more time. But then, he felt, he would have to order another drink, and he was already feeling a bit of a buzz. Better to walk it off and get back to the office, he thought. He signed his tab and left extra on the table.

Even at 8:15, the temperature was still in the nineties. He carried his coat. His tie was already loosened. The light at Ninth Street was red for his direction, so he decided to walk on up "L" Street, past Capitol Park, with its palms silhouetted in the evening sky, to the cathedral just a block north. J.J. knew his Sacramento history. In elementary school, he would walk almost daily through the State Capitol building on his way to his bus stop. He knew every corner of the building, having viewed its exhibits of the counties and having climbed every stair and explored every level. Similarly, he knew the cathedral from his years as an altar boy. These two buildings, the Cathedral of the Blessed Virgin and the State Capitol, were monuments to the dynamic spirit of California in its early history.

The man who would become Sacramento's first bishop had come from Ireland in 1848 as a hard rock miner. Ten years later, he had entered the seminary and had the good fortune to study at St. Sulpice in Paris. He had returned to California as a priest, and when, in 1886, he had been named Sacramento's first bishop, he had commissioned a San Francisco architect to travel to Paris and to study the Church of the Holy Trinity and use it as the model for the cathedral in Sacramento. The Sacramento Cathedral had been dedicated just three years later in 1889.

The State Capitol building had also been modeled after another famous building—the United States Capitol in Washington, D.C. Started in 1862, just a dozen years after gold had been discovered at Sutter's Mill in the foothills above Sacramento, the State Capitol building had a stormy construction history. As Sacramento was prone to flooding from the rivers that surrounded it, the State Capitol, like much of downtown Sacramento, had to be raised fifteen feet above its site. Originally projected to cost $500,000, it had experienced delays as the money had quickly run out and the legislature, which would meet for only two months every two years, had been unavailable to authorize more. The original architect, Reuben Clark, had ended up in a mental institution where he died in 1866. It was suggested that his insanity was directly attributable to his construction of the Capitol building, which gave credence to the later claim that the California legislature had a long history of mental disorders. But the Capitol had been completed, finally, in 1874, at a cost five times the original estimate.

J.J. marveled at how Sacramento must have looked in the 1880s with these two majestic edifices standing almost side by side in the middle of town. Somehow, it seemed that the grandeur of both had waned over time. Now the Capitol was presided over by a bodybuilder/action movie star and a term-limited legislature that appeared incapable of governing the special interests in the building, let alone the state. The cathedral, like much of the Catholic Church in America, was burdened by priests who sexually abused and exploited children. Still, he thought, two beautiful buildings, despite the people in them.

J.J. stopped in the plaza in front of the Cathedral of the Blessed Virgin. Looking up, J.J. saw a stone Virgin Mary above the entry looking down upon him. He felt as if she were reproaching him. He felt the guilt that was part of his life as a young Catholic and as an altar boy. It was as if she knew that even back then he had said the words of the prayers without believing them or had mumbled prayers during Mass because he hadn't bothered memorizing the Latin as altar boys were supposed to. Above the Virgin was the clock tower; above it, the bell tower; and beyond, the pinnacle with its golden cross. He leaned back, looking up, and had the dizzying experience of viewing the structure against the moving clouds. What a truly amazing structure, he thought. Where did religion go so wrong? he wondered.

People were walking back and forth on the K Street Mall and on 11th Street toward the Capitol or sitting in the open-air areas of the restaurants nearby. None of them—not even J.J. staring up at the cathedral tower—saw the person, sitting, behind the clock face, waiting for the sunset.

J.J. walked down 11th to J and to César Chávez Park in front of City Hall and crossed to his office building. When he got upstairs, a fax was there from Andy. He smiled. Handwritten and signed by Father Ramon J. Gutierrez, it admitted all of the conduct with the boys as Sally had reported it. And Andy was on his way back to Sacramento. He would be available by late afternoon to authenticate the document in court, if necessary.

It's in the bag, thought J.J. Case closed. He thought of his promise to *The Wall Street Journal* reporter, Maureen McReynolds. He reached for the phone to call the Hyatt Regency, where she had told him she was registered. But then he would have to call her room and get her fax number if, as he assumed, she was in a business suite with a fax, as a reporter would be. It all felt a little too intimate, especially after their brief flirtation. As if he was asking to see her later that evening when she got through with her "date" with the executive editor of the *Bee*. But something else stopped him. What if she was sharing information with Dougherty? That signal with the ear. There was no point in giving Dougherty the statement early if she was, in fact, passing information to him. No, he would wait until morning, right before Sally took the stand, when it would be too late for her to share the information with Dougherty and for Dougherty to prepare a counterattack or avoid the trap being set for him.

J.J. realized that there was another reason that he didn't call. He was afraid that if he called her room, she might not be alone. Why was she affecting him like this, he thought, other than that she's tall, beautiful, and smart?

Chapter 31

"The Diocese calls Ms. Sally Conrad," announced Roland Dougherty, in his most serious voice, accompanied by a scowl.

J.J. felt comfortable knowing that Sally was carrying the confession of Father Gutierrez, which supported her original beliefs about the extent of abuse upon which Dr. Leibowitz had based her own opinions. Now, to watch it unfold. He saw Maureen McReynolds reading the copy of the statement he had given her moments before. Her head was down, reading, signaling no one, he noted. Rebel had also returned to the courtroom, saying, "I wouldn't miss this for anything." The stage was set.

"Ms. Conrad, you hold only an LCSW—a licensed clinical social work degree—don't you?" Dougherty asked, starting right off on Sally's limited qualifications.

"Yes, well, actually, I have a Bachelor's in Psychology and a Master's in Social Work and am licensed by the State of California as a clinical social worker."

"Right. You're not a medical doctor like our consultant Dr. Mandel, are you?"

"No."

"And you're not a board certified psychiatrist like our consultant, Dr. Mandel, are you?"

"No."

"In fact, you do not treat abused children in your practice, do you?"

"No, that's why I urged Mr. Rai to get these children—these boys—into a specialist like Dr. Leibowitz."

"So you acknowledged to Mr. Rai from the outset that you are not really medically or psychologically trained to treat children for alleged sexual abuse?"

"Yes, that is correct," said Sally, without hesitation or defensiveness in her voice.

"Yet, you not only undertook to do that here, but came up with psychiatric conclusions contrary to those of a medically trained and board-certified psychiatrist," stated Dougherty. It hardly qualified as a question.

"No, I never undertook to treat these boys. Nor would I. I was asked to meet with them and to give an opinion as to whether they appeared to be in need of treatment for abuse. I felt they showed evidence of abuse, acknowledged abuse, and were in need of a specialist in the treatment of sexual abuse because there were lots of signs, red flags, that suggested serious problems. That was supposed to be my assignment; that was supposed to be the end of my role." She added, "Until you insisted that I testify in this matter, Mr. Dougherty."

"So you hold yourself out as an expert in the signs of abuse, Ms. Conrad?"

"Well, I certainly have special training and experience beyond that of the average person—which is why Mr. Rai asked me to meet with these boys—so I suppose I meet the legal definition. However, I would not feel comfortable treating these boys for sexual abuse. Their problems are beyond my training. I think their problems are severe, and these boys are in need of a child psychologist who specializes in sexual abuse."

Sally added, "I assume it's like the law, Mr. Dougherty. You might know enough law to spot a problem, but it is not what you do, do."

J.J. smiled. Sally was in control. Just to push Dougherty's button, J.J. pretended he did not hear the last sentence and asked the court reporter to read it back. The court reporter smiled upon her own reading of "doo-doo." Dougherty's face grew red.

"You're familiar with the controversy over so-called 'recovered memories,' are you not?" asked Dougherty.

"Yes."

"And you feel these boys somehow 'recovered' their memories but only after talking to their parents, their bishop, and a trained psychiatrist, Dr. Mandel, such that they could tell *you* the revealed truth as to what occurred?" There was sarcasm in Dougherty's voice.

"No, I don't believe their memories were ever missing. First, no one asked the boys fully what occurred."

"The bishop, who has known these boys for their whole lives, asked," countered Dougherty.

"I don't think so. He assumed. But put this in context, in all fairness to Bishop O'Brien. Two pre-adolescent boys are asked about sex with a priest, by a bishop. Especially in the Mexican culture, the bishop's voice is akin to the voice of God asking them about a mortal sin. Much of the guilt generated by the Catholic Church is about sex. I wouldn't expect them to volunteer more than the bishop asked."

"Isn't it true, Ms. Conrad, that Juan specifically denied to Ms. Leibowitz any sexual contact at the cathedral and doesn't even recall any inappropriate conduct on the camping trips? Which, according to you, I suppose, means Juan must be lying. Is that your testimony?"

Sally nodded her head in a manner suggesting patience both with Dougherty and the process. Then she began slowly. "We all know that the conduct occurred on the camping trips; yet, Juan does not acknowledge it. Since it occurred, and he does not acknowledge it, this is one of the red flags that concerns me and suggests that we have a more serious problem. Also, I noted that he is very angry with his brother. That is another red flag of concern."

"Why is he angry?" Dougherty asked.

Sally hesitated. She knew that persons untrained in psychotherapy, like Dougherty and the press—and even the judge, would not understand or might misinterpret her answer.

"His brother's report brought to light and ended the relationship between Juan and Father Gutierrez," she said. "He is angry at his brother for doing this."

Dougherty let the answer sit in the air.

"So Juan wanted to be abused. Is that what you are telling us?" he asked, clearly feeling that the tide had turned in his favor.

"As strange as it may seem, Mr. Dougherty, an abused person can be very protective of the abuser. We see it all the time, especially when a parent is involved. A bond is established between the abuser and the abused. That's why I am especially concerned for Juan and his denial of the abuse."

"If it happened," Dougherty responded.

Sally was getting very tired of the game. She knew J.J. wanted the great discovery of the statement with Dougherty "going ballistic," but she didn't appreciate being a pawn. She looked at J.J. and back to Dougherty.

"It happened, Mr. Dougherty."

Dougherty still didn't see it coming.

"Well, according to you."

"No, according to Father Gutierrez. I have reviewed a complete confession from Father Gutierrez, and he acknowledges the acts I reported as occurring, not just on the trips but also at the cathedral." After a pause, she added, "With both boys, especially Juan."

"What statement? That's not in the statement he gave Bishop O'Brien!" he shouted.

"It's in the statement in my file," Sally said, handing him her complete file.

Dougherty had no choice but to take the file, which she was holding in the air in front of her. He saw the multi-page statement and shot a look at J.J. J.J. looked at him, and then at the judge, as if nothing unusual was happening. Dougherty knew he had been had.

"Your Honor, I request a recess so that I may read what Ms. Conrad is relying upon," Dougherty asked. He did his best to appear in control of his emotions. Yet, his hands were shaking with the papers in them.

"Very well," said the judge. "Fifteen minutes." The judge left the bench, but Sally remained in the witness box and watched as a number of reporters rushed towards J.J. Maureen McReynolds was not one of them.

"Mr. Rai, you have a confession from the priest?" asked one of the reporters.

"Yes," J.J. said. "Secured yesterday in Mexico where the priest is hiding out."

"Do you have copies?" another asked.

J.J. looked at Ms. McReynolds, sitting in the back of the courtroom, within hearing distance. Just in case, he raised his voice a notch. "I'm sorry, but you'll have to get that information from the testimony. I don't have copies, and I'm not sure it should be formally released until it's introduced into evidence." Maureen McReynolds nodded her approval as she held on to the only copy, the exclusive that he had promised her. She pushed the "send" button on her Blackberry, and her story was filed and would be on the wire service within fifteen minutes, under her by-line, as a *Wall Street Journal* story. She didn't want to leave the courtroom in search of a telephone line for her laptop computer. At the moment, she was the only one with a copy of the confession and wanted to get a story, however brief, on the wire, as an exclusive.

Dougherty sat at the counsel table for a few minutes reading the statement. After the first two pages, he turned to the last page and saw that it was signed by Father Ramon J. Gutierrez, and "witnessed" by Andrew "Andy" Miller and one Jose Adame. He abruptly left the courtroom with the statement and called his office and the bishop. When he returned, it was with a young associate attorney. They sat down, their heads close together, talking, pointing to the statement from time to time.

"All rise," the bailiff announced. "Court is back in session."

Sally poured a drink of water at the witness stand.

Dougherty began immediately. "Ms. Conrad, where did you get this statement?"

"From Mr. Rai."

"When?"

"This morning."

"Why did he give it to you?"

J.J. knew he could object to the question since it obviously called for his state of mind, which was not particularly relevant to the proceedings. However, he decided that Sally—armed with the statement—was in full control and he need not object.

"He said it completely supported what I had suspected all along and the opinions I had expressed."

"This is a fax. Where is the original?" Dougherty asked.

He was asking the questions in rapid succession in the hope that she would be tripped up if not given enough time to reflect. Sally, however, was taking her time and answering matter-of-factly, so that she was neither distressed nor forced into a rapid response.

"I don't know," she answered, looking at J.J.

"Mr. Rai,"—Dougherty was standing in front of J.J.— "will you produce the original?"

"Don't have it," J.J. said almost flippantly.

"Where is it?" Dougherty demanded.

"Excuse me, Your Honor, but isn't the procedure to ask the witnesses questions? I'm not the witness," J.J. said, acting plaintive in his request to the judge.

Dougherty, finally, was livid.

"Mr. Rai produces a so-called confession, supposedly written in Mexico last night, plants it in a witness' file, and sits back as innocent as a lamb. We all know what's going on. He's trying to put into evidence an inadmissible document," stated Dougherty, addressing the judge.

"Why is it inadmissible, Mr. Dougherty?" the judge asked.

Dougherty looked at the notes the associate was scribbling.

"First, it's hearsay. Second, if it were admissible, it would only be against the priest, not the Diocese. Third, a document cannot be cross-examined. The witness—the priest—is not present or available. Admission of the document, in lieu of the witness, would violate due process and the Diocese's right to be confronted by witnesses against it and to cross-examine such witnesses. Fourth, the Best Evidence Rule. This is a copy. Fifth, the document hasn't been authenticated. How do we even know who signed this document and under what coercive circumstances."

The judge jotted each point down. Then, he asked to read the document.

"We object, Your Honor. It is not admissible; therefore, you shouldn't read it," said Dougherty.

"Mr. Dougherty, I can't rule without reading it, now can I? If it's not admitted, I won't consider it."

J.J. imagined church bells ringing loudly and the old trial lawyer saying, "You can't unring a bell." If the judge reads it, he'll know forever what the priest admitted, even if the judge says he won't "consider it."

Dougherty moved forward and handed the document to the bailiff, who took it the rest of the way across the well to the judge. The judge took his time. Twice he turned back to an earlier page. Finally, he said, "Madam Clerk, mark this as an exhibit next in order, for identification only at this time. I will reserve judgment on admissibility." Then, he looked at J.J.

"Mr. Rai, are you prepared to authenticate this document?"

"Yes, Your Honor. My investigator, who took the statement, should be available later this afternoon. He is on his way back from Nuevo Laredo, Mexico, and will verify the document as genuine."

Dougherty was up again.

"Your Honor, I also want to point out that Mr. Rai has once again contacted an employee of the Diocese that I represent. That's improper. He has no right to contact Father Gutierrez out of my presence."

J.J. started to speak. The judge stopped him.

"As I recall, Mr. Dougherty, you were asked to produce Father Gutierrez for a deposition, for a statement in your presence, and you refused. I believe the law permits Mr. Rai to contact him since he was not a director or managing agent of your client, the Diocese, and you specifically stated before this court that you did not represent him individually."

While Dougherty was digesting his error in not representing the priest, the judge added, "On the statement, I can say preliminarily that it appears to fall within at least three exceptions to the hearsay rule: as an admission, a declaration against interest, and a declaration against penal interest."

Dougherty responded quickly—too quickly, without thinking.

"Your Honor, these priests run off to Mexico. They know they won't be hauled back. We've had others, years ago who—" His associate pulled on his coat. He realized this was not the best argument.

J.J. pounced. "I bet you have, Roland, and you covered it up like a good little sanctimonious Catholic altar boy."

"You sacrilegious hypocrite," replied Dougherty. "You would—"

The judge banged his gavel.

"Who wants the next word and a fine?" he asked, looking at both of them. "Would anybody like to spend the night in the county jail?" When no one responded, the judge told Dougherty to complete his cross-examination of Ms. Conrad.

Dougherty stood looking at his notes and at the statement. He had to decide how to proceed since the judge hadn't ruled on the admissibility of the statement, although he seemed to lean toward admitting it if J.J. could authenticate the signatures.

Now, Dougherty realized, he couldn't attack Conrad's conclusions since the priest appeared to have admitted exactly the conduct to which she had testified. He had to find another way to limit the evidence as it pertained to the church having any knowledge of Father Gutierrez's conduct. Even if Father Gutierrez committed the criminal acts, the Church was not legally liable unless it knew or should have known. The absence of prior conduct with other boys was important. Nothing in the statement suggested conduct with others. It was the best he could do with this witness. He needed to move on not by denying the conduct, but by denying that the Church had any reason to believe that any such conduct was occurring. Let the priest hang to twist slowly in the wind; protect the Church.

"Ms. Conrad, there is nothing in the statement alleged to be from Father Gutierrez indicating that the Diocese knew anything about his conduct until Felix reported it, isn't that true?"

"I believe so," acknowledged Sally.

"And there is nothing to indicate that there were other altar boys that Father Gutierrez sexually abused, is there?"

Sally shot a glance at J.J. He looked away.

"No, I don't believe the statement mentions any other altar boys."

"Well," persisted Dougherty, "it doesn't mention any other person at all abused by Father Gutierrez, does it?"

Again, Sally looked at J.J. as she took a drink of water. She thought he might object or do something to get Dougherty off this line of questioning. Again, J.J. looked away.

"You are absolutely correct, Mr. Dougherty, it does not," she said, hoping the generous admission would satisfy him. It didn't.

"And you know of no other claims whatsoever of abuse by Father Gutierrez, do you, Ms. Conrad?" he said, his arms flying up in victory. It was, J.J. knew, that one final question that a lawyer often asks and never should.

This was it. J.J. stood. He seemed to be taking his time formulating an objection. Enough time for Dougherty to see him and stand himself.

"Your Honor"—J.J. began.

But Dougherty interrupted. "Answer the question, Ms. Conrad. No one else has ever claimed to have been abused by Father Gutierrez. Isn't that true?"

The question seemed to float through the air as a balloon might over a crowd, and in each instance when the balloon attempted to come down, it was pushed up again.

"Objection, Your Honor," J.J. said and stopped as he turned to face Dougherty. "We are here to evaluate the claims of abuse of Juan and Felix Sanchez."

"Well, now," Dougherty responded, feeling he was on a roll, "that's a strange statement coming from Mr. Rai. He knows full well that there must be some notice to the Diocese of Father Gutierrez's acts for the Diocese to be liable. For Your Honor to properly evaluate this case, even on a Minor's Compromise, you need to evaluate not just the injury but the potential for liability. We have always felt that there was no liability on the part of the Diocese but generously offered $100,000 to these young boys out of compassion. We are asking the court to approve that amount of money in light of the lack of any real liability because of our pastoral concerns."

J.J. responded, "Your Honor, we came in here with the Church acknowledging liability, with only the question of damages to be decided. Now, it seems that Mr. Dougherty wants to change the rules in light of the overwhelming evidence of long-term, persistent sexual abuse of these two boys and argue about liability. We strongly object."

J.J. sat down. His objection was half-hearted—he had to admit even to himself. He looked over his shoulder as he sat and rolled his eyes at his daughter. She looked at the ceiling as if something—perhaps the Archangel Michael—was about to burst through.

Sometimes, J.J. thought, you just have to let the truth come out, even in court. What the hell. He folded his arms.

"I'll permit the question," ruled the judge.

Dougherty smiled. He asked that the question be read back by the court reporter. Sally took a final look at J.J. He shrugged his shoulders as if to say, "He asked for it." Sally knew she had no choice. A direct question, the one that she had not wanted to answer, had been asked. She wasn't going to lie.

"Yes, there is another person who claims to have been sexually abused by Father Gutierrez."

"Who?" Dougherty asked, shocked.

The judge stopped taking notes and looked at Sally.

"Carmen Sanchez, the older sister of Juan and Felix."

Mrs. Sanchez, sitting in the audience, gasped, covered her mouth, and began sobbing. Her husband put his arm around her and stoically looked straight ahead.

"Your Honor, I object," Dougherty said. "There has never been any notice of this; no claim filed. Nothing. I reviewed Ms. Conrad's file, and there is not a single note about any claim by Carmen Sanchez."

Dougherty, his voice rising again, pointed to J.J. and shouted, "This isn't a trial; it's an ambush."

"Mr. Dougherty," said the judge, "you insisted on asking the question over Mr. Rai's objection."

"Yes, but I didn't know—"

"Then maybe you shouldn't have insisted," said the judge.

The judge asked Sally, "Are there any references to Carmen's claims in your file?"

"They are in Carmen Sanchez's file—not in the boys' file. I, too, assumed I was to testify only about the boys. I had no intention of talking about the separate matter of Carmen's abuse. I mentioned it only because Mr. Dougherty insisted."

God, she's good, J.J. thought; no wonder I trust her judgment.

The judge nodded to Dougherty to indicate that he could continue his examination.

"When did Carmen make these claims to you?" Dougherty asked. Having been burned upon the claims of the boys, he no longer referred to the claims as "so-called claims" of abuse.

"On Wednesday, after I was excused from this hearing."

"Where did these conversations take place?"

"As I left the courtroom, Carmen asked to speak to me. We went outside the courthouse, and we spent approximately two hours talking about these matters on a bench immediately outside, near the fountain."

"What did she tell you?" he asked, again no longer trying to lead her in any direction but rather allowing her to testify fully.

When, where, what, J.J. thought. This guy is so predictable when rattled.

"That she was sexually abused and later raped by Father Gutierrez"—at this point, the mother's gasping and crying grew louder— "over a period of two to three years, between ages twelve and fourteen, mostly at her home, which is on the church grounds, especially when her family was out of the house and, occasionally, in a car when Father Gutierrez would give her rides."

"Why did she report all of this to you for the first time in the middle of these hearings?" Dougherty asked.

Again, J.J. noted that he could have objected to the question. It was calling for Carmen's state of mind. The proper way to ask the question would have been to ask whether Carmen had told her why she was reporting this information. Technicalities. There was, now, nothing to hide. Sally didn't need any help.

"I don't know why me or why then," Sally said, "other than I was available and she knew that I had spoken to her brothers about their abuse—and I had interviewed her briefly about them—but she said that these events involving her brothers had gotten her to remember. She also said that there was an event recently. She was in her room and lights flashed across her window, and she remembered Father Gutierrez lying on her; she had seen the lights on the ceiling, in the same manner, when her mother was returning home from Bingo. That apparently brought it all back. She said this memory was of the last occasion when they had almost been caught by her mother having sex and Father Gutierrez had fled the house."

"So this one claims that she did have 'recovered memories'?" he asked, seeing an opportunity to challenge Carmen's claim.

"Yes. It appears that she had repressed the whole episode and her memory was triggered by a particular event of flashing lights."

"And she just happened to remember in time for these hearings?" he asked, his normal sarcasm returning in his voice.

"I assume that is a rhetorical question?"

"No, it just seems everyone remembers for you, Ms. Conrad, but can't remember for a parent or a bishop, another therapist, a lawyer—or anyone else. Do you find that a strange coincidence that you are the source of all of these memories and accusations?"

"I don't have an opinion whether it's strange, Mr. Dougherty."

"Well, did you notice that Father Gutierrez didn't admit to molesting Carmen Sanchez? How do you explain that, Ms. Conrad?"

"Perhaps he wasn't asked."

That drew a laugh from a few of the reporters. The judge quickly banged his gavel.

"Did it ever occur to you, Ms. Conrad, that Carmen Sanchez might be making up the accusations to get on the gravy train she saw her brothers on—for the money?"

"Yes, it did."

Damn, J.J. thought, she always has to be so honest.

"I was skeptical exactly for that reason, Mr. Dougherty. Also, I was skeptical of the recovered memory explanation, as you are. But her description of waking from a sleeping state, at night, seeing lights upon the ceiling, and having what amounted to a flashback is very consistent with an event that can restore memory of events so painful as to be denied and repressed. An example is Post-Traumatic Stress Disorder that many of us associate with the Vietnam War. It applies to sexual abuse, too."

"You'll agree that flashbacks can be internally generated—that is, have no basis in reality—will you not, Ms. Conrad?"

226

"Well, Mr. Dougherty, again, I think that is true. Is memory like a camera that just shoots a picture and stores it or something more complicated? A flashback could even be a memory of a dream or a hallucination. We have to look for external support or corroboration of memory. Carmen Sanchez's accusations deserve a lot more investigation, I agree; but if you look at her life since she came to Sacramento, at age ten, you'll see that something seriously changed, and I would not be at all surprised if it was as a result of sexual abuse."

"And this investigation. You haven't done that, have you?" Dougherty asked.

"Not really. I just took the information she gave me."

"Are you sure you didn't suggest abuse to her with your conduct, Ms. Conrad? Memory can be susceptible to suggestion, can it not?"

"I don't believe I suggested anything to her. But, yes, suggestion can play a role in some cases of so-called recovered memory."

"Are you aware that so-called recovered memories are often false memories according to the psychiatric literature, including the report of the Royal College of Psychiatrists in England?" he asked.

"No, that's not true. Where extraordinary means are used by the therapist, often referred to as recovered memory therapies, such as hypnosis, drug-induced abreaction, dream interpretation, art therapy, age regression, or even survivors' groups, then there is a significant danger that the suggestion, interpretation, or expectations of the therapist or other participants will shape or create a memory. But, like here, most patients report recovering memory of abuse while home, alone, or with a friend—not in therapy. It might be a smell of cologne, a touch of a hand, an experience similar to something that happened during the abuse— like the flash of lights on the ceiling."

Sally paused. "Mr. Dougherty, Carmen came to me with a memory. I didn't do anything extraordinary to create it, except to listen."

Dougherty bristled. "Let's look at a few things. You met with the boys—multiple times—you met with the parents, you interviewed Carmen, all about what each of them knew about sexual abuse by Father Gutierrez, right?"

"Yes."

"Based upon what you tell Mr. Rai, another, more professional therapist is brought in, and she also does multiple interviews, right?"

"Yes."

"By the way, when you first met Carmen, how did she appear to you? Depressed? Suffering from Post-Traumatic Stress Syndrome?"

"She appeared flippant, over-sexualized, and an attention-seeker," Sally replied.

J.J. looked at the judge. He had to be impressed that this was not your normal "professional" expert.

"What did she tell you?" asked Dougherty.

"She told me that she knew I was there about 'the priest jerking off' her brothers and that the tongue piercing that she was wearing was for fellatio. Actually, she pronounced it 'fallecheo,' but I got the point."

Dougherty would not be thrown off track, despite some giggling from the media.

"So she was quite aware that her brothers were going to get money by saying that Father Gutierrez abused them, isn't that correct?"

"She knew they were seeking money because he did abuse them," Sally corrected him.

"Right. The more abuse, the more money," said Dougherty, with a hint of sarcasm.

"I suppose."

"And you asked her if she had been abused, didn't you?" Dougherty asked, taking off his glasses to make the point.

"No, I asked if she had ever seen Father Gutierrez engage in any improper acts with anyone, and she answered, 'No.'"

"And it wasn't until this hearing began that she suddenly remembered 'Oh, yes. I forgot. Me!'" Dougherty stated, his voice rising.

Before Sally could answer, he added, "So when did she get this great revelation about being abused?"

"I had the impression that it was within the last few weeks," Sally replied.

"And do you know of any outside corroboration for this supposed recovered memory by Carmen?"

"No, although she did mention that in the last incident when her mother entered the house unexpectedly when Carmen started to scream, the priest hit her—backhand, I think she said—across the face, which left a scratch which she believes her mother saw. But, again, I have not gone outside of my meeting with Carmen for corroboration. That's not my job."

"Right. You're just the messenger," Dougherty said, looking at J.J. "I have no further questions of Ms. Conrad."

"Your Honor, I think Mr. Dougherty should be admonished to avoid the sarcasm," J.J. said.

Sally added a final, unsolicited comment: "I believe her."

Chapter 32

*D*ougherty was an experienced trial lawyer and knew how to play out the clock. Like a football team in disarray toward the end of the first half, he needed to play defense, not let the other side score any more points, and get the team into the locker room and blackboard a new plan for the second half. He looked around the courtroom. His eyes stopped on Mrs. Sanchez.

"Your Honor, we'll call Mrs. Sanchez." He decided to help her to the stand as she was still distraught from Sally's testimony about Carmen. Besides, that would take a little more time and even make him look caring.

"Mrs. Sanchez, I'm sorry to have to ask you these questions," he began, after Mrs. Sanchez was sworn and seated in the witness box. "You've heard that your daughter, Carmen, has told Ms. Conrad that she, too, was molested by Father Gutierrez and—"

"It's not true," Mrs. Sanchez interrupted, choking back more tears. "She never told anyone that."

"Yes, that's what I wanted to ask you. Did she ever tell you that she had been molested by Father Gutierrez?"

"No."

"Did you ever tell the bishop that you suspected that your daughter had been abused?"

"No, because she wasn't. But she was having sex with everyone. All the boys. I found condoms. She just laughed at me."

"If you had ever thought for a moment that Father Gutierrez was molesting your daughter, would you have gone to the bishop and told him of your suspicions?"

J.J. knew he could object since the question obviously called for speculation. But what would be the point? If she hadn't told church authorities, what she might have done had she known was irrelevant.

"Yes, like I did with the boys. The bishop always helped us. I would have gone to him. But it never happened."

"Right," said Dougherty. "In fact, you've called upon the bishop many times to help you with problems involving your daughter, haven't you?"

J.J. saw Dougherty's momentary glance at J.J. Here it comes, he thought. Dougherty does have information about Carmen. He's prepared. Let's see how well.

Dougherty, who had been in the well halfway toward the witness, retreated to his place at the counsel table and pulled a file from his briefcase.

"Last year, your daughter was arrested for loitering, wasn't she?" he asked, obviously knowing the answer.

"Yes."

"Where?"

"On Stockton Boulevard," came the embarrassed answer. Everyone in the courtroom knew what "loitering on Stockton Boulevard" meant.

"Did you know that a lot of women 'loiter' on Stockton Boulevard at night?"

"Yes, the police told us it's where the prostitutes go," Mrs. Sanchez answered, her head down as she wiped away tears with the tissue in her hand.

"Was she taken to jail by the police?"

"Yes, we had to go down and get her out."

"And when you say 'we,' whom do you mean?"

"The bishop and I. When she got in trouble like this, I always called the bishop. He called somebody at the Sacramento Police Department, and they only charged her with loitering and released her to me without any money for bail. The bishop and I drove her home."

Dougherty looked to his file. J.J. saw a slight smile, as if Dougherty was aware that this was information J.J. did not have.

"And before she was arrested for 'loitering,' there was another time she was arrested, wasn't there?"

"Yes," said Mrs. Sanchez, "at the Arden Fair Mall for shoplifting."

"And she has also run away many times where you've had to call the police to find her, hasn't she?"

"Yes. One time we found her in a homeless shelter after she had been at the river for weeks."

"And had she ever run away before you came to Sacramento?"

"Yes. I forgot. One time she ran away with some friends because she didn't want to leave Delano."

"And these friends, when you were still in Delano, had you ever caught her with them in any inappropriate situations?"

"Yes, once her father caught her in a car with a high school boy. The boy had his hands all over her, and they were doing things. Her father gave her a beating for that."

"Here in Sacramento, did Carmen always go to school?"

"No. When she started high school, she didn't want to go to the Catholic school, so we let her go to Sacramento High School. But then she stopped going to school altogether."

"Did she get in trouble at Sacramento High School?"

"Yes. She got into drinking and drugs. The teachers would complain that she would make cuts on her arms and legs with a box cutter or razor that she carried to school."

"You said that she got into drugs. Did you ever seek help for her drug problems?"

"Yes. She was in a drug rehabilitation program for teenagers when she was fifteen. She went for a while, but she just kept using drugs."

"Did anyone help you pay for the drug program for Carmen?" Dougherty asked.

"Yes. The bishop. He knew the people who ran it, and he was the one who got her into the program. He gave us money to help. And he arranged that we could pay them a little bit each month." Mrs. Sanchez turned toward J.J. and stated, "We are still paying for that."

"You heard your daughter testify to an event that she said you witnessed. Did you ever see anything, anything in her room or in the house or any marks on her face or any part of her body, to indicate to you that your daughter was having sex or being molested in your very home?"

"Never!" Again, she looked at J.J.

"Has Father Gutierrez ever been in your home?" Dougherty asked.

"Only for dinner with the whole family. Never alone with Carmen."

"Did you ever see him leaving your home at any time when you hadn't been there?"

"Never!"

"Did you ever see a mark, a bruise, a scratch on your daughter's face when you entered her room and saw her there?"

"I don't remember ever seeing any scratch. I heard what the lady testified to. No, I don't remember anything like that."

J.J. looked at the witness. Never; never; never…I don't remember.

"We're adjourned for lunch; 1:30, gentlemen," announced the judge.

J.J. saw that Maureen McReynolds remained sitting at the back of the courtroom as others were leaving. He slowed down his own packing so as not to appear obvious that he was stalling. When it was just the two of them, he walked to the door. She joined him there but stood blocking the door.

"You're holding out on me," she said. "You never told me about Carmen. I went to the wire service midmorning with the priest's confession. Now the locals are going to beat me with their live feed on the noon news from the front steps of the courthouse with the story about Carmen being raped."

"You heard Ms. Conrad. We were not planning on using it until Dougherty begged and begged," J.J. said.

"Yeah, right. Like you didn't set the whole thing up."

"Right now," J.J. confessed, "I don't know if I set it up or if I am being set up."

"By Dougherty? Why? How would this help him?"

"I haven't figured that out except that if one claim is proven false, maybe he thinks that all of them may seem false. He didn't know we had the priest's confession until he walked into it with Sally on the stand."

"Stepped into it, I would say," Ms. McReynolds replied.

"Yeah. That was worth watching, wasn't it?" J.J. laughed.

"But maybe Dougherty is right and it's Carmen who is trying to get on the money train."

"That could be the other setup I was referring to," J.J. said. "Head-line: 'Famous Attorney J.J. Rai Outfoxed by 17-Year-Old,'" he announced, framing the image of a headline with his hands. "That is a headline that has me worried, and I wouldn't put it past you to run it."

She stepped aside, and he opened the door. He leaned in to smell her hair. She knew and smiled. "Well, since you've been scooped at noon, how about lunch?" he asked.

"Mr. Rai, that was not the deal; you have not won yet," she said with a smile, "although you're looking less of a loser all the time." She left him holding the courtroom door.

Chapter 33

"What do you suppose Dougherty will do this afternoon?" Rebel asked her father. They had ordered sandwiches from the café in the park to eat in the office. Actually, only Rebel was having a plain turkey sandwich; J.J. had opted for his regular Caesar salad with chicken smothered in anchovy dressing—"Hold the anchovy."

"Well, he's out on a limb," J.J. said. "If he keeps denying sex with the boys, he knows that Andy is on his way back to saw it off. If he claims they are all lying, he makes it an all-or-nothing game, and Carmen gets carried in on the boys' evidence. If he attacks just Carmen, the boys get a free walk. I think the best he can do is argue that the Diocese knew nothing about any of it."

J.J. took a bite of his baguette after dipping it into his salad dressing.

"But then," he added, thinking out loud, "how does he explain Carmen and the sexual abuse for years right under their noses—behind the bishop's rectory—before Father Gutierrez got started with the boys?"

He pondered. "If they have a surprise, I don't know what it could be."

"Where do you think the judge is in all this?" Rebel asked.

"Don't know. Hard to read. I think he respected Sally's testimony. I just don't think he likes me."

"Dad, it's not always about you."

"That's where you're wrong, peanut. If a jury likes you, and you keep them laughing, they'll go with you."

"Dad, you've got no jury, and this judge doesn't laugh."

235

"I know. That's what's worrying me," J.J. said in all seriousness.

They did get a surprise when they returned to court. Two surprises. The first was that Bishop O'Brien was in the courtroom. The second was that Roland Dougherty asked J.J. if he and the bishop could speak with him privately.

The three of them walked out of the courtroom, just as Mr. and Mrs. Sanchez, and Carmen, were coming down the hallway.

"Come to my office," J.J. said, as he led them toward the stairwell. They entered the fourth-floor landing together. "What can I do for you gentlemen?" J.J. asked as they stood on the landing.

Dougherty spoke. "The Diocese is prepared to pay $250,000 to each of the boys to end this case now."

J.J. looked at the bishop. Funny, he thought, the three of them together on a landing, much like the vestibule of the cathedral where he and O'Brien snuck a little wine now and then, on cold mornings before serving Mass as altar boys. Roland, or "Rolly-Polly" as they called him, wouldn't have any of it. So, instead, he was the butt of their jokes and pranks.

"What about Carmen?" J.J. asked.

"She's not a party to this case. It is only the boys," Dougherty said.

"Three children are abused by the same priest and only two—the boys—recover? That doesn't sound like justice," J.J. said, looking at Dougherty.

Bishop O'Brien entered the conversation.

"J.J. don't push this. It'll come back and bite you. You cannot trust Carmen."

"Why not?"

"I'm just telling you, as a friend. Consider the boys. Carmen's case, if she has one, can wait until another day. Don't sacrifice the boys for her," said the bishop.

"Don, what is it?" J.J. asked. The earnestness with which Bishop O'Brien had made his statements left J.J. feeling very uneasy. Already, J.J. had been surprised by revelations about Carmen's past behavior. There obviously was more.

Dougherty interrupted and put a hand across the bishop's chest.

"Look. We are here to talk about the cases before this judge. You have been appointed guardian for the boys. So what is it? Yes or no to a half-million dollars?"

J.J. didn't see his case for the boys getting worse, but maybe better.

"No," he said, "I want a million dollars each."

"That isn't going to happen," Dougherty responded immediately.

"Fine," J.J. shot back. "Then, let's go back to court."

He started to leave. Dougherty looking almost smug, replied, "I'm compelled to notify the court that you have rejected $500,000 since this is, after all, a formal offer to compromise claims of minors."

"Fine," said J.J. again, "and, as you said, I have been appointed their guardian by the court. I do not accept or recommend your settlement offer."

The bishop put his hand on J.J.'s arm.

"Don't do this, J.J."

Again, J.J. had a very uncomfortable feeling. Was there anything that they could do at this stage to upset the very compelling presentation that he had made on behalf of the boys? He didn't see it.

As he walked toward the courtroom, he saw Carmen sitting alone on a bench at the far end of the hallway. He nodded to her without speaking. She smiled at him, looking almost contrite. For the first time, he saw her wearing a dress—and a rather modest one at that.

He noticed more media were now present, including representatives of the Spanish-language television channel. Apparently, raping a girl made bigger news than sodomizing boys. Or had people come to expect sodomy of boys by priests? He wasn't sure which was the case.

"Buenos tardes, Luis. ¿Que tal?" J.J. said, addressing the news reporter and exhausting his Spanish.

"Señor Rai. Perhaps an interview after court?" Luis requested.

"Perhaps," he said. J.J. looked back at Carmen sitting at the end of the hall. Obviously, the media did not realize who she was, or they would have been all over her with their questions.

When court resumed, the judge acknowledged learning the latest offers to settle and J.J.'s rejection on behalf of the boys. The judge did not make public the amount of the offers or their terms.

Dougherty, far from looking troubled by J.J.'s rejection, seemed almost to relish it and to gain confidence from it. He stood and recalled the bishop as his first witness of the afternoon.

J.J. turned to Rebel, who was sitting in the audience, and shrugged his shoulders. He had expected Mrs. Sanchez to be followed by Mr. Sanchez. It just seemed the natural order of things—at least in the tidy little mind of Roland Dougherty. Instead, Dougherty had brought the bishop back.

The bishop stepped forward and raised his right hand to be sworn. J.J. smiled. Apparently, the bishop was not accustomed to testifying and didn't realize that he needn't be re-sworn, as he had already been sworn. But the clerk, seeing the bishop with his hand raised, instinctively swore him again.

The first time the bishop was sworn, he had looked like he was blessing the crowd. This time, with his right hand raised only to his shoulder and his left hand behind his back, he looked more like a soldier at parade rest. J.J. studied his old friend. He doodled a sketch of the witness, as he often did, in his trial binder.

"Bishop O'Brien," began Dougherty, "during the years that you have known Carmen Sanchez, did she ever report to you that she had been molested by Father Gutierrez?"

"No," said the bishop softly.

"Did you ever have any suspicion or see anything to suggest that such was the case?"

"No," answered the bishop. He shook his head with the answer and stared directly at his counsel, Roland Dougherty.

"Did her parents ever suggest to you that Carmen had been molested by Father Gutierrez?"

"No."

"Did the boys, in any conversation that you had with them ever suggest that Carmen had also been molested or abused in any way by Father Gutierrez?" Dougherty asked. Clearly a script had been worked out, carefully, even if only over lunch.

"No, they did not."

Interesting, J.J. thought. Dougherty now appears to be giving up on the boys and perhaps even Carmen and just trying to show that the Church didn't know. He's conceding, J.J. thought. It was the path that J.J. and his daughter had discussed at lunch as the most probable and reasonable, given the strong state of the evidence of abuse.

"If you had obtained any information that Carmen was being molested or abused in any way, what would you have done, Bishop O'Brien?"

"Immediately suspended Father Gutierrez. We would then have investigated the accusations. We would have confronted him. If we believed the accusations were true, we would have dismissed him, returned him to his Order, and recommended that he be thrown out of the priesthood. That's what we would have done; that's what I did do here once I had any information that he was molesting a member of the family—specifically, the boys. We never had any such information about Carmen."

"You have observed Carmen over the years, haven't you Bishop O'Brien?"

"Yes, I have."

"How would you describe her?"

"I think she's a very troubled girl. We have all tried to help her. I pray for the parents and for Carmen," he said, looking at the parents.

Nice, thought J.J. Don't dump on her. Dougherty has already done that through the mother. Let the bishop and the clergy be above that kind of thing. Let them pray. The lawyers can do the shit work.

"No further questions," Dougherty said, ending, it seemed to J.J., on prayer for the lost lamb.

That's it? thought J.J. Why was he warn me off? What is there about Carmen that we haven't yet heard? Is he waiting for me to ask the wrong question?

"Any questions, Mr. Rai?" the judge asked.

J.J. stood. He walked to the well. The bishop was watching him closely. The courtroom was silent with anticipation.

"Why didn't you call the Sacramento Police Department when the two altar boys told you that they had been sexually molested by a priest?" asked J.J.

It was a question that J.J. had not prepared. It was something that came to him as he saw the bishop be sworn and take the stand that afternoon. He was asking it, as if over drinks—an afterthought—between two friends.

The bishop appeared surprised by the question.

"Well, I…uh…I don't know. I suppose I acted more like a priest than a policeman. I was concerned about the boys. As soon as I found out that one of my priests had done this, I threw him out. Then I sought to take care of the boys."

J.J. went back, sat down at the counsel table, and studied his friend in the witness box. Then he looked at the image doodled on his legal pad: the bishop being sworn with one hand behind his back. "Oh, God," he thought.

"No further questions," he finally said.

"May the bishop be excused?" Dougherty asked. "He needs to get back to prepare for evening services."

"Yes, you're excused, bishop," said the judge after hearing no objection from J.J.

J.J. continued to sit quietly at the counsel table, looking at his legal pad.

The bishop left the courtroom, whereupon Dougherty called his next witness.

"Mr. Octavio Sanchez."

Mr. Sanchez looked older than his forty-four years. His life in the fields was evidenced from his damaged skin. The hand he raised to be sworn bore the calluses of hoeing and shoveling for a living. Certainly, being janitor of the cathedral was a step up and meant an easier life, but with the loneliness of the job he didn't have the opportunity to speak English a great deal. His English-language skills were not at the level of those of his wife, who, as greeter of official guests of the bishop and, as his scheduler, assistant, and housekeeper, interacted with the public, priests, service people, and all those who had business with the bishop.

As he took the stand, under the guidance of the clerk, Mr. Sanchez looked distraught. His wife remained in the audience, crying occasionally. This must be terrible, thought J.J. He couldn't imagine, as a parent, how he would handle these proceedings if it were one of his children who was abused, let alone all of his children, as in the case of the Sanchezes.

Dougherty was solicitous at the outset.

"Mr. Sanchez, I'm sorry to have to ask you these questions."

Mr. Sanchez nodded.

"Did your daughter Carmen ever tell you that Father Gutierrez molested her?" Dougherty asked, as his very first question, by-passing any questions about the boys.

Mr. Sanchez was listening intently. He seemed to be repeating the words quietly to himself.

"Sex with priest? No, no," he responded.

"Did Juan or Felix tell you about—" Dougherty adopted Mr. Sanchez's verbiage—"'sex with priest?'"

"No, no. They speak to my wife."

"Did you ever see Father Gutierrez do anything with your children, Carmen, Felix, or Juan?"

"Sure, the *padre* all the time in house."

Dougherty wasn't sure the answer was responsive to the question. "No, Mr. Sanchez, I mean did you see any bad—*mal*—things with priest and your children, *niños?*"

J.J. decided to make things a little more frustrating for Dougherty.

"Your Honor, I object to Mr. Dougherty's Spanish. It's really bad."

For the first time, he got a slight smile from the judge.

"Mr. Dougherty, would you like to use the services of a Spanish-speaking translator?" asked the judge.

"No, Your Honor. I don't think it will be necessary. Let me try again."

Mr. Sanchez looked back and forth at the judge and Dougherty. Then he said, "*Niños?*"

Dougherty started over. He changed the subject.

"*Señor.*" He looked at J.J. The judge looked up at Dougherty with a frown. "Mr. Sanchez..." Dougherty began again.

"*Sí?*"

"Mr. Sanchez," Dougherty didn't pause this time, "is Carmen a good girl?"

"Carmen?" He launched into Spanish. "*Carmen es una cualquiera. Una prostituta. Una puta. Se droga. La he pescado mil veces con chavos y con hombres. Se vende por dinero. Y es una mentirosa.*"

The court reporter got the first few words until she looked at her simultaneous printout from her stenograph machine to her laptop computer screen and realized that she was typing in Spanish. Everyone watched as Mr. Sanchez delivered an obviously heated castigation of his daughter, obvious even to non-Spanish speaking listeners. Only the Spanish speaking T.V. reporter was writing—furiously.

When the witness finished, or stopped to take a breath, *The Sacramento Bee* reporter leaned over and asked the Spanish-speaking reporter what Mr. Sanchez had said. Still writing, he replied too loudly in the quiet courtroom, so everyone heard: "He says she's a whore and a liar."

"Okay, Mr. Dougherty," said the judge, "we are going to get a translator up here. Ten-minute recess."

Mr. Sanchez left the stand to comfort his sobbing wife.

J.J. went over to his daughter. "Did you see I got a smile from the judge?"

"Barely," Rebel replied. "Where is Dougherty going? 'Liar' helps him, but 'whore' doesn't."

"I don't know, but he doesn't seem to be making much headway getting there."

J.J.'s phone vibrated at that moment. He looked at the number. It was the office with a text message: "Andy just landed. Sacramento. He'll be at court in an hour."

J.J. showed the message to Rebel. "Great," she said. "Uncle Andy. This should reduce the trial to a new low."

"Hey," J.J. replied, "he came through with the statement. He's a little eccentric, but he has a heart of gold and a fervor for justice."

"Yeah, yeah. You know my view," she said, giving up.

"Remain seated," said the bailiff, as court resumed. The judge motioned to Mr. Sanchez to come forward.

"Mr. Sanchez, if you will come back up here, we are going to start over in Spanish but this time with a translator. Do you understand?" The judge directed the translator to repeat what he had said.

Mr. Sanchez nodded. The judge, in turn, nodded to Dougherty to resume his examination.

"Now, Mr. Sanchez," began Dougherty. The translator repeated, "*Señor Sanchez....*"

"Did your daughter Carmen ever tell you that Father Gutierrez had molested her?"

"No, never."

"Did your boys, Juan and Felix, ever tell you that Father Gutierrez had molested them?"

"No, but Felix told his mother he didn't want to go to camp. Or be an altar boy."

"Is your daughter Carmen a good girl?"

This time the answer was shorter and more abrupt. "She's a whore and a liar."

The Spanish-speaking television reporter looked over at his fellow reporters and smiled. "See? I told you."

"Why do you say that about Carmen?"

"Because all the time I catch her with the boys. She does drugs and drinks. And she has money for drugs and clothes and everything, but she doesn't work. She lies all the time about where she is or where she is going. She never went to school. Instead, she was stealing at the mall or getting money from men."

"When did you catch her with boys?"

Mr. Sanchez looked confused at the translation and addressed Dougherty with the word, "*Primero?*"

Dougherty answered, "*Si. Primero.*" The translator looked confused, then repeated in Spanish, "The first time."

"When she was eleven, I caught her in the car. She had no...the panties...and her skirt was up. The boy was rubbing all over her."

"Was this in Sacramento?"

"No, no. In Delano."

"Did you punish her?"

"Yes, with a belt."

"On her buttocks? With the belt?"

"Yes, on the butt."

"Were her panties on when you punished her?" Dougherty asked.

The translator hesitated. The judge looked up from his note taking. The question was stated in Spanish. Mr. Sanchez looked confused. The translator repeated the question. Mr. Sanchez continued to look confused and did not answer.

"Mr. Sanchez, when you whipped Carmen with the belt, were her panties down?" Dougherty asked, rephrasing the question.

Where was Dougherty going? J.J. wondered. This didn't seem like inadvertent inquiry. Dougherty was insistent. He was going somewhere deliberately and methodically. And it involved a time period before Carmen ever met Father Gutierrez. Don't tell me, J.J. thought, Dougherty is going for the "she wanted it" defense against a child? Wouldn't put it past him. The sick son of a bitch.

"Sure," replied Mr. Sanchez.

"And did you ever tell anyone you were sexually aroused by that?"

Again, Mr. Sanchez looked confused and had to have the term "sexually aroused" explained to him. Finally, he answered, "No," and looked at his wife with embarrassment.

"Did you ever watch your daughter get undressed, Mr. Sanchez?"

"I don't watch her. Sometimes, I've seen her, sure. It's a small house. We have only one bathroom."

"Did you ever tell anyone you were sexually aroused seeing your daughter naked?"

J.J. could see that Dougherty was reading from a typed list of questions.

"No."

"And did she sometimes walk from the bathroom to her bedroom naked?"

"Yes, and her mother told her to stop doing that. It's not good for her brothers to do that. She doesn't care. She just laughs."

"Did you ever tell anyone that you got sexually aroused seeing your daughter walking around the house naked?"

"I tell her to stop. Her mother tells her to stop. All the time. I see her. No."

"You work on Saturday nights when your wife goes to Bingo, don't you, Mr. Sanchez?"

Dougherty got up from the counsel table and stood behind his chair. J.J. had noticed that Dougherty customarily did this when he was getting into an important area of testimony.

"Yes, not just Saturday night; every night," Mr. Sanchez said through the translator.

"But Bingo is Saturday night, and your wife regularly goes and takes the boys, doesn't she? She's been doing that for years, hasn't she? All the time you've been in Sacramento?"

"Yes. And I work late in the cathedral to get ready for Sunday."

"Mr. Sanchez, have you ever come home on a Saturday night and found your daughter in bed?"

"When I come home, I don't go to her bedroom. So I don't know. Her door is always closed."

"Well, Mr. Sanchez," asked Dougherty, leaning on the chair back in front of him—here it comes J.J. thought—"haven't you had impure thoughts about your daughter for years?"

"What does that mean, 'impure thoughts'?" Sanchez asked the interpreter. She repeated his question in English for Dougherty.

"You know, Mr. Sanchez, dirty, sexual thoughts of having sex with your daughter. Like when you go to confession and say, 'Bless me Father for I have sinned. I have had many impure thoughts about my daughter, Carmen, being naked.' That's what I mean."

"Sometimes you think lots of things. You can't help, as a man. That is between man and God."

"But you have gone to confession to Bishop O'Brien and told him your lust after your daughter, Carmen, haven't you?" Dougherty demanded.

J.J. was up. "Objection. No foundation. This is entirely inappropriate. Penitent-priest privilege. What happens in the confessional is inadmissible. My God, judge, I can't believe an attorney for the Catholic Church would be privy to what might have been said in confession. Where is the bishop? I want to put him back on the stand right now!"

245

J.J. was furious. He knew full well that this was innuendo and nothing more, since if he called the bishop to the stand, the bishop would surely refuse to testify as to what had been said in confession. The bishop was bound by church rules, Canon Law, and the Evidence Code of the State of California to assert the privilege. It was inviolable. So, the net result was that Dougherty could make up anything and imply that it was coming from the bishop who had heard it in confession from the witness.

Is this why the bishop testified first, so he could be excused and not be cross-examined about Mr. Sanchez and his so-called confessional statements? J.J. wondered.

"Mr. Dougherty," said the judge, "how do you propose to prove what went on in the confessional? Is the bishop prepared to testify if called by Mr. Rai?" Clearly, the judge saw through the ploy, thought J.J. He was not going to permit this.

"No, Your Honor. The bishop has no intention of violating the sanctity of confession. But Mr. Sanchez can waive the privilege if he wants to and tell us what he told the bishop, or another priest, in confession."

The judge didn't wait for J.J. "By asking the question—which I agree is impermissible—you have implied that Mr. Sanchez has, in fact, said these things, and he has no way to defend himself but to waive the privilege. You cannot force that choice upon him."

The judge looked at the court reporter.

"I am going to strike all of the testimony about what might have been said in confession. Also, Mr. Dougherty, it appears that you are asking questions without a basis or a good faith belief to support them. These are serious charges, and I am warning you, you better be prepared to demonstrate a good faith belief and a basis for them, or I am going to sanction you severely."

Dougherty held his head down as he was berated by the judge. However, when the judge was finished, he appeared less than apologetic.

"As an officer of this court and as an advocate for my client, I can represent that I have a good faith belief in the falsity of Carmen Sanchez's claims against Father Gutierrez and a factual basis for my questions of Mr. Sanchez."

"It'd better become evident, and soon, Mr. Dougherty," replied the judge. "Proceed."

Through all of this, the interpreter was translating for Mr. Sanchez, as fast as possible. Mr. Sanchez clearly did not understand the fine points and nuances of the law. Suddenly, however, a burst of Spanish poured from him, which was translated by the court translator: "Why does the bishop tell everyone what I told him in confession?"

The judge turned to him in an attempt to explain the situation.

"No, Mr. Sanchez, the bishop told no one anything."

"But he just said all these things. I am watching my daughter getting undressed. I want to have sex with my daughter. I heard the bishop told everyone I said this in confession."

Again, the judge tried to explain. "No, Mr. Sanchez. Only Mr. Dougherty said that. Not the bishop."

"Then how does Mr. Dougherty know all this?" Mr. Sanchez asked.

It was a question that momentarily stumped the judge. Finally, he said to the translator, "Tell Mr. Sanchez that Mr. Dougherty was guessing. The bishop told nobody anything."

The translator explained.

"Then it was just a trick?" Mr. Sanchez asked, looking at Dougherty as if he could kill him. "And he said it to my family, my wife, and all the people in the courtroom. The reporters. Everyone."

The judge had no further response. His explanation didn't really satisfy Mr. Sanchez; it didn't satisfy anyone else in the courtroom either—all of whom suspected that Dougherty had to have received the information somewhere. Why else would he ask these specific questions?

"Do you have any other questions, Mr. Dougherty?" asked the judge.

Dougherty got up as if nothing had happened. "Mr. Sanchez, on any Bingo night, or at any other time for that matter, did you go into your daughter's room and have sex with her?"

J.J. stood, although he couldn't think of an appropriate legal objection. The judge held up a hand as a referee might while looking into a fighter's eyes to see if he would let the fight continue.

"What kind of a man do you think I am, you ass?" Mr. Sanchez shouted at Dougherty as the translator repeated. "Do you think because we are poor we have sex with our children? It was your priest. How can you say these things to me?"

Mr. Sanchez abruptly stood and came out of the witness box toward Dougherty. The bailiff rose. Dougherty moved toward J.J.'s side of the table. Mr. Sanchez, however, didn't attempt to hit or attack Dougherty. Instead, he spat on him and walked out of the courtroom. Mrs. Sanchez sat crying. As Mr. Sanchez left, J.J. could see Carmen through the door; she was sitting on the bench, apparently oblivious to what had transpired. He looked at Dougherty and saw that he was also looking at Carmen.

As if on cue, Andy Miller walked through the courtroom door and gave a salute to J.J. He, too, had no of idea what had transpired, or of Carmen's allegations, as he and J.J. had not spoken for days.

J.J. stood and advised the court, "Your Honor, my investigator, Mr. Andy Miller, has just arrived from Mexico and is now available. If you would like me to put him on for the purpose of establishing the genuineness of Father Gutierrez's confession, I would be glad to do so."

The judge looked at Dougherty. "Mr. Dougherty, do you have any other witnesses or may Mr. Rai proceed on this foundational matter?"

"I see no reason to interrupt the orderly process of witnesses. At this time, the Diocese would like to call Carmen Sanchez as our next witness. I believe the bailiff will find her in the hallway."

Mrs. Sanchez looked shocked and turned to see her daughter entering. She watched as Carmen walked in, smiling. J.J. wished he could have prepared her for what was coming as she was about to be blindsided. But there was nothing he could do to help her.

Carmen took the witness stand and sat on the edge of the seat. Back straight, her hands folded in her lap. She had no body piercings or tattoos—visible. She smiled at the judge.

"Ms. Sanchez, may I call you Carmen?"

"Yes, Mr. Dougherty."

"Carmen, you claim that Father Gutierrez molested and raped you when you were about twelve through approximately age thirteen or fourteen; is that right?"

"Yes, he did."

"And you didn't tell anyone about these claims until earlier this week—after you knew that your brothers were getting money from the Church because they said that they were molested, isn't that right?"

Her polite demeanor registered no change in the face of Dougherty's not so subtle suggestion.

"I told the nice lady therapist, yes."

"Why didn't you tell anyone sooner?"

"I think I just didn't remember it for a long time. I put it out of my mind. And with all of this going on, I remembered that's why I was always so upset, into drinking and drugs and sex and everything. It just came back to me like a nightmare."

Pretty good, thought J.J. This kid not only cleans up well, she's no dummy. Convincing. She's going to be a match for Dougherty.

"You just remembered? Like poof, I remember I was raped by Father Gutierrez?" Dougherty snapped his fingers in the air as he began the last sentence.

Andy was sitting in the back of the courtroom listening. He started moving forward, one row at a time, trying to avoid the bailiff's notice.

"No, it was more like a flashing light. I was lying on my bed. It was dark. I was partly asleep, and the lights of a car shined on my ceiling, like when my mom would get home from Bingo, and I suddenly felt this weight on me, and I remembered the times he would come to my room and was on me, and one time when we weren't watching for my mom to come home, and suddenly I saw the lights. Then it just all came back, like a long, bad dream. I was crying and saying, 'No, no, no.' Just like before."

"And this went on for years?" Dougherty asked, using his voice to mock the prospect, "him raping you in your house and no one ever suspecting? Is that what you're telling us?"

"No. At first, he was just nice. Giving me a ride home from the store or something. Giving me money. Then he started just touching me, like on the back, even at church. Then he would accidentally touch my butt or my chest. Sometimes he'd hold my hand on his lap. And then one night he walked me home from Bingo and rubbed my breasts and kissed me. He did lots of other things, too. But then, he started coming to my room when my mom was at Bingo. He'd sit me on the edge of the bed, so I could watch for my mom's car, and do things to me or sit me in front of him on the bed. Then, finally, he started having real sex with me. That's what was happening when we were almost caught, and he didn't come back after that."

"Did he use a condom when he had sex with you?"

"Sure," she said with a shrug of the shoulders. "He showed me how to put it on so I wouldn't get pregnant with boys."

"Why didn't you tell anyone when this was going on?"

"Who was going to believe me? He was a priest. My parents were so involved with the Church, they probably would punish me for lying."

Andy was now at the corner front seat behind the attorneys' section.

"Psst," he whispered to J.J.

"Carmen, you actually started your sexual escapades with boys before you ever met Father Gutierrez, didn't you?"

"I messed around. Just kid stuff, like everyone else, but I didn't have real sex until Father Gutierrez."

"And you started running away from home down in Delano before you ever came to Sacramento, didn't you?"

"Just one night. My dad whipped me, and I didn't want to come up here anyway," she said, starting to get a little surly.

"When did your dad start touching you, Carmen?" Dougherty asked, as if impatient and wanting to end the charade.

"What? What are you talking about? He didn't do nothing to me," she answered, appearing shaken for the first time.

"Aren't you angry with your father, Carmen?"

"I told him I never wanted to come to Sacramento. This would never have happened if we hadn't come." Tears started to well up in her eyes.

"Isn't it true that you've been molested for years, but not by Father Gutierrez?"

"No, it was Father Gutierrez, just like he did to my brothers." She was now leaning on the rail in front of her as if to get closer to Dougherty and in his face. It was clear that she had no fear of him, or of any other man, and could likely bite or scratch him if he got too close to what now appeared as her witness cage.

"Psst, psst," whispered Andy. J.J. finally looked back. The bailiff was also looking over. Andy was trying to hand J.J. a note.

"Didn't you think you could confide in your mother, if these things were actually going on?" Dougherty asked.

"I told you, my parents wouldn't believe me. Besides, she knew." Carmen gestured toward her mother who was still sobbing.

"What do you mean, she knew?"

"How could she not know? She washed the sheets. She saw the blood and the other stuff. She was always gone on Saturday nights and took the boys. She never came home early. She knew, and she didn't stop him. Then the last time. She saw my face. The scratch from the ring. It was bleeding."

Carmen was now shouting, and her mother's sobbing was growing louder.

J.J. pushed his chair backward. Andy handed him the note and finally sat back down. J.J. opened the paper on which Andy had scrawled, "What the fuck is this bullshit!!"

Chapter 34

"Mr. Rai, you have a witness, I believe," said the judge.

J.J. had decided not to cross-examine Carmen. Between Sally's prior testimony of recovered memories and the expected testimony of Dr. Leibowitz on the effects of childhood abuse, he really expected to cover everything necessary through other witnesses. As to Carmen, her "case" was not really before the court. The only reason for her testimony was that it had been insisted upon by Dougherty—albeit through a little detour over a tiger trap set by J.J.—and was designed to show that the abuse by Father Gutierrez was pervasive and extended beyond some occasional groping at altar boy outings.

Now it was time for J.J. to put on witnesses, and the surprise confession of Father Gutierrez needed to be authenticated.

"Yes, Your Honor, since he has just arrived, I would like to have five minutes with my investigator, Andy Miller, before putting him on. That way, I am sure we can shorten his testimony and facilitate the court's schedule."

The judge looked at the clock. It was already 4:00 P.M. and on a Friday, no less. "Five minutes," the judge agreed. "Then we will resume and complete Mr. Miller's testimony."

Andy started for the door. He knew the drill: Find a corner out of the way, unoccupied, or a stairwell. J.J. followed. They went directly to the stairwell.

"Andy, good trip?" J.J. asked as they entered the stairwell, and he looked up and down to make sure they were alone before engaging in a confidential communication.

"Don't get me started. I trailed Ken Lay for three days, and that son of a bitch…"

"Andy. Andy. Later about Ken Lay. I promise. What's with the note?"

Andy calmed himself and sat on the red painted fire hydrant protruding from the floor behind the door. "There is no way that our priest raped that girl," he stated definitively. "You sent me to talk about the boys. Where did the girl come from?"

"She's the sister. He molested and raped her first when she was about the same age as the boys."

Andy listened. He shook his head vigorously. "It didn't happen. No way."

"How do you know?"

"Because our priest is a real homo-erectus, a queer, a fairy, a cocksucker, a fag. There is no way this guy would cross the sidewalk to lie on a nude Madonna. And I mean the real Madonna—not Jesus' mother."

"Is this just your usual homophobia coming out, where you think all priests, college professors, and persons who don't follow Cal football are homos?"

"No. Listen, pal. You don't know what I had to do to get this statement. This priest tells me I have to go down to Nuevo Laredo in Mexico to meet with him. First of all, Nuevo Laredo is like the most dangerous place in the world. It's total anarchy, run by drug lords and the criminal element. And even as bad as the people are down there, when I asked directions to this place where he told me to meet him—La Telaraña— even they are appalled. When I find the place, I go in, and I'm looking around, and everybody is looking at me. First, I realize it's all guys. Not even a cocktail waitress. Then I see these booths and guys sitting in them— and, get this—with little Mexican boys, I mean ten or twelve years old, and there are a bunch of the other guys in the back on computers lined up against the wall."

J.J. listened, his stomach tightening—the feeling of a trial lawyer facing disaster—and realizing he has only a few minutes before court is to resume.

"Andy, I am going to put you on the stand for one thing and one thing only. You will verify that this is the statement you took from Father

Gutierrez and that this is his signature. End of testimony. If Dougherty asks you about Carmen's accusations, just tell him that you knew nothing about them when you went down there and that you had no discussion with Father Gutierrez about them. No mention of 'homo-erectus,' got it?"

"Got it," said Andy. "Just thought you should know. It didn't happen."

They returned to the courtroom. Everybody was already in place.

"Your Honor, we will call Mr. Andrew Miller," said J.J.

Andy strutted up to the witness stand, stopped to raise his hand to be sworn, and winked at Dougherty as he turned his back to the judge to mount the witness stand.

Andy just couldn't miss a chance to antagonize an opponent, thought J.J. He gave Andy a slight, disapproving look.

"Mr. Miller, you were asked by me to locate a certain priest named Ramon J. Gutierrez, were you not?"

"Yes, I was."

"And did you do that?"

"Yes, I located him in Mexico—well actually in Laredo, Texas, at his mother's home—but he agreed to meet me in Nuevo Laredo, Mexico, which he did last evening."

Andy turned to the judge. "Judge, you just cross over this Freedom Bridge from Laredo into Nuevo Laredo, which means New Laredo, and it's right there." He gestured with his hands as if crossing a bridge. "You hardly even notice the border."

The judge nodded.

"Let me show you a statement marked for identification," J.J. said, approaching the stand. "Did you personally obtain this statement from the priest in Nuevo Laredo last evening?"

"Yes, I did," said Andy, putting on his bifocals.

"Did the priest sign it in your presence?"

"Yes, he did. Right here," he said, pointing to the signature and holding it up as if to show it to Dougherty. When Dougherty didn't respond, he turned and showed it to the judge.

"Thank you, Mr. Miller," J.J. said, attempting to rein Andy in. "Your Honor, I'd like to offer this statement in evidence. I have no further questions."

"Mr. Dougherty?" invited the judge.

Dougherty retrieved the statement from Andy's outstretched hand.

"Mr. Miller, are you a licensed investigator?"

"No, I'm primarily an aviation litigation consultant, but I work for Mr. Rai as an investigator from time to time."

"You're a disbarred attorney, aren't you, Mr. Miller?"

"That, too," answered Andy without further explanation.

"You were disbarred for submitting false evidence to a court, weren't you?"

"I plead guilty, with an explanation."

"I think guilty is sufficient, Mr. Miller."

Dougherty handed the statement back to Andy and asked, "Who wrote this statement?"

"Father Gutierrez. He had a very nice pen. I believe it said 'Diocese of Sacramento' on it."

Oh, Jesus, thought J.J. Can't he play anything straight? Don't ham it up. Just get off the fucking stand!

"How did you know that the person was actually Father Ramon Gutierrez, formerly of the Diocese of Sacramento?"

"Well," Andy began, "because he said so; his mother said so; and all the guys at the bar called him 'Father Ramon.' In addition, I asked to see his driver's license—he still had his California license—and I compared his signature with the documents Bishop O'Brien gave Mr. Rai from his personnel file. A match."

J.J. relaxes a little. That's our Andy, he thought. Sucker them in with that good-old-boy act. Maybe Dougherty will stop questioning.

"And," Andy added, after a suitable pause and a glance at J.J.—as if to say "watch this"—"I took our picture together." He held up his cell phone.

"Who is this person identified as a witness on the statement?" All the while, Andy was holding up his cell phone in offer to Dougherty, who was having none of it. So Andy turned to the judge and said, "That's

Father Gutierrez in the middle, me on the right, and the witness on the left." The judge looked at the cell phone picture and thanked Andy for showing it to him.

Andy resumed his response, "The witness? He was the bartender."

"Of what establishment?" asked Dougherty.

Andy threw a quick glance at J.J. Then he answered, "The one we were in."

"Yes, I understand that. But what was the name of the establishment frequented by Father Ramon Gutierrez in which you obtained this statement regarding his abuse of these two boys."

"You know, I can't remember the name right offhand. My Spanish is lousy. I'd have to check my luggage which, I'm told, is somewhere between Houston and Sacramento."

Dougherty looked through his notes and then made a show of looking through his briefcase.

"Your Honor, I have some more questions for this witness, but it appears, I, too, have left papers behind somewhere, I believe in my office. In light of the time, I wonder if we should conclude for the day?"

"Very well," said the judge. "We'll continue Monday morning at 9:00 A.M., and I want to finish this case on Monday, so have all of your witnesses here."

Dougherty walked directly to J.J. as soon as the judge had left the bench.

"I'm doing you a favor, J.J., but only because the bishop asked me to. I have some more questions for your investigator. I hope you don't think that you're the only one with an investigator who has visited La Telaraña." He dropped a picture in front of J.J. of what could only be the inside of the bar with a sign above a bank of computers on a far wall and a room full of men.

"Take the $500,000 for the boys and forget about the girl. You persist, and come Monday, we're gonna show that your witness Carmen is a liar and your expert Sally Conrad doesn't know a rape victim from a hooker."

J.J. attempted to show no weakness or tip his hand. "Thanks, Roland. Nice of you. I'll let you know Monday at 9:00 A.M."

"Fine with me. It's your funeral."

"Nice to know you and the bishop will be there to administer the Last Rites."

"It's what we do, J.J.," Dougherty replied, finally getting in a reasonably decent retort.

Andy came over. "He's charming, isn't he?" gesturing toward Dougherty, who was leaving the courtroom.

"He can't help it. God made him that way," J.J. answered.

"Isn't that a country western lyric?" said Rebel, approaching them. J.J. smiled at his daughter.

"Well, if it isn't, it should be." Then, reaching for Andy's cell phone, he added, "Show us your damn picture."

The picture showed the priest in uniform—his collar on, Andy next to him smiling, with a Negra Modelo beer in his hand, and, on the other side a handsome, shirtless, young man who was apparently "the witness" to the confession. Behind them, over a wall of computers, was a large sign. It read: "NAMBLA."

Andy realized, on taking a second look, his mistake in offering the picture. "Good thing Dougherty didn't get a close look at the picture. Well, he probably doesn't know what NAMBLA stands for anyway."

"He didn't have to look at your picture," said J.J. "He's got his own."

"NAMBLA stands for North American Man / Boy Love Association," Andy whispered to Rebel.

"By the way, Dougherty showed me a picture of the bar with the name La Telaraña across one wall. Do you know what that translates to in English?" J.J. asked Andy.

Andy looked around to make sure that no one could hear his sudden recollection of the bar's name.

"Yeah," he said. "It translates to 'The Spider Web.'"

Chapter 35

"I'm exhausted," J.J. admitted. They were back in the office. "We started with a case with two altar boys the Church admitted were fondled. The Diocese offered $15,000 each for a total of $30,000. Almost immediately, Dougherty admitted the Diocese really meant to offer $50,000. Then he goes to $100,000. Three days into the hearing, the Diocese concedes there was more involved and wants us to take $500,000. But now the sister claims that she was raped and molested, too, to which Dougherty responds that her own father did it. How did we get here?"

His secretary walked in as he was talking. "I think it was because you walked over to the courthouse to do a poor immigrant family a favor," she said, picking up on the conversation.

"I'm too old for this," J.J. said. "Trial work is for younger men."

"And women," Rebel corrected him.

"Right, when you take over my practice."

"Not going to happen for you, dad. Sacramento? Are you kidding?"

He gave up on Rebel, for the time being.

"Andy, we need to get on the river this weekend. I'm going home tonight, but what do you say we get together on the boat tomorrow afternoon and sort this thing out?"

"Sure thing," Andy answered. "You want to join us, Rebel?"

"No, you two have fun. Share war stories. Lie to each other. Whatever it is you guys do."

"That's all we can do anymore," Andy lamented.

"Speak for yourself, Andy," J.J. interjected. "I find when I drive a fifty-five-foot teak Hatteras upriver and pass a few restaurants, the women wave at me. I must be better looking now than I've ever been."

"Maybe it's the boat," Andy said.

"You think so?"

"You know what they say," Andy began, "big boat…"

Rebel, often critical of her father, never hesitated to defend him from others, and cut Andy off. "Dad, you've always had lots of women friends."

"You have women friends?" Andy asked.

"Sure, I enjoy women," J.J. replied.

"It's true," Rebel said. "Dad likes women. Don't you have women who are friends, Andy?"

"Nah," he said. "I don't sleep with my friends."

Rebel gave up. "That's it. I'm out of here. See you Monday, dad. Have fun."

"So, what's the plan, Captain?" Andy asked after Rebel had left.

"Well, I'm going to head out to the spread tonight. Tomorrow, I've got to prep Dr. Leibowitz for Monday's testimony. I should be through by noon, and we can meet at the slip. Let's get aboard and take off. You bring the booze, and we'll cruise, hit a few bars, eat some bad food, play some pool, and park on the American River for the night. Sunday, I'll run over to Tower Books and pick up some newspapers, and we'll vegetate. It's supposed to be 105 this weekend, so no better place to be in Sacramento than on the river."

"Then do we get to talk about Ken Lay? I've got a problem I might need your help on," Andy said.

"You didn't shoot him, did you?"

"No, but we need to talk."

"You've also got to tell me about our priest. I need it all. Monday is looking like the big day."

"And we're going drinking all weekend?" Andy said.

"Yeah." J.J. knew what he meant. In the old days, they would spend the entire weekend preparing for Monday morning. Reading every scrap of paper. Going over every question with every witness. Letting the wives take the kids to swimming tournaments while they worked. Now, was it that they were experienced litigators or that they no longer gave a shit?

Andy had his answer.

"I read this book *Oil and Honor*. Best book I've ever read about trial work. Joe Jamail in Texas. He's getting ready to do his opening statement in the Texaco-Pennzoil case the next morning. Eleven billion dollars at stake—billion, not million. It's like 9:00 or 10:00 at night, and he sits down to write his opening statement, and there comes a knock at the door. He opens it. Standing on his doorstep are Willie Nelson and University of Texas coach Darrell Royal, and they want to drink with old Joe. Damn if he doesn't invite 'em in to share a few drinks! The next morning, he gets up and gives that famous opening statement—'A promise is better than a contract'—that won him that case and $11 billion."

"What are you saying, Andy?"

"I'm saying we need to get really drunk and, like your daughter said, lie to each other. That's what friends are for."

"What else is there?" J.J. agreed.

Andy shook his head and grinned. "I don't know. I've been looking, and I still haven't found it."

Chapter 36

*O*n Saturday morning, J.J. called Dr. Leibowitz from his home for their scheduled testimony prep. He told her of the developments since they had last spoken: the confession of the priest confirming the extent of sexual interaction with the boys and the new accusation by Carmen.

"Does the priest admit the acts with Carmen?" she inquired.

"We didn't ask him, but I have to tell you that all the evidence suggests that his primary interest is in little boys. The Church is pointing the finger at dad, assuming anything actually happened to her." On the one hand, he didn't want to give her all the details; on the other, he couldn't risk her being blindsided.

"Well, I can't help you. I've done no workup on Carmen. I'm not prepared to testify that she is a victim of abuse by anyone. I'm certainly not going to accuse the priest. That looks like a dead end. Frankly, off the record, most child abuse is incest, which, if you think about it, makes sense. Who has the most access to young children? Parents. Relatives."

"Sally Conrad has testified that she believes Carmen was abused," J.J. informed her.

"If Carmen lied to Sally about the abuser—which, from what you tell me, she did—it would seem to follow that she is lying about the abuse," said Dr. Leibowitz. "Not to tell you the law, Mr. Rai, but false in one area, false in all," she said, paraphrasing a standard jury instruction.

This witness was clearly an experienced professional witness, thought J.J. She was also an astute one.

"Sally feels that she shows all the signs of abuse," J.J. offered.

"Ms. Conrad is a little out of her area of expertise. It's an axiom of childhood sexual abuse that you cannot work backward from so-called signs of sexual abuse to abuse. For virtually every so-called sign or symptom there can be another explanation. You have to work forward from the facts of abuse to its consequences, not from supposed consequences back to the conclusion that the child must have been sexually abused."

J.J. saw that the witness was going to go nowhere that she did not want to go.

"The best I can do," she concluded, "is to say that certain behaviors or consequences are consistent with childhood sexual abuse. But I would be destroyed as a witness in this and future cases if I were to testify that I believed Carmen was, in fact, abused. I'm not going to do that."

"I understand." At this point, J.J. realized that once Dougherty cross-examined Andy or brought in his own investigator to show that in addition to being a Catholic priest, Father Gutierrez was a avid fan of NAMBLA—the association that preached a twisted homosexual perversion of love between adult men and boys—Carmen's case was dead anyway. Dr. Leibowitz's testimony could, if she was willing, add support to Sally's belief that Carmen may well have been a victim of childhood sexual abuse. This would maintain Sally's credibility. Even if mistaken about Father Gutierrez as the perpetrator, she had a reasonable psychological basis for her opinion. Apparently, Dr. Leibowitz wasn't willing even to go that far.

After previewing her testimony of the serious problems the boys could expect throughout their lives—with each other, their parents, with anyone with whom they sought to have an intimate relationship, with their own guilt and shame, and with their own children, were they to have any—J.J. realized more than ever the devastating effects of childhood sexual abuse.

"It not only robs a child of childhood," Dr. Leibowitz told him, "sometimes freezing his or her development at the stage of abuse, it inserts itself into every relationship the child will ever have in life. None will totally get over the conduct. Some will repress it. Some will use alcohol or drugs to escape it. Self-medication, we call it. Some will escape into insanity or suicide. Those who function will still be left with shame, guilt, anger, a 'why me' feeling. When the abuse is at the hands of a priest, the child may lose his faith and, thus, in the words of the church, his everlasting soul."

A little much, thought J.J., but it was good to have an advocate with credentials. After testimony, he figured her bill would probably top $15,000. It was worth it. Sally had only billed $950 for all of her meetings with the children and parents, and $350 for a half-day of testimony. At either's rates, this, he thought, was the best argument he could think of for higher education. It's doubtful, in the long run, that crime paid. But being an expert witness certainly did.

Driving back into town, J.J. thought of calling Sally just to leave her the message, "You were wrong about Carmen," but decided that there was no point in irritating her over the weekend. The focus of the case was back where it had started: on the boys. Monday, he would bring in the big gun, Dr. Leibowitz, and her testimony of a lifetime of despair and failed relationships, caused by the Diocese's failure to supervise a priest having sex with altar boys on and off the premises of the cathedral.

He knew, however, that his case for the boys would be stronger, on the question of the Church's knowledge, if he could prove the long history of abuse to Carmen. He had no prior acts, no prior complaints, to show that the Diocese had notice of Father Gutierrez's conduct with the altar boys. Without notice, the Church technically would not be liable. His remaining argument, however, was that given the history of abuse nationally in the Catholic Church, there needed to be greater supervision of a priest's interactions with altar boys. Ironically, the Diocese noted that in a prior case, two priests were abusing altar boys, so having one priest chaperone another wasn't necessarily the answer. The fall-back argument was that the abuse had gone on for so long—years, in fact—that someone should have known. If there had been a proper system of supervision—all priests on alert watching each other—someone would have surely noticed something. Constructive notice. It was the best he had.

When he arrived at the marina, on the Sacramento River just above the Virgin Sturgeon Restaurant, he found Andy sitting aft, Willie Nelson singing on the CD, and a half-dozen bottles of Mexican beer chilling in a metal tub full of ice. Andy was singing "Georgia" along with Willie, holding a half-full plastic tumbler. From the straw hat he was wearing,

J.J. guessed that Andy was drinking margaritas. The salt on the rim of the glass, and the sliced lime, confirmed it.

"Permission to come aboard," J.J. said.

"Hell, it's your boat, Captain. Permission granted."

"How long have you been waiting?"

"All night. Hope you don't mind. I went to Chevy's last night after I left you. Well, I stayed there till they closed, and they were concerned about me leaving. So I told them I was meeting you at the boat, and they gave me a ride. It's part of their new policy of looking out for drunks ever since they got sued over the death of some college kid."

"And I suppose you told them that you were in college? Is that where you got the straw hat?"

"Well, not exactly. She gave it to me," Andy said, pointing toward the cabin.

J.J. turned and saw a woman, maybe in her early fifties, in a bikini, mixing a new batch of margaritas in the blender.

"Esther, this is the famous lawyer, J.J. Rai, I told you about." She smiled and waved. J.J. waved back.

"I'm going forward to change. I'd like to shove off pretty soon," J.J. said, motioning to Andy to do something about Esther.

"Esther's shift starts pretty soon, so she's just making me one last batch, and she's out of here, right hon?"

Esther gave J.J. a margarita as he walked down the steps toward the forward cabin.

"Nice to meet you, Mr. J.J. Gotta run. Thanks." She picked up some clothes, put her sandals on, threw on a shirt over her bikini, and was gone when J.J. came out in his bathing trunks and a Mills College T-shirt.

"Nice girl," J.J. said.

"Yeah, cocktail waitress. Divorced. I only date divorcées. They're so thankful," Andy said in all seriousness, as if this were a conclusion he had reached after a long period of study and backbreaking labor.

"Can you untie the lines and push us away without falling in?" J.J. asked.

"Sure, but as soon as we are away, you've got to listen to me. I'm in some trouble with this Ken Lay thing."

"If you and your sombrero are on the boat when I leave the dock, we'll talk."

Andy showed surprising agility—J.J. had thought he'd have trouble standing—in handling the lines, and they departed with no problem. Andy walked to the starboard side and pulled up the bumpers, and they were underway. Reaching mid-river, J.J. turned the boat and headed down river, past Chevy's and Old Sacramento and under the Tower Bridge— Sacramento's pathetic answer to the Golden Gate. An old vertical lift span bridge, the Board of Supervisors had decided to paint it gold and to light it up at night. But they just couldn't quite find the right shade of gold. Baby-shit yellow came to mind, as they passed under it. When they cleared the bridge, J.J. upped the RPMs, and they were on their way toward the Delta. J.J. came down from the flying bridge, which he always used when casting off, to the controls in the cabin. There, they were in air conditioning and out of the hot sun, and the purring of the engines was subdued. They could talk in normal conversational decibels.

"Okay," J.J. asked, "what is it?"

"I think I may have hurt Ken Lay," Andy said.

"Wasn't that the idea? You said you were going to kill him, remember? I tried to talk you out of it."

"Yeah, but…"

"Did you kill or just maim him?"

"Well, neither exactly," Andy replied, reluctantly and with some embarrassment.

"Then what?"

"I think I may have given him whiplash."

"Whiplash? Are you kidding? You tell me you're going to Texas to kill Ken Lay, and all you do is give him whiplash? You know, in the annals of assassins, Andy, you are going to go down as a freakin' failure." J.J. was laughing.

Andy seemed genuinely embarrassed.

"You were drinking when you rear-ended his limousine, weren't you?"

"Why would you assume I was drinking?"

"Because you were awake? That was a clue," J.J. responded, still laughing.

"It's professionally embarrassing," Andy admitted. "I was stalking—surveilling—as part of my plan to know his routine. I had gotten used to tailing him when he left his condo in River Oaks. Usually, he'd go directly to his country club or this LaGrigha restaurant all those rich guys in Houston go to. This time, his driver swerved at the last minute and took a freeway on-ramp. I don't know, maybe he 'made' me following him again. I moved closer so as not to lose him in traffic. I swear the driver hit his brakes! Anyway, I hit the rear of the limo. I was in a rental car, so I showed them a phony ID and got out of there as soon as I could. I parked the rental car at the lot, but didn't tell anyone I'd brought it back. Later, I called the rental lot and reported that the car was stolen. I figured they'd find it on their lot and assume that some joy rider brought it back—damaged. Then I got the hell out of Texas."

"Can I ask you something?" J.J. said. "Seriously. Was this just one of your big games, or did you really expect to harm Ken Lay?"

Andy looked into his glass. He wiped the salt on the rim with his finger and licked it.

"J.J., this time, I really don't know. I found myself getting more and more involved. I even bought a 30-ought-6 high-powered rifle. I left it in the rental car when I abandoned it. It still had the scope on it."

"What do you mean 'this time'?"

"Well, I've acted out my anger about the justice system before. After O.J. was acquitted on the criminal charge, I was so outraged that I wanted to do something. I went down and read the complete court transcript, looking for evidence that might help convict him, at least in the civil case. I got a lead on those ugly shoes that O.J. said he never wore. I went through every newsreel I could locate. When I found the one that showed him wearing those shoes, I sent the information to the lawyer prosecuting the civil case. In the meantime, I have to admit, I started following O.J., trying to find anything I could.

"After O.J., I just followed up on other cases where I thought justice hadn't been served. Usually it was just trying to uncover new evidence.

When the law shifted and evidence of Battered Women's Syndrome was allowed, I tried to help find lawyers for women in prison who had never been allowed to raise the issue in their original cases. Sometimes, I gave money to investigators instead of investigating myself. I found it enormously satisfying to see real justice done."

J.J. interrupted. "But why Ken Lay?"

"When this whole Ken Lay thing came up, it just enraged me. I felt that this guy epitomized what is wrong with capitalism or rather our system of government that's been bought and paid for by these capitalists. Then they went after Martha. That was the final straw."

"You have a thing for Martha Stewart?"

"No, that's not the point. She might be a bitch—probably is—but she did not threaten America. The Ken Lays of the world do. And it just seemed that they need to be stopped before it's too late."

"Enter Andy Miller, Executioner?"

"Andy Miller, Restorer of Sanity and a System of Justice with Consequences."

"Do I need to remind you that you were disbarred from our system of justice?"

"What justice? I was disbarred from a system of law, not justice. There is a difference, and I make no apology," Andy answered firmly. "Look at this priest case. I'm in Mexico saying, 'Please, Father, could you just give me a statement?' so I can go back and get some money from a church that clearly condemns his conduct, just as the law does. Why do I have to be nice to him? Why can't we drag his ass out and whip him with a cane in front of a church, with parishioners, seminarians, and other priests looking on? No, we ask an insurance company to give us money. This is civilized behavior? It's certainly civil, but I find it barbaric."

Andy took a sip of his margarita.

"And Ken Lay, and all those CEOs making tens, hundreds, of millions a year! Any system that permits that is insane. Even then, they still steal from the futures of widows and retirees! Line them up, like Spartacus, and put their heads on poles along Wall Street. That's justice. That's deterrence. But what happens? Martha Stewart gets prosecuted for selling a few thousand shares of stock on hearing bad news from her broker. If she had listened to a lawyer, she would have said, 'Yeah, of course, I sold. My broker told me to dump it. So?' And she would never have been indicted. Instead, she lies to the feds and basically goes to prison for being arrogant and stupid. And Kenny and the smart ones are still out there."

J.J. nodded. Clearly, Andy had a point.

"So, would I have done it? Would I have killed Ken Lay? I don't know. I'd like to think that I still have enough integrity in me and a yearning for real justice and the future of America to have done it, J.J.," Andy said, now downing what was left of the ice and the salt of his drink.

Chapter 37

*A*ndy and J.J. spent the afternoon on Steamboat Slough, south of Clarksburg, just off of the Sacramento River. When the margaritas were gone, on the way down, they switched to the Mexican beer and then to sipping cold white wine from bottles in the tub full of ice. The serious drinking would need to wait until they were anchored for the night on the American River, a good hour and a half back upstream, near the confluence of the Sacramento River with the American River at Sacramento. Knowing this, they paced themselves with a variety of deli items that J.J. had picked up at Corti Brothers, Sacramento's leading purveyor of fine foods and wines. J.J. settled for a nice Pinot Grigio, and some manchego cheese and Serrano ham that he put on slices of a French baguette. Occasionally, he would pop an olive or a salted almond in his mouth as he turned to Saturday's *Sacramento Bee* newspaper. Andy seemed to be happy alternating between a large bag of potato chips and a one-pound can of mixed nuts while watching the end of his fishing rod leaning on the transom for evidence that a Sacramento River catfish might join them for lunch.

John Kerry was coming to Sacramento—for money, not votes, since California was a deep blue state. J.J. couldn't recall a single commercial on television, or even on the radio, for the presidential election. The Iraq war was grinding on with more marines dead. J.J. shook his head and turned to the Metro section of the paper.

His priest case was page one, Metro, above the fold, but just one column wide on the left side. He noticed the article did not carry the byline of the regular courthouse reporter who had been in court on Friday, but the byline of the Capitol Bureau. Odd, he thought.

The Sacramento Bee story appeared to summarize *The Wall Street Journal's* in many respects, including references to him and Dougherty as former altar boys who were in parochial school together. Inside, the story continued, under the heading: "Church: Reliable Evidence Father Molested Girl."

"Damn it," J.J. muttered. It always bothered him how reporters or headline writers could misunderstand the law and mislead so boldly. Dougherty has asserted that he had a "good faith belief" and a "factual basis" for his questions, nothing more. No one had ever seen, let alone ruled, that there was any reliable evidence to support a charge made only in a question asked by Dougherty which, as every lawyer knew, was not evidence "except as it gave meaning to the answer." And the answer, to Dougherty's question, was "no."

J.J. read on: "Earlier, witness Sally Conrad, a licensed clinical social worker, testified to her belief that the older sister of two molested altar boys was also a victim of abuse. Church testimony suggests that this abuse was by the father of the victim, not the priest alleged to have molested the boys."

Dougherty did this, J.J. thought. It would be just like him to call the metro editor—going over the reporter's head—as if being helpful, but not wanting to be quoted.

"According to informed sources, the Diocese, without admitting any liability, had offered the boys $500,000 to settle their claims," began the next paragraph, "which their court-appointed attorney, J.J. Rai, has refused to consider."

"Dougherty is trying to pressure me into settling," J.J. said, showing the paper to Andy. "That settlement amount was never publicly disclosed. No one knew about it except the parties, and I certainly didn't tell anyone."

"You want me to kill him?" Andy asked, pouring himself another drink.

"With your batting average, Dougherty would show up in court Monday morning in a cervical collar. No, I'll handle him in due course."

In this case, as in almost every other case in which he had been involved, J.J. had opposed a gag order on the attorneys. Therefore, he was in no position to object to Dougherty's statements. Generally, it was he using the media, and being quoted, with the other side trying to silence him. Ironic, he thought.

J.J. and Andy spent the afternoon "lying to each other," as Rebel had called it, reminiscing about trials and tactics, gags and stunts, and what each one had done to maintain his own sanity in a system that was much like sailing: ninety percent boredom and ten percent sheer terror. They agreed that a trial lawyer had to be able to find the humor in a situation—or create it—and drink. In anything from nuclear arms negotiations to a hostage standoff, "send in a good trial lawyer" was their consensus.

"Waco didn't have to happen," Andy said. "I could have brought them all out alive—well, maybe not David Koresh—but the rest."

In the spirit of competition that fed them, J.J. added, "I could have brought out Koresh, too, and maybe even negotiated a tank ride for him."

"Well, he'll never get a tank ride now. The stupid religious fanatic is probably in Hell."

"You think tanks are only in Heaven?" asked J.J. "What's your concept of Heaven?"

"I don't know; I think of Heaven as a place you hang out for all eternity and can have anything you want—except sex. I guess, since that is reserved for marriage, and if you were married to one person for all eternity, that would be Hell, not Heaven."

"Maybe the rules for sex in Heaven are different," replied J.J.

"Or maybe Hell is where all the sex is, but you don't enjoy it. Kinda like a job. I mean, have you ever seen those religious paintings in European churches showing Hell with naked people everywhere, being humped by animals or whipped in nine different positions or put on the rack? If it's Hell, how come they are all getting it on?"

"So, what do you want to do for all eternity?" asked J.J.

"Well, we could just sit here on a boat, drinking, just us guys."

"For all eternity? Just sit here?"

"How about we take up golf?" asked Andy.

"I hate golf," replied J.J.

"Well, what do you want to do?"

"I don't know; what do you want to do?"

Andy didn't answer. They sat silently, looking at the river. Finally, J.J. broke the silence.

"And this is Heaven? Coming up with something to do every single day—for all eternity?"

"Yeah, I see your point," replied Andy. "Hell is looking better all the time. At least there they have planned activities."

By late afternoon, they were tired. Andy was falling asleep in his chair in the aft deck. His fishing rod had long disappeared overboard and probably had been dragged halfway to San Francisco by a large catfish. J.J. decided it was time to weigh anchor, head back to Sacramento, and find some dinner on the way. As he turned the boat, he decided to accelerate quickly. It had the expected effect: Andy fell backward in his chair onto the deck.

"Andy, work on your sea legs. We're going up to Courtland for dinner on the dock."

Andy moved forward to the head.

By nine o'clock, after dinner, they were passing Miller Park at the end of Broadway and the entrance to the downtown area of Sacramento. Small boats were tied together, their occupants still partying on the beach. Water skiers were packing it in, as the sun had set, and, despite the bright red and yellow skies, it was too dangerous in the water, especially with drunk drivers this late in the evening.

J.J. geared down to avoid the wake and started into a slow sequence that would take them under the Tower Bridge and to the American River. At Discovery Park, at the confluence of the American and the Sacramento, campfires and barbecues glowed. J.J. eased down further and joined the line of boats heading up the American River to park for the night. The Sea Ray Club, consisting of a dozen or more Sea Ray boats, were all tethered together. Their occupants had obviously been there all day, judging from their premier location and level of intoxication. They would go late into the night with the occasional "man overboard" or, more likely, "nude woman overboard," followed by a half-dozen splashes.

"Did you ever think, when we were in law school, that we'd end up sitting together on a boat on the American River in God-forsaken Sacramento?" Andy asked, when they had anchored and sat looking at the sky from the aft sitting area.

"Hey, you're talking about my town," J.J. said, smiling.

"What's here, anyway?" Andy asked.

"Well, there's these rivers. What do you have in San Francisco?"

"We have the San Francisco Bay and the Golden Gate Bridge," said Andy, after a silence to take in the warm breeze.

"We have a bridge. You just went under it."

"We have Golden Gate Park, museums, theaters, you name it."

"We have Capitol Park, the Railroad Museum, and the Music Circus."

"The Music Circus? Is that the theater in a tent?"

"They have enclosed it."

"Well, we have some of the finest restaurants in the world, in San Francisco."

"We've got…two," J.J. replied. They both laughed.

"You know what the best thing about Sacramento is?" said Andy.

What, thought J.J., he's going to concede? "What?"

"It's just ninety miles from San Francisco."

"You're right, and ninety miles from the Sierras and Tahoe and sixty miles from the Napa Valley and a short commute for those of us living in the foothills. So, I guess it's not so bad being here when you can be everywhere," J.J. said, as if trying to convince himself. He added: "You know, I could have been in San Francisco. I was offered the opportunity after law school. Maybe it would have turned out different, I don't know. But I settled for being a big fish in a little pond. So don't knock my pond."

Andy turned serious. "You're more than that, J.J. A lot more." Then, as men do with feelings, Andy broke the unease with humor. "In fact, if I was a homo like your priest, you'd probably be my type."

"Ah, our priest. They really called him 'Father Ramon' down there in that place in Mexico?" J.J. asked.

"Yeah. Even the bartender. One of the guys mentioned that there was someone in a chat room looking for Father Ramon, and they all laughed. It's no secret. He's not hiding his identity. Or, if he's hiding, he's hiding in plain sight, on the World Wide Web."

J.J. got up and climbed to the flying bridge.

"Why would Carmen lie?" he asked Andy, who had followed him.

J.J. looked up at the clear night sky. He breathed deeply at the sight of the Milky Way.

"Money," came Andy's delayed response.

"And Juan denying everything that happened—when we all know it did. What do you think that's about?"

"Maybe he's just embarrassed. I mean, did you ever talk about sex when you were twelve or thirteen?"

"I didn't know what sex was when I was twelve or thirteen. No, Juan is just too adamant. There's got to be more to it."

J.J. had an unsettling thought. The priest's confession admitted everything Felix had told them happened. So he must have done it. Unless...J.J. looked at Andy.

"Andy. About this priest's confession?"

"Yeah? What about it?" answered Andy, finishing up a bag of potato chips and looking around for another.

"You didn't happen to put words in the priest's mouth, did you? Just to help out?"

Andy gave a look that said, "What kind of investigator do you think I am?," but must have realized the weakness of this defense and instead took a sip of his beer. "J.J., trust me. For the record, I didn't put anything in that little homo's mouth, not even words."

They sat without talking. There was a gentle lapping of water against the hull and a splash to the gunwale as a Sacramento County Sheriff patrol boat went slowly by.

J.J. followed its movement and could see its technical equipment mounted in the console, lit up much the same as it would be on the screen of a squad car: the soft, crisp illumination in its cabin of a liquid crystal display touch-screen computer.

Suddenly, J.J. got up and retrieved his cell phone. "Oh, my God. What if..." he started, as he dialed. "I'm going to call Rebel. I need to talk to a young person." He took the cell phone and went down to the forward cabin.

When he returned, after fifteen minutes, he was carrying a folded page of *The Sacramento Bee*. He shook his head and poured himself a new drink. "Andy, we can't keep up with these kids. Have you ever picked up the paper and seen one of these full-page ads from Fry's or Best Buy? You look at all that technical stuff, and you don't even know what it does, let alone whether it's a good price?" He didn't wait for an answer. He could hear Andy opening a fresh bag of potato chips.

"Do you know what a Pentium 4 processor with a motherboard is?" he asked Andy, reading from the newspaper ad.

"Sure," Andy answered, his speech slurred. "Pentium is a new sub-atomic element recently discovered in Africa and added to that chart of elements we studied in high school. Right after Uranium." He hesitated, questioning his own answer. "No, that's not right. It's a planet."

"What's a gigahertz?"

"No idea. And I don't care."

"Why would I need a motherboard?"

"To get the kids off to school in the morning?" Andy guessed.

"Or an optional portable hard drive?"

"I got one of those," Andy answered confidently. "Ask Esther."

As he was speaking, J.J. picked up his cell phone and punched in the home number of Cindy Harrison, an old friend, occasional symphony date, and now District Attorney of Sacramento. He got her answering machine.

"Cindy. This is J.J. I'm sure you know I'm in trial with the Diocese. I need your help. I think our priest is still abusing one of the boys—from Mexico."

He knew he could count on her to call back before court on Monday morning and to put the necessary people on the case to explore the criminal conduct he suspected was occurring.

Andy listened and waited for an explanation.

"Computers," J.J. answered his look when he hung up the phone. The one word appeared to satisfy Andy. He opened another beer.

J.J. awoke on Sunday morning just as the sun rose behind Arco Arena, over the levee, and put a glare upon the American River, illuminating the pollen on the water from the willow trees along the banks. It was going to be a hot one, he knew. He checked on Andy, who had chosen to stay outside on the upper deck to sleep. He was snoring. J.J. went to the galley and ground some fresh coffee and made a press pot. He threw on a short-sleeved shirt and a pair of shorts over the swimming trunks that he had worn to bed, put on his deck shoes, ran some water through his hair so it would fit into his "Mills College Dad" cap, and started up the twin engines. He could see that most of the other boats were still anchored and only a few had people sitting on deck drinking their morning coffee. He was the first to be moving this morning, and he eased backward carefully to take the tension off of the rear anchor. After retrieving it, he did the same forward and was underway to the dock. He was determined to get some croissants and the Sunday papers, not only to catch up with local news, but also to enjoy the level of world reporting of the "Week in Review" in *The New York Times*, a level not generally available in Sacramento. Then, of course, there was *The New York Times Magazine* that would occupy a good part of the day. Since he planned on returning to the American River, he tied up at the Virgin Sturgeon dock and took its gangway rather than returning to his regular dock. Andy was still asleep.

Chapter 38

*I*n downtown Sacramento, directly across from the Cathedral of the Blessed Virgin, it was not the bells ringing that woke "K Street Gus" that morning; it was that they didn't ring. His eight o'clock wake-up call never came. He counted on the bells each morning to wake him so that he could get out of the way of people who wanted to use the storefront doorway in which he slept. On Sundays, he didn't have to move since the store was closed. Rather, he enjoyed watching the church goers enter the cathedral and would harass as much as panhandle them as they entered or exited with their renewed religious fervor. To those who avoided eye contact, he asked, "And you call yourself a Christian?" He could recite the Beatitudes—"Blessed are the poor"—but would not do so unless drunk, which was every day except Sundays. He found that he did better panhandling at the cathedral sober and, as an ex-Catholic, he had no reason to recite the Beatitudes while sober since he did not believe in them.

Gus awoke wondering why the bells had not rung. Like waking up to an alarm clock, exactly on time, and wondering why the music wasn't playing. He stood up, got out of his sleeping bag, and watched the last stragglers going to Mass. He looked down at his warm leg. "Damn," he said, as he realized he had wet his pants while sleeping. Then, Gus looked up at the towers of the cathedral—above the Blessed Virgin, above the clock. A rope. He followed the rope back down to the face of the clock. A body was hanging—dangling—still, on the face of the clock. Gus looked around to see whether anyone else was looking up or whether he was the only one seeing this apparition. People continued walking up the steps and into the cathedral.

"Hey! Hey!" he started to say in a quiet but confused voice. As usual, people avoided him.

"Hey, look!" he exclaimed, pointing to the dangling body.

No one seemed to notice the body, and his shouting just caused people to scurry faster. Besides, Gus smelled bad. Only a child looked up and, pulling on his mother's hand, said in unison with Gus, "Look! Look!"

The mother's screams caused others, who had not done so for Gus, to look up and to see the lifeless body of a person hanging from a rope from the tower, the arms of the clock either clasping or penetrating the body at twelve o'clock.

J.J. left Tower Books on Broadway after picking up a *New York Times*, a *Sacramento Bee*, and—for Andy—a *San Francisco Chronicle*. He headed uptown on 16th Street to the bakery. At "I" Street, it seemed that all hell was breaking loose, and sirens converged from all sides. Turning west on I and pulling over to make way for the emergency vehicles, he saw a hook-and-ladder fire truck cross 11th Street. After the emergency vehicles had passed him, he followed them to the 11th Street intersection and found that 11th was blocked by officers erecting traffic barricades. He could see that the activity was to his left, around Cathedral Plaza. Probably a heart attack in church, he thought. Why do fire departments send a huge hook-and-ladder truck for a medical emergency? Don't they have anything smaller? What that must cost taxpayers. He drove on down "I" Street and onto the I-5, over the American River, back to the boat dock.

Andy was sitting, looking refreshed, drinking coffee, and listening to his country music station. "Howdy partner," he said. "Great morning."

"You showered already?" J.J. asked, handing Andy the *Chronicle*.

"Nah, I stood up and fell overboard. But it was as good as a shower. It's got to be eighty or ninety degrees already, and it's not even nine o'clock."

J.J. untied the lines and pushed off. "Let's get back on the American and park. That water is always cooler." Coming down from the Sierras, it was both cooler and cleaner than the Sacramento that flowed through the Valley, picking up farm discharge until it reached Sacramento dark and muddy. At the confluence, a beautiful blue, crisp, and clear American River was lost in the muddy depths of the Sacramento.

As J.J. maneuvered the boat to turn in the middle of the river, he saw the owner of the Virgin Sturgeon waving to him. He hit his horn and waved back. Now, he realized she was shouting and gesturing for him to return to the dock. He had a bad feeling.

"J.J.," Lori said as he pulled alongside the dock, "something terrible has happened at the cathedral. I just heard it on the news. I thought you would want to know. With your case in the news and everything."

"What is it?"

"A body hanging from the cathedral tower."

"Who?"

"They haven't said. The television shows a fire truck with a long ladder going to the clock face, but the body is draped in a sheet. It's really gruesome. The reporter said the police have to leave the body hanging because it's a crime scene, and they are bringing in medical and other crime scene specialists."

J.J. quickly shut the boat down, tied up, and left with Andy for the cathedral.

"Who do you think it is?" Andy asked.

"Could be anyone with what's been going on in this case. One of the boys. Carmen. Her dad. Her mother. Anyone except Dougherty, unfortunately. Or maybe it's not even related to our case," J.J. said, wishing for but doubting a coincidence.

J.J. pulled into the alley on 10th Street, expecting that it would be blocked on 11th in front of the cathedral. He ran ahead of Andy into the Cathedral Plaza and looked up at the clock tower. The rope was in place, ending at a sheet, which appeared to have bungee cords wrapping it around a body. A ladder extended from a City of Sacramento fire truck, but no one was on the ladder. It was a pathetically lonely sight, he thought: death.

He looked around and realized that the police had erected barriers at each end of the street. Television trucks were in place at each end of the plaza, on 11th Street, at J and K, but the alley he had entered had been overlooked. He was in the middle of the yellow police taped, restricted area. As he realized this, the door of the rectory opened. He immediately recognized Mrs. Sanchez accompanied by her two boys and a priest he did not know. As they were led away toward the waiting car, all looked back at the hanging body. Mrs. Sanchez was trying to turn the children's heads as she herself kept looking over her shoulder and wailing. The priest attempted to keep them all moving.

Then Mrs. Sanchez saw J.J.

"You did this," she screamed at him. "You did this!"

Pointing to the body, she added, "See what you have done!" The priest put them in the car and came around to the side on which J.J. and Andy were now standing.

J.J. asked the priest, "Where's Carmen, her daughter?"

"Gone," said the priest, as he got in the car and drove off.

Chapter 39

The Chief Investigative Officer was surprised, as he opened the door, to see two men in shorts on the front steps of the rectory of the Diocese of Sacramento on a Sunday morning, especially since the entire area was supposed to have been sealed off as a crime scene.

"Who are you?" he asked.

"J.J. Rai, attorney for the Sanchez family, and this is Andrew Miller, special investigator."

"Special investigator with who?"

"With me."

"You're not supposed to be here. Who let you in?"

"We just walked in. If this involves the Sanchez family, then I think I have a right to be here."

At that point, Bishop Donald O'Brien moved forward. "It's all right, Officer Douglas. Mr. Rai and his associate are working with me on the Sanchez matter. Come in, gentlemen," he added, holding the door.

"What can you tell me, officer?" J.J. asked, ignoring the bishop's offer and remaining outside on the step.

The officer looked at the bishop, who nodded.

"Male. Mexican. Identified as Octavio Sanchez, custodian for the Diocese of Sacramento. Probable death by hanging. Most likely suicide. Time of death—maybe midnight."

"*Most likely* suicide? *Probable* hanging? *Maybe* midnight?" J.J. repeated. "You're not sure with a guy hanging one hundred feet in the air with a rope around his neck and impaled on two clock hands stuck at 12:00?" J.J. asked, his voice demonstrating some incredulity.

"Mr. Rai, we let the coroner make the definitive death determination. You know how we would be criticized in court if we jumped to conclusions only to have the coroner say that he drowned, and was hung out to dry, and that it happened at noon, not midnight. So I'd say, your guess is as good as mine. Probable suicide. At midnight. Either killed by the rope or being impaled by the clock, or both."

J.J. understood that this was both a meticulous answer and a criticism of criminal defense attorneys who nit-pick and with whom the officer had obviously dealt in court before. He decided to let it go.

"How did he get up there anyway?" J.J. asked, looking at the tower. He guessed it was about two hundred feet high.

Officer Douglas noticeably relaxed.

"Actually, he seems to have enjoyed the tower over the years. To get to the clock tower, he went up the stairs of the adjacent, smaller tower and out onto the roof, which is approximately ninety-two feet off of the plaza. From there, he entered the door to the main tower and climbed up to the clock platform. From the evidence we found, he had been doing this for years."

"What evidence?"

"Well, there is a platform at the point of the clock. To get there from the roof, he had to climb wooden ladders, in the dark, about thirty-five feet through other smaller platforms. At that point, he would have been approximately 127 feet above the plaza. I went up there myself. Imagine a small room, maybe fourteen by fourteen, but with a hole in the middle of the floor, where you enter. There are huge old bells sitting on the floor, no longer connected, and the inside of a clock face on all four walls. It's rather surreal. Reminds you of that old silent movie with Harold Lloyd. I think it was called *Modern Times*."

J.J. looked at Andy with a look to suggest, "Is this a fucking movie review or a murder investigation."

Andy rolled his eyes.

"Anyway, in this 'room' is a chair, a small table, just big enough for an ashtray, a cup, a flashlight, and some books in Spanish and diagrams of the night sky. Planets, stars, the stages of the moon, that kind of thing. Really secluded and a beautiful view of the city's horizon and, of course, the night sky. Hanging above, in the dark, is a huge bell that I am told bears an inscription to the first bishop of Sacramento and was apparently hoisted up there through the tower in the 1890s."

"Did anyone know to look for him up there?"

"Apparently not. No one knew he hung out up there. Not even his wife or any of the employees."

The officer hesitated, realizing that the term "hung out" might not have been the best choice of words.

He continued when no one mentioned the *faux pas*. "The bishop and the priests have never themselves been up there. There is really no reason to go up there. The last report of work that we can find took place years ago when the bells were disconnected and a sound system substituted to play bell sounds in time with the clock. Before that, it looks like the last work was in the 1930s. I can tell you the ladders I climbed felt like they were originals, possibly from the 1890s."

"But how did he get up to the top where the rope was attached?" J.J. asked.

The officer turned to a younger uniformed officer. Gesturing to him, he said, "Officer Curran went up the rest of the way with one of the fire department personnel. Frankly, I am afraid of heights, and the rest of the way up was in a very confined space, as the tower narrows toward its steeple. I'll let him tell you."

"Yes, sir," answered Officer Curran. "I directed the fire search-and-rescue worker to assist me. Since it was a crime scene, I entered first, with him providing support to the ladders. We had to climb five more old ladders to traverse the next sixty feet. But the last ladder was a modern twelve-foot, lightweight aluminum ladder that accessed a hatch onto the last platform. The hatch was open; the ladder was in place, sticking about two feet above the landing from where we believe he jumped." Then he added, "It's a spectacular view."

"Why do you believe he jumped from that point?"

"Well," began the officer, "it was as high as he could go without climbing onto the outside of the steeple. We doubt he did that."

"Tell him why," interjected Officer Douglas.

"We found cigar residue on the ledge, as well as a half-empty bottle of Souza tequila."

The officer was holding some items in his hands. He now showed them to J.J. "We also found these: pictures of his children, one of the twin boys and one of his daughter."

J.J. wanted to throw up.

"Also, the rope was attached at this point, so there was no reason for him to go higher. Instead of using just one corner of pillars to attach the rope, he used two: the two on the corners facing west."

J.J. looked up. He could see the significance immediately. By tying to both pillars and centering the line, Mr. Sanchez—with enough rope—would hit the clock centered below on the tower.

Officer Douglas could see J.J.'s glancing calculations. "It could be a coincidence, of course," he began, "but it is also possible he measured the rope to hit the clock. That clock location seems to have had a lot of meaning for him, looking at the stars, contemplating and all. The sky would likely have been the last thing he saw as the rope jerked his neck up at its end."

"To heaven," said J.J., looking at Bishop O'Brien, and then turned to leave.

"J.J., can I have a minute?" the bishop said, following him down the steps.

"Sure, see you in court."

The bishop continued to follow until they were out of earshot of the officer. "J.J., wait," the bishop said as he grabbed his arm.

J.J. stopped. "What?"

"You blame me for his death, don't you."

"The thought had occurred to me." Then he added, with irritation, "Why does his wife blame me, for Christ's sake?"

"She believes Carmen is lying," said the bishop. "And you and I know she's right."

J.J. looked away. "And if that lie had not been put forth by you and your consultant, none of this would have happened," added the bishop.

"I never wanted Carmen's claim to come out. Dougherty was the one who insisted," said J.J., knowing, however, that he had set the trap for Dougherty and had enjoyed watching him fall into it.

"Do you remember, J.J.? I warned you. I begged you. I told you do not go down that road. I couldn't tell you everything, but I warned you."

"Well, I never expected you would defend the Church by breaking the secrecy of confession. You're the one who accused Carmen's father, not me, and in a way that went against everything you supposedly hold sacred about confession, penance, and forgiveness."

The bishop shook his head. "You know, J.J., you have hated Roland Dougherty since we were in the fifth grade and were altar boys together. Because of your feelings, you have underestimated him. I didn't discover Carmen's lie; he did. I didn't tell him anything that her father had told me in confession. He figured it out for himself. It was a bluff on his part. He actually believed that Carmen may have been abused and concluded that it was most probably incest—especially after his investigator told him that Father Gutierrez was interested only in little boys. So if you need a scapegoat, I guess you can blame Roland, but maybe you should have made sure Carmen was telling the truth before you let that testimony into evidence."

J.J. was stunned. It hurt. He knew he had not investigated Carmen's claim; it came up in the middle of the hearing. But if he had investigated the priest better, he would have known the claim was untrue. Yet, he allowed it into testimony through his own consultant, whose credibility would now be damaged beyond repair once it was shown that her opinion about Carmen being abused by Father Gutierrez was utterly wrong. If she was wrong about Carmen, perhaps she also was wrong about the boys and about the extent of their abuse, which she supposedly "discovered" in her interviews with them. After all, one of the boys—Juan—had totally repudiated the suggestion that he had been abused by Father Gutierrez. The girl was a liar; Juan denied the abuse ever occurred. It was only Felix's testimony—"discovered" by Sally—and, ironically, corroborated by the pedophile's confession—that supported J.J.'s case.

Had his dislike of Dougherty blinded him to the evidence? he wondered. Was the game overshadowing the truth?

"I tried to warn you," repeated the bishop as J.J. walked away.

J.J.'s cell phone rang as he and Andy got into the car.

"Yeah?" he answered. It was Sally Conrad.

"J.J., I just heard. The television said it was the father. What's going on?"

He explained what had occurred in court, told her about the accusations that the father may have molested Carmen—"if she was molested at all"—and the fact that Father Gutierrez had an obsession with little boys, but no interest in girls.

"Are you sure?"

"Yes, the priest is an avid fan of young boys. He's even on the Internet soliciting through some group known as NAMBLA. Have you ever heard of them?"

"Sure. Real sickos. They have a whole philosophical/historical justification for man/boy love that they relate back to the Greeks or earlier. If he's really into that, then you're right, it wouldn't fit that he molested Carmen, and, certainly, he would not have raped her."

"Well, Sally," J.J. said, his voice betraying impatience, "it's a little late for you to be telling me this now, don't you think?"

"J.J., I repeated what she told me. That was my testimony. I was just the messenger."

"Then you added, at the end, that you believed her. That is now going to come back and bite you in the ass and discredit all of your other testimony."

"The essence of my testimony was that Carmen was molested and abused. I believed her. I still do. I have no way of knowing, or stating, as a therapist, who did it. That's your job, J.J. So don't blame me."

She hung up.

The Sunday television news at noon didn't have much trouble deciding who did what.

"A father, accused of molesting his daughter, hanged himself from the Cathedral of the Blessed Virgin this morning," said the announcer on the lead story. Behind him was a live shot of a covered body dangling from a rope on the cathedral tower. The story reported that the father had been despondent since a court hearing on Friday, when he had been accused by church officials of molesting his own daughter.

"After watching a television report on the Spanish station on Saturday evening, he left the family home and did not return. On Sunday, a transient, identified only as 'K Street Gus' discovered the body. The daughter, whose name was not given because she is a minor, has not been seen since Friday," said the reporter.

Even on Sunday, the otherwise tepid talk shows were referring to Mr. Sanchez as the "hanging molester." Callers to KFBK talk radio suggested that the body be left hanging to warn other child molesters that Sacramento was a "zero tolerance" child molester city. Were there "mildly tolerant" child molester cities throughout the United States, J.J. wondered.

The body was removed at about 3:00 P.M., and the clock resumed its function, starting with the hourly bells. Someone noticed the similarity to Good Friday, when at 3:00 P.M., Christ had died and the world had turned dark. In Sacramento, however, it was bright, sunny, and the temperature hit 109 degrees. Not a day for hanging around outdoors in the sun.

Chapter 40

"What do we do now?" J.J. asked Andy, as he turned off the news reports. They were back on the boat.

"How would I know?" asked Andy. "I'm a disbarred lawyer, remember?" He threw up his hands in a gesture of submission. "Maybe you can just take the money and call it quits."

And let Dougherty win? was J.J.'s first thought. It was the immediate and instinctive response of a trial lawyer, and one, it appeared, that may have contributed to a man's death. "Maybe," his mouth said, though his mind shouted, "Never!" The trial lawyer in him asked how he could turn this event against the Church, against Dougherty, and in favor of his client.

His cell phone rang. "You did say call anytime." J.J. recognized the voice of Maureen McReynolds. "I've been in San Francisco all weekend, visiting family. I heard the news and jumped in the car. Can you tell me anything, J.J.?"

Up until now, he had avoided any on-the-record quotes. Instead, they had exchanged favors. She clearly deserved anything he had since she had taken the lead on what would otherwise have been a local story, at best. And she had kept her word with him.

"Maureen, at your hotel, there is a main bar in the lobby. Very public. Then there is a quieter bistro and bar to the left as you enter. Why don't we meet there? I'll give you an on-the-record interview."

They agreed on 4:00 P.M. J.J. figured few people would be in the bar at that hour since the lunch service would have ended and dinner not begun. He knew also that her deadline was three hours ahead, on eastern time, and he wanted the story to appear on Monday morning.

When he hung up the phone, Andy asked, "Why are you going to talk to her, J.J.?"

"We need to breathe some life into this case and give the Church a reason to settle, now."

"Like what?"

"Like we are going to threaten to pull out of this compromise hearing and demand a full-blown trial with a jury and full discovery, with subpoenas and demands for production, for all three children. This judge can't force me to stay in this hearing even though he seems hell-bent on doing so."

"Yeah," said Andy. "I never understood where he was coming from, either, other than he seems not to like you."

"The Diocese can't be happy with the image of a dead Mexican hanging from its cathedral tower. If we start over, by filing lawsuits on behalf of each of the children, conduct depositions of all the priests in the Diocese, and bring in multiple psychiatric experts, this story will be on the front pages for the next eighteen months. Other children may come forward. The Church will lose control of this matter. It can't help but get bigger, especially if it appears that Dougherty had no basis for charging Mr. Sanchez with raping his daughter or if it comes out that the bishop is supposedly telling the Diocese's lawyer what people say in confession."

"You're a devil," said Andy, smiling appreciatively.

"No, Andy. I was raised on Catholic teachings, went to parochial school, to Confession—'Bless me Father for I have sinned. I had three impure thoughts, etc., bullshit'—and received the Holy Ghost with the Sacrament of Confirmation. I even went to the seminary for a week to see if I had a 'calling.' I was an altar boy, chaplain in the Sea Scouts, and married in the Church—all of it. Catholicism was like a weight that held me under water. I was drowning. Fighting to be free. Of guilt. Of doubt. Of death, even. What I had was not a faith in a loving God, but fear of a monster who knew my every thoughts and was ready to roast me for all eternity for one errant act or even thought. And, of course, I had those thoughts. So I came to fear death, not as the natural chapter of life that it is, but as the beginning of suffering for all eternity. So, if sex was enjoyable, it was equally morbid and sinful. Nudity was synonymous with impurity. Now, the priests who enforced the laws of God are exposed. Clearly, they not only do not practice what they preach, they don't even believe it. So, here's to the Catholic Church that condemned so much of our lives to guilt. I'm coming after you. I am not the devil, Andy. I am an avenging angel."

Andy looked at him quizzically. "What the hell was that rant? Your final argument? If so, I suggest you not get carried away with the avenging angel bit. People will think you're crazy."

J.J. went below to shower and dress to meet Maureen McReynolds. He looked in the mirror. Tanned. Not bad looking. He slapped on a little cologne and undid an extra button on his Italian short-sleeved shirt.

Pulling into the Hyatt Regency, he handed the keys of his Jaguar convertible to the valet, who was dressed sensibly in navy blue shorts and short-sleeve shirt. "Be about an hour. Could you just keep the car down here, in the shade?"

As expected, the bistro was empty. The hostess was gone. Only the glasses hanging upside down in the horseshoe-shaped bar greeted him.

He walked to the back, sat in a booth, and waited. She appeared in just a few minutes, stopping at the entry to take off her sunglasses and adjust her eyes to the darkness of the bar. She had on a summer dress with spaghetti straps and carried a cloth bag with a shoulder strap and wore matching green Manolo Blahnik mules. She likes color, and bright colors like her, J.J. thought, admiring her appearance.

Her red hair was pulled back and up off her neck as it had been when he saw her at Frank Fat's restaurant. Her bare arms and shoulders had a smattering of freckles. She looked warm. Hot, he thought.

"Hope you haven't been waiting long," she said. "I was at the cathedral. Horrible. The rope was still there, but, fortunately, they had taken down the body. God, is it hot in this town?"

"Let me get you some water," J.J. said. He went to the bar and called to the back, as there was no server. He brought back two glasses.

"I guess you weren't able to get a picture, then."

"Oh, the *Journal* would never run a picture of something like this. We are not a tabloid, Mr. Rai. We report news," she answered, taking the water.

"Actually, I have wondered why *The Wall Street Journal* is here."

"We go where the news is," she said, pulling a tape recorder out of her bag.

J.J. reached over and put his hand on the tape machine. "Let's just talk first."

She looked at his hand. "I hope you didn't invite me here just for a drink. I understood this was to be an on-the-record interview."

"It is. I'm going to be honest with you. I am hoping to plant some information in your story for Monday morning's *Journal* to influence the settlement of these cases. I don't want you to find out later that I used you. I want to be upfront. I just didn't want to say that on the tape."

She looked at him as if to say, "You poor boy," and laughed.

"Do I look like a virgin to you, Mr. Rai? We all use each other. So go ahead; use me. But don't lie to me. I might use your information in this story; I might not. If I do, it could get cut by the copy editor anyway. So, you can tell me what you want, but I can't promise you that it will make the paper."

"You lived up to your end last time."

"So did you. We now have a track record. One for one. But, Mr. Rai, I have no illusions. If it would help you win your case or even make you look better professionally here in Sacramento, you would double-cross me in a heartbeat. What have you got to gain, otherwise?"

"That date with you."

"Yeah," she smiled, "but only if you win. If it comes to a conflict, the case or me, I know what you'll do. You're a trial lawyer. You'll pick winning the case every time."

She hit the start button on the tape recorder. After asking J.J. to state his name, the date, place, and time and to pronounce and spell his full name and confirming that she was taping with his consent, she began.

"Mr. Rai. How does the tragic death of Mr. Octavio Sanchez today affect the case of his daughter, Carmen?"

"It doesn't, because Carmen has never filed a claim against the Catholic Church. She has testified that she was molested by a priest, but has done so solely as a witness for her brothers against the Diocese and

Father Gutierrez. In response, the Diocese made despicable, unsubstantiated charges against her father, for which there was no basis. As a result, it appears that Mr. Sanchez was driven to suicide. When Carmen brings her own lawsuit, the Diocese will have to prove its accusations or be held accountable not only for the abuse that she suffered at the hands of clergy, but for the Diocese's wrongful conduct that led directly to an innocent man—her father—taking his own life."

Ms. McReynolds raised her eyebrows as he spoke. She knew that his charges were both explosive and designed to be quoted for the use that he had described off record. Self-serving or not, they were clearly newsworthy.

J.J. continued.

"We are researching both a wrongful death claim on behalf of the surviving spouse and all three children, not just Carmen, as well as a malicious prosecution action against the Diocese for knowingly presenting a false defense in this case. We are also considering withdrawing from these proceedings and filing three separate lawsuits, one for each child, so that these matters may be decided by jurors from the Sacramento community. We will make that determination Monday, once this matter resumes and all persons are in court before Judge Gerald Vincent."

J.J., by inserting the judge by name, wanted the warning to extend to the judge since it had appeared from the beginning that Judge Vincent had his own agenda in the case and had been hostile to J.J.

Ms. McReynolds turned off the tape. "So, did you get it all in there, the plant and all?" she asked.

J.J. nodded. "Yeah, I think that about covers it."

"Do you really think Carmen was molested?"

J.J. looked down and noticed that she had not reached for the tape recorder to turn it back on.

"Yes," he said, looking directly at her.

"Do you believe the priest did it?"

He didn't answer.

"Is there something you aren't telling me?" she asked.

"Yes. There are a number of things underway that I can't talk about. But when I can, I will tell you first. Like last time, with the confession."

"Fair enough. But like I said, I'm no virgin. I've been around. If you have to dump me in favor of your case, I'll understand. Just don't lie to me."

She packed her bag, stood up, and patted his arm. "But then you won't get that date, and you'll have to live with that the rest of your life."

Chapter 41

*M*onday morning's *Sacramento Bee* didn't surprise him. Front page. Headline with a half-page high, three-column wide picture of the Cathedral of the Blessed Virgin with a rope and a covered body dangling at its end. The clock, the fire department ladder, all of it. The headline blared: "Accused Father Hangs Self."

J.J. picked up the copy of the morning's *Wall Street Journal* story that had been faxed to him and compared the single-column story on the front page of the *Journal*, entitled "Priest Molestation Case Takes Tragic Turn." He read Maureen McReynolds' bylined story. She had broken his quotes into sections, but they were all there.

> According to Mr. J.J. Rai, attorney for the abused children, the
> tragic death of Mr. Sanchez will only cause him to dig deeper into
> the widening scandal. Mr. Rai noted that all three children accused
> Father Gutierrez of molestation and stated that there is absolutely
> no evidence to the contrary, and certainly nothing to suggest that
> the suicide of Mr. Sanchez was motivated by anything but un-
> founded accusations for which, he claims, the Diocese will ultimately
> be held accountable.

J.J. glanced through the rest of the article and felt satisfied. She was a professional, he saw, upon whom he could count.

He didn't bother reading *The Sacramento Bee* article but put it in his briefcase to display prominently before Dougherty in court this morning. On the ride in, he rotated through the talk stations and the news.

They were all talking about the suicide and the fact that it arose out of claims of sexual abuse by a Catholic priest at the Cathedral of the Blessed Virgin.

He called Kitty O'Neal at KFBK from his car. With fifty thousand watts, the station covered much of the Diocese that extended almost to the Oregon border. From years in trial work, he was well known to the media, and Kitty was one of his favorites. She was also one of Sacramento's favorites and, he knew, was probably being listened to this morning by other participants in the case.

"We've got J.J. Rai, the lawyer for the molested children, on the line," she announced. "Good morning, J.J., is there any basis to the claim that this suicide was related to the charge by the Catholic Church that this young girl may have been raped by her father?"

"Absolutely, Kitty. But it is not because this father molested his daughter. Rather, it is because the Catholic Church hounded him with false accusations in order to protect itself from its own growing sexual abuse scandal. An innocent, falsely accused father was driven to suicide by shame, not guilt. The Church is going to be held responsible for this malicious claim."

"Wow, J.J., that is a serious charge!"

"It is, Kitty. And we are prepared to prove it."

He thanked her for the chance to straighten out the record and hung up. He turned the radio volume back up and caught his own last words on the delay, along with Kitty's close: "That was J.J. Rai, one of the top trial lawyers in America, blaming Catholic Church officials for the suicide of the man who hanged himself yesterday at the Cathedral of the Blessed Virgin."

He imagined Dougherty and the bishop listening. Everyone listened to Kitty.

At the office, his secretary brought in his tea and toasted raisin bread. "Thanks, Natalie. Any word from Andy?"

"He left a message on my voicemail. Said he was multi-tasking and would be a little late for court. Said you would understand." J.J. nodded.

J.J.'s friend, the District Attorney, had called him back earlier that morning and set up a meeting for later in the morning with something called the "Joint Task Force." J.J., in turn, had called Andy and gotten him out of bed for the meeting and explained, in detail, his theory. The call to Rebel from the boat Saturday had confirmed that it was very possible and, more importantly, provable. But it would take law enforcement and specialized, technical people to run it down. The D.A. had just the persons: twin brothers that she referred to as "cybercops." Yes, she had agreed, they were like Click and Clack of public radio, whom J.J. regularly listened to on Saturday mornings, in that they could get "under the hood" and locate the problem.

J.J. picked up his briefcase and headed to court. With the dramatic suicide of Mr. Sanchez, media attention to the hearing had increased significantly. Television trucks, their dishes raised, occupied the entire east side of the courthouse. Hard news television personalities—not the occasional feature talent that generally reported on "Pet of the Week"—posed with the courthouse backdrop. Radio reporters interviewed people walking along the sidewalk for "man on the street" reactions.

Unlike prior days, J.J. walked directly to the front steps and the waiting media. He turned to create the proper backdrop and waited for everyone to focus their cameras or point their microphones in the right direction.

"I am sad to be walking these steps this morning," he began, "to return to the courthouse where irresponsible accusations were made by the Diocese of Sacramento and its representatives, directly leading to the death of Mr. Sanchez yesterday morning."

"Mr. Rai, what do you expect will happen today?" asked the KCRA news anchor.

"I intend to show that the Catholic Church drove an innocent man to his death," J.J. answered without hesitation.

"Mr. Rai. Did Mr. Sanchez molest his daughter? Is that why he killed himself?"

"Absolutely, unequivocally, no. And the Catholic Church had no basis for claiming that he did."

Satisfied that he had made his point, in print, on the radio, and now on television, J.J. walked into the courthouse. One of the old timers, who had watched the show on the courthouse steps, winked at him and patted him on the back.

"I'll pray for you, son," he said.

"I'll need it," replied J.J.

Both knew that J.J. was playing a bluff. J.J. just hoped that he would not be caught holding a pair of 3s.

Reporters were milling around outside the courtroom itself. He nodded and smiled but said nothing—except to one. "Good morning, Ms. McReynolds."

"Good morning, Mr. Rai." The other reporters looked at her.

Inside, the courtroom was empty, except for the bailiff. None of Mr. Sanchez's family was present. Nor was Roland Dougherty.

"The judge wants to see counsel in chambers," the bailiff told him, as soon as J.J. entered.

J.J. walked past the counsel table and the judge's bench and into the side hall leading to the clerk's office and judge's chambers. In the clerk's office sat Roland Dougherty and Bishop O'Brien. Dougherty seemed almost sedated. He looked at J.J. but said nothing.

The clerk buzzed the judge to announce that all counsel were present. She put down the phone and said that the judge would see them now. J.J. looked at the bishop but received no acknowledgement. They proceeded into Judge Vincent's chambers. The judge was seated with his judicial robe on.

The bishop took one of the chairs in front of the judge's desk; J.J. took the other. Dougherty sat behind them, on the couch. The judge addressed the bishop: "Bishop O'Brien, I understand from Mr. Dougherty's statement to my clerk that you have asked for this meeting. I do not normally meet with clients and counsel off the record or in chambers. However, I am aware of the death of Mr. Sanchez. This is an extraordinary development. Perhaps you can tell me why you requested this meeting?"

"Your Honor, we feel terrible that anything we said may have contributed in any way to Mr. Sanchez's death. Perhaps advocacy on the part of the Diocese, even if conducted in good faith, contributed to this troubled man's taking of his own life. We do not want to be in a position of further destroying whatever good memories these children have of their father by challenging Carmen's claims."

"What are you saying, bishop?" asked the judge.

"We are prepared to settle Carmen's claims on the same basis as the boys', $250,000 each. We realize that Carmen has not presented a claim; however, we want to close this entire matter by resolving any potential claim, without her having to proceed with litigation, since she is, after all, also a minor. I am told that the court has the power to entertain such a settlement on behalf of a minor," added the bishop, looking at J.J. for the first time.

"What do you think, Mr. Rai?" asked the judge.

Looking better than a pair of 3s, thought J.J. But he kept his poker face.

"I'm not willing to discuss Carmen's claims," J.J. answered. "After she's been abused for years, her life destroyed by a priest, the Diocese denies the abuse, kills her father, and then says 'Gee, maybe we went too far.' I think Carmen, her mother, and the boys may well have a wrongful death claim against the Church for the acts of its counsel, Roland Dougherty, and the abrogation of the secrecy of confession by Bishop O'Brien."

Roland Dougherty finally spoke, but in a calm, measured, and quiet manner.

"Don't be silly, J.J. You know that everything in court, including my questioning, is absolutely privileged. You cannot sue me or the Church for that. Civil Code Section 47. You've used it yourself many times in your free speech claims—and to defend your buddy, Andy Miller."

J.J. turned in his chair to face Dougherty on the couch. "I think you may be right, Roland, and that's why I was glad that our research showed that we could state a cause of action for malicious prosecution for your frivolous defense. As you know, under the wrongful death statute, the family can't get punitive damages. But for malicious prosecution, the sky is the limit."

He was happy that Dougherty had spoken up. It allowed him to concede the obvious regarding the wrongful death claim, but to counter with a more serious claim of malicious prosecution that would allow punitive damages. What looked like a concession simply increased the Church's exposure.

This was not missed by the bishop. "We are willing to add some compensation to the mother, too, to end this tragedy."

Three 3s, thought J.J. He addressed the judge.

"Your Honor, we are in a hearing about Juan and Felix and proper compensation to them. Until I know that they have been taken care of, I can't be discussing some other hypothetical claims and settlement of those claims, which I have not yet filed."

"But we want it all over," said the bishop. "We don't want to start up again next week with another lawsuit for Carmen and then a month after that with another lawsuit for the death of Mr. Sanchez. We are trying to start the healing now, for the whole family, not drag it out for another year or two with litigation. We owe this to the family. We have a spiritual duty of pastoral care, as you have legal duty, J.J."

"If we can settle the boys' claims, we can talk about the rest. If we can't settle the boys' claims, we can't settle anything. It's that simple," said J.J.

The judge stepped in. "The only thing before me is the petition to approve the compromise and settlement of the molestation claims of the two altar boys. I have to add, those claims are now complicated by a possible separate claim related to the death of their father. Perhaps, Bishop, you and Mr. Dougherty should step outside and discuss your position on settlement of each of these separate claims."

The judge turned to J.J. "What is your demand for settlement for each of the boys?"

"$1,250,000 each."

"You said $1,000,000, Friday!" exclaimed Dougherty.

"That was before you killed their dad," J.J. responded.

"We didn't kill him. And we had no prior knowledge, notice, or suspicion that Father Gutierrez was molesting these boys. That's a valid defense."

"Fine," said J.J., standing. "You walk out of here today without settling, you're going to be explaining that to a jury."

The bishop nodded to Dougherty in a manner that clearly indicated he was to be quiet.

"Is there some place Mr. Dougherty and I can talk, your honor?" the bishop asked.

"Certainly: the back hallway. Mr. Rai can wait in my clerk's office. I prefer no *ex parte* communication in the absence of adverse parties."

"Thank you," replied the bishop as he stood up. J.J. followed him out of chambers but stayed in the clerk's office as Dougherty and the bishop walked into the back hallway. It was empty as it was used only by the judges to come and go, out of public view, to the below-ground parking or for the transport of those in custody at the county jail to their assigned courtroom on the secure special elevator.

Now the bishop, a prisoner of clergy abuse, was using the hallway, out of public sight, to avoid further damage to his church.

Occasionally, while waiting, J.J. strolled to the open door of the back hallway. He couldn't hear the conversation, but he could see Dougherty was on the phone. Obviously, they were in contact with someone. Probably a senior claims representative at the insurance company. At this level of proposed settlement, J.J. knew, the call would be to the home office, in New York. When he looked again, he saw the bishop was personally on the phone, too.

It was forty minutes before Dougherty and the bishop returned. They looked drained.

This time, Dougherty did the talking.

"Your Honor, if the defendants offer $1,250,000 for each of the boys, Juan and Felix, will you approve that amount in full settlement of all claims that they may have?"

"If it is recommended by Mr. Rai, yes," replied the judge.

All turned to J.J.

"Do you recommend it?" Dougherty asked.

Full house, J.J. thought. Then he answered, "Yes."

"Then I am authorized to offer $1,250,000 for each boy in settlement of all claims that they may have and for a full and complete release of the Catholic Church, the Diocese, and all of its representatives, officers, agents, attorneys"—Dougherty looked at J.J. with the inclusion of attorneys—"and employees, arising out of any claims of molestation, abuse, the death of their father, or any other matters."

The judge looked to J.J. J.J. nodded. The judge wrote on the morning docket and then stated: "Having read the reports and heard the evidence, I will enter a Minute Order approving the settlements for the children identified as Doe 1 and Doe 2 in the amount of $1,250,000 each for a full release of all claims of every kind whatsoever against the defendants. Mr. Dougherty, you will prepare the appropriate releases and deliver them to Mr. Rai."

"Now," said the bishop, anxious to resolve all matters, "that leaves remaining only the claim of Carmen. Can we settle her now, J.J.?"

"There is also the possible claim of the surviving spouse, Mrs. Sanchez, I believe," said the judge.

This time it was Dougherty with the surprise. "We considered that possibility, Your Honor, especially as Mr. Rai was making his claims in the media. We have already settled for a confidential amount with Mrs. Sanchez. Since she is an adult, that does not need court approval. She has been taken care of."

The bishop was right: Sometimes, J.J. underestimated Roland Dougherty. All J.J. could do was shake his head. He knew what had happened. She'd been bought off cheap. Poor, devout, silly woman. Whatever it was, he could have gotten her so much more, he knew. So did Dougherty. Maybe that was one of the phone calls in the hall, J.J. thought. Maybe they had even gotten to her when the priest had rushed her off in the car, with the children, as her husband was still hanging from the cathedral. He wouldn't put it past Dougherty—or the Church.

"Do you have a suggestion on the value of Carmen's claims, Mr. Rai?" asked the judge.

"More than the boys' since we know for sure that her life has been devastated by abuse. She's been medicating herself with alcohol and drugs, prostitution, stealing, and acting out for—"

"And committing perjury," interrupted Dougherty. "You know we can prove she's lying."

"How?" asked J.J. "The priest confessing his guilt with the boys is admissible evidence; if he denies that he abused Carmen, that would be hearsay, unless he testifies personally, in court. How are you going to get him to do that? He knows if he shows up in court, he'll be arrested. If you want to fly to Mexico for a deposition, I can guarantee you that I will have the Federales and the Sacramento County authorities on hand to arrest him and extradite him. So tell me, how you are going to do it, Roland? Blame the dad, again?"

The bishop interrupted. "How much, J.J.?"

"I can't recommend less for Carmen than her brothers are receiving," J.J. said, looking at the judge.

"Let's talk," the bishop said to Dougherty, getting up and returning to the hallway and their phones. This time, J.J. heard their voices, which were often loud and sounding more desperate. At one point, J.J. heard Bishop O'Brien telling someone on the phone, "You don't understand the damage that this could cause the Church."

When they returned, the bishop asked J.J. to step into the hallway with him for a moment. Dougherty made no objection. When the bishop and J.J. were alone, the bishop said, "J.J., the insurance company is balking. They don't believe Carmen's claim. If she was abused, they think it was the dad. They have the same information that you have, that Father Gutierrez is a pedophile and molester of young boys, and they do not believe that he would have molested a girl, whether we can prove it in court or not. They won't go over $500,000. Give me thirty days to put pressure on them. I need to go back to New York and meet with them personally. I can't do it on the phone."

"Let's tell the judge what's happening," said J.J., putting his hand on Bishop O'Brien's back and guiding him toward the judge's chambers. He purposely made no comment on the bishop's request.

"What do you think, Mr. Rai?" asked the judge after the bishop explained the problem.

"I think the time is now or never. I can't say what Carmen will do once we file suit for her molestation and the death of her father. At this point, however, I recommend $1,250,000, the same as each boy is receiving. Take it or leave it," said J.J., clearly speaking to Dougherty and the bishop, but maintaining eye contact with the judge.

"We'll take it, subject to getting the insurance company to agree," said the bishop.

"No conditions," said J.J. "The insurance company is your problem. Sue it. Do what you want, but after you pay Carmen."

"Gentlemen," said the judge, "it appears that unless you accept the recommendation of Mr. Rai at this time, concerning the proposed settlement with Carmen, there is nothing pending before me. I don't mean to be harsh. Take it or leave it, as you wish, but we need to conclude this hearing at this time."

The bishop looked at Dougherty. Dougherty looked defeated, as if the events of the weekend and his role in them had finally sunk in. He shrugged his shoulders. It was up to the bishop.

"We'll accept," the bishop said finally. "Complete release. She never, ever again can make any claim of any kind against the Church. Right, J.J.?"

"Right, Don," replied J.J., for the first time using the familiar as if they were all friends again.

"Is Carmen in court?" asked the judge.

"No, Your Honor. She is missing, actually. She, too, apparently was very affected by the accusations made on Friday and, I'm sure, by the events of the weekend. Therefore, I would request that the court enter the proposal as a non-revocable offer to settle and to give me a few days to find her and explain the proposed settlement to her."

Now it was Dougherty's turn to object. "We were told 'take it or leave it,' Your Honor. Now Mr. Rai is saying that he's not authorized to make the settlement and wants more time. He wouldn't give us time," Dougherty said, raising his voice and pointing at J.J.

"Are you saying, Mr. Dougherty, that you are rescinding the offer to settle made by the bishop?" asked the judge.

Again, it was the bishop: "No, we are not. You have your time, J.J. Please get a hold of her as soon as possible and tell us that this matter is behind us."

"That will be the Order," said the judge.

"Can we have a confidentiality agreement, Your Honor?" added Dougherty.

"Once the settlements are entered, they are public records. I don't do secret settlements. Sorry," said the judge. "The names of the children, however, will be maintained in confidence as they are minors. Carmen will now be listed as Doe 3."

The judge turned to the bishop. "Bishop, I think you have done the right thing for the Church and for your Diocese. You could have litigated for years, or you could have stepped up to the plate, as you have done, and taken care of this very serious problem for your Church and for these children. I want to commend you on these settlements."

The judge stood, and the participants knew that the hearing had ended. They proceeded out of chambers. The judge held the door. The bishop went first, then Roland Dougherty, and then J.J. As J.J. walked by, the judge reached out and touched his sleeve and said quietly: "Good work, Mr. Rai."

"How did it go?" asked Andy, when J.J. walked back into the courtroom.

"Straight flush. It would have been a royal flush if Dougherty hadn't beaten me to the mom. How was your morning?"

"We have liftoff," replied Andy. "Computers are marvelous things with meticulous memories, able to scan long distances with a single stroke."

"What the hell does that mean, Andy?" J.J. asked.

Chapter 42

It had come to J.J., suddenly, on the boat. A shudder as much as a thought. Andy's description of the bar scene in Mexico, complete with online computers, had sparked the inquiry. Could Father Gutierrez still be in contact with Juan, the abused altar boy who was denying any impropriety? If so, was Juan protecting his abuser, as Sally had said happens, because he was still in a relationship with him? The parents had mentioned, early on, that Juan was always on his computer. Was this the continuing connection through which Father Gutierrez maintained control over Juan? Felix had broken out of the abusive relationship; Juan might still be in it, if only through the computer connection. This might explain his refusal to admit anything or to give up his abuser.

J.J. had to admit that he knew little about computers. That's why he had called his daughter, Rebel, the night on the boat, and asked her if it was possible.

"Dad, where have you been?" she had said. "Of course. They wouldn't even have to email; they could connect through a chat room."

"What is a chat room, exactly?" J.J. had asked.

After a fifteen-minute crash course on computers from his daughter, he had been convinced of two things: first, that technology had passed him by; and, second, that computers were an instrument for good—and evil. That's when he had called the D.A. Now, with Andy's report at court, that "We have lift off," J.J. knew that the police had confirmed the connection.

The District Attorney had listened to J.J.'s recitation of the abuse. As she had followed the story in the newspaper, she had been annoyed, she told J.J., that the bishop had not contacted law enforcement.

"I don't like finding out about child abuse occurring in my jurisdiction by reading *The Wall Street Journal*," she had told him. "It makes me look like I'm not doing my job. Even if the bishop doesn't know there are mandatory reporting laws, I would expect Roland Dougherty to know better."

"What can I say? The Catholic Church invokes the First Amendment 'free exercise of religion' to claim discipline of priests is its exclusive right. You know, hate the sin, love the sinner," J.J. had told her.

"We'll show them," she had told J.J, "when we get that little stiff-collared butt-fucker back within my jurisdiction," displaying the strong language of an experienced prosecutor who had spent her career around cops and the criminal justice system—a side of her disguised by a pretty, petite body and an electable smile.

J.J.'s call had been welcomed. When the D.A. had called him back and set up an appointment, it had been with the lead consultant for something called the Sacramento Valley Hi-Tech Crime Task Force. "You'll like Byron. He's not your normal 'geek.' He's been with the Sheriff's Department for years. He got into computers with the GRS-80 way back when they were sold to the public almost exclusively at Radio Shack. He looks like a surfer dude who would be more at home on a big board or at a beach bar than in a computer lab."

J.J. had sent Andy to the meeting to work with Byron while J.J. was in court.

The search hadn't taken long. "Father Ramon" had been found in an advanced search of chat rooms, news groups, blogs, and sites frequented by pedophiles. "I didn't even have to do it with an IP address; he's using his real name," Byron had told Andy. "I found him with Coprenic; it searches beyond Google, but anyone can use it." Like hundreds of other perverts, this one had been open and available. He hadn't been hiding. He had been trolling.

"One out of four kids on the Internet is going to get propositioned at some point," Byron had told Andy. "And right under their parents' noses. These guys don't have to hang around school yards anymore. They have a direct line into kids' bedrooms while the parents are down the hall watching television in the den."

"Can't you shut them down?" Andy had asked.

"No. In cyberspace there is no 'there' there. The only way is if they come out of their hole," Byron told him.

"So, how do you get 'em to come out?"

"Bait. Warm, young meat."

"Isn't that risky, with a kid?"

"A kid is not involved. One of our people becomes the kid on the Net. That's why it would be good to have Juan's computer. We'll become him. We'll even use his spelling, his phrasing. Slowly, we let the perv set the trap. We call it cybersnare," Byron had told him.

By bringing in the District Attorney while the civil case was still going on and informing her of the criminal aspects, J.J. had caused the matter to become a criminal investigation. He had wanted the information only law enforcement could get—possibly as leverage against the Church in his civil case—but also in a way he wouldn't have to disclose his theory about the computer contact. Since it was the District Attorney who would be getting a criminal subpoena, entirely outside of the civil process, Dougherty would not necessarily know, unless he got wind of the police taking the computer. J.J. hoped that aspect could be buried in the general search of Juan's room so that not even the Church would know that the focus was upon the computer. Now the civil case had abruptly ended with the settlement, so, even if he had wanted to, J.J. couldn't stop the criminal investigation. He didn't want to.

Andy took J.J. to the headquarters of the Sacramento Valley Hi-Tech Crime Task Force to meet Byron or, as he was known throughout the community, "Cybercop." The Task Force, originally housed in the county jail building, then at the work release building, now had acquired its own one-story headquarters, beyond the Sacramento city limits and out in the county. Ironically, J.J. noted, the facility devoted in part to fighting pornography and perversion on the Web was located—he calculated with his odometer—1.7 miles from and on the same street as one of Sacramento's busiest topless bars, which boasted at least thirty cars when they drove by at two o'clock in the afternoon. And, perhaps because it was guarding "cyber" instead of real space, the Task Force facility apparently did not warrant any of the physical security precautions of the Federal

Bureau of Investigation housed immediately next door, with its electric gate and guards and cameras that could read a license plate a mile away.

To J.J., the Task Force offices looked like any government office, even a Department of Motor Vehicles, with its cubicles. On closer exam, however, he noticed that most cubicles had at least two and as many as four or five computers with LCD screens lined up in series with multiple printers. Byron saw J.J. peeking in the carrels. "Let me take you on a fast tour," he said. In order to decide on which presentation to give, he asked, "How much do you know about computers?"

"I do email—so I can communicate with my kids. I can Google. That's about it."

"Well, if you can type, send email, and Google, then you know enough to meet a pervert on the Web. Or for them to find you."

The first room they entered—or actually stood at the door in order to preserve the "chain of evidence" requirement and not contaminate evidence in the room—was the forensic lab.

"This is where it all happens," Byron proclaimed. "No matter what they do with it, no matter how much they think they've erased, if we have a computer hard drive, we can almost always find what we're looking for. We can trace where they've been, the names they've used, the conversations they've had, and, despite screen names designed to hide, proxy service, anonymizers or dead ends off-shore and elsewhere, we can find them. But it's because they think they're anonymous—and they are to most people—that they're so bold. But, like all criminals, they make mistakes."

"I thought I could erase or delete things or put them in the trash," J.J. said. "My son showed me how."

"I can retrieve anything with enough time and money. You have to understand computers are just ones and zeros; positive and negative, everything is in temporary space. Say you burn or shred a document. There are still ways to read it or put it back together. 'Delete' just means the space is available to be written over. Even with a new message on top, the positives and negatives don't cover exactly the same space. Fragments of the old message remain, usually enough to piece together clues, if only with an electron microscope."

"But even if you know what was said, how do you find the sender?"

"If he's perfect every single time, we don't."

"That wasn't the answer I expected. I mean this technology is impressive."

"Yeah, but it goes both ways," Byron said, laughing. "A perv can trace back our IP address—it's the number that appears on every email and identifies the user—and locate us by longitude, latitude, town, and neighborhood. If we give a street address in a decoy setup, the perv can run a check on Google Earth Search and look at the address from a satellite. For $80 bucks, he can do a fly-by so tight he can read the license plate of a car in the driveway."

"This doesn't sound promising."

"Like I said, they make mistakes. One time, I had this perv checking the email of a young girl he had taken as a sex slave. I sent her an email. When he opened it, in another state, I had him, since anyone reading email leaves an IP address back to the sender. I sent the cops to his house, and they found her in his basement."

"So is that the main thing that you do here—track pedophiles on the Internet?"

"No, that's part of what we do. However, this group involves over fifty-four agencies, starting with local police, sheriff, and D.A. and going all the way up to the FBI, Justice Department, Customs, and every conceivable law enforcement or governmental regulatory agency in between—you name it—as a coordinated effort because hi-tech crime knows no boundaries. People commit bank robberies, breaking into the bank just like an old-time criminal, but with a computer, and instantly transferring the money through a series of accounts into a final destination, somewhere in the world—and all from a keyboard, without ever leaving home. They can hack into credit card sites or a warehouse to have cargo sent to them or a million different things. Virtually all businesses now rely upon computers. They are all vulnerable, to one degree or another. The list is endless. But the use that is so prevalent and open is pornography, solicitation of sex, and, specifically, solicitation of children. Any kid can access pornography, and every kid on the Internet is a target—even when he doesn't go looking—of these perverts."

They walked over to a cubicle, and Byron sat in front of four computer flat screens that were lined up side by side. They were all on the Internet, available to receive a command from Byron. "These are dual monitors on each PC, so we can do two things at once. I can be talking to a pervert on one, tracing back the person on the other, talking in a chat room as a third person engaged in a conversation—or even talking to myself—and staying in touch with another law enforcement agency with whom I might be working on a particular matter. We always have the printers available, so I can print anything at any time for a continuing chain of evidence to use in court as these conversations progress."

Byron hit a key and, as he did, said, "Sit down, I'll give you an education on pedophiles on the Web."

"We'll go into Instant Messenger. You can do this on Yahoo, AOL, any of them. He typed in "Sara, 14, home sick, lonely, chat" and hit the "send" button. Within thirty seconds—he counted out loud—six hits came back.

"Hi Sara. I am lonely, 2."

"Hi Sara. What are u wearing?"

"Sara, u sound sick. Want to play?"

Byron punched in the response, "I'm only wearing panties."

Immediately—three seconds—the reply flashed. "Do you have a video cam?"

Another image entered the scene, seemingly uninvited. It was of a naked man, maybe forty, clean cut, handling himself.

"This is disgusting," said J.J. "Do kids really do this?"

"Yeah, it usually starts out innocent enough, but they get drawn in. Sometimes with a promise of money, clothes, or the newest gadget from Best Buy."

"Jesus."

"Some kids play with these guys. Like the one who asked if 'Sara' had a video cam. If we played him along, he would probably purchase one for us and send it so he could then see 'Sara' in her panties. After that, he might send lingerie or a dildo."

"I never knew it was so easy."

"Nor do most parents."

As Byron spoke, he punched six letters into a search engine, and immediately the "official" homepage of NAMBLA came up. The lead article was about the "persecution" of that loving pedophile, Father Paul Shanley of Boston, "wrongfully convicted" for loving boys too much. In other articles, young boys "spoke out" in defense of their relationships:

"He really listened to me; not like my parents." Morgan, age 13

"It shouldn't be a crime to make love." Terry, age 11

It appeared that the pedophiles of NAMBLA didn't disclaim the name for their "pedophile" perversion, but wore it as a progressive badge. After all, Socrates had been a pedophile went the explanation on the group's website.

Man/Boy Love can be positive beneficial and satisfying to both as long as it is consensual. Studies show that it is not the pedophile that causes injury but the inappropriate anti-sexual attitudes of parents, police, psychologists, lawyers and the like. Damage to children from consensual sex with adults is 'an urban myth' created by hysteria.

Another site spoke of "Club Ped," which turned out to be a so-called orphanage in Bangkok acting as a front for child pornography and sex. Young boys were being provided to sex tourists.

Byron hit another key, and the screen displayed "An Open Letter To Children" from the Pedophile Liberation Front.

J.J. had never seen anything like it.

"Why you shouldn't tell anything," began the letter to children. Because "your friend might go to prison for life and his life would be ruined. You wouldn't want that. And you, well 'you go to therapy' and they keep asking you questions until you get upset, and they will 'calm you down' with drugs and 'you become a sick person.' So, don't tell adults about doing things with your special friend."

"I never knew it was so blatant," said J.J.

"You wouldn't believe it. Now there are teachers, ministers, businesspeople united together—Molesters, Inc. They really do incorporate as non-profit corporations—in their perversion. They are available 24/7 on the Net. Welcome to cybersex. And these Man/Boy guys peddle it as free choice, a loving relationship, with a consenting nine-year-old! Right. Their slogan: 'Sex by 8 or it's too late.' What does that tell you about informed consent?"

The screen went blank, and Byron stood up.

"Get me this kid's hard drive, and I'll tell you everything you need to know. A priest? Jesus! I'll find him and give him what he wants. That spider will leave his web to come looking for a meal."

Chapter 43

"Sally Conrad on the phone," Natalie announced.

It was Wednesday, and the media was still carrying stories of the death of Mr. Sanchez at the Cathedral of the Blessed Virgin. Bishop O'Brien was repeatedly reported as comforting the family. In fact, Mrs. Sanchez had quietly taken the boys and moved back to Delano, where she intended to bury her husband. No one had seen Carmen since she had walked out of court the previous Friday. *The Wall Street Journal* was the only newspaper that carried the full story of the settlement: "Church to Pay Millions to Abused Children." It carried, of course, the dateline of Sacramento and the byline of Maureen McReynolds. Where is she getting her information, he wondered, as he had not revealed the amount of the settlements. Not that he was above leaking information. He just did not want Carmen to read about the settlement in the paper until he had a chance to talk to her and explain it fully. Maureen McReynolds had said that she fully expected him to ditch her for the good of the case. He couldn't blame her, in turn, for running an exclusive story that she had obtained from another source. She had never agreed to pass up a story any more than he had agreed to take an action not in the best interest of his clients.

"Sally, I'm sorry about our last conversation," J.J. began. "I wasn't blaming you."

"She's here," said Sally, ignoring his apology.

"Who is?"

"Carmen. She was waiting for me, once again, when I came in this morning. I thought you would want to know. She's safe."

J.J. was both surprised and relieved.

"I really need to talk to her. Can she come by my office?"

"No guarantee that she wouldn't change her mind on the way. Maybe you should come here."

J.J. thought quickly. He made it a rule never to meet alone with a client, or even a witness, in an abuse case. After all, these were people who had accused or were about to accuse someone of sexual abuse. The next accusation could have been against him if he met alone with a witness or client. Protection. Always have someone present. A secretary. A young associate attorney. Or, better yet, he thought, the person's therapist. Why not? "I'll be right over."

Sally's office was on the second floor of a remodeled house divided into professional offices overlooking McKinley Park. The chairs, located toward the back of the room, spared Sally and her patients the view of the road and, instead, gave them a view of the duck pond, the joggers on the trail once used by President Bill Clinton during a visit to Sacramento, and, beyond, the rose garden. It was a soothing vista.

When J.J. entered Sally's office, the inner door to the counseling room was open. He could hear voices.

"Sally?"

"In here."

He entered to find Sally sitting, her feet folded under her as he remembered she did in therapy, a cup of coffee in hand. Carmen was sitting across from her, on the couch, her feet similarly positioned. She appeared relaxed.

"Hi, Carmen," he said.

"Hello, Mr. Rai," she said politely.

"I'm sorry about what happened in court last week. I had no idea that they would make accusations against your father."

"I know. It's not your fault. I should thank you for all that you've done for my brothers and me."

"Well, I need to talk to you about that. Do you mind if we discuss all this in Sally's presence?"

Carmen looked at Sally. "No, not at all. I've been telling Sally I would like to see her regularly to help me deal with all of this. So I guess we can start now, since it looks like I can afford her." She allowed a smile with the statement, more of irony than happiness.

"Let's start with the proposed settlement," he said.

"What do you mean 'proposed?' I read in the paper that I am going to get over a million dollars."

"'Proposed' just means that you need to understand and agree to the settlement before the judge approves it. Since you weren't around, I worked out the settlement for the boys and you, but there was no one to agree on your behalf. If you accept this, you can never sue the Church, the priest, or anyone else for the alleged abuse, ever again."

"What do you mean 'alleged abuse'?" said Carmen, putting her feet on the floor. "You still don't believe me, do you, Mr. Rai?"

She seemed to become, suddenly, both defensive and combative.

"'Alleged' only means that the Church does not admit liability, and the term is used to refer to any claim that you might make in the future relating to similar or other abuse that you might claim occurred in the past involving anyone else in the Church. That's all. It's standard language."

"When do I get the money?"

Now, this is the old Carmen, J.J. thought.

"It will be placed in a trust, subject to court supervision, until you are eighteen. Obviously, that's only a matter of months. Then you get it. All of it. Unless, of course, you would like me to assist in setting up annuities or some other form of structured settlement so that it can provide for you over your life. I would recommend that. I'm going to make a similar recommendation for the boys, and I expect the court will adopt it for them. I will be personally involved, supervising their care, treatment, education—as much as I can as an attorney—since they are so young. But with you, however, since you are seventeen, it really is up to you."

"What do you think, Sally?" Carmen asked.

J.J. was a little surprised. He fully expected that she would demand the cash, immediately.

Sally took a sip of her coffee. "I think perhaps the idea of spreading it out over time and giving you a guaranteed income for life, for college and other things, makes sense. Perhaps Mr. Rai could put together some proposals. I think it would be wise of you to consider the concept."

Carmen nodded her head. "Okay," she finally said, "but I do want it settled, now."

J.J. had prepared a petition acknowledging the settlement for her to sign. He handed it to her. She signed it without reading it. He put it in a folder and leaned back in his chair.

"Now that the litigation is concluded, Carmen, and you are about to start therapy with Sally, don't you think it's time you told the truth?" he said, looking directly at her.

She stared back, unflinching. A slight smile crossed her face.

"Mr. Rai, if you didn't believe what I said, you wouldn't be sitting here giving me over a million dollars of the Church's money, and the Church wouldn't have paid it, now would they?"

"Unless the bishop had no choice," J.J. replied.

Sally was watching both of them. She saw a slight twitch in Carmen's smile.

"Your dad didn't know anything about any of this, did he, Carmen?" J.J. said.

She didn't answer.

"And Father Gutierrez never raped you, did he?"

Again, she didn't answer.

"In fact, Father Gutierrez showed no interest in you whatsoever; isn't that true? For your information—and the Church knows this but nevertheless agreed to settle with you—Father Gutierrez has no interest whatsoever in little girls, just little boys like your brothers."

"I was raped! I was molested!" Carmen suddenly shouted. She looked like she could jump from the couch and thrust a knife into J.J.'s heart.

"You don't know what it was like. I tried to tell my parents. I didn't want to come to Sacramento. I begged my father not to bring me. He didn't listen. I left things out for my mother to find. She never asked. She didn't want to know. I had nowhere to turn. He was a priest. My parents were honored that he came to our home—honored that he showed attention to me. And then, when I started getting in trouble, they appreciated that he bailed me out, got the charges dropped, or brought me home from a drunk or drug trip. No one would have believed me. But when it happened to my brothers, they believed them. Well, I was abused, too."

She took a deep breath and seemed to collapse into the couch.

"I know you were, Carmen. Sally convinced me of that," J.J. said softly. "I believe you. But why did you lie about Father Gutierrez?"

"What difference does it make? They're all the same."

Sally's head jerked at these words and she asked, "Who did this to you, Carmen?"

Again, Carmen didn't answer. She looked at Sally as if pondering whether to say the words out loud. J.J. did it for her.

"It was Bishop O'Brien," he said, maintaining his gaze on Carmen for a sign of submission. He saw none. So he continued.

"You saw your chance when the boys were abused and Father Gutierrez was blamed. The priest fled to Mexico, and the Church admitted that he was a child molester and offered the boys money. You decided that you were entitled to compensation from the Church, too, for what had happened to you. Since the Church was willing to give money to your brothers, without a fight, you figured that Bishop O'Brien would be only too happy to include you to keep you quiet. Right so far, Carmen?"

Carmen looked at J.J. and then at Sally.

"I never thought they would accuse my father," she said, finally. "Oh, my God. I never knew that they would do that to him. And then he goes and hangs himself. It was like a warning to me. That they would do anything to protect Bishop O'Brien."

Sally left her seat and, in a move J.J. thought uncommon for a therapist, put her arms around Carmen.

"I thought they would just give me some money. I never wanted a lot—I thought maybe $25,000—like they were talking about in the beginning for the boys. Mr. Rai, when they started talking hundreds of thousands of dollars, it was too late. I couldn't change my story. Who would have believed me? After my father died, I damn well couldn't say, 'No, it wasn't my dad; it was the bishop,' after I had already said it was Father Gutierrez, now could I?"

"You're right, Carmen," J.J. said. "That's why they settled. They are paying you off. If you had decided to refuse the settlement and sue, saying that it was Bishop O'Brien, no one would have believed you, since you had already lied about Father Gutierrez. But it would damage Bishop O'Brien and the Church just to have you make the claim. This settlement releases everyone, including Bishop O'Brien, which in a way is why I have no ethical problem with your settlement. As far as I am concerned, it is for the bishop's conduct that you are being paid this money, and he is included in the release. You can't sue him later. You don't need to. The Church is paying you for the molestation regardless of which priest did it. That's the way I see it."

Carmen seemed relieved finally to have someone accept the truth.

"All the things I said, Mr. Rai, about being raped, everything, it was all true—but it was Bishop O'Brien who did it. He would come to my room. It was as if my mother got the kids out and set it up so no one would be there when she went to Bingo. He would come over and do the things I said. I would lie in the dark, knowing he would be there a little while after she left. It was like a movie, slow motion, and I'd be watching from the ceiling. I wasn't part of it. It was happening to her, the girl in the movie—not me. When I would see him later, we'd never talk about it. Most of the time, I tried to stay drunk or on drugs or under some other man who would give me money to lie on me while I watched from the ceiling."

She pulled out a cigarette and looked at Sally. "I'm sorry," she said and fingered the cigarette instead of lighting it in Sally's office. "I'm a mess."

"What are you going to do now?" J.J. asked.

"I don't know. My mom and the boys have headed down to Delano. I don't think I can go with them." She shook her head. "You know, Mr. Rai. I don't really know my brothers. Father Don started with me in Delano when I was about ten. I started drinking when I was eleven or twelve. I don't think I've been sober or clean a week since. I don't really remember the boys. One day, they were ten like I had been except they were going off to be altar boys. By then, I'd had it with the hypocrite priests. But not my mother. She kept on having Bishop O'Brien to the house for dinner. She will never admit that he could do anything wrong. Her bishop. He chose her family. She knows. I was offered up."

Carmen looked at Sally. "Funny, ain't it? I was his Blessed Virgin."

The room was silent. J.J. thought he saw a tear run down Carmen's face, but it quickly disappeared as she threw her head back and laughed: "I guess I showed him."

Chapter 44

Sally Conrad excused herself to walk J.J. out.

"J.J., I hope you have no problem with this, but I am planning on taking Carmen home," she said, as they reached the hallway outside of her office.

"You mean for dinner, or what?"

"No, I mean to live with us—indefinitely. Right now, she is very vulnerable. She is potentially a danger to herself. I am not comfortable leaving her alone, and I am even less comfortable pulling a 5150 on her and placing a mental health hold. It might sound old-fashioned, but I think she just needs a mother right now. And I seem to be the one she has repeatedly chosen. Not that I am the best choice. But maybe I am all she has."

"Jesus, Sally. As you have always told me, you hate children."

Sally laughed. "Well, that's still true, but Carmen is special. She is a child who's been robbed of a childhood. She seems so mature and self-confident. Even cocky. But there is still a little child in her who just wants to be loved."

"I repeat, you hate kids."

"Look, I'm as confused about this as you are, J.J. Maybe at our age, I've given up on social justice, saving the world, and think maybe it would be satisfying to save just one child."

"What does Rose say?" J.J. asked, referring to Sally's partner.

"Funny you should ask. She told me—and I didn't know this—that she had wanted children when she was married and thinks taking Carmen in would make us a more complete family. It doesn't hurt, either, that both Rose and Carmen are of Mexican heritage. Hell, they can pass for mother and daughter. Explaining me will be the problem."

J.J. thought about it. Explaining two lesbian women taking in a young girl could become *his* problem. Sally seemed to sense J.J.'s hesitation.

"We are not talking adoption, J.J. Nothing legal. Just a place to stay, off the street, for now. Maybe we can provide a little stability, a sanctuary from harm—and some parenting—as long as she is willing."

"Have you discussed this with Carmen?"

"Not yet. I wanted to ask you first."

"Well, the court only has jurisdiction over her money, not her, and even then only until she's eighteen. After that, she's an adult and can do as she pleases."

"I told you, I have no interest in legal proceedings. I don't want to have anything to do with her money. You advise her on that. I guess what I'm asking, J.J., is do you approve?"

His expert psychological consultant-turned-witness and the primary proponent of Carmen's claim was asking whether she and her lesbian partner could take a seventeen-year-old abuse victim-turned-millionaire home in a clergy abuse case that had garnered national media attention. There were so many angles from which to consider this potentially explosive development.

"You know she lied about Father Gutierrez?" J.J. said.

Sally waived her hand dismissively. "Lawyers. You are so hung up on what you call the truth that you lose track of reality. She was abused. As a child, she did the best that she could to tolerate it. Why would you expect any more honesty of a child than was shown to her by powerful adults? She was taught duplicity. Finally, she used it to her advantage. We therapists would call that progress: the beginning of healing. Striking back. Your system of so-called truth would punish her further for covering up what really occurred. I have no problem with what she did."

J.J. couldn't think of a more convincing response.

"I don't even fault her for using me," Sally added. "In retrospect, her choice might suggest that she felt I was an adult who could be trusted.

So, perhaps, I should be honored that I was of assistance to an abused child."

"But can you trust her?"

"No, but that's the wrong question. The question is 'can she trust me?' If I demonstrate to her that she can trust an adult, perhaps she will have a chance."

"Okay."

"Okay, what?"

"Okay, I approve."

Sally smiled. "Thanks, but in the last few minutes I've worked myself up to where I don't need your approval; but I'll take it."

Then Sally did what she had done with him only once before. She hugged him. The last time that she had done this had been at the conclusion of his own personal therapy with her, twenty years earlier.

"I just hope you don't always dress her in pants," said J.J., attempting to deal with his own personal discomfort.

Sally punched him lightly on the shoulder, laughing, and said, "You have a lot to learn. Haven't you ever heard of lipstick lesbians? Just kidding. Even lesbians have straight kids. It's just not that big of an issue as it is for you heterosexuals. But, to ease your mind, I can tell you, Carmen loves clothes—girly clothes—and shoes that you would never catch me wearing. So, I think you'll approve there, too."

Sally shook her head. "I never thought I'd have a child."

"Me either, Sally—me either."

Chapter 45

*E*ven though Ken Lay had finally been indicted on July 8, 2004, way later than Martha Stewart, Andy hadn't immediately given up on his quest for justice. But working with the Joint Task Force and Byron was a welcome diversion. He and Byron hit it off and, while he was not really of much assistance, Andy was invited to sit with Byron at the computer as law enforcement began its sting of Father Ramon Gutierrez.

"So I could get dates on this thing?" Andy asked.

"Yeah, but it might turn out to be a sixty-year-old guy in his underwear," replied Byron.

"No, that's what they would get with me," answered Andy.

Juan's computer had been in the possession of the Joint Task Force for just days, and Byron had downloaded everything that had ever passed through its memory chip. Byron had also reconfigured its receiving transmissions and set up a proxy so that all contacts would be passed along to a special computer at the Joint Task Force, manned by Byron. Now Byron *was* Juan. He continued using the computer for games and occasional Internet searches, much in the same way that Juan had done. This, he explained to Andy, was in case anyone was watching. He had detected and deleted spyware and thus knew that Father Gutierrez was not the only party to the lurid conversations, even if the others were only silent observers. He began to watch "Father Ramon" in his transmissions to the broad network of pedophiles to which the priest belonged. Naked pictures of young boys were freely exchanged on sites that might exist for days or even hours before they were discovered and shut down while pedophiles moved on, essentially unobstructed, worldwide. Those using cell phone instant messaging or broadband cell phones capable of downloading entire movies couldn't be touched as, unlike computers, cell phones left no content record.

"Jesus," said Andy. "Why can't these guys be normal and subscribe to *Hustler* magazine like the rest of us?"

Father Ramon had shown some discretion in meeting Juan in a chat room instead of using direct email. Also, he had never attempted to have Juan use a video camera with his computer—an addition that might have seemed odd to his parents. Nor did he send pictures of himself and, as best as Byron could tell, did not share pictures of Juan—if he had any—with his fellow pedophiles.

But he had left a religious memento. A rosary. And his messages were draped in the language of the Catholic faith: "Kneel at your bed. Recite the 'Our Father.' Handle the beads of the rosary. Do this in memory of me." A consistent theme was the purity of love: "And the greatest of these Commandments is to love one another as I have loved you."

"It's like brainwashing," said Andy.

"It is, or at least a form of it. The abuser becomes an object of love for the abused," replied Byron.

Byron, logged on as Juan, had been in a chat room for about an hour when the first contact from Father Ramon was received. As requested, "Juan" went to a private chat room. It was instantly clear that Father Ramon was up to date and following events in Sacramento:

Dear Juan. Thank you for not telling of our love. It is our secret. Sacred. Soon, this will be over for you. May your father rest in the Lord's arms. You will be my loving son.

Over two weeks of nights, Byron alluded to and gradually worked up to telling Father Ramon: "I want to be with you."

Byron had discovered on Juan's hard drive that he nightly had frequented a Harry Potter chat room where kids—or persons pretending to be kids—apparently with a common interest in the Harry Potter phenomenon went to talk. Using screen names reminiscent of Potter characters—like "very-serious" this or that or "her-my-knee" number something or "hog-wartz" or "moaning-mona" or some derivation, they seemed mostly intent on insulting each other. But when someone—especially someone like "Father Ramon," who appeared by this monogram as Andy said he had in Mexico, wanted privacy, a PM—private message—alert sprung up on the recipient's computer.

"You have been invited to a private chat, do you accept?" it said.

"Don't think these pervs are in just one chat room," Byron said, as he answered "yes" to the invitation.

"They are chat-scrolling multiple chat rooms at the same time with multiple windows open on their screens. With enough band width, they can have anywhere from five to sixteen screens open, and every one of them operating a web cam. They are looking for the best prey to take to a PM site."

Byron typed:

My mother wants to take us to Delano. I don't want to go. I'll never see you again. Please, don't let her take me away from you, Father.

The object was to get Father Ramon across the border and preferably to Sacramento. But it had to be his idea and on his terms, or he might suspect a trap.

"These guys aren't stupid. But they have a weakness: little boys. So put it together. Let him think he is stealing a little sex slave from the church that just fired him, one in need of a 'Father' to 'love him' now that his real dad is dead," said Byron.

Andy cringed. "Byron, you've been working around these perverts too long. You're sounding like one."

"I know what you mean. It scares me, too, that I can think like them, but if I'm good at it, I get them."

The next night, Byron typed to Father Ramon:

I'm going to run away from home. I know you can't come for me, so I will look for you. I've packed a few things. I won't be able to take my computer so it may be harder to contact you.

The response was immediate.

No, son, do not leave. Let me help you. When are you to leave for Delano?

"The end of the week, Friday," replied Byron. It was Tuesday.

"I will email you tomorrow. Be ready," came the reply, which, while taking ten minutes, kept Andy staring at the computer screen the entire time.

Andy imagined the festivities at La Telaraña in Nuevo Laredo. Father Ramon was about to score a child. Negra Modelo beer all around.

Byron leaned back. "He's nibbling on the bait."

"What do we do now?"

"Wait. It's got to be on his terms, else some defense lawyer will claim entrapment."

On Wednesday evening, Andy was early, arriving at 6:00 P.M. at the Joint Task Force Center. Byron had put in a long day on other matters and had left word that he would return at 7:30 P.M. So Andy excused himself to drive the 1.7 miles to the topless bar on Auburn Boulevard.

"What do you mean, no drinks?" he asked.

"It's the law," replied the topless server. "We have juice."

"What the hell am I supposed to do with juice? Jesus, I can't watch nude college girls, sober. They got dads—or granddads—my age."

He got up, left, and found a McDonald's. If he was going to eat sober, it would be in the company of fully clad young people.

Andy returned at 7:30 P.M., but Father Ramon had not responded.

"He may have gotten cold feet," said Byron, after viewing the screen and seeing no messages.

"Yeah, or a cold dick," said Andy.

"No chance of that. These guys don't need Viagra or Cialis to have a four-hour emergency. They are perpetually hard." He added, as if to signal the start of the evening shift: "Sick motherfuckers."

By 10:00 P.M., Andy had fallen asleep in his chair, and Byron was in his supervisor's office.

"You've got mail," alerted the computer.

It wasn't the regular mail call. Rather, Byron had left the computer on and was signing into the chat room periodically—so as not to look like a cop hanging around for hours. His computer was programmed to speak when a request for a PM or a designated screen name appeared in the chat room.

"I could have had it say 'You've got a sick motherfucker on the line,' but with sexual harassment and hostile work environment laws, I just opted for the usual," Byron had explained.

Andy jerked awake. "Byron! Byron! It's him!" he yelled. Then Andy whispered, "It's him," as if someone was on the other end of a phone line and Andy didn't want him to know he was listening. Byron came over immediately with his supervisor and watched as the screen scrolled its message.

"Damn!" he said as he read the first few lines of the message. It began:

I assume you are in your room. If you haven't already, say good night to your mother, turn off the lights, and wait. In a few minutes, leave quietly. Don't let anyone see you. Go to the Greyhound bus station...

Byron was on the phone, as was his supervisor.

"It's the Greyhound station, 7th and L Streets," barked the supervisor. "Get the decoy to the back of the Cathedral of the Blessed Virgin at 11th and 'K.' Let her walk out alone, in case anyone's watching."

"Check the schedules," Byron was saying.

"No. On the computer. I don't want any cop asking questions at the bus station. What's going out between 10:30 and midnight? And have a helicopter on standby to track the dog."

Andy looked quizzical. "Greyhound," Byron explained.

The computer message continued:

At the gift shop, just inside the café area, you will be handed a yellow bear. Take it to the video games and play "House of the Dead" until it's time for our bus.

"He's coming to get him. 'Our' bus. Do you see that?" said Andy.

"Maybe," said Byron. "Or that's just how he entices Juan to go there. This could be a trial run with someone watching. Isn't there a hotel across from the station, Lieutenant?" Byron asked.

"Yeah, the Hotel Marshall."

"Put someone in there to watch."

"Or he could have traded him off to another pervert," continued Byron to Andy. "A going-away present. We'll have to be ready for all possibilities." He added, "My guess is we'll find out real soon. If he's having the kid ride a bus, it probably leaves within the hour. He doesn't want anyone to miss the child and call law enforcement. That's why he waits till the last minute. He wants to be well ahead of us."

"So what's with the decoy?" Andy asked. "You said 'she'?"

"Yeah, can't use a kid, so the only way for an eighteen-year-old to look like a twelve-year-old boy is to use a girl. We do it all the time. Michelle is a real pro. Actually, she's a college student studying Police Science. Petite. About four-ten. Little boy haircut. She'll be wearing a jacket with a hood and wearing a wire, so we can monitor what's going on. We've had her on standby all week."

"Do you really think he'll show?"

"If the kid is supposed to board a bus, someone's gotta show. While it's easier to get a kid on a bus than on a plane, either way an unaccompanied minor isn't going anywhere without a lot of documentation. It's not likely he had time to forge the necessary documents, to get a kid across state lines, let alone provide a passport to get out of the country. The law against divorced parents kidnapping their own children has seen to that. But even on a bus, intrastate, a kid under fifteen needs parent signatures, designation of person to meet, ID, the works. No, someone has got to accompany this kid for him to get on that Greyhound bus. And, of course, he's got to have a ticket. If it's our priest, we grab him on Michelle's cue, before the bus leaves the depot."

Byron was watching the other screens. The bus schedules came up on one:

Sacramento—Stockton	10:15 P.M.
Sacramento—Reno	10:35 P.M.
Sacramento—San Francisco	11:05 P.M.
Sacramento—San Diego Express	11:10 P.M.
Sacramento—Redding	11:30 P.M.

"The California Highway Patrol reports that it has a helicopter over south Sacramento that can be deployed to assist," his supervisor told him upon returning to Byron's side at the computer.

"I'm going to the van," Byron said, standing and addressing his supervisor. "I'm betting on the San Diego bus. I'll have the computer in the van up in five," he added, as he rushed toward the parking lot. Andy ran behind him.

"Did I tell you I staked out Ken Lay? I didn't have computers, but I did use this device that I could aim at a building or his limo and pick up conversations," Andy exclaimed in his excitement.

"You probably shouldn't tell me about that," replied Byron.

The console of computers lit up as Byron pulled the van out of the parking lot and onto Auburn Boulevard. They headed west, caught the first exit to Highway 80, and sped toward downtown. Meanwhile, on a dedicated channel, Byron followed the events as plain-clothed city police took up positions on foot, near the Greyhound bus station. It was obvious that the agencies affiliated with the Joint Task Force had worked out various scenarios in kidnapping and child abduction situations. No sirens were heard. Rather, an elite group of undercover agents moved into place. Ironically, the Greyhound bus station, in the downtown area, was conveniently located both a few blocks from the Cathedral of the Blessed Virgin and the Sacramento Police Department.

Within the time it took Byron to travel the few miles to the downtown, he heard various officers checking in at their designated locations near the bus terminal. One sat, with a wine bottle in a bag, on the pavement near the entrance—a not uncommon sight around the Greyhound station. Another acted as a more respectable drunk, perhaps even a legislator, leaning upon a woman—a fellow officer—in front of Frank Fat's restaurant, half a block away from the bus depot. A third sat in a car in a parking lot kitty-corner to the depot, which lot, supposedly, if the City Council ever got its act together, would someday be the site of a high rise-building. For now, it was a huge empty parking lot. A final officer sought refuge in one of the taxis parked outside the depot. When he offered to "just sit; I'll pay you," he was told in no uncertain terms by the Sihk cab driver, in a beautiful pale blue turban wrapped to form a triangle at the center of his forehead and showing a bright yellow cloth in the triangle, "Okay, but no jerky-jerky."

All of the officers and Byron could receive on Michelle's wire, but only the officer in the surveillance van monitoring her could speak to her and broadcast to them.

"Michelle is leaving the Cathedral of the Blessed Virgin," was the first transmission from the van. "She's wearing a Raiders jacket, silver and black, with a hat and hood."

Byron looked at Andy. They both knew it was just five blocks from 11th and "K" to the station at 7th and "L." It had been decided that Michelle should travel south to L Street and down to 7th so that she would always be in sight and easier to get to if necessary.

"We prefer one-ways, like L Street. The K Street Mall would be a mess if we had to rescue her," explained Byron.

"In sight," came the reply a few minutes later from officers in front of Frank Fat's.

Byron had reached the underpass on 12th Street and slowed as he entered the downtown. "Where are we going?" asked Andy.

"To Capitol Park. We'll sit at 12th and 'L,' and wait. If they actually leave on a bus, they'll have to go west, to the I-5 onramp near the Crocker Museum, and we'll be just five blocks behind as they start out."

"Michelle is approaching the depot. No subject in sight," came the next announcement.

"Do we have anyone inside?" asked Byron.

"Negative. Wasn't time," came the reply.

"Shit. Someone's gotta go in with Michelle," Byron responded.

"This is wino. I'll go. But I'm gonna have to leave the bottle. Last time, security threw me out."

"Okay," said Byron. "Sit where you can see her, and buy some coffee."

"Michelle entering the depot front door. No subject in sight."

Byron looked at his watch. It was 10:35.

"Wino is in," came the immediate follow-up on the police radio. It was from the officer deployed to the hotel across the street from the station.

The officer designated "wino" kept his head down as if looking at the floor but scanned the café—suitably named the Traveler's Grill— then turned toward the video game area and coughed once as he looked into the gift shop. No one caught his attention. Michelle entered the gift shop area and looked at the stuffed animals as wino ordered a cup of coffee. The café was at least half full with travelers: families that seemed to have all of their belongings with them in beat-up suitcases, a sprinkling of soldiers in uniform, ready for combat, their hair closely cropped, and a young couple, perhaps nineteen, with bedrolls.

A light-rail train turned onto 7th Street, off of the K Street Mall, and from the direction of the Cathedral of the Blessed Virgin. As it passed the window of the depot, wino-turned-coffee drinker radioed, "There is a priest on the light-rail train."

The train passed through the L Street intersection and came to a stop at the station halfway down the block. "Got him," responded the officer in his car in the parking lot. "He's starting to get off." As he said this, he sank down in his car seat and watched the priest exit the train and walk toward the bus depot. At the intersection, each officer acknowledged the subject in sight.

Instead of walking to the depot door, however, the priest turned east, walked along the windows directly outside the gift shop, and looked in. "Shit, he's going to make her out as a decoy in those bright lights," one officer radioed.

"Not if he doesn't know Juan," said Byron, "but get ready to seize him if he runs."

But the priest seemed satisfied and entered the depot. Instead of going to the gift area, he ordered a cup of tea and sat down. He casually looked around, his eyes stopping on the wino, now coffee-drinker, at the end of his table. The officer thought fast.

"Can you buy me a sandwich, Father?" he asked.

The priest said nothing. Rather, he took a gulp of his tea, rose, and went into the gift shop. There, he picked out a yellow bear, paid for it, and handed it to Michelle with a smile but without saying a word. Obediently, Michelle took the bear, went to the video game area, and began playing. The priest returned to his tea cup, picked it up, took it to another table, and sat back down. Occasionally, he looked around.

Various buses, including the San Diego Express, were called as boarding, but the priest sat drinking his tea. At 11:00 P.M., "last call" was broadcast for the 11:10 Express to San Diego. The priest looked at his watch but remained seated. Within a few moments, however, he casually stood, carried his cup to the dirty dish cart, walked over to Michelle, and said, "Let's go Jonathan," as he grabbed her hand. Wino tensed and coughed twice.

"It's not him," said Byron. "It's another priest or someone dressed as a priest, but it's not our perv."

"How do you know?" Andy asked Byron.

"Two coughs."

The priest went directly to the San Diego bus, expressed regret for being late with his nephew, and presented two computer-generated tickets. All of this was viewed through the front of the terminal by the officers from Frank Fat's restaurant, who had moved to a position directly across from the open terminal garage. "It's San Diego," he announced into the transmitter on his lapel.

"You say it was a computer-generated ticket?" Byron asked someone. Receiving an affirmative, he started typing on his computer. He accessed the Greyhound ticket system.

"Can you do that? I mean, legally?" asked Andy.

Byron just passed him a look. Twenty-two names appeared on the passenger list for the bus about to leave. A Father F. Garcia and a Jonathan Garcia, a minor, each had a $56 one-way fare. With another click on Father F. Garcia, the Greyhound ticket system showed that a person with the same name had also purchased a return ticket for a 7:30 am bus returning the following morning from Los Angeles to Stockton.

"They are going to L.A., not San Diego," Byron announced. The San Diego Express obviously stopped in Los Angeles. Makes sense, he thought. If they would have to transfer in L.A., which would mean a delay at the station. Another chance to get caught. This must mean that someone would be meeting "Jonathan" in Los Angeles.

"Sounds like a hand-off to our subject. Let them go. Line up company along the route. I'll follow in the van. Have the CHP helicopter call me on this band," Byron directed. Then he turned to Andy: "Hope you brought a toothbrush; we're going to L.A. tonight."

"Where is Father Ramon?" they heard Michelle, over the wire, ask her abductor as the door to the Greyhound bus closed.

"He's waiting for you," came the reply.

They held their breath at the exchange, neither Byron nor Andy saying anything. These had been Michelle's first words to her abductor. Would he suspect anything?

Apparently, he didn't, for when Michelle next asked if he would like a piece of her candy bar, he answered, "Sure, thank you, Jonathan."

"What if he feels around and finds the wire?" asked Andy.

Byron laughed. "You've been watching too many movies, Andy. We don't tape wires, microphones, and transmitters to the bodies of our decoys anymore. That's Eliot Ness stuff."

"So where is it?"

"In the other half of the candy bar."

They followed the bus through the Valley with a brief stop in Stockton and resumed its course down Interstate 5. The CHP helicopter left them at Lodi and returned to Sacramento. But CHP cars along the route joined in and dropped off, as did county sheriff vehicles, in case backup was needed. The bus was expected to reach Los Angeles at 6:30 A.M. The only further conversation heard from Michelle's wire during the trip down the Valley came a little after 1:00 A.M., two hours into the trip.

"Would you like to put your head on my lap to sleep?" asked a male voice.

Michelle answered, "No."

The silence was next broken just south of Bakersfield, where I-5 meets Highway 99, when Michelle asked: "Where are we?"

"Good," said Byron, "she's alerting us and testing the transmitter before we reach L.A. and letting us know she's okay."

A voice replied from the bus, "Just starting up the Grapevine. We'll be in L.A. in about ninety minutes, if the traffic is not too bad."

Chapter 46

*J.*J.'s phone rang at 6:45 A.M. It was Andy.

"We've got them!" were his first words, when J.J. answered.

"Them?" asked J.J., confused by the statement and the end of a recurring dream in which he had overslept for a college final exam.

"Yeah, these pervs work in tandem. Father Ramon had a fellow perv get the ticket and ride with our decoy to L.A. Ramon drove up from San Diego in a rental car—we had all the computer stuff on that, too. Can you believe he used a Diocese credit card? Anyway, we got them."

"We? I thought this was a law enforcement matter," said J.J., now waking to the news and Andy's obvious excitement.

"Well, Byron—'cybercop'—let me go along. When this little fellow-fucker started running, I ran after him and tackled him. You won't believe this: He started crying. A guy in a priest's outfit—he wasn't a real priest, though—and he's crying, and he wets himself right there in the Greyhound station. A crowd gathers, and people start shouting at me for beating up a priest. Jesus. If they only knew. There were even three nuns looking at me funny. I was worried maybe they were homos in habits working with the pervs, but it turned out they were real nuns. Good thing someone checked because I was getting ready to roll into them like a bowling ball into pins. I didn't know nuns rode Greyhound. I thought they used company cars."

"Why didn't you call me sooner and tell me you were pursuing Father Ramon?"

"You know me. When I'm after my man, time stands still. Sorry."

"But you got Father Ramon, too?"

"Yeah. You should have seen his face when Michelle—she was the decoy—looked up from under her hood. Up to that point, he had been smiling as he walked toward her. The other priest was holding her hand. They didn't realize it wasn't Juan—or even that it was a girl. As soon as Ramon saw Michelle's face, he knew. He didn't even try to run. Just stood there knowing he was about to be arrested. And he was. The LAPD was on top of him."

"What was he wearing?" J.J. asked "I mean, did he have his clerical clothing?"

"Yeah, collar and all. Can you believe it?"

"Did he say anything about the boys?"

"Not a word. The only statement he made was to ask the police to contact the Mexican Consulate when the officers took his Mexican passport away."

"You might tell your contact to make sure the Mexican Consulate is notified. There have been some recent cases where Mexican citizens have successfully appealed because of our failure to contact the Consulate when they were arrested. Apparently, it's part of some treaty or international agreement. We don't want this guy getting off on a technicality. The fact that he asked suggests that he knows and is already planning his appeal.

"Great work," J.J. added.

"Yeah, well, if I had all this hi-tech stuff that these cops have, I could have gotten to Ken Lay before he was indicted."

"Well, Andy. I'm not sure, but I have the impression that there is more celebration in heaven upon the arrest of on errant priest than upon the assassination of a dishonest businessman."

"Yeah," said Andy, apparently resigned to his failure. "You're probably right. Not that either of them is going to heaven. Ken Lay doesn't know this, but getting indicted probably saved Kenny Boy's life."

J.J. smiled. "Come home, Andy."

Chapter 47

*I*t had taken three weeks, and when he knew the sting operation was successful, J.J. placed two calls. The first was to Maureen McReynolds of *The Wall Street Journal*; the second was to Bishop O'Brien.

When she came on the line, he inhaled as if breathing the smell of her hair when she had walked by him at the door of the courtroom. Since he had her direct line, he had not been announced, and in the pause after she said "Hello," while he thought about her, she must have sensed that it was him calling.

"J.J.?" she asked.

"I promised you an exclusive story. I can now tell you. Father Ramon Gutierrez has been arrested in Los Angeles last night. He was arrested shortly after crossing the U.S. border for the specific purpose of meeting our altar boy, Juan. He had arranged transportation on a Greyhound bus from Sacramento to Los Angeles. He intended to take Juan back across the border, into Mexico, and continue his molestation of the young boy. Unknown to him, however, this was a sting operation we set in motion some weeks ago, during the trial, through the district attorney's office, designed to lure him back so he could be arrested. Sorry I couldn't tell you sooner, but we had to give it a chance to work."

"Wow," she said. He could hear her typing quickly on the computer. He wanted to interrupt in order to ask about her, including how she had known it was him on the phone. Had she been waiting for his call? Thinking of him?

"Has there been any public announcement on this? About the arrest? Any of the details?" she asked.

"No, and there won't be until tomorrow. I have been working with the District Attorney, and she will make the announcement when Father Gutierrez is returned to Sacramento tomorrow and booked in the county jail. She's up for re-election and wants to do it personally. To line up sufficient media coverage, she agreed to put it over until tomorrow. She knows that you have the exclusive and that you'll probably run it tomorrow morning. She didn't want me to give it to the local papers because that would scoop her with her press conference. But a *Wall Street Journal* story, she figures, will just bring more media to her press conference tomorrow. So, you can see, it's working out for everyone. She even gave me copies of the police reports with the whole chronology of the operation. I'll be faxing them to you later this morning with my own summary, so you should have everything by 3:00 P.M. your time. If you need any further information—or a good quote—I think you have all my numbers."

Maureen laughed. "Well, I appreciate your efforts on my behalf. I figure you owe me one since you didn't give me the settlement figures, and I had to find another source."

"I've been meaning to ask you about that. So, have you been playing Dougherty in this thing also, along with me?"

"Now, J.J., I don't know if you're jealous or just dumb. No, I never got anything from Dougherty. He wouldn't talk to me. So, if it makes you feel any better, you were—are—the only lawyer in my life."

He sensed that her comment had gone beyond the case, and his mind wandered again.

"So, do you have lots of information for me about the priest? What happened? How did they get him? Details, details," she demanded.

"Yeah, there is a lot to tell. It's all in the reports I'm sending. It involves the Internet, pedophiles, sharing of pornographic files between these perverts; it's disgusting. These pedophiles are really organized. I mean, I'm an ex-Catholic, and even to me, this goes beyond pornography to sacrilege when it involves priests. How can these guys believe in God and defile altar boys on the very same altar on which they profess to offer the body and blood of Christ? I just don't understand."

"J.J.," she asked, "why do you expect an organization of men to have any more virtues or any less perversions than any other cross section of humanity?"

"I don't know. I suppose it's because I want to believe in what I was taught as a child, even though as an adult I have not believed. I want to be proved wrong. I want to finally discover that the Church is right, that there is a God, and that all of life is not hopeless."

She laughed, again. "We humans are something, aren't we? Supposedly at the top of the food chain, capable of controlling everything else in the world, and all we do is anguish over the question: 'Is this all there is?' Do you think birds sail on air currents, high above, despairing that life is all there is? It sure would ruin a beautiful view, I would think."

"May I remind you of something else?" he asked, changing the subject.

"What?"

"I won the case."

"So you did; so you did, counselor."

"May I buy you dinner?"

"I think that was the deal."

There was a silence. She broke it. "I will be back in California in two weeks. Why don't we meet in San Francisco."

"Great," he answered, not hiding his excitement. "Just call me when you know you're coming in." He hung up the phone, pleased with himself. Maybe there is life after law, he thought.

The next call was harder. He had given it a lot of thought. Played it out in his head, each time with a different ending. He didn't know which version would make the final act.

"Bishop O'Brien, please. J.J. Rai calling."

He was acutely aware that the person answering the rectory phone was no longer Mrs. Sanchez. Of course, he knew that she had left. The new voice was a man's. Probably a priest, he thought. Not a good time, with all the recent publicity, for the Diocese to be placing a "help wanted" ad.

"J.J.," said the bishop, as he came on the line, "I was going to call you. I wanted to thank you for the very professional way you handled this case. That's why I was pleased that you got involved in the first place. I knew you would protect the children."

"Thanks, Don. I'm glad it's over, too. But the settlements couldn't have happened without your intervention. You know, Roland and I would still be going at each other in litigation, if it wasn't for you."

"Well, Roland was just trying to protect the Church."

"Yeah, well, I think that unquestioning belief of his might be why I've never liked him much. Although, I suppose, in a way, I envy him. But, I just don't believe."

The bishop laughed. "All of us over here are praying for you, J.J."

"I appreciate that. But I don't think it'll do any good. Listen," J.J. said, changing the subject—and getting to the point—"there is a story coming out tomorrow in *The Wall Street Journal*. I wanted to give you a heads-up. I'd like to discuss it with you, personally." He paused to let the last word sink in. "Could you come by after work? Like five o'clock?"

The bishop was silent. Confused. Stunned, perhaps. "Uh—yeah, sure, J.J., if you feel it's important," said the bishop, no longer laughing.

"It's important, Don." They hung up. J.J. sat looking at the phone—and through it—at his fellow altar boy and friend of fifty years.

It was 5:15 when Bishop O'Brien arrived. J.J. heard him enter the reception area. Perhaps, thought J.J., as he looked at the clock, he had second thoughts about coming. Perhaps he knew that J.J. knew.

"Come on back, Don. The staff is gone," J.J. said in a loud voice without leaving his office. He went to the wet bar and, as Bishop O'Brien entered, said, "The usual, Don?"

The bishop seemed to relax. "Thanks, J.J. Why not? I'm off duty."

"I didn't know priests were ever off duty," replied J.J., pouring the Johnnie Walker Scotch and water back.

J.J. handed the drink and glass of water to the bishop and then mixed a gin and tonic for himself. He joined the bishop in the couched seating area away from his desk.

"Here's to altar boys," J.J. said.

"It's been a terrible ordeal for them, I'm sure, these past few months," replied the bishop, sipping his Scotch.

"No, Don. I was thinking of us. When we were kids, at the cathedral. We had no idea things like this existed. Did we dodge a bullet? I can't even imagine what it would have been like to have been molested—by a priest of all people. I would think it would really test one's faith," J.J. said, taking a long sip of his drink. "I wonder how our lives would have been different if that had happened to us, Don."

"Well, the boys seem to be doing fine. We're going to stay close to them and help in any way we can. Maybe overcoming this can even strengthen their faith. I don't know."

"Gee, Don, you sound like Father Gutierrez. Sex between men and boys, he says, can be beneficial."

The bishop adjusted himself in his seat and reached for his water back.

"Well, I didn't mean it that way. I mean, overcoming adversity sometimes can make a person stronger. Look at the saints."

"Jesus Christ, Don. I feel a parable coming on. Save me the experience." J.J. smiled at the bishop to show that he was joking.

They drank in silence for a while. Then J.J. let him have it. Confrontation time.

"Why did you do it, Don?" J.J. asked, while looking at his own drink.

"Do what, J.J.?" The bishop looked at J.J. but broke off the look when J.J. stared at him, hard.

"Carmen. A ten-year-old child. The daughter of devout Catholic farm workers in Delano. Molesting her and then bringing the whole family here so you could keep on molesting her and, finally, raping her. Why did you do it, Don?"

"She told you that, J.J.? Now Carmen claims it was me? Don't you think her credibility is a little thin, J.J.?" the bishop asked, his voice rising, but hesitant.

J.J. kept his voice low; indeed, he dropped it lower. "I'm not talking about credibility, Don. I'm talking about you. I knew it was you before Carmen admitted it."

"What would ever make you think that, J.J.?"

"A priest instinctively puts his hand across his chest when he blesses the congregation. You did it when you raised your right hand to take the oath the first time you testified. But when you returned, after Sally testified about Carmen's scratched face, you did a very unnatural thing. It was just so out of character, Don, that I even drew a picture of it in my trial notebook. It was as if you were at military parade rest, your left hand behind your back."

The bishop was obviously uncomfortable with his left hand exposed, holding his drink, but he could not change hands.

J.J. pointed. "That's right. The bishop's ring. A symbol of your position. After Sally testified about Carmen being raped and slapped, backhanded, and suffering a scratch from a ring, you hid your left hand. The one with the ring. I was stunned. I realized then that it was you who had slapped her. Which meant it was you who had raped her. Then I understood why her mother immediately reported the molestation of the boys by Father Gutierrez to you, but sat silently by when you, the bishop, the family patron, molested Carmen. I also understood why Carmen pleaded with her father not to allow you to bring her and the family to Sacramento from Delano."

The bishop attempted to deflect the discussion. "J.J., it's over. Carmen isn't going to change her story now and risk her $1.25 million settlement. She's a smart girl. Anything she told you is attorney-client privileged, so you are not going to reveal it. You'd be disbarred, too, just like your buddy, Andy Miller. Let it go," the bishop pleaded, as if they could remain friends if J.J. put aside his knowledge.

"I guess I could let it go if it weren't for Carmen's dad. You and Roland set him up as the scapegoat. You knew I'd find out, sooner or later, about Father Gutierrez and his little boy fetish. So you put Roland on the trail of Mr. Sanchez with that phony confessional admission, didn't you?"

"No, J.J. I told you before. That was Roland's bluff. You remember, the old 'I've had impure thoughts' is every boy or man's standby in confession. He just played it in the hope that perhaps Mr. Sanchez would confess to something, even having sexual thoughts about his daughter. I mean, he probably did. She was a well-developed girl at an early age."

"Roland had no need to blame anyone else. It was enough to prove that Father Gutierrez couldn't possibly be guilty of molesting a girl, unless, of course, the real molester was another priest, perhaps even a bishop of the church. No, Don, you directed Roland, even though, I'm sure, you lied to get him to do it."

"J.J., I'll say it again: It's over." The bishop stood up to leave. "Thanks for the drinks, J.J., even if they have cost the Church and our insurance company $3.75 million." He attempted a smile, but he was obviously too shaken by the confrontation.

J.J. got up and went to the bar. He waited for the bishop to take a couple of steps toward the door.

"It's not over, Don. *The Wall Street Journal* will report tomorrow morning that Father Ramon Gutierrez has been arrested in Los Angeles after coming across the border at San Diego and will shortly be returning to Sacramento to stand trial for multiple counts of molestation of the altar boys. It won't mention Carmen. For your information, he is not going to be charged with raping her."

J.J. made a point of looking at his watch as if calculating the travel time.

"Representatives of the Sacramento City Police Department, Sacramento Valley Hi-Tech Crime Task Force, and that disbarred lawyer you mentioned, Andy Miller, should be arriving in Sacramento in the company of Father Gutierrez on a private law enforcement plane sometime around ten o'clock tomorrow morning. The District Attorney is planning a press conference within a few hours of the booking, but certainly before the five o'clock news hour. I'll be standing next to the District Attorney during that news conference."

The bishop turned back and leaned against a chair. "Where are you going with this, J.J.?"

"That's up to you, Don. When Father Gutierrez is brought back, there is going to be a full criminal investigation. The kind that should have happened when you confronted Father Gutierrez but didn't report his confession to the police. I guess you didn't want the police asking questions. Carmen might have said something. So you let him escape."

"That's not how it happened," the bishop said. He sat down. "I had every intention of turning Father Gutierrez in to the police. I had no reason to believe Carmen would say anything. Even when she had been arrested before, with the drinking, the drugs, the prostitution—everything—she had never said anything about us, and I never expected she would. No, I literally picked up the phone when Father Gutierrez admitted molesting the boys at camp. That's when he told me about Juan."

"What about Juan?"

"Juan told him that he had seen me with Carmen in her bedroom some years ago doing the same things that he and Father Gutierrez had done. Juan thought it meant that it must be all right. He hadn't understood at the time and hadn't told anyone. Father Gutierrez convinced him that this, too, would be their secret and that he was not to mention it to anyone, not even his brother." The bishop reached for his unfinished drink, which he had abandoned earlier. "So, when I picked up the phone, Father Gutierrez grabbed my hand and said, 'Fine, I guess we can tell them about you and Carmen, too,' and demanded I put the phone down. He told me about what Juan had seen. I put the phone down." The bishop lowered his head. "Gutierrez said what he had done was no different than what I had done with Carmen except that, with Juan, he was showing his love for a boy. He made no apology. On the contrary, he began to explain the philosophy of man/boy love, how it was historically rooted, how it was beneficial to children and not at all harmful. I didn't want to hear it. It sickened me. I told him to get out." The bishop paused. "He thanked me."

"Did Dougherty know any of this?"

"No; but just in case, I warned Dougherty that Carmen was a troubled girl and might make false accusations for money. When she claimed that Father Gutierrez molested her, I knew that you or Dougherty, or both of you, would soon find out that this wasn't—couldn't—be true, and I was worried about what Carmen might do then. So I went along with Dougherty on attacking her credibility and didn't oppose his confessional ploy. It provided a heterosexual explanation, besides me, if someone still believed that she had been abused. I never expected Mr. Sanchez to react as he did. But when he hanged himself, it gave me the perfect excuse to settle her case, pay her off, and put the lid on the whole mess. People would believe that it was either Father Gutierrez or Carmen's own father who had molested her, and nobody would believe her if she were to change her story later."

J.J. walked to his desk and sat down. He put his head in his hands, then slowly lifted his head to look at his old friend as the bishop asked: "You're not going to do this to me, J.J.?"

When he had made the call to the bishop, J.J. had not known what he was going to do. It finally became clear. Any Deputy District Attorney would conclude, upon evaluating the evidence, that Bishop O'Brien could not be successfully prosecuted and convicted "beyond a reasonable doubt," even if Carmen could be convinced to testify. If she testified that the bishop had molested and raped her, she would either be committing perjury in the criminal case or admitting that she had committed perjury in the civil case—for which she had received $1.25 million. An attorney representing Carmen would have to advise her that if subpoenaed to testify, she should refuse upon the Fifth Amendment grounds of self-incrimination. Besides, how could a jury side with a young woman who had made a false claim that had resulted in a "further" false claim against her father, which had resulted in him killing himself? What a mess. There was really no hope of a successful criminal prosecution. A civil case was out of the question, in that Carmen had already released—for $1.25 million—Father Gutierrez and "The Catholic church, its agents, employees, and representatives," which included Bishop O'Brien. The bishop had seen to that.

"Let me explain something to you, Don. I can and will, if necessary, publicly state to law enforcement and the media the confession of Carmen Sanchez that you, Bishop O'Brien, molested her since age ten and raped her repeatedly before she was fourteen. In fact, I plan on making that announcement at tomorrow's press conference, while standing alongside the District Attorney of Sacramento County. While you may know your Bible well, you do not know the Evidence Code. You are wrong on the law. The statements Carmen made to me were not privileged. She has always been a witness in my cases. I was appointed by the court to represent Juan and Felix. I have never been Carmen's attorney even though, when asked by you, Roland, and the court, what my recommendation would be for her settlement, I gave my recommendation, which was accepted. You paid $1.25 million to Carmen Sanchez, a minor, who was not represented by an attorney and, in fact, did not even have a case pending. So, if necessary, I will publicly make that declaration and let the chips fall where they may."

There was a silence between them. Each of them was obviously looking at his own cards, and it was the bishop's turn to decide whether to raise, call, or fold. Finally, he spoke.

"If necessary?"

"If necessary. I'm going to give you the same deal that you gave Father Gutierrez. Quit. Leave town. Immediately. Tomorrow. The *Journal* story is about Father Gutierrez's arrest. The press conference is—unless it need be about you—about Father Gutierrez's arrest. But, the next day, I can guarantee, the story will be about you. I think it should be a nice story about your resignation." J.J. let the thought sink in. With sarcasm and sadness and certain tedium toward religion and its pronouncements, he added: "Think of it this way, Don. Maybe it will strengthen your faith. After all, you can't think much of a two thousand-year-old church run by people like you: child molesters."

It was over. The gauntlet had been thrown down. They both knew it. The end of a friendship between two men who had shared an experience as altar boys fifty years ago. They would never share a memory or a drink again.

J.J. watched in silence as Bishop O'Brien put down his drink, rose, and left the office.

The morning *Wall Street Journal* carried, under Maureen McReynolds' byline, the story of Father Gutierrez's arrest. The morning *Sacramento Bee* carried a brief, late-breaking story, obviously inserted late in the evening before, in the Metro section, announcing Bishop O'Brien's resignation. It noted that his mother had been quite ill and that he was leaving the clergy to join his brother on a fishing trawler working out of the San Juan Islands, just off Seattle, where his mother was confined to a nursing home. There was no reference to the just-concluded child molestation case or the recent hanging from the bell tower.

The timing of the resignation, however, did not escape Maureen McReynolds' attention.

"Is there a story there?" she asked J.J.

"Absolutely not."

"Coincidence? I think not."

"Well, perhaps we can discuss coincidences on our date. Like how you ever found Sacramento and this case in the first place."

"I never reveal sources."

"I have my ways."

"Oww," she moaned. "I'll see you in San Francisco."

Chapter 48

Faith was on his mind as he sat down to email his daughter. The trial had pitted him against the Catholic Church—the church of his youth—against his friend, and against Roland Dougherty. Rebel had asked why he felt so strongly about Dougherty and the Church. Wasn't it enough just to walk away? Why keep coming back, like a moth to a flame, if there was nothing there for him? And why the anger?

"The Epistle of Dad," he thought of his email to his daughter. On the one hand, it sounded so Catholic—like St. Paul's letter to the Ephesians. On the other, it was reminiscent of Jawaharlal Nehru, for whom he was named, whose 1929 writings to his ten-year-old daughter, Indira Gandhi—who later became India's first woman Prime Minister—were published in a book titled *Letters from a Father to His Daughter*.

J.J. thought he owed his daughter an explanation. After all, he had not instilled in his children a faith in God—and certainly not a religious creed. The closest he had ever come was to tell them, in the first grade, that if any of the other children asked, to say "We believe in the Easter Bunny because the Easter Bunny gives us candy, but God takes it away." This made Rebel a cynical first-grader, who now had graduated from Harvard Law. Had he failed his children? Did he owe them a faith? Or was it for them to find their own? Something about the trial mandated he profess his.

Dear Rebel,

I believe religion is the culmination of human arrogance, a support group dedicated to placing man at the center of the universe.

347

It is not about God; it is about we humans who imagine a God in our own likeness to support our belief in our supreme worth over all around us.

Have you ever noticed what man's Gods have in common? A preoccupation with what man does and thinks. For example, in the Old Testament, God not only has human emotions—he is so like us—he has some of our worst emotions. He gets angry a lot. He pouts. Why? Because man doesn't worship him enough; or man put other Gods before Him; or perhaps man hesitates when God tells him, as a parent, to kill his children. He appears both angry and insecure. His answer, when not properly honored, is to send a cloud to kill an army, or a flood to drown the whole world, except Noah and his family. Being a control freak, he specifies the exact measurements of Noah's boat. His instruction to the Jews on how to worship him includes interior design down to the curtain in the temple. And, get this, after 40 years of walking in the desert leading "his people" out of Egypt, no promised land for Moses.

Of course, this is just what he is doing with humans here on Earth. Obviously, he has to maintain the rest of the universe. Imagine what it must take to direct an expanding universe, moving at an ever-increasing speed, with black holes sucking in light and gravity—and perhaps time—with billions of stars, planets, quasars, nebulas, and the millions of millions of other galaxies, not to mention supervising ever-evolving life forms from fairy shrimp in wetland pools to whales in oceans, beetles in the Sahara, and bacteria in moon rocks.

And there is the matter of answering prayers. Pat Robertson wants a vacancy on the Supreme Court; the kid down the block wants a new bike; and, each side in every war calls upon him for victory.

Of all of those upon the Earth, about 5,000 years ago or so, he chose a small tribe as "his people." Jews. Then, 2,000 years ago, he had had it with the Jews and chose a new people—Christians—and had his own son, Christ—or is it "the Christ?"—executed. But since both of these groups apparently have got it all wrong, God—now with his new name, Allah—turns, in dreams, to his messenger, Mohammed. Islam did relatively well for about 700 years but apparently fell into disfavor. (Don't get me started on the 70 virgins waiting for suicide bombers as a fast-track to heaven.) And these are just the "great" religions. Heaven knows there are many more. So one has to wonder if all of these Gods are multiple Gods or multiple manifestations of the same God? Or are all religions—except one group—simply worshiping the wrong God? Which one?

Why would a God need our approval? Is he really that insecure? Maker of the universe but pathetic and unloved? No, it is all about us—not him.

By creating a God—creator and master of the universe—who is preoccupied with us, we have elevated ourselves to the primary place in that universe. He did it for us, say the catechisms, bibles, and other holy texts. The stars are there—for us. The animals roam the Earth—for us. He is there—for us. He wants us with him, forever. Life is just a test. The warm-up act.

Of course, we have had a stormy relationship with our creator—God. After all, he can smite us at any time, cause the sun to stand still, or condemn us to eternal fire. And he did send his only son—if you are Christian—to redeem the sins of the world (not obeying his commandments) by dying on the cross. Talk about abandonment issues. It's hard to know whether to love him or just fear him. Either way, he offers us something that no other living thing in the universe can achieve: eternity, an escape from death.

Man looks up at the night sky and says, "There must be a reason I am here. Life must have purpose."

The Milky Way. That great spiral galaxy in which we live. Look at its majesty on a dark, crisp, clear night. What is its purpose? If the creation of the universe is about us, was it put there for our evening enjoyment? The planets, too? Even those in other galaxies, hundreds of thousands of millions of miles away that we know nothing about? Those whose light will never reach us in the time our species will be on Earth. No, we are truly inconsequential compared to the beauty and complexity of the night sky.

We cannot accept that we are no different than the dog splattered upon the highway. No, God loves us. He wants us, above all of his creations, with him for all eternity. He will scoop us up and put us back together, and we will reside in his presence forever. We will never—really—die.

I regard religion, in the words of the philosopher Bertrand Russell, "as a disease born of fear and a source of untold misery."

J.J. finished typing. It all sounded so depressing. He saw the source of his anger. He wanted to believe. He faulted the Catholic Church, not for its creed or its faith, but its failure to convince him. He wanted to believe and be comforted by a faith that promised everlasting life—the comfort Roland Daugherty seemed to accept without question. But he could not make that "leap of faith" over a canyon of hypocrisy and superstition.

He needed to add something. Hope. He resumed typing.

We know from DNA science that we are each a part of a long line and that we shall continue into lives hence. Thus, your granddad's Indian philosophy of reincarnation has a scientific basis. He is in you as I will be in your children's children—and as I am in you and your brother. (I know; thank God for your mother's genes.) The universe seems—I say seems because my understanding of science is limited—to be made up of a finite number of chemicals and energy changing form. When I am gone, physically, the energy of the universe will not be diminished, just, perhaps, redirected or changed into another form. And, hopefully, I will be a fond memory, however brief.

A friend used to say that the proof of the existence of God was the artichoke. "Why the artichoke?" I asked. "Why not?" he answered.

I see a universe unbelievably beautiful and complex. I marvel at even the little that we understand, want to know more, feel so inconsequential in it and the brief time I have—and, I believe, humanity will have—but feel no need to invent a God to explain it. I can, finally, accept that much is unknowable. We are human. We are limited. It is what we don't know, and what we fear, that makes us create gods.

If "immortality" is that period when we are not mortal—before and after life—then you and I are destined for immortality. I can live with that.

In the meantime, find joy in every day.

Love,
Dad

Chapter 49

Maureen McReynolds had called, as promised, and J.J. offered to pick her up at the San Francisco Airport.

"It's the least I can do if you are flying in for our date."

"You do flatter yourself, Mr. Rai. Actually, I am coming in to spend a few days with my stepfather. But, a bet is a bet, and I am obligated to have dinner with you."

"That reminds me. When I called you at your office, you knew it was me before I said anything. Had you been waiting for my call?"

She laughed. "Caller ID."

Undeterred, J.J. pressed ahead. "Well, since your plane arrives in the morning, would you like to have lunch, perhaps as a warm-up to our big date? I was thinking of Nancy Oakes' restaurant, Boulevard, near the Ferry Building."

"So you're familiar with San Francisco restaurants I see," she remarked.

"Actually, I'm not. I have to confess I did some research and asked around. I do want to impress you."

"Mr. Rai, I am a reporter. I did my research on you months ago. You might be surprised to know I even read your speech at the 30th Reunion of your Boalt Hall law class, published in *The California Lawyer*. I'm not sure what impressed me most: the idealism you expressed or your relationship with your daughter. Both came through. So, I was already impressed from reading about you—let alone watching you in the courtroom."

She acquiesced in his offer to pick her up at the San Francisco Airport and to take her to lunch at Boulevard, but insisted that she would need the afternoon to spend with her stepfather.

"Sure, I'll be glad to drop you off after lunch," he offered.

"Thanks, but I'd be more comfortable going alone." He hadn't inquired further. After a brief, uneasy silence, he asked: "How is it that an Easterner knows so much about San Francisco?"

"Well, for one thing, I came out to California and went to Mills College and spent a lot of time at my stepfather's home in San Francisco."

"Really? My daughter went to Mills."

"I know. I told you: I know everything about you. I write for *The Wall Street Journal*, remember?"

"Right, and you're going to tell me why a *Wall Street Journal* reporter showed up at my little old hearing in Sacramento?"

"Let's start with lunch and see where this goes, shall we?"

"I can't wait."

That afternoon, Andy called the office. "What did he want?" J.J. asked his secretary.

"I don't know. He said it was urgent," Natalie told him.

"Can you get him on the phone?"

"No. He was boarding a plane for Bangladesh when he called and said he'll call you from there in the morning, our time."

J.J. told her to have Andy call him on his cell phone as he would be heading for San Francisco in the morning for his date with Maureen McReynolds.

J.J. looked at the day planner on his desk and remembered that Rebel would be finishing the third day of the Bar exam that day. He asked Natalie to call for a pizza delivery, at 6:00 P.M., to the San Francisco apartment that Rebel was sharing for the summer. He knew she didn't eat for days when she was on a task and would need protein and carbohydrates as she crashed from completing the Bar exam.

He went home early that afternoon. He realized he was experiencing something akin to the nervous excitement of a young man about to go on a first date. He hadn't felt this way for years. He decided to pack and drive to San Francisco that evening, instead of fighting traffic heading into San Francisco in the morning. He didn't want to miss her flight because of an accident on the Bay Bridge. Better to get to San Francisco tonight. Get settled in. Nice place. Perhaps the Fairmont. A high floor, one of the signature rooms with a view of the Golden Gate, Alcatraz, and Coit Tower. He even allowed himself the thought of sharing the view with Maureen McReynolds. He booked the room for two nights.

J.J. packed a couple of Italian shirts, an Armani jacket and pants, underwear, socks, a shaving kit, and a bottle of cologne he hadn't used in years and left for San Francisco.

The following morning, having enjoyed the evening in San Francisco and the view from the Fairmont, J.J. got to the San Francisco Arrival Terminal early. Maureen McReynolds' plane was late, so he browsed through the bookstore and picked up John Lescroart's *The Second Chair* in paperback. He glanced at the back cover and smiled. An older attorney sitting "second chair" to a young rookie female attorney. This, he thought, could be him if his daughter were ever to try a case with him. Although, both being so stubborn, it would be a fight as to who would be first and who would be second chair. A fight he hoped to have someday.

With the new airport security in place, he waited at the foot of the stairs when he heard that her plane had arrived. She descended the escalator from the security area as if levitating down into his life. He followed her down with his eyes but didn't have the courage to embrace her. He put out his hand to shake hers. She ignored it and hugged him instead, with one hand behind his neck and her face caressing his cheek.

"J.J., thank you for coming," she said. She seemed less than the confident *Wall Street Journal* reporter he had previously encountered. She looked sad.

They went together to the luggage area and waited silently. Finally, she pointed to her suitcase. J.J. retrieved it, and they walked to the parking structure to leave. He opened her door, and she smiled at him but said nothing.

His cell phone rang as they were pulling onto northbound 101 toward downtown San Francisco.

"Dad, where are you? I'm celebrating. And thanks for the pizza last night."

"Congratulations," he said. "It's my daughter," he whispered to Maureen. Looking back ahead and addressing Rebel, he continued. "I trust you passed the Bar?"

"Cinch, dad. Now, I have four days off before I start clerking at the Ninth Circuit."

"Enjoy them. You will be doing nights and weekends for the next thirty years."

"So I will have an excuse not to go to my kid's gymnastics, is that what you're telling me?"

"Hey! Enjoy your four days. Take a break from abusing your father. Go see your mom." He smiled as he said it.

"I am, but I was hoping to have lunch with you. Your office said you were in town. What are you doing in San Francisco, anyway?"

He looked at the woman next to him. "Well, if you must know, I am sitting next to a beautiful woman, a reporter for *The Wall Street Journal*, and we are on our way to an early lunch—at Boulevard."

"Put me on speaker phone," Rebel said.

"Why?"

"Just do it!"

"She wants to be on the speaker," he said to Maureen. "I am not taking any responsibility for what she says."

He put the phone into the cradle and said, "You're on, Reb."

Immediately, Rebel shouted, "Mom!"

Maureen laughed, and her whole composure changed.

"Rebel! Your dad tells me you're a Mills woman."

"Really? I bet he said Mills girl."

"If he had, I would have corrected him. I'm a Mills woman myself, class of '82." She put a hand on J.J.'s arm.

"Great. Nice going, dad. Think you can handle two Mills women?"

"Why would I think that, when I've never been able to handle one?"

"Rebel," said Maureen, "congratulations on the Bar. Why don't you join us for lunch?"

"No, but thanks, though. I mean, if this works out, I'll probably be seeing a lot of you. If not, maybe at the next Mills all-class reunion."

"By the way, I love your name—Rebel. What's the story behind that?"

"Well," began Rebel in a bit of a Texas twang, "my daddy figured he might not always be there when I was growin' up, and things could be rough, and I'd have to be tough, so he gave me this awful name."

"Sweetheart," interjected J.J., "Johnny Cash is dead, and you shouldn't be stealing lyrics from him."

"Shucks, dad, you didn't have to tell her. But, listen you guys, get acquainted. And dad, I'll catch up with you in the next few days."

J.J. felt a little embarrassed, at least for Maureen.

"Rebel, Ms. McReynolds and I are not 'working out' anything. She is honorably paying off a bet by dining with me."

"Right, dad. You won her in a poker game." Addressing Maureen, she added, "He's actually a pretty decent person, for a man. You could do worse."

"I have." Maureen laughed.

"And dad, two things: First, good job on the Sanchez case. I'm proud of you, and..."

"Thanks, Reb. That means a lot to me," J.J. interjected, his eyes moistening.

"Second, this time, get a valid pre-nup. Love you. Bye." The last word she sung as she hung up.

J.J. just shook his head. Maureen was still laughing.

"She's a piece of work," he said.

"I think she's exactly like you."

They drove a few minutes, both of them smiling. Then J.J. reached over and held her hand. "Are you okay? You looked a little upset when you got off the plane."

"Ah, the trial lawyer. Perceptive. I was." She held up the book on her lap: Anne Lamott, *Traveling Mercies—Some Thoughts on Faith*.

"I picked this up at the airport in New York. The subtitle, 'Some Thoughts on Faith,' caught my eye. With this case of yours, one's faith could use a little propping up."

"And did it prop up your faith?"

"It's a wonderful book. But it has a chapter about Lamott's loss of her father. The hole it left in her life. And the lifetime she has spent trying to fill that hole. It just hit home because I, too, lost my dad as a young woman."

She squeezed his hand. "You know, there is a special bond between a woman and her father. I see it with you and Rebel."

A son is a son until he takes a wife;
A daughter is a daughter for the rest of your life.

After reciting the couplet, J.J. said, "That's a line from a card my daughter once gave me. It's absolutely true."

He noticed that she tightened her grip on his hand as she looked out the window at the City.

She could see his reflection in her side window. "Sorry," she said. "I always get a little sad when I come to San Francisco." She turned and gave J.J. a slight smile.

"I came out to Mills College right after my father died. I did it for him."

"Mills? A women's college?" J.J. said. "That was his idea, not yours?"

"Yeah, funny, isn't it? But he said graduates of women's colleges are twice as likely to be cited for career accomplishments as graduates of co-ed colleges. He suggested two years in California and then a transfer back to one of the 'Seven Sisters' women's colleges in the East. He was all for feminism, but, as a dad, he didn't want me gone from him for four years."

J.J. looked over. He could see her eyes were glossed with tears. He looked back at the road, not knowing what he could say about a daughter's loss of her father.

"I was lucky," she continued after a few miles. "My mom called her first husband, and he looked after me like the daughter they never had together. That was my step-dad. So I've had two dads."

She smiled at the mention of her step-dad and wiped her eyes.

"So, how did you ever end up at *The Wall Street Journal*?" J.J. asked, bringing her back fully into the present.

"What? Oh, that. Well, after Mills, I went to law school at NYU. I wanted to be back in New York with my mom and—"

"I didn't know you were a lawyer," J.J. interrupted, clearly surprised.

"I'm not. I mean, I've never practiced, but I did graduate from law school. Then I followed my mom's very impressive footsteps into news reporting. Did I mention she is assistant director of CBS News?"

"No, I think you neglected to tell me that, too."

"Well, after she and my step-dad divorced, my mom transferred from Berkeley to Columbia and graduated in journalism. My dad was a young professor of English literature. They met at an art opening in The Village and joked that I was born nine months later. Anyway, while he took me as a toddler to his lectures, she was traveling the world as a correspondent for CBS News. By the time I was a teenager, my mom had settled down in New York, working on the evening news. Walter Cronkite was just 'Uncle Walt' to me at barbeques in our backyard."

She stopped, as if remembering good times with her mother and father.

"My first job was with the *L.A. Times*. A phone call from her got me hired, although, I must say, I had a good resume and was a good writer. Of course, I covered the local courts, which is what I wanted to do with my law degree. After two years, I was offered a job by *The Wall Street Journal*, and I took it. Now, my scope is national. I travel a lot but usually get to have lunch with my mother at least twice a month in a great New York restaurant. So, it's pretty much been the best of all worlds."

"Which brings me back to how you found me and my little old case in Sacramento."

She looked ahead. "No, that brings us to Boulevard. I'm starving."

J.J. valeted the car and they stepped across the pavement and entered the antique revolving wood doors of Boulevard restaurant.

"Beautiful, isn't it?" she said as J.J.'s look betrayed his first visit to the restaurant.

"Gorgeous."

"And to think, it was almost destroyed in the 1906 earthquake," she said. "The story is the saloonkeeper bribed the firemen with whiskey and wine not to dynamite the building in their effort to stop the spread of the fire that accompanied the earthquake."

She took his hand as they entered. "It's another classic Pat Kaleto design: mosaics, brick, art nouveau glass fixtures, metalwork. But I still like the view. Let's go to the back where we can sit at a window on the Bay."

"Shall we celebrate your victory with champagne?" she asked, when they were seated.

J.J. nodded and ordered two glasses from the waiter. He picked the Roederer.

"Terrible, isn't it? Celebrating a case where children were molested and their father committed suicide," J.J. said, when the waiter had left.

"It is, truly, an American tragedy. But what else can we do but play it out, each of us playing our role, never really knowing how it will end." He felt she was talking about another tragedy, not the case he had just finished.

"You do the best you can and keep moving ahead, I suppose," she answered her own question, looking at the bubbles in her glass, one finger marking the sign of the cross in the moisture on the outside of the flute.

They talked throughout lunch and sat after, sipping cappuccinos. He admitted he would never have ordered the Ahi tuna tartar, except upon her urging, and didn't realize *salumi* was Italian for salami. They laughed at his cautious eating habits.

Now that they both had played their roles—he the lawyer, she the investigative reporter—he could let down and share information that would not go beyond the table. This was not just the continuation of a professional understanding; it was the beginning of a personal understanding they could confide in each other.

J.J. told Maureen stories of his long relationship with Don O'Brien and Roland Dougherty—many of which she knew—of growing up in Sacramento over fifty years. He gave her more details on the sting that landed Father Gutierrez in the custody of law enforcement, including the tactics and procedures used by the Special Task Force, which had been kept secret so perverts would not fully know how to avoid detection on the Internet.

Maureen told him of growing up with her parents, the death of her father, and many things that came flooding back about her stepfather: how he had taken up the responsibility of being a father to her; had attended school events in which she had participated; had taken her into his home as if she were his own daughter; and had dutifully shared her every achievement, her every sorrow, with her mother. This he had done, despite the fact that, she knew, it had hurt him not to have been, in fact, her biological father.

As he nodded to the waiter for the bill, J.J. brought the conversation back to a nagging question. "You still haven't told me how you found out about my case or why you came to California to what was, initially, a minor hearing about nothing, on paper, and a nominal amount of money."

"Oh, yes, that. You just won't let it go, will you?" She smiled at him. "My mother called me and told me all about it. She suggested that it could become a very big story."

"How would your mother know that when I didn't even know that, initially?"

Maureen laughed. "Oh, J.J., you are so predictable. Once you were set loose on this case, your instincts would lead you to the truth. We all knew that."

"Set loose? No one set me loose on this case."

"Yes, they did, J.J. You were chosen. As I was. Both of us did our jobs, as expected."

Before he could ask by whom, she stood up and excused herself to go to the restroom. When she returned, he wanted to ask her more about the case, her sources, her suggestion that it had somehow all been orchestrated by a unidentified hand. Who? And why? He could see, however, that while she was still smiling, she looked very tired.

"A long flight, champagne, and two glasses of wine and I'm out," she said. "Listen, I need to check in with my stepfather and get a little rest if we're going to have that promised date. Where are you staying?"

"The Fairmont," he answered. "Beautiful view."

"Maybe I'll get to see it tonight," she said with a smile, "but right now, I need to tend to family business and crash for a few hours."

She got up and waved him to sit back down. "You stay and enjoy dessert. I'm going to take a cab. I'll see you tonight at the Fairmont— 7:30, okay?" She came around the table and kissed him on the cheek. "Nice cologne," she said as she straightened up. "Wear that tonight."

It seemed that he was always watching her walk away. Nice watching, he thought. Again, as attractive women often do, she turned to look over her shoulder, as she exited the restaurant. Yes, he was watching. She smiled in appreciation, as she had on all the other occasions when he had watched her leave.

"Damn," J.J. said to nobody, as if caught with his hand in the cookie jar. He was laughing. It felt good—very good.

He finished his cappuccino and returned to the Fairmont to park his car. From now on, it would be taxis for the weekend. No one should ever own a car in San Francisco, he thought. There is no parking. Some people, he had heard, paid more for parking tickets than for rent.

"Shall I send the suitcase up?" asked the doorman at the Fairmont.

"What?" He turned to see Maureen's suitcase on the backseat. He had placed it there at the airport. He wasn't sure whether she had forgotten it or had intended to leave it there.

"Yes, send it up."

God, he thought, how the rules of dating have changed over the years. He shook his head. Here he was, sixty, single, ranked as one of the best lawyers in America, standing in front of the Fairmont Hotel on the famous Nob Hill in San Francisco, one of the most beautiful cities in the world, feeling like a college kid, and wondering what a woman might have meant by the possible innocent act of leaving a suitcase in his car. And hours to kill, he thought, before he could find out.

"Is there a bookstore nearby?" he asked the doorman.

"Borders. Union Square. Straight down," pointed the doorman.

He had been thinking about what she had said earlier. About a book, *Traveling Mercies—Some Thoughts on Faith*. What was faith? He'd asked himself that question ever since leaving the Catholic Church. Faith seemed to be an excuse for not knowing. To make up for what could not be known. Or, perhaps, because there was nothing to know. Some argued that a "leap of faith" was the necessary step to knowing when man reached the limits of his capacity to know. But how could man increase his capacity to know by leaping? What was on the other side that could not be comprehended without the leap? What was in the leap?

Borders, of course, had the book and every other book by Anne Lamott. She seemed to be in favor in San Francisco. He looked at the cover. A white girl in dreadlocks. He bought *Traveling Mercies*.

Walking down California and Powell streets to Union Square had been easy. Walking back up left him perspiring. Even though he had stopped a couple of times on the way up, when he finally reached the top, he leaned over, his hands on his knees, to catch his breath. When he looked up, it was at the gothic structure of Grace Cathedral. He had loved architecture, especially in cathedral designs, since reading Ken Follett's novel, *The Pillars of the Earth*. He looked to the towering cathedral and shuddered. He almost expected to see a body hanging.

The sight of the Grace Cathedral brought back the memory of the famous sixties activist, Bishop James Pike. He had been the bishop of this very cathedral when his body was found in a canyon into which he had gone to hike or pray. Canyons and cathedrals, both seemed to reach for the sky: sheer walls, tall peaks. Compare the Grand Canyon and Grace Cathedral, he thought. Two places of prayer to God, if there be one, with the cathedral emulating the grandeur of nature. Prayer and nature. Pray to nature. Be one with nature. Are we any different than anything else in nature?

He entered Grace Cathedral and encountered a purple labyrinth in a circular carpet, designed, it said, to represent the journey of the soul. While it required that shoes be removed, the sign cautioned, "Unattended belongings may be stolen." So much for the journey of the soul, J.J. thought, as he made his way out of the atrium of the cathedral toward the front pews in the nave, before the high altar.

Sitting in the pew, he reached for the hymnal, which stated it was approved by both the Joint Commission on the Revision of the Hymnal and the Standing Commission on Church Music. Could Jesus have known what he had unleashed? J.J. wondered.

Amazing grace! How sweet the sound,
that saved a wretch like me!
I once was lost but now am found,
was blind, but now I see.

J.J. put the book back.

But the architecture. Magnificent. Gothic arches, like glass candy pulled too thin to support even itself. Delicate. He leaned his head back and looked straight up. When he lowered his head, he saw the small plaque, perhaps three inches square, on this, the front pew:

"Phoebe Apperson Hearst, Benefactress of the University of California"

Best seat in the house.

He spent the afternoon at Grace Cathedral reading Ann Lamott until he fell asleep in the quiet of the cathedral and in Lamott's discovery of faith. Ironically, it was a homeless man who woke him. If it weren't for the homeless, J.J. thought, people might oversleep in public, and there would be no one to notice those who hanged themselves.

"Blessed are the poor, for they are the children of God."

Hard to get a Catholic education out of one's head.

He thanked the homeless man for waking him and handed him the book. He thought Anne Lamott would probably like that.

Chapter 50

*J*J. dressed early, in a new gray Armani suit and added a deep purple tie that he had purchased in Union Square. Cuff links at his off-white sleeves, ¼ inch beyond his jacket. A dab of cologne under each ear and a spray to his upper chest, which he immediately thought was too much and wiped off. He sat, waiting for her call, looking at the bottle of French champagne chilling in ice with two glasses on a silver tray. He had thought of ordering Dom Perignon with which to greet her. But this bottle looked interesting.

At 7:30, he heard a knock on the door. He answered it. It was Maureen. One hand on her hip and the other holding a small Channel purse. Her red hair hung freely. Long dangling earrings called attention to her ears. She was wearing a pale green cocktail dress, with thin straps, and shoes to match her hair.

"Radiant" was the only word J.J. could think of. "How did you know what room I was in? I thought proper hotels did not give out that information to young single ladies anymore."

She laughed. "You forgot, I'm an investigative reporter." She walked into the room. Instinctively, he leaned forward to catch her fragrance. She kissed him lightly as he did and then continued walking in the direction of the windows.

"You weren't kidding. This is spectacular," she said as she looked out onto the San Francisco Bay with Alcatraz directly ahead, its search-light drawing the eye even before dark as it circled, and huge cargo ships from Oakland heading out of the Golden Gate to Asia and other points west.

She picked up a champagne flute, turned, and raised an eyebrow: "Alexandra?"

"Yes, compliments of the hotel. It arrived an hour ago," he responded, walking toward her. The card sat on the table. "Enjoy," it said.

"No, I meant, would you like some? I sent it," she said, unwrapping the cork and warming the neck of the bottle with her hand. Looking again at the bottle, he realized that what he had found interesting about the bottle was its shape. Long necked, a fullness of body. Almost feminine.

"I hope you weren't thinking of ordering Dom Perignon. Why men think it's impressive to order a bottle of champagne you can buy at Costco is beyond me," she said as she turned the bottle in her hand.

His look was a confession.

She laughed. "This champagne has an interesting story. The winemaker kept it a secret for years and presented it at his daughter's wedding. And, of course, her name was Alexandra."

Maureen began to apply pressure to the cork. "Fathers and daughters. It seems to be our fate. But we are the lucky ones, J.J."

The cork popped without a drop being spilled.

"I do hope you are comfortable with a woman sending her date a gift of champagne?"

"I could get used to it, I suppose," J.J. said, picking up a flute. She poured his first and then hers. The champagne was a deep salmon pink in color.

"What shall we drink to?" he asked.

Her eyes looked up, as if she was giving it much thought. Finally, she clinked his glass. "To altar boys."

J.J. pulled two of the large chairs from the table and placed them so they could sit and view San Francisco from the fourteenth floor of the Fairmont—a view unmatched in the world. And here she was, he thought, finally. Sharing it with him. He looked over at her, studying her in profile. She let him look, lifting her head just a little for his satisfaction, as she took a sip of champagne and looked upon the Bay.

"Did I tell you that my stepfather was an altar boy?" she asked.

"No. But it seems everyone was—or at least has an altar boy story."

"Well, his is the story of his life," she said, viewing the Bay through the fog of her champagne flute. Her expression changed. J.J. saw pain.

"He was seventeen. He had been an altar boy for years. Here in San Francisco. He had thoughts of possibly becoming a priest. One evening, he went to the home of a priest to talk about the priesthood. They had a few drinks. He doesn't remember what happened next. Possibly, he was drugged. He woke up in the middle of the night in bed, nude, with the priest asleep next to him. He was sore." She stopped as her voice broke. He leaned over to put a hand on her arm, and she waved him off. "He left without saying a word. He never told anyone. He tried to forget it; pretended it never happened. About two years later, he met my mother when they were both students at Berkeley. They fell in love, she the Mother Earth, save-the-world, pot-smoking social activist, and he, the lost soul in need of saving. They married. It lasted, really, just months, although the formal divorce came later. He fell apart. After having been raped by a priest, he was haunted with doubts about his sexuality. Ultimately, he became sexually impotent. He associated sex with overwhelming shame and humiliation. He attempted suicide a number of times, which was just too much for my mom. She had hoped that she could save him; fix him; bring him back. She finally admitted that she couldn't, which, she felt, made her useless for him. His family had the money to get him the best care, and he was repeatedly hospitalized, medicated, and spent years in therapy."

Maureen excused herself and went into the bathroom to blow her nose. She returned and poured more champagne. J.J. said nothing. She sat back down.

"He did two things as part of his therapy. First, he confronted the priest. He found the priest had been transferred to another parish in Southern California. He flew down there. He sat through Mass and actually received Communion from the priest. The priest recognized him and my dad—step-dad—said he knew everything he needed to know when the priest's hands shook, trembled, and the priest literally fled the altar in the middle of Mass. My step-dad knew then that it had not been his fault."

She stopped as if to regain her composure and her ability to speak.

"The second thing he did was call my mother and explain what had occurred so she'd know that the failure of their marriage and his sexual problems had nothing to do with her. He thanked her for her love. They cried together. They went their separate ways but maintained contact. When my father died, my mother called him and asked him to involve himself in my life and help me deal with my father's death as I began Mills College. He didn't hesitate. He has acted as my father ever since. An important part of my life. In fact, an inspiration to me in many ways and probably the reason that I attended law school."

Finally, J.J. understood why the issues of his case had been so important to her that she would write about clergy abuse from her prestigious position as a reporter for one of the nation's most distinguished and credible papers. And she was not just a good writer but a superb investigative reporter capable of developing sources that permitted her to know and disclose settlement offers that were not public. She obviously must have worked sources, just as she had him, for confidential information that he had not provided her. He was impressed, not critical, that she had not limited herself to him as a single source, even if he would normally wish to control the story by being its only source.

"May I buy you dinner?" he asked.

"J.J., you forgot. I lost this bet. I have reservations at 1550 Hyde. I hope you don't mind."

"Like I said, I could get used to it. Actually, I think I could get used to you."

As she put a hand on his, which had come to rest on her arm, she answered, "Yeah, we should give it a try."

He leaned over, raising his hand to caress her face, and kissed her. She reached back and held his head to keep their lips together. Finally, they broke the kiss, but she kept her forehead against his, her hand dropping to his neck.

"Let's get out of here while we're still dressed," she sighed. They stood, and he put his arms around her, holding her body tightly as he kissed her, harder this time. She reciprocated, and he could feel the contours of her body, her full breasts, her inner thighs as she moved her legs against his. He hardened, and he knew that she knew it when she moaned.

Finally, she dropped her arms behind her to signify surrender. Then she let her head fall back as his lips fell to her neck. She laughed loudly. "Whoa! Well, Mr. Rai, I hope that might be enough to entice you to New York to spend some time with me."

"I'm booking it tonight," he answered, a little out of breath.

"After dinner," she replied. "Let's go."

She reached for his hand. He straightened his clothes. "Right. Dinner. That was the deal. Oh," he added, not sure which voice in his head to obey: the one that said "tell her" or the one that said "don't tell her."

"You left your suitcase in my car. I had it brought up. For safekeeping."

"And I bet you thought I was a little hussy, using that as an excuse to spend the night with you," she said, laughing.

"It had crossed my mind."

"This time, J.J., I just forgot it. Next time, I'll let you carry it in with me. That's if you take my offer to come to New York to see me." She faced him squarely. "You'll find that I'm very direct. No games. Life is too short. J.J., I'd like to spend some time getting to know you better. But tonight, alas, I will be going to my stepfather's home."

"Then we'd better get to dinner. I'll carry the suitcase down."

She gave him another kiss to make sure the correct message had been sent—and received.

"What?" she asked, seeing J.J. looking confused.

"Well, I was just wondering. If I had your suitcase, how did you get dressed so beautifully for our date tonight?"

"You little schemer, Mr. Rai. You really thought having my suitcase gave you control over my wardrobe? You have a lot to learn about women. When I realized I had left my suitcase in your car, I went out and bought new clothes. This date has cost me $1,800 in new clothes so far—not counting the shoes. I must say, it's been worth every penny."

J.J. looked at her shoes.

"You don't want to know," she answered his look.

"I bought a new tie for our date," he offered. "Ninety dollars," he added.

They both laughed.

"Let's just call it even," Maureen agreed.

The phone rang. J.J. hesitated, not wanting any interruption to their evening. She understood his hesitation and said, "Oh, get it. But I want your full attention at dinner."

He answered it. "Andy? I thought you were in Bangladesh."

"I got as far as Munich and found that some son-of-a-bitch Urdu-speaking Pakistani lawyer had signed up all of the clients from the Air Pakistan crash in Bangladesh. Can you believe it? This outsourcing is getting out of hand. Pretty soon, American lawyers won't be able to compete with these Third-World greedy bastards."

"Andy. Andy, I'm really busy. Where are you? I'll call you tomorrow," J.J. said, rolling his eyes at Maureen.

"I'm on your boat, sitting in front of the Virgin Sturgeon. People are asking about you."

"Great, Andy. What do you need? What was so urgent? I've got to run."

He lifted the phone over his head and said to Maureen, "It's my investigator. He's on my boat on the Sacramento River." Maureen nodded. She had seen Andy in court on the witness stand. She sat on the chair next to J.J. and put her hand on his back, at the waist, as he spoke. He looked down and smiled and put his hand on her neck. She moved her head around in his hand as if to signal a massage.

"J.J., I got sued!" said Andy.

"What?" J.J. asked, momentarily taking his hand off of Maureen's neck. She stopped the low sounds that she had been making to the rhythm of his hand and looked up as she heard him ask Andy: "Who sued you, Andy?"

"Ken Lay. Remember? I told you, I bumped his car. He's got a big-time personal injury lawyer in Houston, and he's suing me for cervical myalgia. Can you believe this shit?"

J.J. repeated to Maureen what Andy had said. He covered the phone as they both began laughing.

"Who are you talking to?" Andy asked.

"A beautiful woman. Maureen McReynolds, *Wall Street Journal* reporter, is here in my fourteenth-floor room at the Fairmont Hotel, and you're calling to tell me that Ken Lay is suing you for whiplash? What's wrong with you, Andy?" J.J. asked, holding up his hand and looking up as if appealing for divine intervention.

Maureen signaled J.J. to give her the phone. He handed it to her.

"Andy," she said in a voice that was both hushed and penetrating, "this is Maureen. Andy, I want you to know that just the thought of you gives me whiplash. But, Andy, I only have J.J. here and not you. What should I do, Andy? Tell me."

It was all that J.J. could do not to choke on his champagne. He covered his mouth, coughing and imagining Andy on the other end, standing on deck, holding the portable phone.

Maureen heard a loud splash and handed the phone back to J.J.

"He fell overboard," J.J. surmised. "Don't worry. It happens all the time with him. I'll probably have to buy a new portable phone."

He hung up the phone, and they hugged again. "If you had whispered that to me, I probably would have needed a cold shower, too."

She bit his ear and made a little, playful growl.

"Feed me."

"Right."

They held hands and left the room.

In the taxi, J.J. leaned back, holding Maureen's hand across the backseat. Looking out of the window, he viewed the City in a way he'd never seen it before. He felt content with himself. Life had worked out well. He could travel in any circle, engage in whatever interested him in the law or otherwise, and choose with whom to spend time. More than a successful career—a successful life. What interested him at the moment was Maureen McReynolds. Who knew where it would lead, he thought, but he was determined to take the journey with this interesting woman.

Maureen, for her part, had been attracted to J.J. before ever meeting him. He had been selected, as she had said, because her stepfather had placed his confidence in him, had known that he would represent the children's interests well, and could not have allowed still another altar boy's life to be so damaged, quietly, without accountability, in the name of protecting the Catholic Church. That is why he had asked his gardener, Alfonso, to call the Sanchez parents and urge them in their native tongue to contact J.J. Rai.

He and J.J. had never formally met. But he knew of J.J.'s reputation and had observed J.J.'s career in litigation. It was he who had given Maureen a copy of J.J.'s speech to the 30th reunion of his law school class, wherein he had talked of clinging, even thirty years later, "to an image of the law student at Boalt Hall, at Berkeley, in the sixties...."

Her stepfather also clung to the Berkeley of the sixties, where he had loved and married, and had lost and suffered through no fault of his own. He could not have stood by and witnessed similar suffering in still one more altar boy without reaching out to help. That was why he had picked J.J.

Maureen looked at J.J. now. He had championed their cause—not because it was their cause, but because it was also his cause. Everyone was searching for faith. How dare anyone interrupt that journey? She loved what he stood for. She was beginning to love who he was.

Dinner was splendid. But then, they were not in a critical mood. They resolved to return to 1550 Hyde for an "anniversary" dinner in a year. Neither of them wanted the night to end, but they gave each other the promise of a future. There were still lingering questions. As they drank their decaffeinated cappuccinos, she asked him, "It wasn't Father Gutierrez with Carmen, was it?"

J.J. looked into his coffee. He knew he could trust her. He also felt that she had earned the right to know.

"No."

"Her father?"

"No."

"Then who?" Maureen asked, putting down her cup.

"Bishop O'Brien," he said, after a long pause.

"There is no story," J.J. had told her. There never would be. She understood the deal.

"Take me home, you dear man," she requested, after she insisted on paying the bill. They stood, and she took his arm. The waiter had called a cab, and it was waiting as they exited the restaurant. They got in together, and he said, "The Fairmont Hotel. We've got to pick up a suitcase, and then we'll be dropping off the young lady." The cabbie just shrugged, started the meter, as if to say, "It's none of my business."

At the Fairmont, J.J. went in and retrieved the suitcase from the Bell Captain's desk and returned to the cab. "I'll ride with you," he said. "I'll have the cab bring me back."

She hesitated at first but finally gave the cabbie an address. Then she snuggled up to J.J. as the cab proceeded west on California, across Van Ness, and climbed the hill toward Pacific Heights, just as a cable car topped the crest and came into sight, its bell ringing rhythmically.

As they passed the Victorians for which this area of San Francisco was known, it was not the sites but a smell that consumed his attention. Her hair touching his cheek. He breathed deeply. He leaned into her, just as he had done the first time she had passed him at the courtroom door. It was getting to be a habit.

After what seemed miles, Maureen McReynolds addressed the cab driver.

"Take Presidio and drive in the back way on Lincoln Boulevard."

The driver nodded and pulled into the right lane. If she wanted to go the long way, it was fine with him.

She squeezed J.J.'s arm as she made herself comfortable nestled against him. They were now in the darkness of a park, and the even stronger smell of eucalyptus through the open window struck him. They were winding through the Presidio, and up ahead he could see signs for the Golden Gate Bridge. The taxi looped back, under the bridge entry, and everything to J.J.'s right was completely black. He could hear—and smell—the ocean.

"Where are we?" he asked.

"Sea Cliff," she answered.

The taxi took the first right as it exited the Presidio and entered an area of San Francisco J.J. had never seen. As the taxi slowed, J.J. looked at the homes. These were not houses, they were estates—mansions—from a time when the term "mansion" had meaning. The cab turned at the end of a cul-de-sac, and J.J. looked to see the lights of the Golden Gate Bridge directly ahead. Clearly, the houses before him fronted on the entrance to the Golden Gate—from the Pacific Ocean side.

"Number 20?" asked the cabbie.

"Yes," Maureen answered.

The cab slowed in front of the largest mansion. The low walls, topped with wrought-iron bars, allowed a view of the home while providing security for all within. Cyprus, obviously decades old, hung over the fencing and, as with the lawn, palms, olive trees, and bamboo, was meticulously manicured.

She directed the cab to a gate leading directly to the front door of the home. Immediately, J.J. offered to carry her suitcase, but she declined.

"I'll get it," she said as she leaned over, in the backseat, and kissed him. He got out on his side and came around the cab, and they kissed again, but this time longer and more softly. She hesitated after their lips separated and, with her eyes closed, said, "I need you in New York, soon."

He watched as she went to the gate, pushed a button on the intercom, and announced: "It's Maureen, dad."

She turned, after she had opened the gate, and waved to him and walked to the front door. He waved back. She knew he was watching. She trusted him with the final secret. From her stepfather, she knew the quote of Aeschylus uttered 2,500 years ago: "God is not averse to deceit in a holy cause."

A light came on at the front door, and J.J. saw a figure walk past the window of a room full of bookshelves that appeared to be a library. It was a man, walking toward the door. J.J. recognized him immediately.

There had been another altar boy in the courtroom.

Judge Gerald Vincent greeted Maureen at the door. Maureen hugged him as a daughter might; he had waited up for her as a father would.

Epilogue

*J*udge Gerald Vincent retired from the Sacramento bench after the Sanchez case, effective the end of that year. When not tending to his garden at his home in the Seacliff district of San Francisco, he can often be seen sailing, alone, on the San Francisco Bay.

In the early morning hours of July 5, 2006, Ken Lay died while vacationing in Aspen, Colorado, reportedly of a massive heart attack. The coroner said there was no evidence of foul play despite the conspiracy theories swirling around Lay's death. Andy insisted he was nowhere near Aspen when Lay died. However, in October, when a federal court judge, Simeon T. Lake, III, set aside the jury verdict of guilty against Ken Lay, solely because he had died, Andy was inconsolable. He felt Lay had, in death, "cheated justice."

Andy told J.J., "I should have shot Ken Lay when I had the chance."

J.J. noted that, either way, Ken Lay was dead.

"No," replied Andy, "shooting him would have made a statement." As an afterthought, he added, "And what kind of a name is Simeon for a judge, anyway?"

The death of Bishop Donald O'Brien, in March 2007, in the frigid waters off Alaska, was noted by the *Catholic Herald* newspaper in an article that J.J. thought was surprisingly brief, given that the bishop had led the diocese for so many years. It noted that the bishop had gone out alone, from Seattle, in his brother's fishing boat, and when he did not return in the evening, the Coast Guard was notified. The boat was found a week later four miles off Kodiak Island in the Gulf of Alaska. It appeared functional. But, there was no sign of the bishop. His body was never found. Despite the absence of weather conditions in the area or physical signs on board to explain the disappearance, the apparent drowning was ruled an accident.

The *Sacramento Bee* carried a larger story tracing the bishop's life and service, especially to poor Mexican farm workers and immigrant families in California's Central Valley. It noted, in passing, the altar boy scandal that he had successfully settled for the diocese shortly before retiring and leaving the area.

J.J. pondered Roland Dougherty's quote in the article about their fellow altar boy: "He has been called home by God."

The altar boy in him instinctively thought: "God works in mysterious ways, His wonders to perform"—but then, J.J. knew better.

Acknowledgements

As with my first novel, I have a group I call my "readers" who, after reading the manuscript, submit to a faceless, phone interrogation in which their every word is recorded; I then return to the manuscript with their comments. They include: Catherine O'Brien, Betty Moulds, Mimi Mahoney, Ron Pomares, Karen Sarkissian, Cindy Daly, Russ Solomon, Heidy Kellison, Tom Hedtke, Nancy Sheehan, Wade Thompson, Sally Davis, Peter Kellison, Vicki Lorini, Rebel Curd, Tracy Eastwood, Patty Drosins, Dani Luzzatti, Joy Gough, Jacquelyn Wilson, and Dr. Steven Polansky. Later, Joshua Chapman provided a valuable read.

I want to thank Sacramento County District Attorney, Jan Scully, and her senior deputy, Al Locher, for giving me access to the Sacramento Valley High Tech Crime Task Force, and particularly Michael J. Menz, the real "cybercop," who dazzled—and scared—me with what can be done with a computer to perpetrate crime and, more importantly, to catch criminals. As always, when I needed medical research, I turned to K.D. Proffit of the Sutter Resource Library. This time, the search was of the psychiatric literature regarding repressed and recovered memory. And, thank you to all those who gave me unauthorized access to tall places.

For Spanish translation and Mexican customs, I again called upon Carmen Barnard. For all things nautical or about San Francisco, the call went to (Captain) Bill McCarthy. And, as the book neared completion, I turned to my son, Robert Poswall, for website construction and my son-in-law, Steve Curd, for marketing help. Marketing was made easier by the unsolicited help of two book enthusiasts, Diane and Larrie Grenz.

Of course, there are the tireless and dedicated workers who make up Jullundur Press, beginning with Sally Iannone directing traffic and shipping, Natalie Bradburn typing revision after revision without complaint, Brenda Mojarro getting the manuscript into shape for the printers, Cheryl Steiner bailing us out whenever the computers eat something, chief financial officer Julie Kurtz, and Melinda Arendt smiling on all of them.

Along the way, I have enjoyed the support of many media people, a few of whom I want to thank here: Fahizah Alim, Pam Dinsmore, Kitty O'Neal, Chistine Craft, Stan Atkinson, Donna Apidone, Jeff Metcalf, Linda Birner, and Deric Rothe.

I have also been blessed (pardon the expression) to have the support of three *New York Times* best-selling authors I respect: John Lescroart, John Martel, and Sheldon Siegel. And, in New York, I am honored to have as my agent, Paul Bresnick.

I would not have attempted my first novel, *The Lawyers*, without the critical judgment, editing help, and tutelage of a gifted young writer, playwright, and lawyer—what doesn't he do?—Aram Kouyoumdjian (who also provided the first edit of this novel). I would not have attempted this second novel if it had not been for the encouragement and support of John Lescroart; of Jackie Cantor, now Executive Editor of Berkley Publishing Group; of Vicki Lorini, Regional Sales Manager, Borders Books; and, of Russ Solomon, a legend in the book and record industry. Thank you.

Finally, I couldn't do anything without the patience, love, and support of my wife, Peg Tomlinson-Poswall, who stands by me in both my manic and depressive states.

John M. Poswall
January, 2008

Also by John M. Poswall

THE LAWYERS:
Class of '69
(a novel)

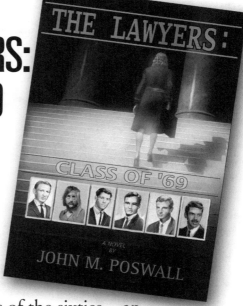

They were the last class of the sixties—an idealistic generation committed to changing the world. What happened?

Tonight, they return for the 30th reunion of the U.C. Berkeley law school class. Brought together once again are Rose, the daughter of Mexican farm workers and one of the few "girls" in the class; Leon, the Marxist son of a longshoremen's union organizer; Michael, the outspoken and often-ridiculed conservative Republican; Brian, the upstate New Yorker who wound up in the South and in a life-changing confrontation with racism; and Jackson, a person of East Coast pedigree who forever regretted not going to Stanford law school. What began in the classroom spills over into their lives.

From divorce court to the Supreme Court, from public demonstrations to private White House conferences: The lawyers of the sixties battle in the legal system—and sometimes with each other—and with the question raised at the reunion: "Did we make a goddamn bit of difference? Did we change the law? Society? Or were we changed?"

For one, as a woman, the challenges have been very different even as she bests the men in school and in the courtroom.

What Others Say about *The Lawyers*:

A complex tapestry of intertwining stories
Midwest Book Review
(Oregon, WI USA)

> "*The Lawyers: Class of '69* is an original and deftly written novel by John M. Poswall that blends reality and fiction into a seamlessly entertaining whole. In the mid-1960s, many Berkeley law school students were intent on changing the world; thirty years later, they meet at a class reunion and question themselves (and one another) as to whether they truly made a difference, and if so, was it for the better? A complex tapestry of intertwining stories, ranging from dashed hopes to life-changing close calls to public demonstrations and private White House meetings, *The Lawyers: Class of '69* is a highly recommended and thoroughly engrossing read."

John Lescroart, *New York Times* best-selling author
of legal fiction

> "I...thought I'd read a page or two. Three days later, I had tears in my eyes as I finished this remarkable book.... It's a beautiful book.... There is a wonderful sense of purpose and idealism, and an awesome sense of lost innocence coupled with painful

growth.... But there is also suspense, humor, excellent characterization.... It could become required reading for the next generation."

Sacramento News & Review

"About as far away from a John Grisham novel as one could get and infinitely more intriguing."

Because People Matter (newspaper)

"*The Lawyers* is a slice-of-life novel with a vivid surface richness. Its subjects, however—how individuals, the law, and the social currents of the times intersect and change—is a deep and complex one, and Poswall does it justice!"

The Sacramento Bee

"John Poswall draws on his life as a crusading lawyer for his first novel."

The Daily Record (New York)

"The story was captivating from beginning to end."

On Amazon

Congressman Bob Matsui called *The Lawyers* "an absorbing cleverly paced book that I could not put down and didn't want to end. This first novel distinguishes its author, John Poswall, as one of fiction's most promising writers"; journalism professor William Dorman described it as "*Paper Chase* meets *Big Chill*"; a woman lawyer from Arizona wrote that Poswall's description of the experience of a woman lawyer was "so accurate I was sure a woman must have written it"; and a judge in Hays, Kansas, said "Poswall compares favorably with…legal novelists such as Martini and Lescroart." The William Morris Agency, in a coverage, recommended it for a TV/cable movie or series.

From Kerala, India

Book reviewer Narayan Radhakrishnan compared Poswall to Scott Turow.

About the Author

John M. Poswall is the author of the novel *The Lawyers: Class of '69* (see inside). He has also been named one of the "Best Lawyers in America" and "Superlawyers of Northern California." *The Sacramento Bee* said, "When David takes on Goliath, he usually calls John M. Poswall." He lives outside Sacramento on fifty acres, where his gardens have been listed on the National Garden Conservancy tour. He is married to food consultant Peg Tomlinson-Poswall.

For more on John the lawyer, writer and gardener
go to www.johnposwall.com.